# THE EMPEROR'S COLOURED COAT

*In which Otto Prohaska, future hero of the Habsburg Empire,*
*has an unexpectedly interesting time while*
*not quite managing to avert the First World War*

## By John Biggins

McBooks Press, Inc.
Ithaca, New York

PUBLISHED BY MCBOOKS PRESS, INC. 2006

*Copyright © 1992 by John Biggins*

First published in Great Britain by Martin Secker & Warburg Limited

Cover painting by Geoff Hunt.

ISBN: 978-1-59013-108-4
1-59013-108-8

Library of Congress Cataloging-in-Publication Data

Biggins, John.
  The emperor's coloured coat : in which Otto Prohaska, future hero of the Habsburg Empire, has an unexpectedly interesting time while not quite managing to avert the First World War
/ by John Biggins.
     p. cm.
  ISBN-13: 978-1-59013-108-4 (trade pbk. : alk. paper)
  ISBN-10: 1-59013-108-8 (trade pbk. : alk. paper)
  1. World War, 1914-1918—Naval operations, Austrian—Fiction. 2. Austria—History, Naval—20th century—Fiction. I. Title.
  PR6052.I34E4 2006
  823'.914--dc22
  2005029520

Distributed to the trade by National Book Network, Inc., 15200 NBN Way, Blue Ridge Summit, PA 17214

800-462-6420

Additional copies of this book may be ordered from any bookstore or directly from McBooks Press, Inc., ID Booth Building, 520 North Meadow St., Ithaca, NY 14850. Please include $5.00 postage and handling with mail orders. New York State residents must add sales tax to total remittance (books & shipping). All McBooks Press publications can also be ordered by calling toll-free 1-888-BOOKS11 (1-888-266-5711). Please call to request a free catalog.

Visit the McBooks Press website at www.mcbooks.com.

Printed in the United States of America

9 8 7 6 5 4 3 2 1

# THE EMPEROR'S COLOURED COAT

*This book is dedicated to Małgorzata, my wife,*
*for putting up with a house full of ghosts*

# ABBREVIATIONS

THE AUSTRO-HUNGARIAN EMPIRE set up by the Compromise of 1867 was a union of two near-independent states in the person of their monarch, Emperor of Austria and King of Hungary. Thus, for the fifty-one years of its existence, almost every institution and many of the personnel of this composite state had their titles prefixed with initials indicating their status.

Shared Austro-Hungarian institutions were Imperial and Royal: "kaiserlich und königlich" or "k.u.k." for short. Those belonging to the Austrian part of the Monarchy (that is to say, everything that was not the Kingdom of Hungary) were designated Imperial-Royal—"kaiserlich-königlich" or simply "k.k."—in respect of the monarch's status as Emperor of Austria and King of Bohemia; while purely Hungarian institutions were Royal Hungarian: "königlich ungarisch" ("k.u.") or "kiraly magyar" ("k.m.").

The Austro-Hungarian Navy followed contemporary Continental practice in quoting sea distances in European nautical miles (6080 feet), land distances in kilometres, battle ranges etc. in metres and gun calibres in centimetres. However, it followed pre-1914 British practice in using the twelve-hour system for times. Its vessels were designated "Seiner Majestäts Schiff" or "S.M.S."

# PLACE NAMES

A GLOSSARY OF PLACE NAMES is attached since frontier and political changes between 1914 and 1947 have altered many of those used in this story beyond recognition. The list merely records official practice in 1914 and implies no recognition whatever of any territorial claims past or present.

Chinese place names are spelt with the former English transliteration system (for example, "Peking") rather than the one employed nowadays.

| | | | |
|---|---|---|---|
| Abbazia | Opatija, Yu. | Lemberg | L'vov/Lwów, USSR |
| Amboina | Ambon, Indonesia | Neugraditz | Novi Gradic, Yu. |
| Antivari | Stari Bar, Yu. | Pancsova | Pančevo, Yu. |
| Batavia | Djakarta, Indonesia | Petwardein | Petrovaradin, Yu. |
| Beneschau | Benešov, Cz. | Podgorica | Titograd, Yu. |
| Castellnuovo | Herzegnovi, Yu. | Pola | Pula, Yu. |
| Cattaro | Kotor, Yu. | Porto Ré | Kraljevica, Yu. |
| Chefoo | Yentai, China | Scutari Lake | Skadarsko Jezero, Yu. |
| Fiume | Rijeka, Yu. | Semandria | Smederevo, Yu. |
| Gródek Jagielloński | Gorodok, USSR | Spizza | Sutomore, Yu. |
| Iglau | Jihlava, Cz. | Temesvár | Timisoara, Rom. |
| Jungbunzlau | Mladá Boleslav, Cz. | Teodo | Tivat, Yu. |
| Klattnau | Klatnov, Cz. | Ujvidek | Novi Sad, Yu. |
| Leitmeritz | Litoměřice, Cz. | Zemlin | Zemun, Yu. |

# 1

# DISTANT ECHOES

SISTERS OF THE
PERPETUAL ADORATION

PLAS GAERLLWYDD

JANUARY 1987

I HAVE NEVER BEEN A GOOD INVALID, I am afraid: not when I was a small child, fighting to survive the routine diseases that used to carry off so many infants in the late 1880s; nor even now, when I have lived so unbearably long that death will come to me as a welcome visitor; and not in all those many times in between when sickness or wounds have put me on my back for a spell.

Bronchial pneumonia laid me low the week before Christmas, while the Sisters were busy preparing the vigil-night supper for us forlorn inmates of this home for Polish refugees. They put me to bed and called Dr Watkins over from Llangwynydd village to attend to me, but this was largely a formality: I was not expected to survive the next day, despite an injection of antibiotics and the use of an oxygen mask. It was not even considered worthwhile to call an ambulance to move me to hospital in Swansea. Quite sensibly, I thought: I might as well die here as there, especially in the middle days of December when the ambulance men have their hands full dealing with road casualties. In any case, I was little disposed to argue, lying there fighting for breath and wondering like a shipwreck survivor in a freezing sea how many more waves he can be expected to breast before he gives in to the inevitable and goes under for the last time. It is by no means an unpleasant sensation, this dying, at least as I experienced it: rather like waking early in the morning, then realising that it is Sunday and stretching lazily in one's hammock in the knowledge that the bugles will not blow Auspurren for another hour. I was conscious of faces about me, and of people coming and going, but of little else.

Then they brought Father McCaffrey to administer extreme unction. Now, I have nothing against the reverend father, who is a pleasant young Irishman with a permanent smile and a shiny pink face, rather like a slaughtered pig that has just been scalded and had its bristles shaved off. Also he was conscientious enough to drive thirty kilometres late on a wet, cold night to offer the last meagre comforts of Holy Mother Church to a withered old husk of an agnostic like myself, baptised and confirmed as a Catholic—like all other subjects of the Noble House of Austria who didn't claim to be anything else—but otherwise (like most Czechs) a Hussite at heart and a sceptic as regards the head. But it was the extreme unction itself which did it—though I think not quite in the way they intended. I served in both world wars and in several conflicts in between, and I am strongly of the opinion that the wanton administration of religion to helpless sick and wounded men lying in hospitals is a practice which ought to be outlawed under the Geneva Convention. I remember, at any rate, having a strenuous and most enjoyable argument on this point about twenty years ago with the Matron at the Stanmore Orthopaedic Hospital, when I was laid up with a broken hip and a gang of well-heeled Samaritans turned up to dispense Christmas carols and condescension to the inmates. Anyway, on this occasion, far gone as I was, having Father McCaffrey smearing me with embrocation and muttering incantations over me was more than I could take. I pushed him away—to the horror of the assembled Sisters—then managed to sit up and gather enough breath to tell him to leave me alone and be about his business attending to people who have asked for his ministrations. It was disgraceful, I know, but the anger worked like some marvellous elixir upon me. The exertion brought about a profuse sweat, my heartbeat grew strong and regular again, my breathing eased later that night and I recovered over the next few days to a point where, just before New Year, I was taken off the danger list and officially declared a convalescent.

I am still confined to bed, however, until further notice, and Sister Felicja is enforcing the order by impounding my clothes. Really, I think that with someone of my age—a hundred last April—they ought to let me get dressed and wander out into the snow to perish like an aged and toothless Red Indian brave. But their minds appear not to work that way—like those of prison warders who take away a condemned man's shoelaces and belt and braces for fear that he should hang himself and save them the trouble. But now it looks as if they will merely turn out to have substituted death from boredom for death from cardio-respiratory failure, because the truth is that I am finding my time in bed extremely tiresome. I cannot read a great deal these days, because of cataract, and I find that the wireless soon palls once one has listened to the fifth or sixth afternoon play about the problems of blue whales and single-parent families.

However it must be admitted that, even if I were allowed to get up, there would not be a great deal to do at the moment, for last Monday the weather suddenly changed. On Saturday afternoon it was the usual January half-gale and drizzle along this stretch of the Welsh Atlantic coast. But then on Sunday the wind began to veer round and turn into a raw, iron-grey north-easter, moaning steadily about the house up here on the headland and ruffling the trees and bushes against their gale-bent grain like an invisible hand stroked the wrong way along a cat's back. By Monday evening the snow had begun to fall: not the usual large, wet, sea-scented flakes of these parts but a solid, steady cascade of fine, harsh powder almost like that which falls where I come from in the middle of Europe. By Tuesday morning the roads were impassable, the sunken lane to Llangwynydd village buried two or three metres deep along its entire length. The local people who have managed to struggle up to the Plas these past few days say that they have not seen worse in twenty-five years.

Not that it has affected me a great deal, lying here in my upstairs room. I was aware of the pallid, grey light reflected on to the ceiling when I awoke that morning, then of the branching fingers of ice on the window panes. But it was not until I managed to hoist myself out of bed, when the Sisters' backs were turned, that I looked out of the window and saw the rock-terraced gardens about the house smoothed to a gently undulating expanse of white, and the great ridge of the Cefn Gaerllwydd beyond turned into the back of an albino whale standing out sharp and livid against a sky of tarnished pewter. The sea—commanded by the wind off the land to an unaccustomed calm—lapped sullenly at the shores of Pengadog Bay below the house, leaving a fringe of broken ice-shards as the tide went out. All was stillness and silence.

Movement to and from the Plas has been impossible these past few days, balanced as we are out here on the very tip of the peninsula, far from even the secondary roads and with only a couple of farmsteads between us and Llangwynydd. Earlier today there was a great clattering overhead as an RAF helicopter came over to drop fodder to the sheep up on the ridge; but apart from that we have been quite isolated from the rest of the world, except for the telephone and the wireless. Not that it matters a great deal though, in a place inhabited by ten nuns and eighty or so aged and impoverished Polish émigrés, most of them hardly less feeble and decrepit than myself. No, we have supplies for a month or so I believe, and central-heating oil for longer, so cannibalism will not be necessary, by my reckoning, until about the end of February. Likewise the suspension of milk and postal deliveries is no great hardship to us. Coming from Central Europe, we take lemon in our tea. And being of our accursed generation, we receive little mail, having precious few relatives or friends left alive to send us any. In fact there has been a certain end-of-term levity about the place these past few days. Yesterday a couple of the younger and more frivolous Sisters were even induced to take part in a snowball fight with Major Koziołkiewicz and a few of his fellow-gallants, then help him build a snowman. An old biretta was dug out from somewhere to turn it into the semblance of a priest, with an empty vodka bottle tucked under one of its arms and a breviary under the other. But when a carrot begged from the kitchen to represent a nose was turned into something else altogether, Sister Felicja felt that the fun had gone far enough and came out to send the nuns about their duties.

As far as I am concerned the sudden onset of the blizzards and our subsequent isolation from the world has had one unlooked-for benefit. My young friend Kevin Scully, unemployed ex-naval rating and part-time handyman about the Plas, drove across from Llanelli on the Monday afternoon to fix a leaking tap and was stranded here as the snow began to drift in the lanes. He has been here for six days now. Not that he seems to mind very much: he has no job, and his "on-off" relationship with his girlfriend appears to be going through an "off" phase. And anyway, as an ex-serviceman, he has come to appreciate that the one great merit of military life is its irreproachable idleness. He has dug a few paths clear about the house and thawed out a pipe or two, and he is conscientious in his twice-daily checking of the boiler and heating pumps in their outhouse. But otherwise he seems happy to sit up here in my room, well away from Sister Felicja, talking with me about this and that or just reading quietly. He is the ideal sickroom companion: instinctively tactful and unobtrusive, with none of these irritating ideas about having to entertain me or otherwise justify his presence. Strange really, when you think about it, that just as I am about to depart this life, after having outlived all my generation, I should take such comfort from the mere presence of this uneducated, mannerless foreign youth. When I was a submarine captain back in 1918 we were once called to assist a torpedoed Austrian troop-ship off the coast of Albania. We arrived too late to do anything but retrieve a few dead bodies, and I remember how, when we dragged them aboard, we found that several of them had some pathetic everyday object—a pencil or a cigarette lighter perhaps—clutched in their lifeless hands, as if they had clung desperately to this last token of the world of mankind just as they were slipping out of it. But whatever the reasons, Kevin has been a great comfort to me in these exhausted post-illness weeks; likewise my friend and confidante Sister Elisabeth, who comes up to sit with me whenever her duties in the kitchen permit.

It was Kevin Scully and Sister Elisabeth who twisted my arm last autumn to tape-record my reminiscences of my career as k.u.k. Linienschiffsleutnant Ottokar, Ritter von Prohaska, First World War U-Boat Ace and officially certified War-Hero of the Austro-Hungarian Monarchy. You may perhaps listen to these memoirs one day, if you are interested in that sort of thing and if anyone ever considers them worthy of editing and setting in order. But if you do ever hear these yarns you may wonder, like Kevin Scully to whom I first told them, why it is that they commence in the spring of 1915, by which time I had been a career officer in the Habsburg Navy for the best part of fifteen years and had already fought nine months of the world war which eventually brought about the collapse of my country. I had told Kevin that when the war broke out at the end of July 1914 I was in the Far East, at Tsingtao on the coast of northern China with the cruiser *Kaiserin Elisabeth*. But I avoided going into details, for if I had told him about my experiences there, and about my subsequent six months of adventures on the way back to Europe, it would have been necessary to tell him how I came to be there in the first place. And that, I am afraid, is a long and complicated story; also one which, at the time, I had a particularly strong personal reason for not wishing to tell. However, I say "had," because the day before yesterday, late in the afternoon, just as it was beginning to get dark, a curious thing occurred which has, I think, set me at liberty to relate this tale—provided of course that whatever residual deity oversees the affairs of agnostic ex-Austrian, ex-Czech, ex-Polish stateless persons grants me the breath and the time necessary to tell it.

I was sitting up in bed as Sister Elisabeth came to draw the curtains then went downstairs again to the kitchen. Kevin had brought me a couple of the last newspapers to arrive at the Plas on the Sunday before the snow came. I was browsing through these as he sat in the armchair leafing through a colour supplement. I had just put aside that infinitely tiresome London-Polish journal the *Dziennik Polski* and had picked up a Friday edition of *The Times*. It was the usual thin post-Christmas stuff; and anyway, if you ever get to my age world events will not interest you a great deal since you will have seen it all so many times already. I scanned a couple of pages in a cursory fashion—then felt my eye being dragged back up the page, like a jersey sleeve caught on a nail. It was in the obituaries column—not something I normally bother with, since all my contemporaries have been dead thirty years or more. It lay among the collection of minor entries down at the foot of the column, beneath those lucky enough to be given star billing: the obituaries written about those worthies who were too obscure to attract any notice while alive, but whose death is regarded as being of just sufficient importance to merit a few lines near the bottom. It read:

## PROFESSOR ALOIS FIBICH

The death was announced on 23 December at Limburg, Nebraska, of Alois Fibich, Emeritus Professor of Econometrics at the University of Omaha from 1947 until 1963.

Professor Fibich was born in Klagenfurt, Austria, in 1897 and served as a lieutenant in the Austro-Hungarian Navy during the First World War. Following the collapse of the Habsburg Empire in 1918 he studied economics in Budapest and emigrated to the United States in 1929, becoming a US citizen two years later and serving on President Roosevelt's economic staff during the New Deal years. His paper "Towards a Multiple Regression Analysis of the Demand Deficit Curve" (1948) is now widely regarded as placing him among the founders of the science of econometrics.

"Al" Fibich will be sadly missed by colleagues and by several generations of students, not only for his sterling contributions to modern economic science but also for his great personal charm and courtesy, which brought even to a windswept mid-western university campus a distant echo of that long-vanished world into which he was born. He is survived by a wife and three daughters.

Kevin looked up from his magazine. Sensing that something had happened, he got up and came to my bedside, and saw my fingertip resting on the page. He seemed to know instinctively.

"Someone you knew then, was it?"

"Yes, Kevin . . . yes, I think that I must have done. Surely there cannot be many people with that name. I remember, but somehow . . ." Recollections were beginning to swirl and surge inside my head, like the incoming tide in that little cove down among the rocks below the Plas.

"Funny coincidence that, like. Mate of yours, was he? Did you know him well then?"

"No, no, not well at all. If this is the man I think it must be, then I can only have met him for five minutes at the most. It's just that there was . . ."

Kevin had walked over and was pulling the armchair up beside the bed. He paused.

"Want to tell me about it, then? Bugger all else to do there is. They reckon on the weather forecast we're in for some snow tonight, an' if I go downstairs that ol' cow Asumpta'll only start chewin' me bollocks off for missin' the exposition of the blessed bloody sacrament." He grinned. "'Ere, tell you what, I've got a little water-heater thing down in the car, and some real coffee in a tin, just nice like. I'll nip down an' get it, then we'll have a brew-up here on the quiet while ol' Felicja's orderin' 'em about downstairs gettin' supper. Real rotten I call it, stoppin' you drinkin' coffee an' all. How long do they reckon you're . . . Sorry. I din' mean . . ."

I laughed. "You mean it doesn't make much difference at my age? Quite right: the Sisters are never happier than when they're denying some-body something. It suits their instinct for ruling. They are determined that I shall be the healthiest corpse in the graveyard. No, go ahead and bring up your things and start making coffee. Then sit down and perhaps I shall be able to tell you about it."

"You sure, like? You aren't any too well, they reckon."

"What does it matter? I am already dying from inactivity here. It helps pass the time. And anyway, perhaps telling you about it will clear a load from my chest before I pass on."

"Like goin' to confession?"

"Precisely, like going to confession. Except that I shall not expect Father Kevin to maintain secrecy. In fact, come to think of it, in case I drop dead half-way through, we had better have Sister Elisabeth's tape recorder here with us this time."

# 2

# A SAILOR'S LIFE

NOTHING HAS HAPPENED FOR THE PAST FIFTY YEARS . . ."
The wicker armchair creaked as Linienschiffsleutnant Stefan
Kaszała-Piotrowski stretched out his elegant silk-pyjamaed
legs and yawned. ". . . And the thing to realise, my dear Prohaska, is that
there is not the slightest reason to suppose that anything will happen in the
next fifty." It was there, I suppose, that these curious adventures of mine
can be said to have begun, that drizzly Sunday evening in the spring of the
year 1912; there in that cramped little stern cabin on the lower deck of the
Imperial and Royal battleship S.M.S. *Erzherzog Albrecht,* lying at anchor in
Pola harbour. It had been a miserable, damp day and I was in lower spirits
than usual, so I was not a ready or grateful recipient for the beautifully
modulated Weltschmerz which the lieutenant—a Pole from Cracow—had
made into such a wardroom speciality these past few months.

"Rubbish Kaszała: you're spreading alarm and despondency again
like the subversive Polish minor aristocrat that you are. Everyone says
there'll be a European war by 1915: us and Germany and Italy against
England and France and Russia. And if we aren't going to have a war,
will you please explain to me why all the governments of Europe are
spending money on armaments as if it were rainwater? Even our own
tight-fisted rulers have coughed up the money for a fleet of modern
battleships; vessels—if I may be permitted to observe—whose quarter-
decks your own feet may one day grace as a senior officer. So what's
it all for if it's not going to be used one day? The latest opinion in the
*Reichspost* is that it will start in the summer of 1915 and last perhaps as
long as two months; maybe even three." He laughed, and took another
puff at his cigarette.

"Really Prohaska, at your age. Twenty-six last week and you already sound like a retired colonel in a Graz coffee-house—or one of your asinine editorials in the *Reichspost,* come to that. Subversive Polish aristocrat indeed: that sounds marvellous coming from a Czech, aristocratic or not. I doubt whether the entire Danubian Monarchy contains another nationality as thoroughly disloyal—not even the Italians, who are half the time not really serious about it in my opinion . . ."

"What about the affair at the New Year's party in the wardroom? You could have ended up being court-martialled, toasting the Emperor's portrait as 'a tedious old fart.' If the GDO had understood Polish you'd have been in real trouble; and as it was all the rest of us had to perjure ourselves swearing that 'stary pierdoła' means 'wise and venerated monarch.'"

"I'd just had rather too much to drink, that's all: a harmless escapade. But really, Prohaska, it just won't do. For all your Kaisertreu speeches and your black-and-yellow underpants, you're far too bright not to see the truth."

"What truth?"

"The truth staring you in the face: that war's a thing of the past as far as Europe is concerned. No, they can all strut about in Pickelhaubes and dragoon cuirasses as much as they please: the fact is that a century of education and public health and piped water and tramways have abolished the possibility of a general war. We might still go out and shoot a few black men in the jungles of Africa, but the fact is we're now far too highly developed a civilisation for wars at home. They'll all snarl at one another and threaten and hold military parades without end, but it's all a great delusion. I read a book recently which proved conclusively that even if a war started by some accident, it would grind to a stop after a week."

"Why?"

He smiled knowingly: the smile of someone party to a secret denied to the understanding of the vulgar herd.

"Because, quite apart from anything else, the money would dry up. The modern world's run by the Jews and the stock exchanges, and the economic life of the industrial nations is far too delicate a mechanism for war to be of any use to it. If you read anything more in the papers than your stupid editorials you'd have noticed that the German steel industry has recently formed a cartel with the French ironfields. So that rules out war between France and Germany straight away, whatever rubbish the Kaiser cares to spout. No, you can depend upon it: at the first sign of serious trouble the financiers would turn off the money supply to any country that disturbed the peace. And even if troops got into the field they'd never endure the hardships or face up to modern weapons. Battles went out when our beloved Emperor and Louis Napoleon were both sick at Solferino."

"But what about armaments? The Great Powers are arming as never before. Even the k.u.k. Armee is building a 30cm howitzer . . ."

"Public works, pure public works: nothing but a way of redistributing tax revenues back into the economy. If they weren't building battleships and guns and fortresses it would have to be mausoleums or pyramids or something—anything so long as it absorbed money. But the socialists would kick up a row if governments nowadays went around building palaces like Versailles, so it has to be spent on something that puts money in the factory worker's pocket."

"I see. So if what you say is true, where precisely does that leave us?"

"Us? I will tell you, Prohaska. It leaves us as two young—but no longer quite so young—decorative and absolutely pointless mannequins aboard a sort of floating reform school swinging at anchor somewhere off the tip of the Istrian Peninsula: futile officers of this, the most deliciously, gloriously useless fleet the world has ever seen—the Imperial, Royal and Cataleptic Navy of the imperishable, petrified, land-locked Austro-Hungarian Monarchy, a desiccated mummy so fragile that its very existence is proof of how peaceful a place Europe has become, that it can tolerate such a ludicrous fossil." A note of seriousness began to tincture the elegant banter. ". . . Two young men, watching our glorious youth trickle away from us as we fritter away our days making boorish Croats and faithless Italians scrub their hammocks and polish brightwork and wash behind their ears; crashing away at gunnery drills as if we really expected to be doing it for real one day; bleeding grey with boredom and scraping together a few Kronen from our salaries each month so that we can pay a visit to Frau Mitzi's Tea Rooms and pick up a dose of something which we then have to pay the ship's surgeon to cure for us." He paused, staring at the rivet-studded deckhead above us, "God, such a waste. Such a terrible waste. Surely this can't be the only life there is? Why didn't I press on with the piano at the Conservatoire instead of letting my aunt frog-march me into sitting the Seeaspirant's exams?"

"Come on, Kaszała old man, cheer up for goodness' sake. It must be the weather. Anyway, you could always go back to music . . ."

"No good I'm afraid: too old now." He grinned, and drew upon his cigarette. "Anyway, you mustn't take too much notice of me and my melancholia. You're half Polish yourself and you understand what gloomy buggers we are—never happy unless we're miserable, 'the Martyr-Nation' and all that. Anyway, mustn't go on jawing like this. I'm officer of the watch for the diana, so it's time I turned in."

The four strokes of the ship's bell sounded dimly above us, sad and infinitely distant in the fine, sound-muffling drizzle, like the cathedral bells of some long-drowned city. Kaszała-Piotrowski stubbed out his cigarette—despite his pretensions to refinement and his amber cigarette holder he had to smoke the awful throat-corroding Ägyptianers like the rest of us junior officers—then he took off his dressing-gown and hung it on a hook behind the cabin door, swung his long legs up into the top bunk (which he occupied by virtue of his year's seniority over myself), wished me good-night and drew the curtains. He was soon snoring peacefully, happy to have spread a little dejection before retiring for the night.

I was left sitting by the folding desk, alone with my thoughts under the brass-shaded light of the reading lamp. I looked about me at the steel cube which had been our home these past six months. In truth it was not a particularly inviting nook: a poor compromise between the requirement for living space of two young men and the cruel steel exigencies of a warship; a bed-sitting room that might one day be a compartment in a floating fortress, slippery with blood and filled with the smoke and din of battle. One complete side was made of mahogany panelling—solid enough to look at, but in fact a removable partition which could be taken out when clearing for action and thrown overboard to reduce the risk of fire. Piping, ventilator trunking and cable ducts snaked across the steel ceiling, not quite high enough for Kaszała-Piotrowski (who was very tall) to avoid banging his head unless he walked slightly stooped. A single porthole, now curtained against the weeping night, provided light in daytime and also some measure of ventilation—though never enough in an Adriatic summer, when the cabins on the sunward side of the ship could be used to bake bread by mid-afternoon. An air shaft for the after magazine's cooling system obtruded into one corner of the cabin and reduced the already inadequate wardrobe space which had to hold our sizeable collection of clothing: gala, parade and service uniforms as well as field dress, overalls and tropical rig. Apart from that, our living arrangements consisted of two drawers, one apiece, beneath the lower bunk; a folding desk; a collapsible wash-stand which had a disconcerting habit of collapsing when in use; a couple of small lockers; a hard-backed chair; and a second-hand wicker armchair which we had clubbed together to purchase. All things considered, it was a pretty cheerless hole. The two of us had done our best with it, pinning up a few pages cut from the risqué Viennese journal *Pschütt* and other such periodicals; but it was still about as home-like as the average public lavatory.

And it was noisy: surrounded on every side, day and night, with all the myriad sounds of that great echoing steel hulk, ten thousand tonnes of ship packed tight with machinery and armament and stores, and with seven hundred men trying as best they could to fit themselves into the spaces that remained. Even at rest in harbour, as on this particular evening, the ship was never still. Water gurgled in pipes, ventilator fans hummed, donkey engines throbbed to work the electric generators, voices and footsteps echoed in distant passageways and on steel ladders above and below us in the great labyrinth. Massive hawsers groaned softly to themselves in their fairleads as the ship swung gently at her buoy. Even now, before I had turned in, the Phantom Scrap Dealer was getting down to his night's work: the man who seemed to be aboard all battleships, but whom one never met, who passed the hours of darkness by dragging a crate full of old rigging shackles, chain links and other such items into a compartment directly above one's head, then setting to work to sort them into piles on the bare steel deck.

You will perhaps have gathered from the foregoing that Linienschiffs-leutnant Kaszała-Piotrowski's elegant pessimism, though irritating, had not fallen upon entirely unreceptive soil. For the truth is that over the past few months my adolescent love affair with the seafaring life had begun to come under strain for the first time. Up until the autumn of 1911 I had enjoyed a remarkably promising career as a junior sea-officer in the small but now rapidly expanding fleet of the Austro-Hungarian Monarchy. Gazetted Seefähnrich on leaving the Imperial and Royal Naval Academy in 1904, I had almost immediately been posted to the China Station and had become embroiled in the closing stages of the Russo-Japanese war; creditably enough, at any rate, for me to be promoted on my return to Fregattenleutnant, a year earlier than normal. I had spent six months in England in 1907–08, studying submarine construction with the Royal Navy and Messrs Vickers at Barrow-in-Furness. There had then followed a succession of subordinate postings until at last, late in the year 1910, I was given my first independent sea-going command, the torpedo-boat S.M.S. *Haaifisch* based at Teodo on the Gulf of Cattaro.

Those had been glorious months for me aboard that little vessel, even though she was really nothing more than an enlarged, herring-gutted canoe made out of tinplate and powered by a single, grossly oversized triple-expansion steam engine. Day after day, night after night, we would steam at a hissing, vibrating twenty-five knots along the treacherous rock-studded channels between the Dalmatian islands, slicing through the waves with the sensation of speed made all the greater by our closeness to the water. I read somewhere a few years ago that naval historians now consider the torpedo-boat to have been the precursor of the submarine. And as one of their few surviving captains I can certainly confirm that, at speed in a head-sea, a torpedo-boat always seemed to spend more of its time underwater than above it. Sometimes we were never dry for weeks at a time. But for all the cramped discomfort aboard we were a happy crew, those twenty men and I: packed too close on top of one another for the exercise of Old Austrian discipline and having too many hardships and dangers in common for there to be any great distinction between ward-room and fo'c'sle. Then in the summer of 1911 my happiness was made complete: S.M.S. *Haaifisch* (Lschlt Otto Prohaska) was selected to be leader of a torpedo-boat division for two weeks during the summer naval manoeuvres in the Quarnero Gulf.

Nothing lasts forever though, either good or bad, and there were numerous other newly gazetted Linienschiffsleutnants below me, hungry for sea experience and their first command. All too soon I had to walk down the gangplank bound for Pola and the next stage in my educa-tion as a naval officer, which Fate and the Marine Section of the k.u.k. War Ministry had decided would be as a gunnery officer aboard a real ship-of-the-line.

The battleship S.M.S. *Erzherzog Albrecht*, 10,350 tonnes, launched at Trieste in 1906, was the result of a characteristically Austrian solution to the Imperial and Royal Navy's perennial problem of meagre annual budgets. Throughout most of its century or so of life, the k.u.k. Kriegsmarine had been crippled by official indifference and lack of money. Some said that it was all to do with our aged Emperor, who had nursed an intense mistrust of salt water ever since he had been dreadfully seasick on his first (and only) sea voyage—to Port Said in 1872 for the Suez Canal opening celebrations. Certainly it was true that, alone among European monarchs, Franz Joseph possessed no naval rank or uniform and used to say that quite frankly he felt queasy at the sight of a paper boat floating in a wash-tub. But perhaps it was rather that of all the European Great Powers in those days, Old Austria was the most mentally land-locked: ignorant and mistrustful of the world beyond Europe, with neither the means nor the will to stir its arthritic limbs in acquiring itself colonies. The result was that Vienna could never quite make up its mind whether it required a navy or not. As for Budapest, forget about it: if Austria had but a tepid interest in the sea and the lands beyond it, the Hungarian half of the Dual Monarchy had none at all. It was difficult enough year after year to get the Magyars to pay their share towards the upkeep of the k.u.k. Armee, so there was no hope whatever of getting them to cough up for a proper navy as well.

Relations between Vienna and Budapest had been more than usually strained when the 1903 defence budget came up for debate in the Imperial Reichsrat. The k.u.k. War Ministry had not quite managed to squeeze enough money out of the Magyar delegation to build two battleships to the standards current in the rest of the world's major navies. So a typically Austrian half-solution was arrived at, whereby, instead of two decent vessels, three almost-battleships were built instead, too weak to fight their foreign contemporaries and not quite fast enough to run away from them. Then, when the ships were laid down on the slipways and already too far advanced to be started again, insult was added to injury: the Royal Hungarian budgetary slot-machine unexpectedly disgorged the money for a fourth ship of the class. She was finally christened the *Erzherzog Albrecht* after the doyen of the House of Austria, the regulation-obsessed martinet who had beaten the Italians at Custozza in 1866—and (it was said) accidentally burnt his own daughter to death when he caught her smoking and she had tried to hide the offending cigarette beneath her crinolines. His portrait used to glare down at us disapprovingly as we dined in the wardroom, the thick Habsburg lower lip curling in disapproval and the hooded eyes narrowed behind the half-moon spectacles as he searched for a carelessly fastened button or a collar set a half-centimetre too high or too low.

The *Albrecht* and her sisters were certainly smart enough ships to look at, and quite adequate for summer flag-showing cruises around the Mediterranean ports if for no other purpose. But appearance is no sure sign of what the Royal Navy used to call "a happy ship," and I must say that my own six months aboard the *Albrecht* had been decidedly miserable ones. My position in the ship's staff was that of Gunnery Officer for the starboard intermediate battery: a broadside-firing group of six 19cm guns arranged amidships in two turrets at upper-deck level and four casemates set in the ship's side on the battery deck. My post in action was the starboard midships conning tower, a small, heavily armoured cupola, rather like one of your street letterboxes, set in the side of the ship above the intermediate battery. I would crouch inside this with a telephone clamped to my head and a rangetaker NCO beside me, peering out through the narrow vision slits and trying to direct the fire of the six guns. The arrangement was that I gave the rangetaker a target and he gave me the range. I then added the bearing and telephoned this down to the captains of the six guns, each of which had a crew of five men around it, with a further twelve or so below handling ammunition up from the magazines. This meant that I would be in a highly responsible position if we ever got into action, with nearly a hundred men under my command and perhaps a fifth of the ship's total firepower dependent on my judgement and eye-sight to guide it to its target. In practice, though, I soon found that my position as Gunnery Officer, Starboard Intermediate Battery, was rather like that of a constitutional monarch vis-à-vis his ministers: required to sign things and endorse decisions already taken, but still liable to be called upon to lay his head on the block when things go wrong. For the truth is that our range-taking and fire-control systems were still indifferent by British or German standards—admittedly better than in the good old days twenty years before, when each turret captain aimed the guns himself and blazed away as he thought fit (usually missing the target with at least nine shells out of every ten as a result), but not much better. Likewise the long-service gunnery NCOs on whom a battleship's fighting efficiency largely depends had been moving around with unsettling frequency of late, now that the Habsburg battle fleet was starting to grow after decades of neglect. Artillery NCOs—even senior gunnery ratings—were in great demand now, and the result aboard the *Albrecht* in the last months of 1911 had been an apparently endless game of musical chairs among the turret captains of my battery as petty officers left to be replaced by promoted ratings—who were soon promoted again and left just as they were getting to know their job. In the circumstances it is scarcely surprising that our results during a series of practice shoots in the winter of 1911–12 had been the worst of a very poor lot. In fact on one nightmarish afternoon in early March, south of Fort Peneda, my battery's fire-control system had broken down completely and we had ended up showering our shells around pretty well at random until the Captain, incoherent with rage, had ordered us to stop. The result had been a week's board-arrest for myself and a month or so of merciless ragging for my men, who were dubbed "the Peacemakers" and who got involved in a series of bar-room brawls in Pola town after being offered lessons at fairground shooting galleries.

It was a sorry state of affairs, to be sure. But I was young and inexperienced and had not yet come to understand that chaos and flux and constant low-level incompetence are the natural conditions of organised mankind; that for every happy ship, whether afloat or ashore, there are a dozen unhappy and perhaps three dozen indifferent ones. I felt flat and stale, and began to wonder for the first time whether seafaring life—at least as embodied in big-ship routine in the peacetime fleet of a venerable and almost land-locked empire—was quite what I had envisaged all those years ago as a sea-struck small boy in a small town in Northern Moravia, reading *Treasure Island* in German translation and building rafts of cabbage barrels to try and drown myself in farm ponds. As Kaszała-Piotrowski had been kind enough to point out, I had passed my twenty-sixth birthday the week before. The irresponsibility of adolescence, of being a snotty-nosed midshipman with farthings in my grubby pocket and the whole wide world before me, had slipped away and been lost. I still had farthings in my pocket (a Linienschiffsleutnant's monthly salary barely covered boot polish once the wardroom bills had been paid), but little now of the careless *joie de vivre* of youth. The world seemed to have narrowed lately to a dismal tunnel walled in by duty and routine and the service regulations, a tunnel with no light at the end of it save for the faint, infinitely distant glimmer of a Korvettenkapitän's cuff-rings some time about 1919.

Promotion in the k.u.k. armed forces was always achingly slow. We had no colonies, of course, and therefore no colonial wars, with their gratifying tendency to loosen up the seniority list a little through yellow fever or a few native spears in the back. And, then as now, people in Central Europe had a marked tendency to live until they turned to stone. With an eighty-two-year-old emperor in the Hofburg, how could it be otherwise? Seventy was the official retiring age for naval officers above the rank of commodore, but quite a number lingered on until they were in their eighties, by special permission of the Emperor. As for marriage, forget about it: I had no private means, so that nice girl and the small villa in the Borgo San Policarpo would have to wait until the mid-1920s at least.

No, it was scarcely an enticing prospect that seemed to stretch before me that drizzling spring evening in Pola harbour. And not having the skills of a clairvoyant, I had no way of knowing that in the end it would all turn out to be infinitely worse (though admittedly more interesting) than anything I could possibly have imagined that night. I undressed and prepared to turn in for the night. My cabin-mate was snoring steadily, while the nocturnal chainsmith was already about his work chink-clunk-CLANK-tinkle somewhere a deck above us. Five bells sounded as I prepared to turn out the light and get into my bunk. But as I did so, something jolted my thoughts. It was a white dove perched on the bare arm of one of the thinly veined *Pschütt* lovelies stuck up on the bulkhead. I opened my tiny desk drawer as quietly as I could and drew out a bundle of papers. Ah yes, here it was: k.u.k. War Ministry (Marine Section) circular GRM15/7/203(b) of 27 March 1912. I read it again, considered awhile, then placed it in my letter case for safe keeping. Perhaps it would be best to sleep on it until tomorrow, I thought. But why not? After all, they could only say no.

The bugles blew Auspurren at 5 a.m. sharp. Our shared servant, a surly Croat reservist called Bajželj, knocked and entered with my morning tea and a can of hot water for shaving (Kaszała-Piotrowski was taking the morning watch, the diana, and had risen and left at 4 a.m.). Bajželj was in appropriate Monday-morning form.

"Obediently report that it still rain, Herr Schiffsleutnant, and Matrose Quirini he come back last night all-over blood from bottle-fight in café. He with Oberschiffsarzt now—need ten stitches, maybe twelve perhaps."

I groaned inwardly, dismissed Bajželj, got up and drank my tea. Then I consulted the duty roster. We were on harbour watches now, so it would be normal working hours for me until Tuesday, when I was on for the middle watch. I poured the hot water into the treacherous wash-basin, stropped my razor and shaved in the dim light, then dressed and set off to perform my duties as officer commanding the starboard watch of the Foretop Division.

I think that scarcely anyone alive nowadays can begin to conceive of the precision with which life was organised aboard one of those pre-1914 battleships—seaborne symbols of the state's prestige at the end of a century of unparalleled peace and progress, floating microcosms of the ordered and stable society which (in theory at any rate) was supposed to prevail ashore in those now barely imaginable days of the gold standard and constitutional monarchy and Newtonian physics. Aboard the *Erzherzog Albrecht*, seven hundred men lived their daily lives to a time-table regulated to the last second, precise and closely packed as a Swiss pocket watch. The buglers would blow "Tagwäche und zum Gebet" at 5:00: fifteen minutes to turn out and dress, then fifteen minutes to lash up and stow the hammocks and tidy below decks. Then breakfast for the ratings: a half-kilogram of bread and a litre of syrupy, viciously strong black coffee. Breakfast finished, Schiffsreinigung commenced at 6 a.m. precisely: water streaming across the decks from hosepipes and cascading from the scuppers as four hundred bleary-eyed, barefoot sailors, trousers rolled up and boots hung about their waists, scrubbed and holystoned the decks and swabbed down paintwork and polished brass. By 7:30 the ship would be immaculate, wet and reeking of carbolic soap and metal polish. Then it was the men's turn, jostling one another to wash and shave by divisions in the ship's echoing, overcrowded fo'c'sle washrooms as the petty officers bellowed at them to hurry up and get on deck. Then 8 a.m.: eight bells, and the solemn start to the day, the red-white-red ensign of Imperial Austria hoisted at the stern as the ship's band played the "Gott Erhalte" and a platoon of sailors presented arms. That ceremony concluded, the boats were hoisted out, the post was distributed on the battery deck, awnings were spread (if the weather required it) and everyone not on watch set about his daily work.

There would be no awnings required this morning: it was drizzling steadily and the decks still gleamed with water hours after scrubbing had finished. My half-division went below for weapon-cleaning—scouring up cutlasses and boarding-pikes for all the world as if we still expected to grapple an enemy battleship and send boarding parties scrambling over the railings. At 9:00 I went on my morning rounds. The men were blank-faced: mostly Croats and Italians from the Dalmatian coast and islands, with a higher proportion of conscripts than usual. A good few of my men were first-year recruits, and therefore resentful of naval discipline, while a lot of the remainder were in their final year and therefore in that state which I think you used to call "demob-happy": not disposed to take the constraints of shipboard life too seriously when freedom was only a few short months away.

Matrose Quirini, the broken-bottle enthusiast, was one of the latter class. Once I had finished my rounds I went down to visit him in the ship's lock-up, accompanied by a petty officer clerk so that we could take a written statement. We found him sitting with his head swathed in bandages, woefully hungover and with an aggrieved air about him. It appeared that he had gone for a corporal of the Fortress Artillery after an argument over football and had got the worst of it; also that the corporal's fellow-drinkers and a number of civilian witnesses were willing to swear on oath that he had drawn his bayonet before making the assault. I took his statement, got him to sign it, assured him of a month's board-arrest with daily punishment-rowing thrown in, then left to take Divisional Officer's Report at 10 a.m. It was the usual sad chronicle of petty crime and folly, longer than usual on a Monday as all the derelictions of the weekend were reported to me. I finished only at 10:45, giving Steurmatrose Wenzliček a week's board-arrest for having removed the wire stiffener from inside the top of his cap in order to cut a more dashing figure with the girls over in town.

Next came clothes-washing, for this was Monday morning. I always hated supervising the washing of clothing and personal effects, overseeing the brutal process by which eighty or ninety young men knelt on the wet deck-planks and cleaned their second-best whites and underclothing by scrubbing them to destruction with hard bristle brushes. Soon the scuppers on the fo'c'sle deck by "A" turret were bubbling with an evil-looking sepia-coloured liquor unpleasantly reminiscent of the morning's breakfast coffee. Their hearts were not in it, though, this chill, damp morning, and I had to keep sending men back to do it again when they held up items of clothing for my inspection. About half-past eleven the Gesamt Detail Offizier, Fregattenkapitän the Freiherr Moravetz-Pellegrini von

Treuenschwert, came on his rounds and gave me a mild dressing-down because my men were so slow about their washing. He was followed by a messenger boy who handed me a note saying that in answer to my request, the Captain would be pleased to see me in his day-cabin after dinner, at 1:15 p.m. SHARP. So I saw the men to their dinner at 12:00. It was Monday, and everyone knew what was on the menu: the universally despised rice with peas—"risi-bisi"—of which the only good thing that could be said was that it was not quite as awful as the sour lentils which our economy-minded Proviantmeister offered the crew on Fridays. But a groan still went up from the crowded mess tables slung beneath the deck heads as the Backgasten carried up the steaming tins from the galley. Then the bugles blew to summon the officers to dinner. I finished eating as quickly as I could and went to see that my half-division were settled down for their hour's after-dinner rest. It was wet today, so they would not be able to spend the time in their preferred manner: some dozing on the warm deck-planks beneath the Mediterranean sun with their caps tipped forward over their faces while others sat around in groups playing lotto or wrote letters to their girls back in Linz and Czernowitz.

For my own part, I had some writing to do as well when I got back to my cabin, penning a formal request on one of those peculiar sheets of paper known as "Kanzlei-Doppel" on which all the myriad transactions of that paper-bound empire of ours were supposed to take place. I signed it, pressed it on to the blotter, then folded it carefully and placed it in the inside pocket of my jacket. I glanced at my watch: 1:11 already. I gave my hair and moustache a last nervous comb, straightened my bow-tie and set my cap square on my head. Then I made my way with palpitating heart to my interview with the Old Man.

In the many years since its downfall I have often heard the opinion expressed that the Austro-Hungarian Empire was nothing but a mechanism to enable a German master-race to lord it over a host of subject peoples whom it treated as little better than serfs—a sort of European South Africa in fact. This is utter nonsense of course: the old Dual Monarchy had many faults but (in its Austrian half at least) discrimination on grounds of birth or language was not one of them. However, it has to be admitted that within the Habsburg officer corps there was certainly massive over-representation of one nationality: the Croats. And of all the House of Austria's thousands of Croat land- and sea-officers, it would have been hard to obtain a finer specimen than our commanding officer aboard the *Erzherzog Albrecht,* Linienschiffskapitän Blasius Lovranić, Edler von Lovranica. Old Lovranić—a burly, red-faced man in his mid-fifties with protuberant eyes, en-brosse hair and a black moustache like the horns of an African buffalo—was a representative of that now long-forgotten tribe the "Alte Grenzer": the poor but ferociously proud Croat petty nobility settled by the Habsburgs as military colonists along the wild Turkish frontier back in the seventeenth century. Even goats were hard put to it to browse a living from the stony hillsides of the Lika district, so for generations past Lovranić and men like him had earned their bread as officers in the Austrian Army and fleet, rarely rising above the rank of major, since their courage and loyalty was usually equalled only by their dim-wittedness. Our Captain was a fierce disciplinarian and a minute stickler for naval regulations, perhaps an even greater terror to his subaltern officers than to the lower deck (who at least saw less of him). But it has also to be said that he was a fine seaman, scrupulously honest within his narrow mental limits and outstandingly brave. For one of the few things he and I had in common in the year 1912 was that we were both among the tiny handful of serving Austro-Hungarian officers who had ever heard a shot fired in anger.

For old Lovranić it had been in July 1900 in Peking, when he had been GDO of the cruiser *Temesvár* lying at Tangku and had been given the job of leading a detachment of sailors to guard the Austrian Legation in the Chinese capital, where trouble was reported to be brewing. On arrival he had fallen his men in at the railway station and set off towards the legation compound. Something was already afoot though: hostile crowds jostled them along the way and soon shots were heard within the city walls. Then as they passed through the city gates and reached the Mongol Market they suddenly found themselves facing a howling mob of a thousand or so Boxer fanatics, armed to the eyebrows and screaming for the blood of the long-nose devils. There was no line of retreat. Most men would have closed their eyes at this point and prayed that it would all be over quickly. But not Lovranić. Perhaps too unimaginative to grasp the appalling odds, he drew his sword, ordered his men to fix bayonets, then charged towards the British compound on the other side of the square. Forty-one men set out; a mere three arrived at their destination: Lovranić and two ratings, one of whom died soon afterwards from his injuries. A swathe of dead Boxers lay behind them. Lovranić, who had taken eighteen sword- and spear-wounds, survived to be awarded the gold Signum Laudis and was promoted two ranks by imperial decree when he returned to Austria. His other souvenirs of the Boxer Rising were a livid sword-scar across his forehead, half an ear missing, and an unshakeable opinion that he had a unique understanding of what war ("D'you hear that young man, WAR!") was all about.

As he rose from his desk to receive my salute I thought what a pity it was that Nature, which had given him the heart of a bull, should also have endowed him with a bull's intellectual equipment. He returned the salute brusquely, then picked up my petition from the desk as if holding up the corpse of a rat by one of its legs. He regarded it for some time with one half-closed eye before he spoke.

"Hmmph! Train as an aeroplane pilot! What the devil do you mean by this, Prohaska? Never read such a lot of damned eyewash in my entire life. Is this some kind of joke? Because I warn you . . ."

I swallowed nervously: the scar was beginning to grow livid, always a reliable barometer for approaching tempests.

"I most obediently report that if the Herr Kommandant would care to look at the attached War Ministry circular, all would be explained."

"Yes I have read it, thank you very much, Prohaska, and I still want to know what's the meaning of this. Life in the battle fleet not to your liking, eh?"

I tried to restrain my desperate urge to flee and seek refuge in the sick-bay, pleading temporary mental disturbance. "I obediently report that not in the least, Herr Kommandant. It's just that aviation has begun to interest me lately, and since the War Ministry is keen to encourage officers to qualify as pilots I thought—"

He cut me off short, but, to my surprise, more with a tone of hurt bewilderment than of bellowing anger. I sensed in fact that instead of browbeating me into submission he was trying in his clumsy way to reason me round. "Aeroplanes, Prohaska—complete and utter nonsense. Whoever heard the like of such drivel? Look here, I'm no opponent of progress: I grew up in the sailing navy—in ships without even auxiliary engines when I was your age—yet I still command one of the Monarchy's most up-to-date warships. Oh no, I can assure you, the Old Man may seem a chump to you young fellows, but there isn't much that he doesn't know about steam and torpedoes and breech-loading artillery . . ." (he tapped the side of his head knowingly) ". . . In fact, between ourselves, I can tell you that even electricity holds few mysteries for old Blasius Lovranić!" (I was suddenly reminded at this point of an incident a few weeks before when a fire had started down in the stoker's flats after the Captain had ordered the Elektromeister to rewire a fusebox with 2mm copper wire "instead of that miserable tinsel stuff you imbeciles insist on using.") "But aeroplanes, Prohaska—for God's sake man, where's the sense in it? None whatever. If a fellow really wants to break his neck then as far as I can see he might as well take up tightrope-walking for all the good it'll do the Emperor and the Fatherland."

"But Herr Kommandant . . ." He ignored me, seemingly anxious to talk me around to his way of thinking, rather than bawling me out of his office and giving me two weeks' arrest for being an insubordinate young whelp.

"I grant you, aircraft may have some limited utility for reconnaissance purposes—though quite frankly I fail to see how they can be of much use to the Navy since they can only venture a few miles out from land and are at the mercy of the lightest breeze. Likewise I have it on the authority of the ship's surgeon that the speed and altitude will make the blood accumulate in the airmen's brains and cause hallucinations. But as for their alleged applications in attacking ships—" (he snorted furiously) "—I ask you: a moth might as well hope to damage a blacksmith's anvil by butting it with his head!" He reached out and banged the white-painted steel bulkhead with his fist, causing it to ring dully. "For heaven's sake man: a wretched thing made out of bamboo and sailcloth, so flimsy that it's almost transparent, trying to threaten ten thousand tonnes of chrome steel with a six-centimetre armoured deck—they're all mad, I tell you." He paused awhile, mentally exhausted by this unaccustomed recourse to argument instead of a loud voice and naval regulations. It looked hopeless: request refused, and yet another black mark against me, this time as a crazed visionary as well as an incompetent gunnery officer. Then he turned back to me.

"Well Prohaska. I don't mind saying it, but you are one of our more promising young officers and I don't want to lose you." I nearly fainted with surprise at this, having believed myself to be on the edge of a court martial after the practice-shoot fiasco. "You've coped very well these past six months in a difficult command, and I'd rather you stayed with us. In my opinion the k.u.k. Kriegsmarine doesn't have so many lieutenants of your calibre that it can afford to squander their lives trying to make bird-men out of them. But there—I shall not stand in your way if you wish to kill yourself. My only stipulation is that you will first serve out your posting here aboard the *Albrecht*." He bent over his desk to sign the request—then paused with his pen in mid-air.

"No—not just now. Come back in an hour after you've thought it over. They tell me that it's a long way to fall; and that you only fall once."

By the time I came off duty at six bells my heart was considerably lighter than when I had awoken that morning. I descended the gangway to the officers' launch with the official request—now countersigned by the Captain as promised—in my jacket pocket. As the boat puttered past the long line of moored ships towards the Molo Bellona in front of the Marineoberkommando building on the Riva I looked again at the War Ministry circular:

GRM15/7/203(b) (Marine)    27/III/12

APPLICATIONS TO TRAIN AS NAVAL AEROPLANE PILOTS

In accordance with k.u.k. Ministerial Resolution of 13/XI/11, concerning the increasing relevance of flying machines to the conduct of modern warfare and the consequent need for the Dual Monarchy to build up a nucleus of trained fliers, the k.u.k. Minister for War has decided to increase the annual budget allocation for such training above the levels envisaged in the 1910/11 military estimates. In consequence of this, a further round of applications is invited from suitably qualified land- and sea-officers to be considered for possible places as trainee aeroplane pilots.

It is envisaged that training will commence in the early summer of 1912 and will be imparted, in the first instance, at civilian flying schools pending the establishment of an Imperial and Royal military flying academy.

Then came the paragraph that was troubling me:

Applicants should be aware that in view of the high failure rate on flying courses during the year 1911, and the limited availability of funding for the present year, trainee pilots will henceforth be required to pay for tuition themselves, receiving only board and lodging allowances while undergoing instruction. The cost of the tuition (currently estimated at 800 Kronen) will later be fully refunded by the k.u.k. Ministry of Finances, BUT ONLY UPON SUCCESSFUL COMPLETION OF THE COURSE AND ATTAINMENT OF A VALID PILOT'S LICENCE.

A fellow-Linienschiffsleutnant had been sitting next to me on the bench perusing the circular. He was a cheerful, open-faced fellow called Felsenberger from near Salzburg. Sensing my concern, he laughed and pointed at the paragraph with the stem of his pipe.

"Know what that means, don't you Prohaska old man—they've had to scrape so many of the poor deluded sods off the Aspern flying field that the War Ministry's getting fed up with paying for the funerals."

"Is that really so then, Felsenberger?"

"Fact. My brother's there with the Army and he says that the last one was so flattened they simply rolled him up like a Persian rug."

The launch bumped up against the limestone quayside and I stepped ashore. My first port of call was the post office building on the corner of the Arsenalstrasse. I was loath to do it, and a telegram to Vienna would blow a gaping hole in my parlous mid-month finances. But my Aunt

Aleksia had always said . . . So I sent the telegram. I did not expect a reply until next day, but I met a lady acquaintance in the main hall and stopped to pass a few pleasant minutes of light flirtation with her. Just as I was about to kiss her hand and bid her goodbye a clerk called to me from the telegraph booth:

"Herr Schiffsleutnant Prohaska? Telegram for you from Vienna."

I rushed across and tore open the envelope. It read simply, "Of course."

I concluded my business in the Marineoberkommando about 5:00, submitted my request in triplicate, gave the necessary financial guarantees, spoke with the necessary officials, then departed. It stands out vividly in my mind even now, three-quarters of a century later, because as I walked down the steps of the building and on to the Riva Francisco Giuseppe I saw a crowd gathered around a newspaper kiosk on the edge of the harbour. The evening edition of the *Polaer Tagblatt* had just come out. Wondering what was up, I crossed the road and tried to get to the stand to buy a copy. No luck: they were already sold out. But glancing across a reader's shoulder I saw the headline. It read, LINER *TITANIC* SINKS—GREAT LOSS OF LIFE. The twentieth century was not far off now.

## 3

# CLIMBING IN CIRCLES

ELECTRICAL CONTACTS?"
"All contacts open. Everything ready?"
"Ready for take-off, Herr Leutnant."
"Start the engine then."

There was a pause, then a shudder as the mechanic swung down on the propeller blade with the whole weight of his body. The engine coughed and backfired as the propeller turned once or twice then jerked to a stop. The mechanic took another swing at it, and this time, after a moment's hesitation, the engine spluttered into life. Smoke spat from the exhaust pipe and was followed by a metre-long jet of flame, blue and green as a peacock's tail feather in the early-morning half-darkness. The flame shrank back to a steady pulsing red-and-gold glow as the four cylinders of the Hieronymus-Warchlachowski engine settled into their rhythm. I let it idle to warm itself up and turned to the four mechanics waiting behind me.

"Right, lift her round then."

Two of them lifted the tail while the other two seized the wingtips to turn the aeroplane's nose into the faint breeze which was stirring the wind-vane on the other side of that still dim expanse of Bohemian cow-pasture. There was light enough now to see the end of the field—and also the copse of young larch trees beyond, its even, saw-edged skyline broken here and there by the gaps which marked errors of judgement on the part of earlier pupils at k.k. Fliegerschule Arány und Seligmann. I looked out across the port wing to where two men stood. One was dressed in the fur-collared blue-grey winter jacket and crimson breeches of a dragoon regiment; the other was a bowler-hatted civilian with gold-framed spectacles, wearing an inverness cape. These were the proprietors of the school, an unlikely enough pair on the face of it. Major Gyula Arány, Graf von Aránya, was a wealthy young officer in one of the smartest k.u.k. cavalry regiments. His partner was Herr Lucian Seligmann, a Jewish financier and industrialist from Brünn. They had been drawn into this venture of theirs by a common interest in aviation, Arány as a flier—he held one of Austria-Hungary's earliest pilot's licences, dating from 1910—and Seligmann as a patriotic man of business, struggling in the face of massive official indifference and hostility to set up an Austrian aircraft industry. The flying school was the outcome of their shared passion, Herr Seligmann providing the funds and Arány the necessary contacts and social cachet.

Well, no point in delaying it any further, I thought, for my seafarer's instinct told me that there would be no stronger wind that day. So with an apprehensive eye and a trembling heart I looked towards the line of trees in the distance, like a rider surveying a high fence from the back of an unreliable horse. Arány shouted to me above the noise of the engine.

"Good luck, Prohaska. May you break your neck and your legs!"

His companion was less disposed to such bonhomie. "Yes, Herr Leutnant!" he called. "Bend me another wingtip like the last one and I'll personally break your neck and your legs for you—before going on to do every other bone in your body!" It was barely light, but I could sense that he meant it.

I turned to the mechanics holding up the tail. "Very well then, let's go."

I pushed the throttle forward, and the engine roared with all its surging eighty horse-power. The aeroplane began to lurch forward across the uneven grass, its tail and wingtips steadied by the ground crew. It gathered speed, rocking and jolting as its four bicycle wheels bounced over ruts and molehills. Twenty metres, and the mechanics let go of the tail. Thirty metres, and the wings were beginning to flex and tremble. Fifty metres—I stared desperately at the copse ahead, trying to judge the right moment to pull back the control column: too soon and I would stall and crash; too late and I would hit the tree-tops and crash. Sixty, seventy . . . Now! I lugged at the column with all my strength, heart pounding and mouth dry with fear. I felt the motion smooth suddenly as the wheels left the ground, saw the trees rushing towards me—yes, we had made it, though only just, since

I distinctly heard the dry rattle as the undercarriage brushed the topmost twigs. I felt the sweat of fear chill suddenly in the rushing air as I turned the steering wheel on top of the control column to bank away over the larch wood. I was safely airborne: the difficult part was over.

It was about 7 a.m. one grey morning in the middle of November 1912 as I climbed laboriously away from that primitive flying field, just outside the southern Bohemian town of Iglau. It was nearly seven months now since I had applied to train as a naval pilot, but it had taken me this long to get as far as my final examination, what with the delays as papers were passed from desk to desk in Pola and Vienna, and then the difficulties of getting released from my posting aboard the *Erzherzog Albrecht,* then the wait for a place to fall vacant on a flying course. It was not until mid-September that I had made my first flight at Steinfeld flying school, just outside Vienna. I had flown solo after a week, and gained my civilian pilot's licence after two weeks—a speed, I might add, which was not a result of any exceptional skill on my part but rather of the extreme sketchiness of the instruction that could be offered in those far-off days when flying was learnt largely by doing it, like riding a potentially lethal bicycle, and bare survival was convincing enough proof of aptitude. And now I had come here to Iglau to take my military Flugzeugführer's examination. The k.u.k. Armee had not got around to establishing its long-promised flying academy, so army and naval pilot-training was still being contracted out to the civilian flying schools that were springing up everywhere across the Dual Monarchy, some of them quite reputable, others run by charlatans who might be receiving a secret subvention from the Guild of Undertakers to judge by the amount of business they put their way.

The previous day I had successfully completed Part 4 of my examinations, which required me to take the aeroplane ten times in succession up to a thousand metres—a process which involved climbing in a shallow spiral for about half an hour each time—and then cutting the engine to glide down and land between two telegraph poles spaced about twenty metres apart on a field. All had gone well until the last landing, when a sudden side-wind had caught me just as I was about to touch down and had caused me to clip one of the poles with a wingtip. The mechanics had been obliged to stay up half the night busying themselves with glue and wire and sailmaker's needles. Herr Seligmann had not been one bit pleased. He had given me a black look over the top of his spectacles, sighed, and noted down the sum carefully in his leather-bound notebook. It was going to cost me 250 Kronen, I was told—the best part of a month's salary. And I was already 850 Kronen in debt to my Aunt Aleksia for the course itself. The Imperial and Royal Ministry of Finances—the Ärar—would certainly refund the cost of my course once I had passed, and perhaps also the damage money. I knew though, both from experience and from hearsay, that it might well take years to get around to it.

But that could look after itself, I thought, now that I was already several minutes into the fifth and final part of my examinations, the map-reading exercise. This involved a cross-country flight over a course of a hundred kilometres from Iglau north-westwards to the Bubentsch flying field just outside Prague, carrying a sixty-kilogram sack of sand in the seat behind me to represent a passenger. On arrival at Prague I would hand the aeroplane over to another examinee, who would fly it back to Iglau while I returned by rail.

The aeroplane was a curious contraption called an Etrich Taube, or pigeon; a monoplane designed by an Austrian called Igo Etrich and notable for the fact that it had wings and a tail quite deliberately shaped like those of a dove, on the grounds (which I must say struck me even at the time as being logically questionable) that, if a bird flew looking like that, then so would an aeroplane. When I remember it now I tremble to think that I should have been foolhardy enough to take to the air in such a flimsy machine, a confection of such pathetic, damsel-fly fragility that when the Germans used one to drop bombs on Paris in 1914, the people on the ground thought that a gas-main had exploded because their assailant was almost transparent against the sunny sky. I sat waist-deep in a sort of wicker hip-bath and steered with a wheel, mounted upright on the control column, which banked the aeroplane not by means of a pair of ailerons but by twisting the whole of each wing via an elaborate system of wires and pulleys which ran to a pylon in front of me. As for instruments, I had a fuel gauge and an oil-pressure indicator and a crude sort of altimeter. But I quickly learnt that a pilot's best friends were his trailing scarf and a musical ear. The scarf was an excellent direction indicator: when we were going up it trailed down, when we were going down it trailed up and in between times leeway could be estimated by whether it trailed port or starboard. As for air speed, the most reliable means of judging it (I found) was the singing note produced by the wind rushing through the numerous bracing wires. Years later, when I was in the Home at Iddesleigh Road, I would often sit out in the garden on summer days and watch the jumbo jets thundering overhead from Heathrow, several hundred tonnes of aircraft and three hundred passengers blasted into the sky at forty degrees by engines, a single one of which would produce as much power as a thousand Etrich Taubes lashed together. And I used sometimes to smile and think, God speed you on your way my children and enjoy your package holiday. And spare a thought for the decrepit old fool down here with the funny accent, because if you can breakfast in Slough and eat your lunch in Tenerife you owe it in some small measure to people like me. For even if I cannot claim in all honesty to have been one of the pioneer aviators, I was still in the first rank of those who came along behind them.

The first hour of the cross-country flight passed uneventfully enough, cruising along at an altitude of six hundred metres and an average speed of fifty knots. It was one of those dreary Central European days in late autumn when high pressure stills the air and a thick, even blanket of grey cloud hangs over the landscape with such mournful, monotonous density that every trace of colour seems to have drained from earth and sky. But at least there was little wind—an important consideration when piloting an aeroplane that was really not much more than a powered glider. On I droned towards Prague, about an hour and a half from Iglau by my reckoning. As instructed, I was following the road: a white pin-scratch wandering through the matchstick-like field strips and dark-grey forests of the Tabor Plateau. I had already flown over Vlasim, a sudden knot of roads and houses below me. I would soon be at Beneschau, where I would pick up the main railway line and fly along that until I saw the spires of Prague in the distance. Arány had said that if I timed it right I should be able to follow the 6:30 Vienna-Prague express. I checked the fuel gauge. No trouble there: tank still half-full. Oil pressure was normal, but I thought that I detected the engine firing a little less evenly than before. Dirt in the carburettor, perhaps. But no matter: my watch told me that I was running ahead of time, so if the worst came to the worst I could always land in some field and clear the trouble—as I had done on several occasions already—then take off again and still reach Bubentsch within the time limit.

I looked up from the instrument panel. About two kilometres ahead the sky and landscape were blotted out by a haze of drifting white smoke. Perhaps the local peasants were burning stubble after the harvest, or perhaps a wood was ablaze somewhere (it had been a very dry autumn that year). At any rate, the smoke-bank was too high for me to climb over now, and too long for me to fly around. There was nothing for it but to take a bearing with my pocket compass and head straight into it, hoping that it would not be too wide. So into the sour, bonfire-reeking grey murk I flew, bearing north-west by north. I coughed from the smoke and pulled down my goggles to stop the smarting of my eyes. I suppose that I was in the smoke-cloud only a minute or so, and the bearing still read true. But when I emerged into the clear air beyond, it dawned upon me that the terrain below now bore no very evident relationship to that on the map clipped to its board balanced on my knee. I had lost the road. But that was soon the lesser of my troubles. As if it too objected to the smell of burning vegetation, the engine was now spluttering quite alarmingly, and I was patently beginning to lose altitude as the revs fell. A forced landing would soon be necessary. I looked ahead—and my heart sank even faster than the aeroplane. Before me loomed a great expanse of dark green pine forest: tall, mature trees and seemingly without clearings among them. This was extremely unwelcome, for unless I could keep the Taube airborne long enough to clear the forest and land in the pasture and stubble fields on the far side of it, there was going to be a crash, with Linienschiffsleutnant Ottokar Prohaska quite possibly ending a promising career impaled on the top of a Bohemian fir tree. At the very least 3,000 Kronen worth of aeroplane would be written off and I would be required to pay for it. Vistas of iron-bound poverty seemed to stretch before me, reaching into the early 1950s at least. "Come on, come on, you can do it," I muttered under my breath to the aeroplane, like a rider encouraging an exhausted horse to make a last jump. The engine coughed and stopped altogether, then burst into life again after a few turns of the propeller. We were over the forest now, close enough to make out the individual tree-tops below. The serrated line of its far edge was about a kilometre away, I thought. If only we could stay up . . . I bit my lip to blood and squeezed the breath in my lungs, as if this would somehow keep up the failing engine. As if in response to my frantic urging, it choked and backfired several times— then stopped completely. There was only the keening of the wind in the wires now as I drifted towards the menacing blue-green spikes reaching up at us like a cat's claws towards a bird.

But if the aeroplanes of 1912 were little better than powered gliders, this did at least have the advantage that when the engine failed—which was very often the case—they could still skim along for quite some distance on their own. I was thankful now for the tedious climb-and-glide-down examination of the previous day, as I struggled there with the control column, trying to prevent the Taube from stalling and urging it desperately towards the level fields in the distance. I thought that we were going to hit the tree-tops at one point. But some faint, freak updraught of air gave the Taube a tiny amount of extra lift—barely discernible, but just enough to offer some prospect of clearing the forest's edge. It was a couple of hundred metres now—yes, we were going to make it! As we glided over the forest fringe, almost brushing the topmost twigs, I saw a sudden explosion of birds below, scores of pheasants rising ahead of me squawking with terror. Then as I skimmed over the very edge of the treeline the air was suddenly filled with noise and whistling as the ground below broke out in a rash of bangs and flashes and puffs of white smoke. A metre-square section of wing near me disintegrated into a shower of splinters and shreds of fabric, then the rudder bar went limp beneath my feet as something hit the tail. The Taube suddenly lurched to port, mortally wounded and out of control.

I have often noticed during my life the curious phenomenon that, as disaster approaches, time seems to go into slow motion, so that one has all the leisure in the world to study the badge on the radiator of the bus which is about to run one over. And it was just so that morning. It could not have been more than five seconds or so in clock-time, but I was able to take in every tiny detail of the looming catastrophe: the wide stubble field, and straight ahead of me the rectangular enclosure of straw bales around two long trestle tables spread with white cloths and with silver and glassware and bottles all neatly set out. I saw the green-coated attendants unpacking things from wicker hampers. And I noted with curiosity how they paused from their work to turn round and stare at my approach—then leapt over the bales and scattered in all directions like hares in a cornfield. I made one last despairing attempt to try and miss the enclosure, which seemed to be drawing me towards it like some fateful magnet. But the rudder was done for, the control wires shot through. All that I could do now was duck my head down and shut my eyes tight. With an appalling noise of splintering wood and rending linen, the aeroplane made contact with the yellow soil of the Tabor Plateau. The undercarriage collapsed beneath us and the Taube proceeded to skid across the field on its belly.

I have little recollection of what happened next, only of a tremendous impact and a mighty crash of crockery and glass and cutlery and exploding champagne bottles as we hit the enclosure. Then stillness, and silence, and a swirling ochre fog of dust. Gradually it dawned upon me that I was still alive: bruised and cut and winded, but still alive. Gingerly, I worked my fingers and toes, then each arm and leg in turn. No broken bones so far as I could make out. But I was trapped in the wreckage by the sandbag, which had slid forward, and by the intricate cat's cradle of control wires, which had collapsed on top of me. This was not good: the aeroplanes of 1912 might have been deliberately designed as firelighters; and, not a month before, one of my fellow-pupils at Steinfeld had been cremated alive, trapped in the debris of a Taube after a heavy landing. The smell of burning flesh seemed to sting in my nostrils once more as I struggled to free myself. I could see little for the dust. Also the talc lens of one side of my goggles had shattered, and my flying helmet had slipped down over the other eye. So I could make out only dimly the shape of the figure clambering over the wreckage towards me.

"Quick!" I yelled. "For God's sake help me out—the plane might catch fire at any moment!" But to my astonishment, instead of trying to drag me free, my rescuer fell upon me with a bellow of rage, seized the lapels of my flying tunic and proceeded to shake me until my head nearly came off.

"Scum! Filth! Canaille!" he roared. "You miserable horse-turd! You lousy rotten vermin-infested blackguard! What do you mean by this outrage, you hooligan? By God, I swear that I'll get you ten years for this, and sue you for every last Haller in damages!"

I must say that I rather lost my own temper at this ruffianly assault on a helpless survivor of an air-crash. I had one arm free, so I lashed out at my assailant—and caught him a nice satisfying thump in his ample midriff. With a loud "Ooof!" he staggered backwards, waving his arms—then sat down ignominiously in the dust some way off. I felt that I should give him a piece of my own mind now.

"Hooligan yourself! What do you mean by shooting down passing aircraft, you fat imbecile, then attacking the survivors like a common street bully? Damages—I should think so too! I'll have to pay for this aeroplane, and I swear that I'll have the money out of you with costs even if I have to drag you through every court in Austria to do it!"

I had managed to push up my goggles now, and the dust had settled enough to give me a clear view of my assailant, who had got to his feet and was brushing himself down, puce-faced with rage and gobbling incoherently like an infuriated turkey-cock.

In those far-off days before television, when cinema newsreels were a novelty and even magazine photographs still uncommon, we ordinary folk were far less familiar with the features of the great than people are today. We had only a few stiff, heavily retouched official portrait-photographs to go on, with perhaps an occasional glimpse from afar during a procession if we were lucky and lived in the big cities. Also it was very much the custom there in Central Europe that our rulers should hardly ever appear in public without being dressed in military uniform of some kind. So there was a few moments' hesitation before recognition dawned upon me. There could be no doubt about it though: he wore a green Homburg hat and was dressed in a long jacket of loden cloth with corduroy knee-breeches and

Tyrolean stockings and ankle boots, but there could be no mistaking that jowly face and the wild-boar moustache and the curious dead, blank eyes which stared coldly down at us from a hundred official portraits. Even so it took some time, sitting there in that Bohemian field amid the ruins of the Taube, for the full ghastly skin-crawling realisation to dawn upon me: that the man whose shooting picnic I had just devastated and whom I had then assaulted and abused was none other than Franz Ferdinand von Habsburg-Lothringen, Archduke of Österreich-Este, Heir-Apparent to the Imperial Throne of Austria and the Apostolic Crown of St Stephen of Hungary. I swallowed hard and closed my eyes as a chill sweat broke out down my back, hoping desperately that the aeroplane would catch fire after all.

The Heir-Apparent had by now recovered his breath sufficiently to let me know what he thought of me. "Punch me would you, eh, you lout? Not content with smashing up my luncheon without so much as a by-your-leave? Well my fine sir, I can promise you a hot time of it and no mistake. This may be the age of democracy, but punching a level-crossing keeper and assaulting an archduke are still not quite the same thing . . ." He paused. The sleeve of my flying tunic had torn open and the three gold-braid cuff-rings of my naval jacket were visible beneath. A smile spread across the archducal features: a curiously unpleasant and (I later learnt) rarely observed grimace in which the upper front teeth were slowly bared as the moustache-points closed upon the nose like the pincers of a stag-beetle. "Aha, so you are a naval officer, are you? Or should I say, *were* a naval officer? Because if I don't use my position as an admiral to get you locked up for life in Pola naval prison then my name's not Habsburg!"

You may perhaps have concluded that, in the circumstances outlined above, there was no possible particle of horror that could have been added to the predicament in which I found myself. But you would be mistaken, for a second figure had walked up to join the Heir-Apparent as he berated me. And if there had been some momentary hesitation in recognising the Archduke, there could not be a single instant's doubt as to who this was who stood before me. The spiked moustache and the deformed left arm were instantly recognisable, likewise the rather ludicrous quasi-military hunting get-up with the feathered hat and the ornate dagger at the belt and the Cross of the Order of St Hubert hung below the high Prussian collar. It was Wilhelm II of Hohenzollern, Emperor of Germany.

I squeezed my eyes tight shut. I am sure that you also have experienced it: the sensation of being in some hideous nightmare, knowing perfectly well that it is only a nightmare, yet being unable to find the lever which will allow you to drop out of it and wake up. Well, it was just like that. Yet I was curiously composed and resolute now. I would count up to ten and then open my eyes. If they had gone away (of which I was fairly confident), then it was only a dream. If they were still there, then I was resolved that I would struggle free of the wreckage, seize the Heir-Apparent's shotgun (which lay nearby), place it beneath my chin and blow my own head off. Eight, nine, ten . . . I opened my eyes, half expecting to find now that I had crash-landed in St Peter's Square, killing the Pope and the American President. But no; they were still there. I gazed, dismayed, as the Kaiser stared at me in disbelief, turning red in the face. Then to my utter astonishment he flung back his head and let out a bellow of laughter the like of which I have rarely heard before or since. He roared, he howled, he sobbed with laughter. He doubled up with merriment. Tears rolled down his cheeks as he laughed to a point where his attendants had to thump him on the back to prevent him from choking. At length he recovered himself sufficiently to fling his arm about the shoulder of the Heir-Apparent, who had stood by during this display of hilarity looking very confused and unsure of himself.

*"Du lieber Gott!"* he gasped. "Oh Franzi, it was priceless . . . Merciful heavens, I don't think I've laughed so much in years . . . to see you sit down on your fat arse like that in the dust . . . Oh dear . . . oh my goodness . . . What a sight!"

By now others had come to join the Kaiser and the Archduke. First to arrive was a slim, tall, middle-aged woman dressed in a tweed suit with a fox-fur stole and a wide, heavily veiled hat. She was accompanied by a girl of about twelve and two younger boys, both wearing smart brass-buttoned sailor outfits with cap-ribbons lettered S.M.S. SANKT GEORG. They stared at me. Then the woman spoke.

"Really, you men—just standing there gawping. Haven't you the sense to help the poor man? Honestly . . ." She turned to the two boys. "Maxi, Ernst, help the poor Herr Leutnant get out, quickly now. And you, Soferl, run and get the first-aid box, then tell the Head Keeper to send for the motor car!"

Maxi and Ernst needed no second bidding: they scrambled across the ruins of the Taube and set to work disentangling me from the confusion of wires. A couple of beaters came to help them, and before long I was lying on the stubble field as the Heir-Apparent's wife and daughter expertly slit open the leg of my breeches to apply bandages and iodine to a long but fortunately shallow graze on my shin. Half an hour later I was reclining on the middle bench-seat of a large yellow Mercedes touring car as we lurched along a rural cart-track. The Duchess of Hohenberg and her daughter fussed over me while the Kaiser and the Heir-Apparent sat in front misdirecting the harassed chauffeur. As for the two boys, they fairly devoured me with questions. Was it very cold up in the air? How fast did an aeroplane fly? Did I get dizzy? Had I ever flown upside-down? What were clouds like inside? Would I promise to take them up for a flight one day, please oh *please* Herr Leutnant . . . Their excited cross-examination only ceased as the motor car drove across a bridge and through an echoing gate-arch. We had reached the Heir-Apparent's country residence, the castle of Konopischt.

At dinner that evening, by his own special request, I was seated next to the German Kaiser. I scarcely managed to get down a forkful, however, amid the barrage of questions he fired at me throughout the meal in that famous peremptory, no-nonsense bark of his, questions (I soon divined) which were designed not so much to elicit information as to impress me and all within earshot with his masterly and up-to-the-minute grasp of aeronautical science, the development of aircraft and their potential civil and military (especially military) applications. It was difficult to give intelligent answers; partly because he would keep answering the questions himself, and partly because it appeared that at the moment he had a number of grasshoppers inside his Pickelhaube concerning the relative merits of airships and winged aircraft; also a number of frankly bizarre notions on the subject of aerodynamics.

"Of course, Prohaska, any imbecile can see that heavier-than-air machines will never be able to grow much bigger than the Taube in which you flew here so inauspiciously today. It's all to do with the density of the atmosphere. There comes a point, d'you see, at which the air is no longer thick enough to support an airfoil."

I knew that royalty must never be contradicted, but I felt I had to point out that according to all the aviation magazines, Professor Sikorsky in Russia had already built and flown a giant four-engined biplane which could carry twenty passengers or several tonnes of cargo. The All-Highest merely ignored this, however, and pressed ahead with his discourse, explaining that the universally recognised inability of the air to support large aeroplanes—and also the well-known scientific fact that aeroplanes would never be able to fly faster than two hundred kilometres per hour without their wings snapping off—was the reason for Imperial Germany's massive investment in Zeppelin airships.

All in all it was a very trying few hours, particularly since my numerous bruises and abrasions from the crash were now beginning to stiffen and ache. Worse than the injuries though, once I had got over my initial relief at having emerged from the accident alive and largely intact, was the awful realisation that I had written off not only the Taube but also a large amount of the Heir-Apparent's silverware, glass, crockery, provisions, wine and table linen. How on earth was I ever going to pay for it all? At my request an aide had telephoned to Iglau with news of the crash. He reported that Herr Seligmann had thrown an epic fit at the other end of the line and promised (i) to emasculate me publicly in front of Iglau Town Hall and then (ii) to sue me for my very last farthing and the shirt on my back by way of reparation. I longed to get to bed and seek some escape at least from my troubles in the arms of sleep. But even when dinner was ended there was still no respite, for I was obliged, once the ladies had left, to join the Kaiser and the Heir-Apparent and their respective entourages (for the most part painfully aristocratic cavalry officers) in the smoking room for a display of that awful, elephantine North German bonhomie.

The Kaiser was still full of the day's unusual events and his part in them. Already I could sense that the story of my forced landing in the stubble field was being furbished up for eventual inclusion in a coy little volume entitled *Merry Anecdotes About Our Beloved Kaiser* or some such syco- phantic hogwash, which a generation of German schoolchildren would be forced to read and which would be bought (and left unread) by all monarchy-loving German households. The Kaiser was enjoying himself hugely; but the Heir-Apparent, for his part, was still eyeing me with cold dislike, no doubt remembering the buffet in the stomach and wondering at what point he could decently take me aside and talk seriously about com- pensation for his devastated shooting picnic. For the moment though, so long as the Kaiser had attached himself to me, I knew that I was safe.

"My dear Prohaska," he boomed, throwing his sound arm around my shoulder, "tell me now, how do you feel after your little accident?"

"Your Imperial Majesty, I have the honour to report that . . ."

"Come on man, don't look so down in the mouth. Have some more champagne. You look like a dog that's just had a good thrashing. What's the trouble?"

"Well, Your Imperial Majesty, I have to confess that I am rather trou- bled over paying for the loss of the aeroplane and the damage to His Imperial Highness's property. I have no private means, you see, only my naval lieutenant's salary . . ."

He roared with laughter. "Just a little joke, Prohaska—knew about it all along. Only teasing. Don't worry yourself on that score: all that's being taken care of. I shall personally pay for everything."

"Your Imperial Majesty is too kind . . . I . . ."

He laughed. "My Germany is a wealthy country. In fact, Count Hohenstein was on the telephone not an hour ago speaking with your lousy Jewish flying school proprietor. He has been assured that by tomor- row at the latest he will have received in compensation not one but two— mark you, two—brand-new Taube aeroplanes, courtesy of the Rumpler Aircraft Company and the German Imperial Household. That should shut his nasty Israelite mouth for him. There is just one condition though."

I swallowed hard: the Kaiser was notorious for making people perform humiliating forfeits in return for favours granted. "Might I obediently enquire what that is, Your Imperial Majesty?"

"Well, since the remains of the crashed aeroplane are now, technically speaking, your property, I want you to let me have the propeller and sign it for me so that I can hang it up among my other trophies in the lodge at Rominten. I want all the future generations of Germans to be reminded of the day Kaiser Wilhelm II bagged his largest pigeon!"

Although exhausted, I slept badly that night, what with my bruises and sprains and all the excitements of the day. But at least it was a crushing weight off my mind to know that the German Kaiser—who after all claimed to have fired the fatal shots—would pay for the damage. After breakfast the next morning the Heir-Apparent, clearly not wishing to be outshone in magnanimity by his guest, took me on a guided tour of Schloss Konopischt, with the Kaiser tagging along behind to contribute his two-pennyworth at every possible juncture. I rapidly came to the conclusion that the Kaiser was a compulsive attention-seeker, determined to be the bride at every wedding and the corpse at every funeral. He struck me that morning as someone who might have made a tolerable actor, but who was—to say the least of it—a rather disturbing character to find in charge of the greatest military and industrial power in Europe.

But then, I have to say that his host was pretty peculiar as well. As we trooped through the rooms of the castle Franz Ferdinand held forth to us on what he had paid for the contents of each. And in truth, it was all more like an ill-managed department store than the principal family residence of the heir-apparent to an empire: every salon and every chamber crammed from floor to ceiling with a suffocating, indigestion-provoking, cloying profusion of antiques and bric-à-brac—vases, paintings, statuary, Turkish rugs, Arabic silverware and Chinese porcelain; objets d'art, objets trouvés and plain objets; the Ottoman Room, the Tyrolean Room, the Italian Room; genuinely priceless art treasures (mostly looted from his Este estates in Italy) mingled promiscuously with junk that would have been remaindered at any flea-market in Vienna's 16th District. And everywhere, stuffed animals: mementoes of the hecatombs of wild creatures slaughtered by this tireless huntsman. The Archduke, it soon became clear, could recite the price of each item from memory, but had not the remotest conception of the intrinsic worth or worthlessness of any of them. There was something bizarre, gross, almost psychotic in this relentless accumulation of things for the mere sake of accumulation. Most peculiar of all, I remember, was the Saint George Room, crammed with hundreds of representations of the warrior saint on everything from stained-glass windows to ashtrays. Saddest of all was the stuffed corpse of a duckbill platypus—about the size of a smallish cat—which the Heir-Apparent boasted of having despatched with a single shot one morning on a creek north of Sydney during his 1892 world tour.

We reached the third floor, and here the Heir-Apparent stopped to open the door of a lavatory leading off a stone corridor. I assumed that he wished to leave us for a couple of minutes, but to my surprise he beckoned us inside and closed the door behind us.

"Finest view in the whole castle, from this window," he said. "There —magnificent, isn't it? The largest rose-garden in Europe, and all my own work. I had to demolish a village to get this vista, and I've even had five hundred wicker muzzles made so that the damned tenants' cows can't browse the bushes. No ploughing within three kilometres of the Schloss, that's my rule. And if the villagers don't like it they can sell up and go to America. Had some impertinent bugger of a Czech deputy asking questions about it last week in the Reichsrat. Hah! Soon dealt with him: 'Watch your step, my man,' I said. 'I shall be Emperor before long, and I certainly don't intend taking any lip from your sort.'"

It was a tight fit for the three of us in the lavatory, which like most such offices had been designed for only one occupant at a time. The Kaiser and I had to edge around one another and the Archduke to admire the view. Suddenly the Kaiser spoke.

"Franzi, I've been thinking."

"Oh?"

"About the young Herr Schiffsleutnant here. You were saying only a few days ago that you need an assistant naval ADC on your staff to deal with marine aviation. Well, who could be a better candidate than Prohaska here?"

I could scarcely believe my ears. The Heir-Apparent was clearly reluctant though.

"Oh . . . er . . . yes . . . Well, I suppose I did say something of the kind. But . . . well, frankly I had been thinking of someone rather more senior and . . . er . . . of a more appropriate background."

"Yes Franzi, but you aren't going to find any naval officer much more senior than this with a pilot's licence. And anyway, I was speaking with your wife and she's rather pleased that Prohaska here is a Czech by birth, like herself."

"Well . . . yes . . . but . . ."

"Franzi, you owe me a favour or two. Be a generous host and grant me this."

"Oh well . . . hang it all . . . All right then."

And thus it was that only twenty-four hours after taking off from that Bohemian cow-pasture, I, k.u.k. Linienschiffsleutnant Ottokar Prohaska, son of a Czech postal official and with barely two Kreuzers to rub together in my pocket, landed in the entourage of the heir to, if no longer the most powerful, then still the grandest and most venerable monarchy in Europe.

# 4

# FIRST SOCIETY

ALL THINGS CONSIDERED, my appointment to the Archduke Franz Ferdinand's Military Chancellery as Assistant ADC (Marine) was remarkably swift. In the normal course of events in Imperial Austria these things would take months or even years as the relevant papers were passed from in-tray to out-tray to in-tray on a hundred desks in a score of government departments. But in my own case the whole process had a powerful driving motor behind it in the form of the Heir-Apparent; because even if Franz Ferdinand himself was evidently unhappy about my appointment, the mere mention of his name had a remarkable effect on the weed-clogged channels of the Habsburg bureaucracy. Not only were all civilian officials, from departmental head to filing clerk, in awe and some terror of him as the man who would soon be their lord and master; the Heir-Apparent also had considerable leverage in the War Ministry and particularly in its Marine Section.

Alone among the numerous members of the Noble House of Austria, Franz Ferdinand had taken an interest in the Fleet. The last Habsburg to occupy himself with maritime affairs had been the Emperor's brother Ferdinand Max a half-century before, the one who had met his end in front of a firing squad after a half-baked attempt to have himself crowned Emperor of Mexico. Come to think of it, perhaps Franz Ferdinand would have done well to have heeded that unhappy precedent. But instead he wore an admiral's uniform on public occasions, busied himself with the Flottenverein and other such causes, and used his influence in the ministries and the Reichsrat to try and get budget allocations which would do something more than replace antiquated ships with ones which were merely obsolete. It all stemmed (I was told) from the Archduke's round-the-world tour in 1892 when he had been incensed to see how easily the arrogant English milords—whom he detested—controlled the world's oceans with their mighty fleet. What he had never thought through however, as far as I could make out, was exactly how he proposed remedying this state of affairs, since if the Dual Monarchy spent its entire national budget each year on battleships the British would merely build more. Like most of the Archduke's personal dynamism, for which he was so regularly praised in the Catholic press, it was dynamism which led nowhere.

It has to be said, however, that during the time in which I served the Heir-Apparent as junior naval ADC with responsibility for marine aviation, I had very little contact with the man himself. Franz Ferdinand had already built up a kind of semi-official government-in-waiting at the Belvedere, his official residence in Vienna, and by the time I arrived on the scene there were some forty or so military aides on the Archduke's staff, forming what was called "the Military Chancellery" under the direction of Colonel Bardolff. My duties, as a very junior Linienschiffsleutnant of less than glittering social origins, were chiefly concerned with gathering information on the development of naval flying elsewhere in Europe (largely from press cuttings, where my knowledge of English and Italian came in useful), feeding stories to the Heir-Apparent's pet newspaper journalists and handling correspondence pertaining to marine aviation—with the various ministries, and with the hundreds of industrialists, inventors and downright lunatics who were trying to sell their products and ideas to the Austro-Hungarian Navy. I shared a small, stuffy outer office at the Belvedere, not with the chief naval ADC but with a young army captain called Count Belcredi who was also dealing with aviation, but this time from the side of the k.u.k. Armee. Hauptmann Belcredi was on secondment from a Jäger regiment; not your common-or-garden Feldjägers like my brother Anton's regiment up at Leitmeritz, but the crack Tiroler Kaiserjägers—the ones with the curled-brim hats and the plumes of cock's feathers.

He was a rather reserved fellow, but amiable enough, and over the weeks a certain guarded camaraderie grew up between us. His great-uncle had been Austria's Prime Minister back in the 1860s, and he—unusually for an army officer—also seemed very interested in the Viennese political scene, reading the newspapers avidly each day and spending a great deal of time in conversation with the various *hommes d'affaires* who frequented the Belvedere. I suspected him of perhaps harbouring an intention of leaving the Army one day and entering political life himself.

My only release from desk duties came in December 1912, when I was sent south to the Adriatic to do some serious flying. I had successfully retaken Part 5 of my Flugzeugführer's examinations the week after the crash at Konopischt and had duly gained my brevet as a naval pilot. The First Balkan War was now in full chaotic swing, so I was despatched to the Gulf of Cattaro at the Archduke's behest to try out one of the k.u.k. Kriegsmarine's recently purchased French Donnet-Lévèque flying boats. Austria was officially neutral, so my excursions down the Montenegrin coast were for observation purposes only. But I shall still always remember those early-morning flights from Teodo Bay: climbing into the rushing thin cold air as the first light of the winter sun shone over the snow-capped peaks of the Lovčen range, its rays producing such colours as one would never even have thought existed. One day I circled for twenty minutes and watched as the Turkish cruiser *Hamidieh* shelled the Montenegrins below in Antivari.

In general though, back at the Belvedere, my duties were not onerous. So for the first time I was able to get to know our great capital city, which I had previously visited only for a few days at a time. Ah, Old Vienna: I think that there has never been a city in the whole world whose memory has attracted such extremes of love and loathing. In the years since, a thousand syrupy popular songs and third-rate films have portrayed it as a dream-kingdom of gaiety and music and laughter. Likewise library shelves full of memoirs and learned articles have described its dreary tubercular slums and the national hatreds that festered within them; the stuffy, airless, over-furnished rooms and the swarms of prostitutes on the Kärntnering and the coffee-house philosophers talking vaguely of final solutions to the Jewish question. But I saw it in those last years; and while it is true that the drains were bad and the Imperial Parliament even worse, and that syphilis was as much a local speciality as Apfelstrudel, I still think that for a young man like myself life in the imperial city before the world war was about as near an approximation to paradise as this earthly existence allows.

Vienna in those years was a city which never simply *was,* like Edwardian London, but one which was endlessly, fascinatingly not-quite. The city was solidly anchored in the very centre of Europe, yet I found that living there was curiously like my first voyage on a sea-going ship, when I was about eleven: that same odd, rather disturbing sensation as I walked across the deck and found that the planks were not quite where I expected them to be when I put my foot down. Outwardly it was a German capital; yet three quarters of its people were Czechs or Poles or Magyars or Italians, first-generation German speakers at best. The actors at the k.k. Burgtheater set the world standard for spoken German. Yet when people asked for directions in the street it was often difficult to tell which language one was being addressed in, let alone what was being said. Capital of the most hidebound, mummified bureaucracy in Europe, it still contained in those years the little knots of scientists and philosophers and artists who were busy inventing the modern world, in every domain from nuclear physics to psychology and from economics to music—totally ignored by the Viennese themselves, who slumbered on in their cosy little cocoon of waltzes and Schlagobers as if nothing would ever disturb their bovine tranquillity. The city had some of Europe's most daringly modern public buildings, and electric trams and motor buses and one of the best-planned city railways in the world. Its public water-supply was so excellent that the fluid which came out of its taps could have been bottled and sold as mineral water anywhere else. But still the place had an atmosphere of the Balkans about it rather than of Western Europe. One would sit outside a café watching the bowler-hatted, ostrich-feathered crowds on the Mariahilferstrasse, indistinguishable from those on Oxford Street or the Unter den Linden—then suddenly see a sheepskin-clad Slovak herdsman or a Moravian children's nurse in her short pleated skirt and brightly embroidered bodice; or a platoon of Bosnian infantrymen in their red fezzes marching back to barracks; or even (if one was very lucky and it was early in the morning) a Herzegovinan kitchen-maid making her way back from the Naschmarkt with her purchases contained in a basket balanced on her head.

It was not the soft, gentle, warm place of popular myth. The city was grey and sooty, and constantly swept by winds—either the cold gritty north-easter from the plains of Moravia or the sticky, irritating wind blowing down from the Alps which would set off the suicide epidemics that were such a feature of local life. Yet to me it was a place which could suddenly thrill the heart: quite unexpectedly, as when one looked out on a snowy morning from the windows of the Neu Hofburg on to the panorama of the Ringstrasse, its theatrical splendour all the more engaging (I found) because of its schizophrenic inability to decide exactly how it would impress the beholder, whether with fake German Gothic or fake classical architecture, or with that odd ochre-painted pattern-book version of Neo-Renaissance which distinguished the public buildings of the entire Monarchy. While I was in Vienna they were just completing the Ringstrasse project with a final triumphant flourish: the great pompous pseudo-baroque hulk of the new War Ministry down at the Stuben Ring end, with its giant double-headed eagle perched precariously on the parapet as if it were about to crash down on to the pavement beneath. Carved below it on the architrave, grandiloquently set out for the benefit of wondering posterity in metre-high letters, was the date MCDXIII.

Oh, it was all designed to impress. And it was, I have to admit, very imposing to the casual beholder; for never did Habsburg Austria look more confident or vigorous than in those last years. I witnessed what I suppose must have been the old Monarchy's last great military parade, along the Ringstrasse in—if I remember correctly—October 1913, to mark the centenary of the battle of Leipzig. Even now I still see them marching past, a river of dark blue and grey behind the black-and-yellow eagle-banners and the glittering regimental bands, those men of the old Imperial Army, rifles slung on their shoulders and sprigs of green fir behind their shako rosettes: Germans and Magyars and Czechs and Slovenes swinging past the round-shouldered old man in the green-plumed hat, taking the salute in front of the Schwarzenberg Monument. Gone, all gone before long: vanished like so much smoke. The Polish mud and the crater-fields of the Isonzo would soon swallow them up as though they had never been. Nothing remains of them now but a distant echo in an old man's ears, of the steady tramp of their nailed boots on the granite paving slabs and the brazen blare of those incomparable marches: "Schönfeld" and "Erzherzog Albrecht" and "Trenk Panduren."

My naval ADC's duties obliged me to spend a good deal of my time away from the capital accompanying Franz Ferdinand and his family on their journeyings about the lands of the Dual Monarchy: from Vienna to the family's rural seat at Arstetten on the Danube, then up to Konopischt, then down to Schloss Miramar at Trieste for fleet reviews, then back to Vienna. Like most of the activity around the heir to the throne, however, this ceaseless travelling involved a great deal of noise and bustle but seemed in the end to lead to very little. The Archduke was always everywhere at once, with his loud, rather high-pitched voice and his strange, dead, fish-like stare—as if the irises of his blue-grey eyes were in fact portholes and some small animal sat inside his skull, peering out and operating a wheel and levers to steer him around. On photographs he looks a large man, but in fact he was neither very tall nor very heavily built. The photographs were always cunningly taken from some way below eye-level, and the bulky appearance was largely a result of tailor's padding, the girth around the chest constantly being expanded to make the middle-aged paunch less conspicuous. By the time I met him, when he appeared in a military tunic (which is to say, nearly all the time), the padding had produced a very noticeable disproportion between the upper and lower halves of his body, as if the torso had absent-mindedly put on the wrong pair of legs.

I had little direct contact with the Heir-Apparent myself, but at least I got to know the archducal family quite well in those months. As I suppose most people remember from school, Franz Ferdinand's marriage was a rather odd one, in that his wife and children were not officially part of the Habsburg family. When the Heir-Apparent had met and fallen in love with Sophie Chotek von Chotkova she had been a penniless lady-in-waiting—a countess to be sure, but most emphatically not of a rank or degree of inbreeding that would qualify her to marry an archduke and produce even more half-wits with protuberant lower jaws. In the end, after several years of rows at court, they had been permitted to marry only on condition that their children were debarred from the succession and took their mother's title of Hohenberg. As to the Duchess of Hohenberg herself, opinions varied a great deal. The Archduke's toadies in the clerical party newspapers made her out of course to be a beautiful, gracious angel of light. Others whispered that she was tight-fisted, petty and a Catholic *dévote* whose religious bigotry outdid even that of her husband. For my part I must say that I found her a decent enough person, within the narrow mental confines of the Bohemian-German lesser nobility. She always had a certain soft spot for me because she considered us to be fellow-Czechs. I cannot say why she should have cherished this opinion though, because the Chotek family were Czechs in nothing but name, survivors of the old Bohemian nobility who had managed to hang on to their lands after 1620 only at the price of becoming completely German in speech and outlook. She spoke some Czech, but with a thick accent, and with all verbs in the imperative mood since she had learnt it through giving orders to servants. As for the rest, I think that much of it was malicious gossip on the part of her social superiors against a glorified servant who had scooped the pool in snatching the Heir-Apparent. She was indeed rather economical—but then, like myself, she had known what it was to be hard-up, so I was ready to forgive her that. She was certainly brighter than most of her class—though that is not saying a great deal—while as for the charge of excessive Catholicism, well, I think that perhaps she merely took it all more seriously than her court contemporaries.

The children—Sophie the eldest and the two brothers Max and Ernst—were pleasant company, and their exclusion from the Noble House of Austria seemed to have done them only good, at least to judge from the little archdukes and archduchesses whom I also met at the Belvedere about this time, and who struck me as pitifully dull, desiccated, lifeless automata, descendants of those poor sawdust-filled little infantas who stare out so miserably from the paintings of Velázquez. The Hohenberg children were not like that at all. The two boys in particular were excellent lads: lively, intelligent, active and passionately interested in flying. So of course, in those days, my position among them as a real live airman was one of near-deity, as if an astronaut had parachuted into a modern junior-school playground. I am happy to report that their later lives seem to have borne out this early promise—though not quite in circumstances that I would have wished. My fellow-resident Mr Witkowski met them many years later, sharing a barrack-hut with them in Dachau concentration camp, and he tells me that their courage and generosity were a constant support to their fellow-sufferers.

The Archduke's love for his wife and children was deep and genuine— no one who knew him can deny that—as if all his severely limited stock of affection was reserved for these four people. But then, the same was true of Himmler and Eichmann; and I have to say that in all other respects the Archduke Franz Ferdinand of Österreich-Este was one of the most poisonous human beings I have ever had the misfortune to run across even in a lifetime as long as mine. For years before I joined his staff I had heard tales of the Heir-Apparent's faults of character: of his permanent ill-temper; of his overbearing, erratic rudeness; of his tight-fistedness, which extended to haggling with market stall holders and leaving hotel bills unpaid; also of his insatiable lust for the blood of furred and feathered creatures, which was of such psychopathic monstrosity that it aroused comment even in those days of seemingly limitless game and minimal scruples about killing it. Until now, I had taken little notice of these stories: I was an officer of the House of Austria, and therefore not interested in politics, and also a democratic Czech, and therefore not much interested in the doings of royalty. In so far as I took any cognisance of the rumours about the Heir-Apparent I put them down to the normal backbiting and reptilian malice endemic to old Austria, the instinctive desire of a notably feeble and introverted society to run down anyone who showed any signs of energy or ability or a desire to change things. But that was before I met the man in person.

Certainly Franz Ferdinand and his shadow-court were in an awkward position as 1912 turned into 1913. The old Emperor had lived to turn to stone, and since he would let no one else run the country for him, the government of the Danubian Monarchy had long since succumbed to advanced arteriosclerosis, the channels of state chalked up solid like the pipes of some ancient central-heating system. Everyone knew that the Old Gentleman could not live much longer. But everyone had known that for years, and still he got up at four each morning, winter and summer, to sit for the next sixteen hours at his army field-desk signing papers, Supreme Bureaucrat of the Empire of Chair-Polishers. Meanwhile the cabinet-in-waiting at the Belvedere waited . . . and waited. It was enough to try the most patient of men. However, even if the rising sun rises with painful slowness, it still attracts worshippers, and over the years the very best and brightest and most dedicated of the Monarchy's politicians, writers and men of affairs had tried to attach themselves to the Belvedere, seeing in Franz Ferdinand the man whose reputed energy and determination would haul Austria out of the swamp into which it had sunk. But after a year or so they would always drift away, reduced to baffled despair by the Heir-Apparent's aimless, despotic violence and by the sheer scope and intensity of his hatreds. In the end only a dispiriting collection of sycophants and minor politicians-on-the-make remained in the Archduke's entourage.

Franz Ferdinand was a true democrat in one thing if in nothing else: he detested everyone more or less equally. Democrats, Freemasons, free-thinkers, free traders, republicans, atheists, liberals, anti-clericals, trade unionists, academics; Italians, Poles, Jews, Germans, non-Germans, Serbs, Americans—all were the victims of those sudden barking eruptions of toxin-filled, red-hot lava. I suppose that, in fairness, a good deal of this was not the man's fault but rather a result of heredity. Generations of first cousins had been mated to produce the House of Österreich-Este, while the Heir-Apparent's paternal grandfather had been that appalling old ruffian King Ferdinand "Bomba" of Naples, who used to manifest his love for his subjects by means of the occasional artillery bombardment. But in this extraordinary catalogue of hatreds there was one conspicuous gap. Most other nationalities the Archduke merely hated; but the Hungarians he loathed with an intensity and fervour that bordered on the religious, to a degree where the mere mention of a Magyar name would send him into fury. No one was left in any doubt that when the day came for Franz Ferdinand to ascend the throne, he was going to make short work of *that* lot—though as usual, precisely how was never specified.

As to the stories about the Heir-Apparent's murderous obsession with killing game, I had my first chance to verify them one day early in January 1913 when I was commanded to take part in a shoot on an estate near

Jungbunzlau in Bohemia. Like most people who have once in their lives driven a bulldozer through protocol and correct form, Franz Ferdinand had since become a minute stickler for it in relation to himself. So it was only with the help of yet another sub from my Aunt Aleksia that I managed to kit myself out in the correct rig for these occasions: loden jacket, breeches, brown boots, feathered hat and the rest. Even so I had to borrow a suitable shotgun from a fellow-officer of my elder brother Anton, who was based nearby with the 26th Jägers. The morning came, and we trooped out to the turf butts as a great pear-shaped ring of hundreds of beaters drove all the game over ten or so square kilometres of woodland and scrub towards the stalk-end of the pear where we waited, thirty or so of us, in hiding. Then it began, such a slaughter of the driven, helpless, panic-stricken birds and animals as I never witnessed even on the worst battlefields of two world wars. I see it vividly even now: the Heir-Apparent and his guests blasting indiscriminately at the onrushing, close-packed animals and at the birds that darkened the sky above us (he was a superb shot, and could knock birds down unerringly even with a hunting rifle); bearers handing freshly loaded guns to him and his companions as they fired in a sort of trance; the dead and wounded birds falling all around us like giant raindrops; a wild boar trying to stagger past us on three legs; and terrified roe deer stampeding towards us crammed together so thickly that every shot passed through two or three bodies. It must have gone on for a good ten minutes, until the carcasses were stacked all about us like some nightmarish abattoir and the forest earth reeked and steamed with blood. There was a lull for a few moments. Smiling and radiantly happy, the Heir-Apparent turned to me (the only time that he had spoken to me that morning) and remarked:

"You know, the best of all is when a fellow gets to a stage where he kills automatically, without knowing that he's killing."

Then they came on again, and the carnage resumed. Now, I am no vegetarian and I was always a good marksman in the hunting field. But this was too much. Breaking point came for me when I was bending to reload and a fine cock pheasant plumped dead at my feet. I looked at the iridescent neck-plumage and the perfection of its wing-feathers, and its bright black eyes filming over in death, and I felt heart-sick. Something had to be done. When no one was looking I took some of the gritty, wet clay soil and smeared it over the two cartridges, then pushed them into the breech. I raised the gun, and fired both barrels into the empty air. Then I broke the weapon open. As I had hoped, both empty cases were now quite securely jammed in the barrels, I fumbled a while as the slaughter continued, hoping to escape notice. But it was coming to an end now of its own accord, every local living thing above the size of a fieldmouse having already been exterminated.

The Archduke turned to me and regarded me for some time with his blank, lifeless eyes.

"Trouble with your gun, Prohaska?"

"Yes Your Imperial Highness, I obediently report that both cartridges are jammed."

He subjected me to a long, cold stare. "Hmph! Better pay more attention to cleaning your gun in future—or buy something better. Fellows who can't afford a proper weapon ought not to shoot in decent society." And with that he left me. Like many before me, I had begun to fall from archducal favour—though in my case at least the fall would not be very far.

The bag of game for the day, incidentally, was 179 deer, 327 wild boar, 1,529 hares and rabbits, 1,793 partridges and grouse, 6,357 pheasants, three hedgehogs disturbed from their winter slumber and a domestic cat, which had somehow got mixed up in the carnage. It was reckoned to be good, but not outstanding for its day.

The next week saw me ascend even further in what the Archduke was pleased to call decent society, this time in fact to its very pinnacle. For in mid-January 1913, to my utter astonishment, I received a letter from the Imperial Chamberlain's office in the Hofburg Palace.

It was one Monday morning, I remember, as I went through my post tray in the office at the Belvedere. My room-mate Hauptmann Belcredi and I had just sat back at our desks, dazzled and struck dumb by the splendour of a proposal which had been sent in by a certain Dipl. Ing. von Gergjaszevics from Varaśdin. It involved (so far as either of us could make out) an airship which would combine a totally novel system of propulsion with complete invisibility. Instead of being driven by propellers, the outer envelope of the airship itself would be in the form of a helix, so that the thing would spin on its long axis and bore its way through the air like a gigantic screw through a piece of wood. However, that was not all: the envelope would be painted in spiral stripes of all the colours of the spectrum so that as it went spinning along (Herr Gergjaszevics assured us, with numerous equations by way of proof) its colour would never settle to any particular value and it would thus remain invisible to the human eye. Belcredi whistled in awe as he read the letter, then sat silent for some time. At length he slapped himself on the back of the head as if to wake himself from his reverie and remarked, "Well, there's nothing really to be added to that, is there? Better forward it to the Steinhof mental hospital marked *Urgent* I think."

He took the next missive from the post tray and examined it for some moments: "Another one for you here, Prohaska old fellow. Nice-quality paper and court-script address as well. Perhaps from a better class of maniac this time . . ."

I slit open the envelope and drew out a rather plain handwritten card—then stared in disbelief. It was an invitation to the annual Ball bei Hof.

My first reaction was that there must have been some mistake. Nothing in Old Austria was ever simple if there was any way of making it complicated, and the pre-Lenten carnival season in Vienna saw not one but two court balls held in the Hofburg. Of these the Hofball had become, by 1913, rather like one of your garden parties at Buckingham Palace: a gathering of several thousand people to which not only high society but also a good many worthy commoners were now invited—professors and provincial civil servants and even a sprinkling of the more socially acceptable journalists and Jewish Finanzbarons. The Ball bei Hof was an entirely different affair though: a rigidly exclusive gathering of the Imperial House and the three hundred or so families of the "first society," those great and ancient landed dynasties of Imperial Austria which could boast the necessary sixteen quarterings on their coats of arms. Normally a commoner like myself, a naval lieutenant born of Czech peasant ancestors on one side and decayed Polish petty nobility on the other, would have about as much chance of being admitted to the latter gathering as a pig keeper would of entering the Grand Mosque in Mecca. But the fact was that the survival rate among archduchesses and female members of the first society was markedly higher than that of their male relatives. This meant that there was a shortage of dancing partners, and the deficit was normally made up by inviting officers from the more glittering regiments based in the capital—and also from the staffs of those archdukes who had taken up a military career. Someone from the Heir-Apparent's staff had to represent the Navy, and the senior naval ADC was down with influenza. So in the end, by default, the choice had fallen on me.

We worked the best part of three days, my servant Smrkal and I, to get my gala uniform into a suitable state of immaculacy. Smrkal—a delicious name by the way, which means something like "runny-nose" in Czech—was a good-natured, red-faced young country lad from Moravia, serving his two years' conscription with an infantry regiment in the capital, homesick and delighted to be shared batman to an officer not much older than himself who spoke his own language. He was already at work with clothes-brush and flat iron before dawn on the great day, and as he buttoned me that afternoon into the stiff blue serge of my double-breasted, high-collared gala tunic (a seldom-worn and universally hated item of dress known in the fleet as the "Prachteinband"—the "presentation binding") he was in an agony of nervousness on my part, as if the Emperor would come along and berate him in person if he detected any fault in my turn-out.

"Now remember, Herr Schiffsleutnant, don't sit down because it ruins the creases in your trousers. And don't breathe in too much or the top button'll go."

I arrived by fiacre at the Hofburg at 6 p.m. sharp as instructed, and spent the next half-hour waiting with a few dozen fellow-officers in the entrance hall to the great ballroom. Most, as I had expected, came from cavalry regiments. Bandy legs, braided tunics and inane accents seemed to fill the room. Occasionally one of them would pause and adjust his monocle to survey me up and down—the only naval officer present—then return to his braying. I began to wonder, had I unknowingly committed some awful solecism of dress? The Emperor was known to have a needle-sharp eye for details of uniform and could recite the *K.u.K.*

*Adjustierungsvorschrift* by heart (the only book he had ever read, he used to boast). Even a shoelace wrongly knotted would suffice to have me cast into outer darkness if the Old Gentleman spotted it. A bell rang, and we queued up to have our invitations checked, for all the world like lining up outside the sick-bay for an inoculation. The doorkeeper to this aristocratic holy of holies was pointed out to me: Prince Montenuovo, the chief upholder and living embodiment of that rigid Spanish protocol by which the Habsburg court still conducted its affairs. This was the man who used to make sure that when in Vienna members of the Imperial House travelled in carriages with gold threads wound around the wheel-spokes, a distinction imported from Madrid in the seventeenth century and now enforced by Montenuovo and his assistants with a zeal which seemed to be all the greater for its utter meaninglessness. A highly intelligent man (I was told), Prince Montenuovo was one of those rather embittered people—I have often met them in the armed forces—who have been entrusted with the task of enforcing regulations which they know to be idiotic, and who take a perverse pleasure in upholding them to the very last letter not despite but precisely because of their idiocy. His view of the carriage-wheel regulation, for example, was not that entitled persons might (if they so pleased) have gold threads on their wheels, but rather that all those entitled *must* have them, even if they were driving in a hired fiacre or (on one occasion) riding a bicycle. Montenuovo was reported to have solved the problem of the Heir-Apparent's unequal status with his wife, as regards carriage-wheel decoration, by laying down that only the wheels on one side of the vehicle should be adorned with the sacred threads. The Chamberlain checked my invitation, surveyed me cursorily as if through the wrong end of a telescope, then directed me towards an antechamber with the rest.

Then the magnates themselves began to arrive, each announced by an usher. Soon the room was filling up with grand names: Habsburg archdukes and duchesses, then Schwarzenbergs and Lobkowitzes and Esterhazys and Metterniches and Kinskys and Starhembergs and Khevenhullers and Colloredos and Auerspergs and heaven alone knows what else, three centuries of Europe's history gathered together in a single room. It was the first time that I had seen even as many as two of our great territorial nobility gathered together in one place. Yet the sight was anything but imposing. The overriding impression was one of age, as if the weight of so many ancient names and so much history had brought about premature senility in their owners; of wrinkled, shrunken, toothless faces and withered décollettés and bent shoulders. A faint miasma of mothballs and weak bladders already hung over the assembly. But even the younger members of the gathering were not particularly inspiring to look at: enough protruding lower jaws to keep a team of modern orthodontists in business for a year, and facial expressions which ranged from bovine dullness to downright imbecility. Only a few individuals stood out from this uninspiring mob of nobility. One of them was a tall, handsome man in his late fifties with iron-grey hair and a pince-nez. Almost alone among the men present there, he wore civilian court dress rather than a uniform of some kind. His face seemed vaguely familiar to me from somewhere, and I noticed that as his gaze swept over the assembly it rested for a moment on me.

The Heir-Apparent and the Duchess of Hohenberg were announced. The Archduke nodded curtly towards me and his wife smiled. Then at 7 p.m. precisely the Chamberlain banged on the floor with his staff of office and announced that we were to enter the ballroom. By order of precedence, the first to enter would be the Heir-Apparent. The procession formed up, two by two, and Franz Ferdinand took his place at its head with his wife on his arm. Then I saw from my place towards the rear that Montenuovo and a couple of his henchmen were whispering with the Heir-Apparent. Voices began to be raised. It was difficult to hear exactly what was being said, but I sensed from the sudden hush that something unusual was happening. I saw the Archduke turning red and beginning to splutter with rage; I caught the words "You miserable Italian dung-beetle—how dare you! . . ." Then there was a sudden scuffle, the outcome of which was that an aged noblewoman was attached to the Heir-Apparent's arm while the Duchess of Hohenberg, white-faced and distraught, was being half led, half propelled towards the rear of the procession. The Archduke was clearly going to make a scene, but before he could get started the great double doors swung open, the orchestra struck up and the procession began to march, strut or hobble into the ballroom. I was down at the very end of the line, so far without a partner to escort. Montenuovo and a group of ladies-in-waiting were attending with fans and *sal volatile* to the Heir-Apparent's wife, who was by now trembling and near to tears. The officers were beginning to enter, yet something made me hold back. There were only a few of us left now in the antechamber, and it was clear that if Montenuovo and his acolytes could arrange it, Sophie Chotek von Chotkova would enter the ballroom on her own. At a signal from the Chamberlain—no doubt long and lovingly rehearsed—half of the double doors was swung shut, to underline the humiliation. Then a sudden crazy impulse came over me. I knew little of court protocol and I cared even less. I strode over to her and proffered my arm. She hesitated for a moment. Then she took it and we made our way into the ballroom. As I shoved the half-door open with my shoulder in passing I had one last glimpse of Montenuovo with his mouth hanging open, taken by surprise. We entered the great hall to be greeted by a sudden, intense silence. First to break it were two old parrots near the door. They had their fans to their mouths, but I heard it clearly.

"But this is monstrous—and a commoner too! *Ach, diese g'meine Leute . . .*"

"I know my dear. I always say that human life begins at baron." Then the orchestra began the imperial anthem, the "Gott Erhalte."

Once I realised what I had just done I felt a sudden weakness of the knees. The Heir-Apparent came over and patted me on the shoulder as ostentatiously as he could, but I sensed that even he, being a strong upholder of social degree and precedence where other people were concerned, was in two minds about what I had just done. As for the rest, I had a sudden and rather disagreeable sensation of having become invisible. The ball was now warming up with its first waltz, but I was clearly not going to have a partner that evening. Being a non-combatant did have certain advantages though, in that it gave me the opportunity to observe my surroundings.

The Redoutensaal was as boring as most palace ballrooms: draughty as a barn and lit by chandeliers with hundreds of smoking, guttering candles. Electricity or even gaslight had still to reach this particular wing of the Hofburg. As the dancers swirled through the first few waltzes a powerful smell of boot polish began to pervade the air, a consequence of the Emperor's insistence that all officers present should be dressed exactly according to the service regulations, which made no mention of patent-leather footwear. But at least the smell did something to mask the faint but disturbing odour from the palace's rudimentary drainage system—and from the ballroom's own comfort-stations, which were nothing but two rows of chamber-pots behind screens.

The Emperor came down from his rooms at 7:30 sharp and mingled with the guests for precisely fifteen minutes, as was his custom, before returning to his desk. He asked the usual questions of people selected at random, or perhaps according to some counter inside his head. He missed me, thank goodness, but he stopped to talk with someone near me, and thus gave me my first close-up view of this doyen of monarchs, head of Europe's grandest and most ancient ruling house. And really, the impression that I gained was not at all what I had expected. The sloping shoulders and the side-whiskers and the curious springy gait were familiar enough to me from newspaper articles and official portraits. But it still came as something of a shock to see how closely this descendant of Charles V resembled an elderly fiacre driver; and when he opened his mouth, to hear him speak with a pronounced Viennese kleinbürgerlich accent and idiom, as if your own Queen Elizabeth should speak in the tones of Peckham or Shepherd's Bush. At length he passed on and returned upstairs to his papers, and the ball adjourned for the buffet supper.

The refreshments provided for us were very much in keeping with the rest of the Hofburg's domestic arrangements: an evil-smelling maroon-coloured soup, and plates stacked high with horrible wizened little pies which looked as if they were on loan from some museum. I tried a spoonful of the soup, and nearly choked. It was disgusting: liquor of a Bengal tiger stewed for a week in dragon's blood and seasoned with gunpowder and brass nails. I was trying to abandon my bowl of it as discreetly as I could when I heard a voice over my shoulder:

"Vile, isn't it?" I turned around. There stood the tall, distinguished-looking man in civilian clothes whom I had noticed as we prepared to enter the ballroom. "You know what they call it, I suppose: 'Spanish Soup.' The recipe was brought here from the Escorial three hundred years ago and has been a closely guarded secret of the Hofburg kitchens ever since. I believe that it involves barrowloads of ox's marrowbones stewed in an iron cauldron for two days with a bucketful of garlic and several kilograms of pepper. It seems that they make it like this so that no one will drink more than a few spoonfuls and they can then boil up what's left over for the next function. Some of it must have been going back and forth for years. Have you tried the patties over there?"

"No."

"Well don't: they're even worse than the soup—though of less antiquarian interest since the recipe dates merely from the time of Prinz Eugen. But tell me young man, what's your name?"

"Ottokar Prohaska, sir, k.u.k. Linienschiffsleutnant, currently serving on the staff of the Heir-Apparent."

"Yes, I knew that already. But where do you come from?"

I struggled to contain my surprise. "From a little town up in northern Moravia. I doubt whether you will ever have heard of it: a place called Hirschendorf, near Olmutz."

He laughed. "Heard of the place? I was born and grew up there. But allow me to introduce myself. At your service: Prince Joseph von und zu Regnitz—otherwise known as Professor Joseph Regnitz of the Faculty of Jurisprudence at the University of Vienna." Of course, I thought to myself, that's how I recognised him: the Regnitz family of Schloss Regnitz were the local landed magnates where I came from, and would occasionally appear in town for the local people to doff their hats to them. But how did he know, and why . . .

"Yes Prohaska, I know what you're thinking: what am I doing here? But as you may have heard if you've been back home of late, my elder brother Adolf has recently been declared insane and the title has passed to me."

"Then my congratu—" I bit my tongue. But the prince only smiled.

"Oh, nothing to congratulate me on really, I assure you, quite apart from the distressing circumstances. I teach administrative law at the university and dabble a little in politics and I had no wish to inherit the title and the bother of looking after the estates. And normally I'd steer well clear of occasions like this too. But the Regnitzes have been Princes of the Holy Roman Empire since 1519 so someone has to represent the family; and anyway, one can hardly turn down an invitation from the Old Gentleman."

"But if you will excuse my asking, how did you know that I . . ."

"Oh, I was at the Belvedere a couple of weeks ago on business and someone mentioned your name; said in fact what a scandal it was that a postal superintendent's son from Hirschendorf with a name like Prohaska should be attending the Ball bei Hof. So I made a few enquiries, then remembered that you were looked after when you were young by old Hanuška Jindrichova, the wife of our head forester."

"You are very kind to remember such trifles."

"Don't mention it: we lawyers need good memories. But I thought anyway that I ought to try and comfort you a little after that nonsense when we came in."

I squirmed. "I had hoped that it would soon be forgotten. I acted without thinking."

"Forgotten? It'll be all round Vienna by morning. But cheer up: there will be many who'll say that you did the right thing, taking a crack at the meaningless rituals that gum up this monarchy of ours. But anyway, Prohaska, I was going to ask whether you would like to take supper with me after we leave? I've got a room booked at Sacher's. I was going to discuss some business with one of the Czech deputies, but he couldn't make it."

"Really Your Serene Highness, you are too kind. But I must not trouble you . . ."

He waved his hand. "No trouble, I assure you: the pleasure will be all mine, to be able to talk with someone young and intelligent and not from this pestilential city. Every now and then I have to reassure myself that Austria contains at least a few people under the age of seventy, with brains inside their heads instead of blotting paper and blood in their veins instead of endorsing ink. And by the way, chuck that 'Durchlaucht' nonsense: I don't use my title except on state occasions, so call me Professor, or even Regnitz if you prefer it. Anyway, meet me outside when we leave: the dancing's about to start again. *Auf wiederschauen.*"

The orchestra struck up once more. And if one thing was in order at the Hofburg to compensate for the dingy surroundings and the smells and the appalling food, it was the music. Carl Michael Ziehrer might not have been in quite the same class as his predecessor in the post of k.k. Hofballmusik Direktor, the incomparable Johann Strauss. But he was nearly as good, and he led an excellent orchestra. I suppose that to you, nowadays, the waltzes of old Vienna must sound rather like the dusty crepitation of some ancient bouquet of dried flowers brought down from the attic. But for me who was young when the dew was still fresh upon them they have never quite lost their magic. That curious mixture of the formal and the dizzy, the gaiety tinged with sadness, still breathes to me of youth and adventure and that world now gone for ever. I am quite at a loss though to explain how such a stuffy, arthritic, utterly unadventurous society should have produced such enchanting music, and in such profusion. Perhaps people made up on the dance-floor for their lack of enterprise in the other departments of life, I really cannot say.

I was quite a good dancer in those days. The k.u.k. Marine Akademie had put us through the ordeal of twice-weekly dancing classes when I was a cadet there, afternoons when we clumped gracelessly about the floor of the main hall trying surreptitiously to grope the daughters of the Fiume middle classes, who came to us from their convent schools as partners. But this evening, following my reckless assault on court protocol, it seemed as if I was to have no chance to practise my skills. Not even the most aged or the most ugly of potential partners would deign to notice me.

That is, until the last dance of the evening, the Ladies' Choice, when suddenly there stood before me the smiling, slim figure of the Duchess of Hohenberg.

"Heir Schiffsleutnant, may I have the pleasure of this dance?"

"Why . . . er . . . yes, Your Highness . . . certainly," I stammered as we glided out on to the floor. I hear it to this day. It was the waltz "Wiener Bürger" (in its musical tastes the Habsburg court was a mere three decades out of date rather than three centuries, as in every other respect). And I remember how we whirled sedately about the floor before the aghast stares of the female part of the first society. She seemed not to care though, and had clearly recovered from her unpleasant experience earlier that evening.

"Herr Schiffsleutnant," she said, "I really cannot thank you enough for your gallant deed when we came in."

"Your Highness, it was nothing, I assure you. I merely did what seemed to be my duty."

"Anyway, please do not worry that any harm will come to your career because of it. My husband is grateful and will see that you are looked after. While as for myself, if there is ever any way in which I can help you one day, I shall not hesitate to do it."

And not long afterwards, she was as good as her word.

When the ball ended I collected my overcoat and met Professor Regnitz. It was snowing again, and the frozen slush crunched beneath our boots as we walked to the Hotel Sacher for supper. Ten minutes later we were being ushered into one of the hotel's famous *chambres séparées,* which operetta has made into a device for seduction but which were in fact used largely for the private discussion of political and commercial business—a necessity in a smallish city like Vienna where gossip was a major industry and where who had been seen dining with whom was often as important as the outcome of a parliamentary debate. Supper was brought in, and the waiter departed. It was Tafelspitz—boiled beef with dumplings—a great winter favourite of mine, but a taste which I rarely had the means to indulge. The supper was very good: quite the best meal I had eaten in a year spent cursing the wardroom cooks aboard the *Erzherzog Albrecht* or subsisting on the rather nasty meals provided at the Belvedere, where the Archduke's tight-fistedness led him to keep his staff on the most meagre rations.

"I would always recommend anyone who attends the Hofburg," said the professor, lighting a cigar, "to make arrangements for supper afterwards. People have been known to topple over from starvation during some of the longer functions there. I hear that they don't feed you a great deal better at the Belvedere though."

"The kitchen there is—well, not generous."

"Yes, I would imagine that the Heir-Apparent keeps his men on pretty short commons. But tell me, Prohaska, what do you think of the Archduke?"

"Me? . . . I . . . well, really I don't think that it would be proper . . ."

"Oh, come on young fellow, we're not going to be overheard here. Tell me frankly, does he seem to you to be getting any worse?"

"Worse, Herr Professor? In what way?"

"You know perfectly well what I mean: the violent outbursts and the fits of temper. I ask because it worries me—and also people a good deal more highly placed than I am."

"Since you ask me, I must say that he does always seem to be—well— rather fierce about everything; and although I have only been there a short time and don't see a great deal of him, other people have been saying these past few weeks that he's getting more difficult to deal with. In fact none of the household servants ever seems to stay more than a few months now."

He thought for a while. "Yes, that certainly bears out what other people have been telling me lately. The thing that frightens me most about him, I must say, is not so much the violence as the indiscriminate violence—as if resolving problems by any other means than brute force were a confession of weakness. Believe me, Prohaska, I fear for Austria when that man becomes Emperor, which can't be long now. I understand from my informants that the latest idea is to shut down the Reichsrat, rule by decree in Austria and impose martial law in Hungary."

"I know nothing of this, Herr Professor: I am just a junior naval officer with no interest in politics. I have to say though that some of my brother-officers in the Chancellery do discuss them, and their opinion is that it might be better if someone started ruling by decree, rather than let things go on drifting as they've been the past few years. I've a brother in the 26th Jägers up in Bohemia and he wrote in his last letter that about a third of this year's intake of recruits in the Leitmeritz military district have gone missing or left the country; also that a lot of the men who did eventually turn up at the depot are refusing to go forward for NCO training. In fact some of them are saying quite openly that in a few years they expect to be out of Austria and serving in their own army."

"It doesn't surprise me. I'm a Reichsrat deputy in the Moravian-German Club, for my sins, and I've never in all my days seen such a political slum as we've been in these past four years or so. We don't have government in Austria any more, only administration. Tell me Prohaska, who's the Austrian Prime Minister?"

"Why . . . er . . . Stürgkh, I think . . ."

"Quite correct, though I'm surprised you got it: not many people know that Stürgkh is our Prime Minister—in fact I'm not sure that Herr Stürgkh always remembers it himself. They're certainly a fine lot if you ever get the chance to see them together though, Stürgkh and his cabinet—the very epitome of the Habsburg state anno domini 1913: the Prime Minister nearly blind, Roessler sick with heart trouble, Bráf suffering from palsy and Zaleski dying of nephritis. And of course, Sani Berchtold at the Foreign Ministry, with his fatuous grin and that irritating giggle." He paused. "Have you managed to do any sightseeing in Vienna?"

"Quite a lot. I'm officially billeted at the Belvedere, but I have an aunt in the 8th District and I sometimes stay with her at weekends."

"And have you yet managed to visit the Capuchin Crypt?"

"Why yes, I was there with a lady friend the Sunday before last when it rained and we had an hour or two to spare."

"Did you notice the curious smell there?"

"Now that you come to mention it we did: a sort of sweetish, musty smell. We found it rather unpleasant."

"And you know what that was? It was the smell of ten generations of embalmed Habsburgs turning slowly to dust. But I'll tell you something: I notice that smell everywhere in Vienna now, airless and fusty and cloying. It's risen from the Capuchin vaults to fill all the offices of state in this wretched baroque stage-set of a capital. It hangs over the officials at their desks and fills the corridors of ministries. The smell of the tomb pervades this whole decrepit empire of ours."

"But surely, Herr Professor, you're being too pessimistic. Austria-Hungary is still one of the world's Great Powers."

He laughed. "On paper, yes. But in fact it's largely self-delusion. As powers go, the Monarchy on the way down is soon set to be passed by Italy on the way up. I understand in fact from my contacts at the War Ministry that if war broke out tomorrow the k.u.k. Armee would be able to put fewer battalions into the field than in 1866, when we had fifteen million fewer people. No, my dear Prohaska: Old Austria still looks like a real, living country, but it's really all an elaborate sham. The life went out of the Habsburg state years ago now, and what was once its heart has turned into a hard, dead, inert lump of matter like fingernail or horse's hoof. And soon this crumbling fossil will be made over to the care of our beloved Heir-Apparent . . ." He paused. "I know that I shouldn't be discussing these matters with someone of your junior rank, but I felt that I had to ask what you have observed recently at the Belvedere. You see, there have been rumours floating around for some time past that Franz Ferdinand is wobbling on the brink of outright insanity, stories of his suffering black-outs and slashing railway-carriage cushions with his sabre and even trying to throttle a valet. I asked your opinion, Prohaska, be-cause I believe that matters have now reached a stage where the Duchess of Hohenberg is seriously worried. I understand that she's been consult-ing one of our leading neurologists, but that the Archduke refuses to undergo treatment."

"A nice business," I said after a while. "Perhaps we aren't so badly off with the Old Gentleman after all."

"We certainly aren't. The old boy might have the brains of a rural gendarmery sergeant and we might all laugh at his iron cot and his field-desk and the cold baths at four in the morning. But he's got integrity, everyone grants him that. No one has ever heard him be discourteous, either to a fellow-monarch or to a crossing sweeper; while as for telling a lie, he couldn't do it to save his life. No, Franz Ferdinand and his crony the German Kaiser are creatures from another world."

"Why?"

"I don't know; perhaps a century's accumulation of wealth and weapons has made them think that they really are gods among men after all. You know what the court circulars in Berlin put down now for each

Sunday: 'This morning at 0930 hours the All-Highest will pay his respects to the Highest.' I tell you Prohaska, they frighten me: children of limited intelligence placed behind the steering wheels of powerful motor cars. How long will it be before they start running into one another?"

"But surely, the Archduke and the Kaiser don't want war. At least, they keep assuring everyone that they don't."

"And perhaps they're telling the truth: the Heir-Apparent's a rather timorous character, behind all the bluster, while as for the Kaiser, the man's a pitiful windbag, resolute as a weather-vane and frightened of his own shadow. No, it's not them who frighten me so much as the soldiers behind them—like our own Conrad von Hötzendorf for example. Conrad spends a good half of his working week these days wandering around Vienna buttonholing politicians like me and telling us that only war can save the Monarchy now: war with Serbia; war with Italy; war with Russia; war with the Cannibal Isles so long as we have action. They terrify me, these generals of ours. Because you have to realise that none of them now has ever smelt powder for real or seen a dying man. When they come to me with their little speeches about Salvation through Sacrifice and the Great Idea I tell them about what I saw when I was a lad back in '66, when they were bringing in the wounded from the fight at Klattnau and laying them out in Hirschendorf town square. I often remember the sights I saw that day, and sometimes wish that I could take all the generals and all the cadets in every military academy in the Monarchy back there, to see that there's more to war than sticking coloured flags into maps. But there you are, Prohaska: we're ruled now by people who suffer from a colossal deficit of imagination. Old Austria will die before long, I am convinced of that now. But I fear that with creatures like the Archduke and Conrad and Sani Berchtold in charge she'll contrive to take a great many healthy young men like you with her to the grave."

I bade farewell to Professor the Prince von und zu Regnitz in a thoughtful frame of mind, and took a fiacre back to the Belvedere. It was nearly midnight, but I had packing still to do, for tomorrow I was to leave with the Heir-Apparent and his family for the Adriatic resort of Abbazia. I had been instructed to take my flying kit with me.

# 5

# POLISH BLOOD

THE MAIN PURPOSE OF THE HEIR-APPARENT'S JOURNEY to the Adriatic Riviera was pleasure, the family's late-winter holiday at the resort of Abbazia. However, a modicum of official business was to be mingled with recreation, for it had been arranged that on the last day of January the Archduke and his wife would visit the Ganz-Danubius shipyard at Porto Ré, on the opposite shore of the Quarnero Gulf, to launch two new destroyers for the k.u.k. Kriegsmarine. The Admiralty yacht *Dalmat* had been brought up to Abbazia for them to embark. This may seem odd if one looks at the map; Abbazia and Porto Ré were both near the head of the gulf and were only about twenty kilometres apart by road, perhaps half an hour in a motor car. But the road ran through the city of Fiume. And Fiume was the coast of the Kingdom of Hungary. You will notice that I said "the coast of" and not "on the coast of"; because the fact is that the waterfront of Fiume—four kilometres of it from Cantrida in the west to Sušak in the east—was the entire saltwater shore of the Kingdom of Hungary, allocated to Budapest under the Austro-Hungarian settlement of 1867 even though the vast majority of the town's inhabitants were Italians and Croats. The Heir-Apparent's loathing for the Magyars was so intense that he never missed any occasion, however small, to slight them, and here was a splendid opportunity for a snub: to travel from Abbazia to Porto Ré by sea and cock a snook at the Hungarian Governor in his palazzo up on the hillside overlooking the bay. My part in the exercise, however, was not concerned with injuring the pride of the notoriously touchy Magyars. Instead I was to use the archducal party's sea journey to give a demonstration flight of the Imperial and Royal Navy's latest flying boat.

It was a native Austrian product this time, the Etrich-Mieckl AII: the wings and tail of a small biplane merged with a boat hull rather like that of a plywood canoe. It was powered by a French 60hp Le Rhone rotary engine, in which (for reasons which I once knew but have long since forgotten) the crankshaft stayed still while the engine and propeller spun around it. It was mounted pusher-fashion behind the pilot's cockpit—a matter of intense relief to me, I can tell you, since rotary engines were lubricated with castor oil and several hours sitting behind one inhaling the fumes was apt to have a sudden and violent effect on the bowels. The whole machine was so ridiculously small that one did not so much board it as put it on like a pair of trousers, while it was so feebly powered that in an effort to save weight I did away with the ankle-boots and puttees usually worn by airmen in those days and instead wore stockings with rubber plimsolls.

By the time appointed for the demonstration flight, early in the afternoon of 31 January, I had already taken the little aeroplane up for a couple of trial flights over Abbazia and had found her to be light and pleasant to handle. So I anticipated no difficulty as I took off, about 2 p.m., in the wake of the *Dalmat* as she steamed towards Porto Ré amid a jostle of bunting-decked small boats. It was a glorious afternoon at the very beginning of the early Adriatic spring: the trees on shore still bare, but the sun shining warmly and the air now peaceful and diamond-clear after three days of the bora. I skimmed across the calm, sapphire water of Abbazia Bay and pulled back the control column to unstick the planing hull from the water's surface. I climbed out over the Quarnero Gulf, over the *Dalmat* down below with her silver wake spreading out on either side, then banked to port to head for the coast, still climbing as I went. Soon the cypress woods and bare limestone gullies of Mount Ucka were unfolding below as I turned south to fly back over Abbazia. I would head out over the gulf once more, then descend and land on the water alongside the *Dalmat* before taking off again to return to Abbazia harbour. There was little breeze, so the direction in which I landed was not important. Down I came. I could see the passengers lining the *Dalmat*'s rails and waving as I lined up to land about four hundred metres to port of them. I was now flying five or six metres above the barely rippled surface of the sea. I eased the throttle, then brought the nose up a little so that the first point to touch the water would be the stern of the planing hull. I felt the bump and shudder as it touched down, then the roar of spray as it started to skim the surface.

They told me afterwards that it was a large baulk of timber lost from the slipway a few days before, after a launching at the Bergudi shipyard. But I knew nothing of that: only felt a sudden, tremendous impact from below accompanied by a crunch like a giant boot stamping on a cigar box—then noted, with curiosity rather than fear, that I was still airborne, only this time without an aeroplane around me. The spectators on the *Dalmat* saw me hit the water, bounce once or twice like a stone skimmed across a pond, then disappear beneath the surface in a cloud of spray. My own next recollection is of returning to semi-consciousness dazed, water-logged and with the breath knocked out of me, buoyed up by the bicycle inner tube which served as a life-jacket and vaguely annoyed that my right leg would not work as I attempted to tread water. There was a creak of rowlocks nearby and a voice saying, "Back oars there!" then hands reaching down to lift me into the rowing cutter. They laid me out on the bottom boards as a petty officer slit open the leg of my stocking with a clasp knife. He sucked in his breath sharply and said, "Jezus!" as he saw the mess that lay beneath. I tried feebly to move—and yelped at the first hideous stab of pain from my shin, as if the leg had been cut open and filled with broken bottles then sewn back up again. The noise, I remember, was like the damp, grinding snap of a rotten tree-branch.

I felt faint and sick as I lay in a room in the Fiume hospital that evening. They had injected me with morphine, but I had been conscious enough when the surgeons came to gather that I had sustained an elaborate compound fracture of the right tibia and fibula. I also knew that for such complex injuries in the year 1913 there was only one remedy: the most drastic. The Heir-Apparent and his wife had just been to visit me, the Archduke evidently fighting hard to contain his disgust at having to be on Hungarian territory. He had departed after a few minutes in order to avoid meeting the Governor and had left me alone with the Duchess of Hohenberg. She had spoken with the doctors and was now out in the corridor engaged in intense discussion with the chief surgeon. Meanwhile

I was left with the pain in my leg; and with my thoughts, which on the whole were even harder to bear than the injury. What was I going to do now? There was no place in a twentieth-century navy for an officer with a leg missing below the knee. Dear God—I had survived one crash uninjured, then gone up to tempt Providence a second time—why had I not listened to that old fool Lovranić aboard the *Albrecht?*

Voices were being raised outside the room. The duchess's last words were, "Well, if you wish to be on bad terms with the wife of your future Emperor, then so be it. But I strongly advise you to consider my request." Then she came in, smiling, and stood beside my bed. She bent down and pressed something into my hand. She spoke in thick, clumsy German-Czech, presumably in an attempt to be kind.

"Be brave, Herr Schiffsleutnant, everything will be well. Just pray to Our Lady to support you in your hour of trial, and keep this little medal with you. It was blessed by the Pope himself. Everything will be all right, you will see."

Then she left. I felt even worse when she had gone. The Devil take her and her condescension and her holy medals, the miserable old German trout! Telling me to pray to Our Lady when I was about to have my leg sawn off, then be discharged from the Navy without a Kreuzer to my name and no way of earning my living. Damn and blast her! I flung the holy medal into the wastepaper basket in my anger. A nurse came in with a tray and gave me something bitter to drink. Well, I thought, this is it. They'll wheel me down to the operating theatre and I shall leave half my right leg and my entire career behind on the table. I felt a needle prick my thigh, tried to hang on to consciousness, then gave up in weariness and slid down into a bottomless black well.

I awoke I have no idea how much later. Slowly the events of the past day came back, and the aching regret with them. I tried to move—and was informed by the sudden jag of pain that at least my right leg was still attached to me. Then I realised that I was in fact in a railway carriage, not in a hospital ward, and that we were rattling at some speed through the outskirts of a city in the early light of morning. Buildings and bridges rushed by until the brakes began to squeal and the train slowed down to come into a railway station. They lifted me out on a stretcher. I had a glimpse of a high, soot-clouded glass canopy above me, then I was loaded into the back of a motor ambulance and the doors were shut behind me. Half an hour later I was lying in another hospital bed, this time in Vienna's General Hospital, the Allegemeines Krankenhaus. The door of my room opened, and in walked a group of medical staff led by a shortish man in his sixties, with a trim white beard and that unmistakable air about him of one accustomed to command. This, I learnt, was Admiralstabsarzt Anton, Freiherr von Eiselberg, Chief Medical Officer to the Austro-Hungarian Navy and one of the most eminent surgeons of his day, a pupil of the great Billroth and himself originator of a number of operative techniques which I believe are still in use today. He bade me a curt good-morning, then set to work examining my leg. His hands were delicate, but I still winced with pain as he examined the open wound and the jagged pieces of bone protruding from it. At length he stood up.

"Well, Herr Schiffsleutnant, you have a very nasty compound fracture there. If you'd come to me six months ago I'd have had to amputate, no question of it. But now I think we may be able to do something for you. So I'll put the case to you squarely, as one sea-officer to another. My colleagues and I have been developing a technique of bone repair which might—I just say might—allow us to save your leg. If you consent to place yourself under my care, then we shall try out these procedures on you, and you'll have to accept the consequences if we fail. If not, then I'm afraid it's the saw. But you must make up your mind immediately: with an open wound like that infection will soon set in, and I'll have to amputate by evening at the latest. What do you say?"

I had no hesitation. "Herr Admiral, do with me exactly as you please. I'm yours to experiment upon as you wish."

"Good man, Prohaska, spoken like a true officer of the House of Austria. You'll need all the courage at your disposal these next few months, because even if the operation succeeds the recovery will be long and painful. But I dare say that if it works we'll have you playing football again this time next year."

"I obediently report, Herr Admiral, that you would then have worked a miracle, not a cure. I have never played football in my life."

He smiled. "Well then, riding a bicycle if you prefer it. But I'll tell you one thing: you're a lucky man that the Duchess of Hohenberg was in Fiume. Those butchers were going to have your leg off yesterday evening, but I understand she bullied and threatened until they agreed to transfer you, then got the Heir-Apparent's personal train laid on to bring you to Vienna. You're fortunate to have friends like that. Anyway, we must work fast, so I shall see you in the operating theatre in ten minutes—though by then you won't see me. May you break your neck and . . . well, your other leg."

The nurses prepared me for the theatre. Then I was wheeled along a white corridor into a tiled room. Once more I felt the prick of a needle, then had a rubber mask placed over my face. I felt as rotten now as I had the evening before when they drugged me down for the journey, but this time for entirely different reasons. Would they find the medallion in the waste-paper basket and give it back to her? How would I explain, and what would I be able to say to thank her when I next met her? In the event Fate decreed that I was never to have the chance.

I awoke from the anaesthetic God alone knows how many hours later, and was promptly sick into a basin. I felt dreadful, and my leg throbbed quite monstrously, strapped to a board to keep it immobile and under traction, but as yet without a plaster cast. I dared not look at it. I was given a cup of weak tea and a slice of dry bread, then a sleeping draught which put me out for most of the ensuing day. I awoke next morning just as Eiselberg and his staff entered the room. He was in a jubilant mood.

"Well Prohaska, we worked four solid hours on your leg yesterday, the whole team of us. It's the longest we've ever kept a patient under anaesthetic. But I think we've succeeded in putting your shin back together again. Luckily the fibula was a clean break. Here, look at these: absolute godsend these Röntgen cameras—couldn't even have attempted the operation without one." He held up a number of large, black photographic plates. I winced inwardly as I saw the one which was obviously "Before." The leg was twisted and the shin-bone was shattered into three or four fragments about half-way down, like the stem of a clay pipe. "After," though, looked much more encouraging: the limb had been straightened and although the cracks were still very visible, the bones had been reassembled as neatly as a well-mended china ornament. I was puzzled however by three sharp-edged, dense white bands spaced at intervals down the damaged section. Eiselberg pointed them out with a pencil.

"Strapping. We had one of Vienna's best silversmiths working at a bench with us in the operating theatre. We opened your leg and cleaned out the blood clots and bits of marrow, then put the fragments back in place, then strapped and pinned the whole thing back together. It's a pretty neat piece of work even though I say it myself. We'll have to operate again in about two months to remove some minor bone fragments, but really from now on it depends upon you and your body's ability to heal—and resist infection of course. We shall have to keep the limb immobilized— and I mean totally immobilised—for a month, then see how you're getting on. I don't hold out more that a fifty-fifty chance of your keeping the leg, but at least the most difficult part is over." He paused, and produced another Röntgen plate. "You're going to have problems though with this thing here." He pointed to a fragment about a centimetre in length. "We can't get at this one without disturbing the main fracture, so we'll have to leave it to work its way to the surface on its own. It should take about eighteen months, and you'll need a small operation to remove it when it gets there. Anyway I shall leave you now, and wish you good luck. Also a great deal of patience, because you are going to spend most of the next six months on your back."

As Eiselberg predicted, I spent the spring and summer months of 1913 in bed, completely immobile until mid-March, then in a plaster cast until October. During those first weeks I was in an agony of apprehension at each of the admiral's morning inspections, listening intently to each "Hmmm" or "Aha" and dreading the "Well Prohaska, I'm afraid that I have to tell you . . ." which would presage the operating table and the bone-saw. But slowly, as the weeks wore by, I began to realise that thirty generations of Bohemian peasant ancestors had given me, if nothing else, a sturdy constitution. It was painful though. The after-effects of the second operation were much worse than the first time, while as for my first attempt to stand and place weight on the limb, early in September, it was sheer agony. Months of physiotherapy followed, in which I worked treadles and rode stationary bicycles until my leg seemed fit to drop off at the hip, restoring strength to the calf-muscles wasted by months of inactivity. But I made it. I could have been lame for life of course, even if I kept the leg; but in the event, before the year was out, the injury had almost completely healed, leaving me with no more to show for it than a complicated pattern of scars, a right leg a centimetre or so shorter than the left, a slight limp and an ache which still troubles me in damp weather even to this day. Otherwise, there was little further difficulty. The limb bore me almost without demur through a further half-century of adventures, and long after I am dead and crumbled away in my coffin three bright rings of silver amid the dust will bear witness to the skill of Admiralstabsarzt Anton, Freiherr von Eiselberg and his colleagues. I hope to meet him in the next world, salute and obediently report that the operation was a complete success.

Boredom was the main problem for me, laid up in bed in those interminable months of mid-1913. My father visited me of course: a doubtful honour, to tell you the truth, since he harangued me for two solid hours on the subject of Teutonic racial purity. The old boy was a convert from Czech nineteenth-century liberal nationalism to the twentieth-century and rabidly illiberal Pan-German variety, and now laboured under a delusion that he was blond and two metres tall, when in fact he was a dark-haired, stocky, squarish Slav peasant. Likewise my brother Anton came down from Leitmeritz to see me. It appeared that he was shortly to move with his regiment to southern Bosnia. Most k.u.k. Armee officers would have cheerfully been posted to Devil's Island rather than go to this poverty-stricken and mountainous province, but Anton was not at all displeased. He had become interested in entomology and was now one of Austria's leading experts on beetles, author of a whole series of learned scientific papers on the order Coleoptera—all published anonymously, since the *K.u.K. Dienstreglement* forbade serving officers to issue anything under their own name, and even then only with their commanding officer's permission. Yes, he said, the area was remote and lacking in amenities; but the insect fauna of the region was largely uncatalogued, and he was sure that so long as he had his collecting bottles and microscope with him he would not be bored.

However, since I was a naval officer based far away on the coast at Pola it was but rarely that any of my brother-officers could come to see me. My main contact with the rest of the world during those months of immobility was therefore my Aunt Aleksandra, who came to see me each day. She was my dead mother's oldest sister, a Pole from Cracow by birth but resident for most of her life in Vienna. She had married a baron who had later risen to be a departmental head in the k.u.k. Ministry of Finances and had then died in his mid-fifties, leaving her with a substantial inheritance and a large flat on the Josefsgasse in the 8th District as well as a comfortable pension. A handsome, grey-haired woman, she seemed to have inherited at birth the entire allocation of brains and character provided for her brothers and sisters, who were otherwise an utterly vapid and feeble lot. In those days the status of a widow gave women a degree of freedom they would otherwise be denied, so since her husband's death Aunt Aleksia had become quite a considerable salon-hostess among the Viennese intelligentsia, fostering the talents of a large number of poets and musicians and painters. Most of them were awful, but not all. She was on terms of intimacy with the artist Klimt and had her portrait painted by him: the "Portrait of Alexandra von Rieger-Mazeotti," ablaze with gilding and inlay work, which I understand no longer exists, having been burnt with a number of the artist's other paintings in 1945. Luckily for me in my helpless condition, I had always got on well with Aunt Aleksia, who was excellent company, so her visits were a constant pleasure. For her part she tried to interest me in painting and literature. She maintained that my education had been badly neglected in a provincial hole like Hirschendorf and in the gunrooms of battleships and that my convalescence was a heaven-sent opportunity to fill in the gaps. Scarcely a day passed in which a new book did not arrive on my bedside table. Soon I had worked my way through the German novel and the Polish classics and started on Dickens and George Eliot.

I also received, about the middle of March, a pro forma visit from the Heir-Apparent. With that tact and sense of occasion for which he was so justly renowned, he used the visit—which lasted about ninety seconds—to inform me that my appointment to his staff was being terminated. The reason, so far as I could make out, was that the Archduke had discovered that my mother, though a Pole, had an Italian surname, a fact which in Franz Ferdinand's eyes was grounds for instant dismissal—that is, unless one happened to be a count like my former room-mate Belcredi. I was not disposed to protest. I had no idea at all of what I would do when I left the hospital, even assuming that the k.u.k. Kriegsmarine wished to retain my services. But certainly the Belvedere was one place to which I had no desire whatever to return.

Otherwise, hospital life was rather trying as the long, hot days of the Viennese summer arrived. They moved me into a double room with a fellow-officer, a Polish Uhlan Rittmeister called Malczewski. He was in with a broken thigh, acquired not (as I had at first imagined) as a result of some over-daring feat of horsemanship but on the cobbles of the Stephansplatz, falling off the platform of one of the new motor buses. He was an exceedingly dull fellow who would use the phrase "so to speak" like a sort of nervous tic at least twice in each sentence. But at least he was quiet and left me to get on with my reading. Like most Poles though, he had swarms of relatives: numerous cousins and aunts and uncles resident in and around Vienna who never seemed to visit him at anything less than battalion strength. Most of them were a dowdy lot, middle-aged and scarcely less tedious than Malczewski himself. However, one warm Sunday afternoon early in July the usual posse of visitors contained a really splendid-looking woman in her mid-twenties—tall, graceful, dressed in the height of fashion and very obviously Polish. She made her entry into the room as if she expected to be greeted by a round of applause, smiled graciously at me, then removed her hat and veil with studied elegance before sitting down with the other relatives by the Rittmeister's bedside. Her hair was quite marvellously blond. The majority of Poles are fair-haired, but this is usually a thin, rather washed-out fairness. This woman's hair though was dense as a horse's mane and the colour of a 20-Gulden piece, so golden in fact that I would have suspected artificial help, if the hair-dyes of those days had not been so crude as to betray themselves at first glance. I looked at her shapely back, sighed, thought, Not for the likes of you, Ottokar my boy, then returned to *The Mill on the Floss.*

The conversation started: the normal Polish familial music of gaggling, hissing, snarling imprecation punctuated by appeals to the holy virgin and the saints, which to the unaccustomed ear sounds like the prelude to an outbreak of communal knifing but which in fact signifies little. I was used to it from childhood and could ignore it, much as people nowadays shut out the wireless. After some time though I felt a slight disturbance under the thin summer counterpane—then something stealing across my thigh. Puzzled, I looked up. The woman still had her back to me and was apparently engaged in the on-going family argument, but her left arm had crept under my bedclothes. The hand made its way across to my private parts, whose existence I had almost forgotten in the months since my injury, and there proceeded to perform a number of actions which delicacy forbids me to describe in detail, save to remark that the hand's owner was certainly no stranger to this kind of thing. Then the hand withdrew as stealthily as it had been inserted. She took advantage of a lull in the conversation to glance around and give me a ravishing smile, then turned back to Malczewski and his relatives. For my part I was rather embarrassed than anything else. I was no stranger to women's endearments, but I had never before met with quite such forwardness. Was she perhaps a top-class courtesan taking a Sunday off, I wondered? But surely such women granted their favours only for money . . . As they rose to leave I was half dreading being presented with a discreet envelope containing a bill. But no, she merely smiled and bade me goodbye, in German, then swept out as dramatically as she had entered. None but the two of us knew anything about the incident it seemed. As soon as I decently could I engaged Malczewski in conversation and asked who his lady visitor had been.

"Oh, she's called Bożena Grbić-Karpińska: second cousin of mine. Quite a corker isn't she, so to speak? She used to be an opera singer in

Lemberg, but then she got married, so to speak, to some rich Serb down in the Banat and gave up the stage. Spends most of her time in Vienna now though I believe . . ."

"So to speak?"

"Yes, so to speak."

Apart from this trifling incident, there was little to remark upon during the remainder of my stay in hospital. I got up on crutches for the first time in late August, and began to move about. Then in October—joyous day—the plaster cast was removed and I was allowed to start walking again—clumsy at first as a year-old baby, but with increasing nimbleness as the weeks passed and physiotherapy began to do its work. Early in November I was discharged from hospital and moved to my aunt's flat on the Josefsgasse. My sessions of exercise at the hospital now took up only three days of each week, and the Navy had put me on indefinite convalesence leave, so filling in the remaining four days became rather a problem now that the winter was setting in and made the streets difficult for a semi-cripple with a stick. I knew hardly anyone in the capital. Attempts to telephone one or two lady-friends produced frustratingly little. Fräulein Mitzi from the Carltheater was now engaged to a Bulgarian count; while as for Frau Hanni the corn-chandler's wife from Purkersdorf, her husband answered the telephone and promised to shoot me dead if I came within sight of the place. However, I was not entirely without society, because my aunt's winter programme of artistic soirées was now getting into full swing.

It was at one of these get-togethers in mid-November that my aunt's maid Franzi announced a Madame Grbić-Karpińska. In she swept, like a frigate under full sail, wrapped in a fur stole that showed off her glorious hair to perfection. Her blue-grey eyes under their arched brows swept around the assembled company—which had suddenly fallen silent—as if it were a theatre audience. Then they rested on me. She was not disconcerted even for an instant. My aunt introduced us. Madame Grbić-Karpińska smiled disarmingly, then spoke in her Polish-flavoured German: "Ah yes my dear Aleksia, the Herr Leutnant and I have already met. We enjoyed a brief tête-à-tête during the summer when he was a patient in the General Hospital."

I was tempted to remark that tête-à-tête was certainly a new expression for what had taken place. But I kept silence, merely kissing her hand and restricting myself to the usual polite formalities. Later that evening though, as soon as she decently could, she sought me out: not difficult, because my leg obliged me to remain seated for most of the evening. She was delighted when she found that we could converse in Polish, which I spoke fluently though with a slight Czech intonation.

"My dear, dear lieutenant, what a pleasure to see you again. And how is your poor leg? Your aunt tells me that you injured it in a flying accident. How romantic though—I always think that airmen must be so brave. I would so very much like to be able to fly one day. The speed, and the rushing wind—ah! it must be ecstasy, a rapture like that of love itself. But tell me, are you getting better now?"

"Much better now, thank you, dear lady. I am beginning to be able to walk without the stick. The doctors think that I should be completely cured by the spring. But tell me if you will, madame, what brings you back to Vienna?"

She looked at me obliquely. "How did you know that I had been away?"

"Your cousin Rittmeister Malczewski told me that you live in Hungary, down in the Banat I believe."

She smiled archly. "Oh you wicked, wicked man. Making secret enquiries about respectable married women indeed—I never heard the like of it. Why did you want to know?"

"Natural curiosity, dear lady. I thought it a sad thing though, when the Rittmeister told me, that such a beautiful and charming woman should be obliged to waste her sweetness upon the indifferent maize fields of such a backward province when she should rightfully ornament our capital city."

She sighed like a pair of blacksmith's bellows and cast down her eyes.

"Ah yes, alas, yes, my dear lieutenant. But there; we all have our sorrows to bear in this vale of tears."

"But what sorrows, if I might ask? Surely a woman as attractive and—I understand—as talented as yourself should have little enough to be sad about?"

She lowered her eyes again and was silent for some moments, as if waiting for a cue from a stage prompter. I failed to give it, so she supplied it herself: "Oh yes, the world thinks me to be so. But the blessed virgin alone knows I have enough to be sad about, marooned out there in that wilderness, buried alive in a rotten stinking little pit of a town, surrounded by Serb peasants hardly less uncouth than their own pigs and by a swarm of Jews and gypsies. The nearest railways station is half a day's drive away and the river steamer takes two days to Budapest even in summer."

"But surely, you have a husband and a household to occupy you: perhaps children as well?"

Her eyes flashed dangerously. "Pah! That ignorant boor of a Serb of mine? Holy Mother of God why did I marry him? Yes, yes, I know—for his money. But what is money to compensate me for having to share a house and the marital bed with an illiterate oaf who stinks of tobacco and pig-dung and scarcely knows how to use a knife and fork? Ah lieutenant . . ." (a teardrop began to glisten in the corner of one eye) "dear lieutenant, when I think of what I could have been, and when I look at myself as I am now, then I sometimes want to cry . . ." I thought at this point that she was indeed going to burst into sobs, and looked around in panic. Luckily we were half hidden from the sight of the rest of the company behind some potted ferns. She knelt beside my armchair and gazed up into my face. Her eyes were a steely bluish-grey with a dark ring around the iris, but slightly slanted, with more than a hint of the Asiatic steppes about them.

"Ah, my dear Ottokar—if I may call you that—you cannot understand what moves a woman's heart: no man ever will. But perhaps you may begin to appreciate how much I would give to have the love and companionship of a man who was sensitive and gentle, and who cared for me as a human being and not as a piece of property. For the truth is that my husband married me only to acquire another work of art for his collection: a living one this time, the beautiful young soprano Bożena Karpińska at the very start of her career, the toast of Lemberg, with counts and barons beyond number queuing up to beg for her hand in marriage—and with her glorious golden hair. Hair" (she took a strand and examined it) "which turns a little greyer now with the falling leaves of each autumn . . ." We were interrupted by a call from my aunt.

"*Meine Damen und Herren,* if you please. There will now be a little musical interlude. Madame Grbić-Karpińska will sing for us a small trifle from the lighter repertoire: the song 'Meine Herr Marquis' from *Die Fledermaus.* I give you Madame Grbić-Karpińska." She rose, squeezed my arm in farewell and left to a round of polite applause, then took her place beside the piano as the accompanist sat down and shuffled his music-sheets. She inflated her barrel chest, the pianist gave her a note, and she began.

I am not a particularly discerning judge of voices, but I have to say that as mezzo sopranos of the Wagnerian stamp go, Bożena Grbić-Karpińska was pretty good, with excellent breath control and phrasing. I do not doubt for a moment that if she had not left the stage she could have made, if not a brilliant, then at least a very creditable career in the operatic world. No, the trouble that evening was rather one of personality than of technique, for the truth is that although she was no taller than myself—and I was not much above the average height for those days—she was one of those people who appear to be much larger than they really are. As with the definition of a gas which we used to learn in physics classes at school, she seemed to expand to fill any space into which she was introduced. The operatic style of delivery was much more florid and declamatory in those days than now, of course. But it has to be said that not only were the singer and the song that evening wildly ill-assorted—like putting a cavalry charger to work giving children rides on the beach at Grado—but the performer herself made no concessions whatever to the fact that she was in the drawing room of a Viennese flat, and not trying to reach the back row of a provincial opera-house with bad acoustics. People spoke with awe in those days of singers whose top C could crack a wineglass. Well, Pani Bożena's would have shattered an earthenware flowerpot at twenty-five paces. I observed the looks of pain on the faces around me as she hit the top notes, and was grateful for the first time ever that my spell as a battleship's gunnery officer had at least taken the edge off my hearing in the upper registers. Next morning I was talking to my aunt over breakfast.

"Well, Otto dear boy" (she always used the German contraction, holding "Ottokar" to be a vulgar Czech peasant name), "I see that last night's gathering put some sparkle back into you. You've been looking very down since you came out of hospital. I saw you deep in conversation with Bozena Karpińska, which cheered me up a lot. You need to meet people of your own age more, and not old relics like me all the time. How did you find her?"

"A very remarkable and charming woman, Aunt. She has a very powerful personality."

"Yes, that's true enough. There's nothing mimsy-pimsy or lukewarm about Pani Bozena. But I'm glad you liked her, because she's asked to meet you again. In fact I've invited her here for tea tomorrow afternoon. She would have invited us, but she's staying with relatives in Wiener Neustadt and I don't think that your leg will allow the journey yet."

I could hardly conceal my delight. "That will be very pleasant, Aunt. I hope that she will entertain you as much as she entertains me."

She smiled enigmatically. "She won't have the chance. I'm off to Merano for three days tomorrow morning to visit friends. Franzi and Frau Niedermayer will look after you while I'm away, and Franzi will set out tea tomorrow before she goes out. It's her afternoon off." Really, this was too good to be true. "Anyway Otto, I hope that you'll have a pleasant afternoon."

"Er . . . yes Aunt . . . I'm sure we . . . I mean, I shall. Madame Grbić-Karpińska is going to tell me about her work with Mahler."

She gave me a steady, quizzical look, searching but kindly. "Yes, I'm sure she will. I've told Franzi to put clean sheets on the bed."

The next afternoon came: 2:30, then 3 p.m. and still no sign of Pani Bozena. Had she decided against it after all? She certainly looked and acted as if she might be very capricious and unreliable, perhaps even addicted to cruel little practical jokes. I was just giving up hope when a fiacre clip-clopped to a halt in the street. Then the bell rang. Was it her? I limped towards the door and opened it. Yes, there she stood, magnificent as ever, like some ship's figurehead come to life. A wave of scent almost knocked me off my unsteady legs. She scooped me up in her arms and planted a large wet kiss on my cheek.

"Ah, my poor lieutenant, what a pleasure to see you again. But aren't you going to ask a poor girl inside?" She seemed not to be surprised that I should have answered the door. Could she have known already that the servants were out? She swept past me as I closed the door behind her and hobbled over to take her hat and coat. Then she bade me wait a few moments while she went to the dressing room. I smelt her coat as I hung it up: a wonderful warm, feminine smell, doubly intoxicating to someone whose profession dictated a life spent in the draughty, loud, masculine, carbolic-scented surroundings of ship's wardrooms and naval shore-establishments.

As a twenty-seven-year-old naval officer I was certainly no novice at the delicate business of seduction. And I knew that a certain finesse and regard for the niceties was in order even here, with a woman who was proclaiming her readiness by wireless, semaphore, flags and signalling lamps all at once. So I laid my plans carefully: how one topic of teatime conversation would lead to another; how signals would be exchanged; how I would cautiously reconnoitre the ground and advance stage by stage, working my way around resistance wherever I encountered it until—perhaps even by the end of this afternoon if things went well—hints might be dropped about a further meeting elsewhere.

But these, as I am sure you will have realised, were the standard infantry tactics which were to bring such dismal results in the World War, and I had quite failed to appreciate that in Pani Bozena I was dealing with an early exponent of Blitzkrieg. She's taking her time, I thought, and went out into the corridor—just in time to meet her emerging from the dressing room, naked as Eve in the Garden of Eden except for her golden hair, which she had unpinned and allowed to fall in a shining, corn-coloured waterfall over her shoulders. She brushed a tress of it aside from her face and smiled at me, confident as if she had been fully clothed and wearing her hat and gloves and overcoat. I was not exactly unfamiliar with women in a state of undress, but even so . . .

"Well, dear Ottokar, does the dashing airman like his little Pani Bozena?"

"I . . . well . . . I . . ."

"Oh don't be shy. There's no one here but us. Your aunt told me that it was Franzi's afternoon off. I know that your poor leg must still ache, but really I would have expected a little more—well—initiative. Or is it not true what they say about the virility of sailors?" She frowned slightly. "Or perhaps little Bozena does not appeal to the Herr Leutnant. Maybe he prefers brunettes?"

I stammered that no, really, I had no preferences in the matter, just that I had been taken rather by surprise. I might have added that "little" was hardly the adjective I would have chosen myself to describe Pani Bozena. She was a splendid creature to be sure, but statuesque rather than voluptuous: Bayreuth rather than Bad Ischl. "Strapping" is the English word that would describe her best: big-boned and athletic, like some Nordic warrior-goddess with a hint of Tartar.

She took me in her arms and kissed me.

"Really, cuddling in uniform. Don't you officers ever unbutton? Here's a Polish girl offering her consolations to an injured flying hero and he can't even take his jacket off for her. Here, I'll help you undress. We must mind your poor leg." Her hand slid downwards, and her eyes widened in mock-surprise. "Mother of God, what on earth is this? Are you sure that the surgeons removed all the pieces of bone?"

"I think that you are perfectly well aware what that is. In fact as I recall you are acquainted already."

She looked puzzled for a moment, then laughed. "A mere frolic to pass a dull afternoon with my relatives. Shaking hands does not constitute a formal introduction. But my poor, dear Ottokar: they've been giving exercise to your leg, I know, but how long is it since . . . ?"

"I forget. Well over a year I should think."

"Over a year? Dear God, you'll turn into a eunuch. Come on, let's administer a little physiotherapy there as well, shall we?"

So from that afternoon on, in those closing weeks of the year, Pani Bozena's physiotherapy sessions became a pretty regular affair. Sometimes my aunt—who, as you may already have gathered, was very much a woman of the world—would tactfully go out for the afternoon and give Franzi a few hours off to visit her mother in Favoriten. Franzi was a sweet girl but—well, more than a little soft in the head, and I doubt whether she would have suspected anything even if she had stayed in. She had no idea where babies came from and once, when taken by my aunt on an improving trip to the Kunsthistorisches Museum, had stared for some time in bewilderment at a statue of a Greek athlete before observing mysteriously that she had never realised that Catholics and Jews were that different. Otherwise we would repair to one of the locality's small backstreet hotels. In those days most cities in Europe had establishments which were prepared to let rooms by the hour; but so far as I know only Vienna had hotels which let exclusively on that basis. Divorce was extremely rare in Catholic Austria, so adultery was an almost Church-sanctioned means of blowing off steam. Nobody gave it a great deal of thought so long as the rules of the game were observed and people behaved decorously.

At least I now had the means to book a room for an hour or two or three, and to fund trips to the theatre, where—appropriately enough in my circumstances—Nedbal's operetta *Polenblut* was the sensation of the season. Throughout my time in hospital my back pay had been accumulating (the General Hospital was using me as an experimental patient, so it waived my fees) while my aunt, being a Pole, would have looked with horror upon any offer to pay for her hospitality. Therefore, with no wardroom bills to devour my monthly salary, I had accumulated for the first time in my career a reasonable sum in the bank, even after having repaid my debts to my aunt. This state of affairs was so gratifying that I even considered breaking my other leg to prolong it.

Naturally, we had to exercise a certain caution, she and I. Pani Bożena was not by nature a person to pay heed to things, but even she realised that her prolonged absences in Vienna might be causing her factory-owner husband back in Hungary to wonder, perhaps even to have her followed. Likewise I had to bear in mind that I was myself quite a conspicuous figure on the Viennese streets. Alone of the European powers, Austria-Hungary forbade its officers to wear mufti and insisted that they should appear at all times in uniform, even when skiing or rock-climbing; and Vienna was far enough from the sea anyway for naval personnel to be an infrequent sight there. So we resorted to an elaborate and enjoyable pantomime of changing trams and arriving in separate fiacres and leaving notes to one another in poste restante boxes. Looking back on it, in fact, it was all quite as much fun as the energetic bouts of fornication which were the object of the exercise. After all, the process itself only takes about half an hour; so to my mind how two people get to the bedroom door is usually quite as interesting as what goes on once they are behind it.

Also how they spend the time afterwards. And in this respect I must say that quite the most intriguing aspect of my relationship with Bożena Grbić-Karpińska was getting to know the woman herself. For growing up in the rather grey, solid bourgeois world of a small town in the Czech provinces—a world which by about 1900 was not so very different from that of a similar-sized town in Belgium or Yorkshire—I had never met anyone quite like her: living testimony to the old aphorism that the River San is the western frontier of Asia. She gave herself without reserve in everything she did, and during those weeks together she displayed her remarkable personality to me with quite as little reticence as her handsome body.

Pani Bożena was a wonderful, prime specimen of that extraordinary breed, the Mitteleuropean female; a type scattered in their millions across that vast, amorphous tract of territory bordered by the Baltic, the Adriatic and the Black Seas. A small-town girl by upbringing (she came from a place called Gródek Jagielloński in Eastern Galicia, where her father was a revenue official), she was still a peasant woman at heart: warm, generous, resourceful and immensely brave, but at the same time naïve, credulous, possessive and childishly devious; also capable of a sudden whimsical cruelty which could only be excused by its complete lack of premeditation. In fact I think I never in all my life met anyone less capable of premeditating anything, for she seemed to live entirely by instinct. It was not that Pani Bożena was stupid—far from it. It was just that for most of the time she kept her brain resolutely disconnected and functioned on spinal cord alone.

Her capacity for not thinking about things was prodigious, and endlessly fascinating to a drab, rationalist Czech like myself. I well remember how we lay in bed one afternoon, following a prolonged session of horizontal exercise. She reclined there, her hair cascading over the pillow, while I lay propped up on one elbow, idly constructing a miniature tower of matchsticks around one of her nipples, seeing how many I could stack up before her breathing upset them. We were talking about this and that, the way people do afterwards. Then she got on to the Jews again. Like most Polish small-town people she was virulently anti-Semitic, and (unlike the folk of Vienna) not in the least coy about admitting it. We had reached the crucial phrase "Mowią że . . ."—"They say that . . ."—inevitable precursor to some breathtakingly improbable statement, rather as the rush of air in an Underground tunnel announces the approach of a train long before its lights appear in the distance. According to Pani Bożena "they" (whoever they were) had revealed in recent weeks that the Pope was a Freemason, that King George V of England was a woman and—most baffling of all—that St Francis of Assisi was a Protestant.

"Anyway, they say that . . . What are you doing there? It tickles."

"Building a pagoda. Your breasts remind me of the Moulmein temples."

"Of the what?"

"The Moulmein pagodas. I went there when I was a cadet and our ship put in at Rangoon."

"Where?"

"Rangoon. Burma. Near India."

"Oh. Well, anyway, they say it's a scandal the way the Jews are cutting prices to drive Christian shopkeepers out of business. They're taking everything over here in Vienna just the same as in Galicia. Also the prices they charge are outrageous."

I stopped my pagoda-building. "Wait a minute, Bożena, that's rubbish."

"What do you mean, rubbish? Everyone knows it."

"Look, the two statements you have just made are mutually exclusive. It's possible that both propositions may be untrue—in fact they both sound remarkable nonsense to me. But if that isn't the case, then they cannot both be true."

"Why not?"

"Because logically, neither the Jews nor anyone else can undercut prices and overcharge at the same time: it just can't be done."

"Oh yes it can, if they're Jews; it just shows how cunning they are."

Some time after this we got up, dressed and went for a walk in a nearby park. I could manage quite well without the stick now, though I was still unsteady, and I thought that we were sufficiently far from the city centre for no one to recognise us. The park was on the edge of the Leopoldstadt, the one-time Jewish quarter of Vienna. Suddenly I saw coming towards us along the pavement a Hassidic Jew, complete with hat and sidelocks, and his bewigged, shawl-wrapped wife and small son, also with sidelocks and wearing a yarmulka. Oh dear, I thought, here comes trouble: this pavement is too narrow for both couples to pass. But as we drew near, Pani Bożena suddenly gave a whoop like a Red Indian and rushed up to the Jews to fling her arms about them and kiss them in an excited torrent of Polish and half-Yiddish. Then she knelt down and embraced the little boy.

"Come on, Reuben, aren't you going to give a kiss to Auntie Bożenka?"

At length we exchanged farewells and parted. When they were out of earshot I turned to her. "Bożena, it seems to me that you're either an arch-hypocrite or completely loopy. After what you've been saying about the Jews this afternoon you come straight out on to the street and embrace the first Hassidim couple you meet as if they were long-lost brothers and sisters."

Her eyes suddenly blazed. "How dare you! Calling them Jews. We grew up together in Gródek, Isaiah and Rachel and I, and they're as true a couple of Poles as ever walked the earth. How dare you call them Jews!" I sensed that further debate on this point would be futile.

In the matter of religion Pani Bożena herself was a particularly devout occasional Catholic. By this I mean that for about 360 days in each year she conducted her life with the cheerful abandon of a Tahitian before the arrival of the missionaries. But on the remaining five or so, at certain not entirely predictable seasons which seemed to be determined as much by astrology (in which she believed implicitly) as by the Church calendar, she would take herself to the Gardekirche, which was in those days much favoured by Vienna's large Polish community, and there abandon herself to a period of Latin wailing and rosary-fingering and kneeling on flagstones until her knees were raw, lighting candles and praying before images with a fervour that would be regarded as excessive by even the most besotted of Hindus. She would be like this for a day or so. Then it would be back to assaulting the bed-springs in back-street hotels with just the same cheerful sensuality as before. Occasionally though, religion did manage to seep out a little from its watertight compartment and intrude upon the rest of her life. I remember how, one afternoon quite early in our friendship, while climbing into the saddle so to speak, I enquired as discreetly as I could whether she was taking . . . certain precautions. Such things were not yet spoken of in public of course, except to be denounced from pulpits as unnamed "abominable practices." But even in backward Austria the word had been spreading among the enlightened classes for a decade or more past that a few simple measures would greatly reduce the risk of pregnancy. I liked children, and wished to be a father one day. But not just yet, and certainly not with a woman who was married to someone else. As the significance of what I was asking dawned upon her, her eyes widened in unfeigned horror and she crossed herself.

"Holy Mother of God and all the saints," she gasped, "what are you asking of me? Do you want me to commit a sin?"

So those last weeks of the year passed in a pleasant haze of sexual semi-exhaustion. But as we neared New Year I began to ask myself whether, like the little girl in the fairy story who finds the magic porridge pot, it might not be possible to have too much of a good thing. Pani Bożena was delightful company most of the time, impulsive and generous with her favours. But she also expected a great deal in return, both physically and emotionally, and though I did my best to give it I was still less than a year after a very nasty injury and a prolonged period of convalescence, probably more run-down in body and spirits than I quite appreciated. Suffice it to say anyway that by Christmas I began to feel rather as though I had been boiled for a week and then wrung out in a towel. And there was the constant emotional drain as well, because Madame Grbić-Karpińska possessed a highly strung as well as a powerful personality. She tended to oscillate for much of the time between bouts of mild megalomania, during which she would maintain that she could (had Fate treated her less cruelly) have been the equal of Melba or Jenny Lind, and periods of depression during which she was nothing, nobody and lower than the offal cast out for the dogs. She was prone to the most abominable and unpredictable attacks of the sulks, and she also took a malicious delight in making scenes if she felt that she was not sufficiently the centre of attention. On one occasion, I remember, we walked into a café on the Prater and I happened to meet a lady acquaintance, one Kathi Merizzi, sitting at a table sharing an ice-cream with her small daughter. Frau Kathi was a pretty woman, but of irreproachable virtue: chaste, religious and happily married since she was eighteen to a major in my brother's regiment. Pani Bozena smiled like a tigress and stirred cornflour into her Polish accent, which was usually not too obtrusive.

"Just fancy—another of Ottokar's discarded mistresses. I keep bumping into them everywhere these days." She leant over and her voice sank to a deafening stage whisper. "Tell me, my dear, when was he last up you, then? Quite good at it isn't he? I say though, what a beautiful little girl. Is Ottokar the father? Yes, yes, I think that I see a distinct likeness about the eyes . . ."

That was nearly seventy-five years ago now, but I still break out into a chill sweat when I remember that afternoon: the sudden, profound hush in the café; the hundred pairs of eyes staring at us; Frau Kathi speechless with her mouth hanging open in horror, then bursting into tears; the little girl asking, "Mummy, who is this funny lady? Is this man really my daddy?"; myself desperately trying to recall everything that I had ever read about spontaneous combustion and wondering how one started the process.

New Year's Eve came around—the Feast of St Sylvester as we call it where I come from. She and I went to the Hotel Krantz on the Neuer Markt, where the Polish Club of Reichsrat Deputies was holding a New Year's party. We knew that we would be safe together there since the Poles, though horribly malicious among themselves, would never inform on one another to an outsider. About ten minutes to midnight Pani Bozena disappeared. As the hour neared I went to look for her. Maddening woman: she would miss seeing in the New Year. The street outside was full of revellers and drunkards blowing horns, throwing streamers and hitting policemen or one another to see out the old year. By the hotel entrance a large man was engaged in roughing up a woman, cursing her most violently in Serb and shaking her by the arm. I went over to intervene—then saw who it was. The woman was Pani Bożena, her hair disordered, and the man was a burly, tall, moustachioed individual of rural origin—evidently Grbić himself, up in town from the distant Banat. I hesitated for a moment wondering what to do. I should rescue her. But he was her lawful husband after all; and what if a general brawl started? A brother-officer had been cashiered by a court of honour some years before after he had intervened in such a dispute and the husband had laid a hand on his sword, thus obliging him to kill the man on the spot (which he had failed to do) in order to wipe out the insult to the officer corps. I looked around desperately. Quick, find a policeman. But before I could move, a fiacre had drawn up and Grbić had bundled Bożena into the back of it. I shouted after her, but the door closed and the cab started to drive away. Feeling more utterly contemptible and useless than I had ever felt in my life before, I went back to the hotel, just as the bells of the cathedral and all the churches of the city began to strike midnight. The k.u.k. Minister of Finances, Leon, Ritter von Biliński, climbed on to a table and raised his glass.

"Ladies and gentlemen—fellow Austrian Poles—let us drink a toast, that this new year may bring peace and prosperity to each and every one of us, to our dear Polish Fatherland, to our beloved Emperor and to all the peoples of our Monarchy. Ladies and gentlemen, I give you the year 1914."

# 6

# DANUBE FLOTILLA

THE SUDDEN ABDUCTION OF PANI BOZENA by her husband that New Year's Eve left me feeling very low for some time afterwards. Not only was there the sense of my own wretched inadequacy for having failed to intervene, there was also the feeling of loss now that she was no longer around. For, even if she had often been a very tiresome woman to be with, her generosity and her sheer exuberance had more than compensated for her frequent spells of beastliness.

But as things turned out I had little enough time to grieve over her departure, because in the third week of January I was instructed to report to the Marine Section of the k.u.k. War Ministry, on the Zollamtstrasse, to be examined by a medical board. I needed no second bidding: I was a seafaring man by choice and only twice during the past year had I been afloat on salt water. My injury was nearly healed now and the life of a dry-land sailor was getting to be irksome. I longed for a heaving deck beneath my feet once more, for the distant blue waters of the Adriatic—or perhaps waters even bluer and more distant if I could wangle a posting aboard a ship proceeding on foreign service. Naval aviation was developing rapidly, so who knew? Might there not soon be berths for qualified pilots on the China Station or in the West Indies? The days before the examining board were taken up with weight exercises and vigorous long walks as I tried to remove the remaining stiffness from my leg. I would pass the fitness examination or die in the attempt. The board was a disappointment I am afraid: passed category A3. I suppose in retrospect that this was not at all bad for someone who less than a year before had been within hailing distance of a wooden leg. But it meant (they told me) that I would not return to flying duties in the forseeable future.

"Nothing personal, Prohaska," the Chief Postings Officer had said. "It's just that we've suddenly got more pilots than aeroplanes, so the fitness category has been raised to A2. And there's also the fact that you wrote off one of our newest machines last year. Yes, yes, I know it wasn't your fault. But it makes you look rather unlucky. Anyway, come back for another board this time next year and we'll see what we can do."

"And for now?"

He adjusted his spectacles and looked down at the sheaf of papers. "Yes, what about now. Hmmm, it seems that the only thing available at the moment is aboard your old ship the *Erzherzog Albrecht*." My heart suddenly turned to a lump of clay in my breast. "Report aboard 23 February, say. It's only a supernumerary posting, but we can find you something else while you're there."

So with a heavy heart I packed my bags, said farewell to my aunt and set off for the Südbahnhof to catch the train for Pola. And at 8 a.m. on the morning of 23 February I duly climbed up the gangway of the battleship S.M.S. *Erzherzog Albrecht* to report myself to the officer of the watch.

Going back is something which I have never found easy or pleasant. I was received back into the wardroom cordially enough I suppose, but there were some who laughed up their sleeves. Every prison contains some inmates who will jeer and whistle as an escaper is led back in through the gates, laden down with chains. My former cabin-mate Linienschiffsleutnant Kaszała-Piotrowski was particularly spiteful I remember; a surprise to me, since I had always considered him to be rather feeble and inept, but basically a decent enough sort of character. Scarcely a meal could pass without his making some oblique reference to my recent rapid elevation into high society, and my equally rapid fall therefrom: "Yes, I suppose they all handle their knives and forks like that in court circles" or some such pleasantry. I tried my best to ignore him.

The greatest surprise however was the Old Man, Linienschiffskapitän Blasius Lovranić von Lovranica. I confidently expected a terrible time at the hands of this bull-headed old martinet, what with having ignored his advice about aeroplanes and then come back with my tail between my legs and a damaged leg to show for my folly. On my first evening back in the wardroom he buttonholed me in full view of my brother-officers in that booming, foghorn voice of his:

"Well, Prohaska, back with us once more I see? Evidently flying didn't suit you after all."

I gritted my teeth. It was to be public breaking on the wheel, slow and methodical at the hands of a master executioner, with each blow of the iron bar expertly delivered before an admiring crowd.

"I most obediently report, Herr Kommandant, that flying suited me well enough. It was just that my luck ran out."

He grunted. "Hmmm! Well, since you left I've often thought over what I said to you when you first came to me. And I see what an old fool I was. I still have my doubts about the naval applications of aircraft. But by God I admire your spirit for trying to learn to fly one. After all, where would any of us be, I ask myself, if no one ever tried anything new? Still paddling about in dug-out canoes. And then I think of some of the hare-brained things I got up to when I was your age. No, Prohaska, I'm sorry that it ended badly for you and I'm glad to have you back with us, truly I am. Trouble is though that the *Albrecht*'s up to strength for officers at the moment. Really we haven't a great deal for you to do except general duties."

These general duties turned out to be the usual dispiriting mish-mash of chores commonly assigned to supernumerary lieutenants aboard battle-ships: welfare, leave, inspecting sides of beef at the screens, organising German classes for warrant officer candidates, assisting the ship's surgeon with his magic lantern at a lecture on venereal diseases. I quickly resigned myself to an indefinite stay in this limbo of shipboard life. However, Fate decreed that before the week was out I would be ejected from limbo into purgatory.

It happened one morning early in March, just after eight bells as the post was being distributed in the wardroom.

"One for you here Prohaska—looks official."

It was a buff War Ministry postings envelope. A hush of anticipation fell over my assembled brother-officers as I tore it open, the hush that surrounds someone rummaging in a bran-tub at a fair. At length I pulled out the prize:

K.u.K. War Ministry (Marine Section)
26/II/14 Vienna

Lschlt Ottokar Prohaska, currently serving aboard S.M.S. *Erzherzog Albrecht*, is instructed to present himself at 8 a.m. on 7 March inst. aboard . . .

There was a fold in the paper here. I opened it—and stared aghast.

river monitor S.M.S. *Tisza,* currently lying at k.u.k. Marine Station Budapest, and there report to the vessel's commanding officer Korvettenkapitän Adolf von Poltl.

Substantive post aboard vessel: Gesamt Detail Offizier.

I was silent; pole-axed; *foudroyé;* struck dumb and rigid. The Danube Flotilla. And Adolf von Poltl. The horror of it, the unspeakable horror . . .

"What's the matter, Prohaska old man, bad news?" Someone picked up the letter, which had fallen from my numbed fingers. A groan went through the assembled officers. "Oh Christ no! . . . Der Poltl . . . And the *Tisza* . . . You poor sod!"

Then the moaning turned into a steady, rhythmical chant. I suppose that one of the most basic human instincts—seemingly callous but in fact quite understandable—is that when a member of the tribe gets struck by lightning or devoured by a lion, the survivors should make a joke of it to congratulate themselves on the fact that, this time at least, it was not them. Soon the whole wardroom was shuffling around in a procession, shoulders bowed and jackets pulled up over heads to impersonate Roman mourners, groaning in chorus as Kaszała-Piotrowski picked out Chopin's "Marche Funèbre" on the wardroom piano.

*"Ad-di von Poltl und die Donau Flotil-le, Ad-di von Poltl und die Donau Flotil-le . . ."*

Suddenly the door opened. It was the GDO, Fregattenkapitän the Freiherr Moravetz-Pellegrini von Treuenschwert.

"What the Devil do you young idiots think you're playing at?" he bellowed. Everyone froze to attention. "What's the meaning of this racket?" Someone handed him my letter. "By your leave, Herr Fregatten-kapitän . . ."

He took it and adjusted his monocle to read it. Then he slowly shut his eyes and swallowed hard. He stood like that for a few moments. Then, without another word, he too pulled his jacket up over his head and joined the procession as the mourners began once more to tramp around the wardroom.

Even the process of joining my new ship seemed to be ill-starred. I arrived at Marine Station Budapest on the day and at the hour appointed—but only to find that the Imperial and Royal River Monitor *Tisza* had sailed two days previously, heading downstream for the town of Pancsova, five hundred kilometres away at the confluence of the Danube and the Temes just downriver from Belgrade. So I set off by the next river steamer to catch up with her. But when I stepped down on to the landing stage at Pancsova next day, bags in hand, I learnt that S.M.S. *Tisza* was overdue: in fact, had disappeared without trace. Totally at a loss to explain how 350 tonnes of warship with sixty men aboard might vanish on a river in the heart of Europe in peacetime, I sat down at Pancsova and waited. Two days later the naval station office received a telegram: S.M.S. *Tisza* was stuck fast on a sandbank about forty kilometres up the eponymous River Tisza, in the desolate heart of the Hungarian puszta, and could someone please send a tug to pull her off? A tug was duly despatched, and I settled down once more to wait.

I had considered Marine Station Budapest to be a pretty dreary sort of place, but the sub-station at Pancsova was infinitely worse: a nest of sloth and dereliction such as I was often to see years later on the banks of the Parana River in Paraguay. But then the Imperial and Royal Danube Flotilla was widely recognised as the Austro-Hungarian Naval equivalent of Siberia. Most of the Monarchy's sailors, you see, officers and ratings alike, were in the Kriegsmarine because they had chosen the seafaring life. Only three of the Monarchy's 108 recruiting districts supplied conscripts direct to the Navy. Everyone else had to volunteer to do their national service afloat, and since the term of conscription in the fleet was four years, as against two in the infantry, no one in their right mind would volunteer unless they intended making a career at sea afterwards. So this meant that nearly everyone in the Imperial and Royal Navy regarded a posting to a duckpond fleet like the Danube Flotilla as something close to a professional slur: sending blue-water seamen to crawl up and down a ditch, even if the ditch in question was the wide and frequently treacherous Danube. I suppose that really the most sensible idea would have been to have handed over the Danube monitors—which were really little more than floating batteries—to the k.u.k. Armee, under whose command they would anyway fall in time of war. But the bureaucratic mind does not work like that. Ship equals sailors, so the famous port-cities of Vienna and Linz and Budapest were often treated to the faintly ludicrous sight of parties of blue-jackets walking along their streets, looking as awkward and out of place as Franciscan friars in a bordello.

My chief recollection of my three days' sojourn at Marine Station Pancsova is of sitting in the Kanzlei hut about ten o'clock one morning, wondering when on earth my ship was going to arrive and whiling away the aching hours by filling in a few forms in quadruplicate. The Station Commandant was seated behind his desk on the other side of the room, chin cupped in hands, staring down at a blank sheet of paper resting on the desk, completely motionless. He was an ancient Korvettenkapitän who had been sent here (it was said) for six months in 1879 and then forgotten by the k.u.k. War Ministry, fallen through a crack in the floorboards of official memory. I stole another glance at him. Still no movement: surely he could not have died, I thought, and still remain upright in his chair? Then, as with the iguana in the zoo which you feel sure must really be stuffed, there was a slight flicker of an eyelid. I turned back to my forms. The door opened, and in strolled a cheerful-looking young Linienschiffsleutnant of about the same age as myself, smoking a cigar and with his cap balanced rakishly on the back of his head. He saluted the commandant, who showed no sign of having even noticed his entry, hung up his cap and sword on a hook behind the door, then, with an air of inexpressible ennui, sat down to his desk. Nothing happened for five minutes or so, until a large bluebottle droned in through the open window. The lieutenant watched it with interest. At length it settled on his desk and stood rubbing its feet together. With infinite care, so as not to frighten it, he picked up a pencil and slowly, patiently raised it into the air directly above the insect. Stealthily, gently, millimetre by millimetre, the pencil was lowered, flat end downwards. The fly clearly sensed that something was wrong, but seemed rooted to the spot, presumably unable (since it saw the descending pencil with both eyes) to decide in which direction to make its escape. The pencil got to about a centimetre above the creature, still dithering helplessly, then—tap! It was all over. The lieutenant scooped the insect's corpse on to a sheet of Kanzlei-Doppel, got up and carried it across to the Station Commandant, then placed it ceremoniously on the desk in front of him before stepping back and saluting smartly, but with unmistakable irony.

"Herr Kommandant, I obediently enquire whether there is anything else to be done today?"

I decided at once—I cannot quite say why—that I rather liked this young man. We got talking later, and I discovered that his name was Richard Seifert; also that we were both posted to the errant S.M.S. *Tisza*. It appeared that he was to replace the Second Officer, who had been landed the previous month suffering from acute nervous prostration, while I was to take over from the present GDO, who was in the early stages of a mental breakdown. Yet despite these fearful auguries for my new posting, I felt suddenly that life might not be quite so awful after all with Seifert around. He came from an old naval family—his father was a retired admiral now living in Graz—but his attitude to naval discipline was far from rigid, and he had a refreshingly laconic way of looking at life, seemingly surprised by nothing. I enquired about our new captain, the egregious Korvettenkapitän Adolf von Poltl.

"Good God yes, he's every bit as bad as they say. In fact a lot worse from some of the stories I've heard lately. My old man says they sent him here to the Danube Flotilla because he was too dangerous even to be allowed aboard a sea-going ship, let alone command one. The man's a complete cretin. His only talent is for passing promotion boards. Everywhere he goes his superiors have recommended him for promotion just to get rid of him. They say –" We were interrupted by the distant hoot of a steamer siren from upriver. "Well," said Seifert, "this sounds like our train. Better go out and meet our fate like men I suppose. *'Ave Caesar, morituri . . .'* and all that. No point in delaying the inevitable."

So we walked out on to the wooden landing stage. Away upstream, on the wide, watery expanse of the great river, were two vessels, one a paddle-tug, the other what appeared to be a biscuit tin on a floating plank with a thin, smoking pipe in the middle. The smoke-cloud issuing from this funnel as the vessel steamed towards us was one of the most extraordinary I have ever seen: not an even plume of grey coal-smoke but a great amorphous string of black blobs hanging in the sky and joined together by the faintest of wisps, as if Indian ink were being dripped into a glass of water. The smoke died away completely at one point—only to be followed a few seconds later by an angry, boiling black mushroom cloud and a momentary snort of flame.

"Holy Mother of God," said Seifert, "what the devil are those stokers playing at? Are they cleaning the furnaces out or what?"

The two vessels were nearing the landing stage now. We saw the *Tisza*'s warp-handling party milling on the foredeck, ready to moor at the jetty. Two blasts on her siren told us that she was about to come up to the jetty. Then we sensed that something was not quite right. Seifert stared at the approaching warship. She was not reducing speed.

"Quick, Prohaska, run!"

We dived for safety as the *Tisza* cannoned into the end of the landing stage. It was a glancing blow; the vessel slid past as the mooring party tried desperately to lasso the passing bollards on the end of the pier. One warp was tossed over a bollard and, with a great rending of timber, a large section of the landing-stage planking was torn away from the frame as the river monitor snubbed the hawser, swung round bows upstream like a huge fish on a line, then began to churn against the current until her bows crashed against the downstream side of the stage. There was a wild commotion as men leapt across from the ship to try and secure her to the pier. I saw the tugboat captain on the bridge of his vessel. He was holding his hand over his eyes and shaking his head sadly.

At last, after about twenty minutes and a great deal of activity and shouting, the river monitor S.M.S. *Tisza* was made fast (more or less) to the by now much dilapidated landing stage. A gangplank was lowered, bos'uns' calls sounded and a corpulent, pop-eyed little man with a Franz Ferdinand moustache strutted stiffly down on to the pier. We were about to meet the far-famed k.u.k. Korvettenkapitän Adolf von Poltl.

If nothing else, our introduction to our new captain that morning there on the landing stage at Pancsova certainly set the tone for our future relations. Seifert and I stepped up and saluted smartly to make our report. The salute was not acknowledged: instead purple blotches began to creep up von Poltl's neck as his eyes bulged in fury. He swelled like a bullfrog inside his jacket.

"God damn you, you pair of swine," he shrieked. "Were you saluting me or brushing away flies? Go back the both of you and do it properly this time!"

So we stepped back and did it again in perfect unison, bringing our hands up to our cap-peaks so smartly that our wrist-joints cracked audibly. In the end we had to essay the salute a further five times before von Poltl deigned to acknowledge it. Then he glowered at us for some time in silence. Finally he managed to speak, his voice starting in a menacing undertone but rising to a scream of rage.

"And where, pray, have you been the pair of you for the past FIVE DAYS?"

As GDO-designate I ventured to reply. "I most obediently report, Herr Kommandant, that our posting orders told me to report aboard at Marine Station Budapest on the 7th and Schiffsleutnant Seifert here at Pancsova on the 5th, but that when I reached Budapest on the day the ship had already sailed, and when we both arrived here . . ."

"SILENCE WHEN YOU SPEAK TO ME! Five days late—one month's board-arrest. *Abtreten sofort!*"

So we spent the next four weeks confined aboard the ship. Or, to be more exact, Seifert and I slipped ashore one evening when Poltl was asleep in his cabin—but after making a ten-minute tour of the town of Pancsova decided that we might as well be back aboard anyway. It used to be a constant source of debate in the officers' messes of the k.u.k. Armee (my brother Anton used to tell me) which of the Austro-Hungarian Empire's numerous garrison-towns best qualified for the title of Imperial, Royal and Apostolic Arsehole of the Danubian Monarchy. The choice usually narrowed down in the end to a run-off between a place called Radautz in the Bukovina, a province so poor and remote that no one in Vienna was even quite sure where it was, and the town of Mostar in Herzegovina, which boasted among its other attractions a pestilential, sticky, sub-tropical climate and fleas which would fight a full-grown cat. But if the Imperial and Royal Navy was also to have its acme of provincial squalor and boredom, it needed to look no further than Pancsova. True, the place was on the railway line; but few trains stopped there. Why should they? It was only two muddy streets, a tumbledown hotel, a single store and a couple of slivovica shops.

My month of enforced confinement on board obliged me to get thoroughly acquainted with my new ship. Not that it was a particularly worthwhile acquaintance to have made though. S.M.S. *Tisza* herself was merely a riverine version of that class of vessel—now vanished from the world's navy lists for many a long year—known as monitors, after their progenitor the USS *Monitor* of the American Civil War: a sort of steam-driven armoured raft, of minimal draught and no freeboard to speak of, with a single turret amidships mounting a pair of heavy cannon. Our own *Tisza* had begun life like that, about 1870, but had been modernised since and now carried a single 15cm gun in her turret, plus two army howitzers in barbettes aft. A single thin funnel protruded amidships. There was an armoured conning tower to be used as a steering position in action, there was a folding mast with an armoured crow's nest at the top of it and there were two boats slung on davits at each side: zilles, those curious flat-bottomed, curved rowing skiffs which were used along the entire length of the Danube and which always looked to me like giant wooden bananas with the ends trimmed off. And that was about all. Year in, year out, throughout Europe's long, golden summer afternoon of peace, the *Tisza* had proceeded south each April from her winter quarters at Budapest to patrol the Danube and the Sava, from Brod down to the Iron Gates, along the frontier between Austria-Hungary and Serbia. And each December she had steamed back upriver, fighting against the autumn floods, to be laid up at Budapest once more before the river froze over.

The ship drew only a metre of water and had less than a metre of freeboard above it, so as you may imagine, life below decks was made very uncomfortable by the lack of headroom. I was not a tall man, but even I had to shave in the mornings standing in my cabin with my head and shoulders protruding through a skylight and with the mirror balanced on the coaming edge. The later Austrian monitors had quite civilised accommodation in a deckhouse amidships. Not our *Tisza,* though. Everything was below the armoured deck, and of course the point of armoured decks is to have as few holes in them as possible for hatchways and skylights and ventilation trunking. We rigged awnings whenever the sun shone. Even so, in the broiling heat of a south Hungarian summer the atmosphere below decks rapidly became such that you could have hung an axe on it. All this was tiresome enough, but there was also the fact—as I soon discovered—that the ship's lower deck was made up almost exclusively of ethnic Magyars.

The Imperial and Royal Austro-Hungarian Navy was a genuinely multinational force. For reasons of geography, the largest single national group among its sailors was the Croats, but after that the other ten nationalities of the Dual Monarchy were represented, if not exactly in proportion to their numbers in the Empire as a whole, then not too far out of proportion, and were allocated to ships regardless of their mother tongue. For official purposes the k.u.k. Kriegsmarine used German as its language of command, but in practice we got by in a curious argot known as "Marinesprache" or "lingua di bordo," made up from German and Italian and Croat all jumbled together into a rich compost. The mark of a contented ship in the Austro-Hungarian Navy was one where the crew sat down to dinner at their mess tables with no regard to nationality, a Czech electrician happily rubbing shoulders with a Croat torpedo-man on one side and an Italian telegraphist on the other.

In theory, the river monitors should have been manned in the same fashion, even though they were based in the Kingdom of Hungary. Magyars made up about ten per cent at most of the Navy's total strength, so one would have expected about every tenth man of the *Tisza*'s crew to be a Hungarian. Not a bit of it though. For all its shortcomings, the k.u.k. Danube Flotilla was still a useful military force, and one which Budapest would wish to have in its pocket, particularly if—as seemed likely before long—the Archduke Franz Ferdinand became Emperor and carried out his long-standing threat to cut the Kingdom of Hungary down to size. So over several years, it appeared, bogus cross-postings and other ingenious wangles at Marine Station Budapest had been used to produce a ship's complement in which the only non-Magyars were the Captain and Seifert (both German-Austrians), myself (an Austro-Czech), the bos'un Jovanović, who was a Croat, and the Chief Engineer, whose cerebral cortex had been so eroded by years of slivovica that no one was quite sure what he was. Myself, I have no doubt whatever that if Franz Ferdinand had succeeded to the throne and it had come to unpleasantness between Vienna and Budapest, all of us would rapidly have ended up at the bottom of the river with our throats cut and bricks in our pockets.

This meant that one of the most basic problems of life aboard S.M.S. *Tisza* was that of communication between officers and crew; for even if German was technically the language of command aboard, I soon discovered that an order in German to a Magyar rating would as often as not produce a blank look and a reply of *"Nem tudom"*—"I don't understand"—or at best a reply in a German which was not so much broken as pulverised. Except (oddly enough) at the weekly pay parade, where the crew would start tudom-ing with a vengeance and the Holy Spirit would bestow the gift of tongues in quite miraculous fashion upon any seaman who believed his pay and allowances to be a Kreuzer short. For my part, I spoke seven of the Monarchy's eleven official languages, but Magyar had always eluded me—a pleasant-sounding language, but one which seemed to have been deliberately designed to be as difficult as possible to learn. Our salvation really was Jovanović who, though a Croat, came from a border area of Croatia and had a smattering of Magyar learnt at school.

He was an excellent man, and it was a surprise to find him among this rag-tag-and-bobtail crew aboard the *Tisza*. I learnt that some years before he had lost a torpedo during summer naval manoeuvres and that the Danube Flotilla had been his punishment.

S.M.S. *Tisza* in the spring of 1914 was not a happy ship. One could tell as much from her smoke-cloud, that extraordinary straggle of puffs and sooty blobs which had announced her approach to us that morning as we stood on the jetty at Pancsova. That was always the way with coal-fired steamships: one could gather a great deal about their internal economy by the smoke signature written on the sky astern of them. A well-conducted vessel would leave a nice even grey streak behind her, while a ship with dyspepsia would produce a ragged, uneven cloud as the stokers slacked and the steam pressure fell and the captain bellowed down the voice-pipe and the stokers retaliated by suddenly opening the furnace doors to let the draught blast soot and clinker up the funnel, hoping that some of it would settle on the bridge and the captain's best whites. Suffice it to say, anyway, that S.M.S. *Tisza*'s smoke-cloud was one of the most uneven I had ever seen; evidence not so much of strained relations between bridge and stokehold as a constant state of incipient mutiny.

These bad relations would not have mattered too much aboard a sea-going vessel. The sea is a dangerous place, and even if officers and crew cordially detest the sight of one another, there is still a certain shared interest in avoiding death by drowning. On a river vessel, though, there is not quite that same common urge to make things work. This was short-sighted of us, now that I look back on it, because with her heavily armoured hull and her near-total lack of reserve buoyancy the *Tisza* would certainly have sunk like a granite paving slab if holed in a collision, sucking the lot of us down with her. Likewise the Danube (as I soon discovered) is a tricky river to navigate. Along these Banat-Voivodina reaches it was wide, marshy-banked and fretted with innumerable side-channels winding between low, swampy islands covered in alder and willow. It had a strong current, particularly in spring, when the melting snows of Central Europe were decanted down the river into the Black Sea; and in the autumn, after the rains; but also in between, when a spell of wet weather on one or other of the tributaries would produce unpredictable flash-floods further downstream. Often we would turn out in the middle of the night to find the ship moaning and tugging at her mooring warps as the water rose almost perceptibly up the red-and-white-striped marker-poles on the bank, swirling uprooted trees and dead animals and even entire peasant huts along on the sinuous chocolate-coloured flood.

It was one of these floods, early in April, which brought Seifert and me an unexpected diversion from the monotony of life aboard. We found her one morning stuck in the branches of a tree on the bank near the Pancsova landing stage, a beautifully constructed, very expensive and almost undamaged Red Indian-style canoe planked in cedarwood. She had no name plate and not the slightest indication of where she had come from, so we claimed her as our lawful prize and spent the next fortnight of our off-duty time repairing and revarnishing the little vessel while Poltl combed the *K.u.K. Dienstreglement* for some regulation that could be used to stop us.

I think that in time I might have overcome my initial distaste at being posted to a fresh-water ship and set to work with a will at acquiring the skills of a river pilot, which are very different from those of ocean navigation. Always though there was the presence of the Captain, strutting around the bridge or sitting in his cabin perusing the service regulations and thinking up new ways of oppressing us all. For the truth is that "der Poltl" was an officer such as could only have been produced by a country that had been at peace for half a century. I think that, even if the old k.u.k. Kriegsmarine was a small fleet and permanently strapped for cash, the quality of its officers and men was generally excellent and its standards in seamanship and navigation the equal of any in the world. But in all services there are exceptions. I was quite well acquainted with the Royal Navy in its Edwardian heyday, when it was without question the most professionally competent fleet on earth. But even there I heard wardroom tales of dangerous imbeciles who had somehow—no one was ever quite sure how—managed to pass successive promotion boards until they ended up in a position where they were able to inflict real damage. Some people subscribe to the "bloody fool" theory of naval and military incompetence. But for my part, having had many years to observe these things and to ruminate upon them, I have come to the view that the truly lethal idiots in this world are in fact people who are moderately bright, but who have some fatal flaw of character—a sort of loose wire in the brain—which turns even their intelligence into a potential murder weapon. Usually they are people who are quite clever in examinations (but not nearly as clever as they think they are) and totally devoid of that mysterious quality called common sense. Likewise they are invariably energetic. Stupid people on the whole are rather lazy, and most lazy intelligent people can be coaxed or bullied into doing a good job if one works on them hard enough. The really dangerous ones though are the industrious maniacs, the people who combine utter incompetence with unquenchable, dog-like zeal. Adolf von Poltl was one such.

His path into the k.u.k. Kriegsmarine had been (it seemed) a circuitous one: first as a warrant officer Aspirant in the artillery—until an inexplicably double-charged howitzer had exploded and wiped out half his battery—then in the Fortress Artillery, that notable cemetery for the living, then in the Naval Ordnance Service (Austria had no marines, but soldiers frequently served at sea as artillery specialists), finally in the Navy itself. He was about fifty-eight when I met him, a pompous, bulging-eyed little tyrant whose life was ruled in every detail by the *K.u.K. Dienstreglement*—all fourteen volumes of it—much as an Orthodox Jew's life is ruled by the Talmud and the Torah. According to Korvettenkapitän von Poltl (he always used the mysteriously acquired "von" as if it were an integral part of his surname; to Austrians a rather vulgar North German habit) there was not a single problem in the whole universe—not medicine, not philosophy, not economics, not theology, not even mathematics—that could not be resolved by reference to the service regulations. And if the *Dienstreglement* made no mention of it, why then, by definition it could not be a problem. He knew every paragraph, every line, every word of it by heart. In fact, if the *K.u.K. Adjustierungsvorschrift* had permitted it he would undoutedly have worn a miniature copy of the *Dienstreglement* as a phylactery bound about his forehead. Unmarried but chaste and abstemious in his personal habits, he lived a life which anyone else would have regarded as barely human, but which for him seemed, like that of a monk I suppose, to fulfill all his needs—chiefly the need to contemplate the endless perfections of the *Dienstreglement,* and when not doing that to torment those around him by trying to make them conform to it.

He was also quite outstandingly bad at his job. In fact the bare adjective "bad" hardly scratches the surface of the man's awesome incapacity. The root of the trouble, as far as I could make out, was that even if he had somehow achieved the eminence of Korvettenkapitän in a Great Power navy, and with one half of his mind was dazzled by his own excellence, with the other half he knew perfectly well that he was a remarkably poor officer and an object of pity and contempt to those around him. Thus, in order to bolster his high opinion of himself, it was essential above all that he should always be right in every particular, no matter how trifling; that when, for example, he had wedged his ship securely on to a sandbank forty kilometres up the River Tisza (which he had entered after mistaking it for the Temes) he should insist that this was exactly what he had intended in the first place, and sit there incommunicado for the next two days admiring the view. In fact they would probably be there still if the wretched GDO had not taken time off from his nervous breakdown to steal ashore under cover of darkness, then trudge twenty kilometres to the nearest post office and telegraph Pancsova for help. This, I think, is where the folly of women differs from that of men: that even if women are marginally more prone to fall into bêtise, they are also much quicker to fall out of it again, as if they possessed some kind of in-built self-righting mechanism. With men, though, I have often seen in this dismal century that there comes a point at which lunacy starts to generate itself, where the fact of having behaved like an absolute imbecile becomes in itself a reason for behaving even more like an absolute imbecile, until disaster supervenes.

I do not think that any of us, officers or ratings, would have minded sailing under the command of a ferocious old martinet like Blasius Lovranić aboard the *Erzherzog Albrecht.* We might have feared his rages and grumbled privately about his strictness, but we would all have recognised his essential fairness and, above all, felt safe in trusting our lives to

his professional judgement. Adolf von Poltl, however, was a very different proposition, not only disliked but despised by all who knew him. He
roared and blustered and threatened everyone around him with the most
savage punishments, but there was no substance to it: discipline aboard
S.M.S. *Tisza* was in fact remarkably poor. Even the most ferocious tyrants
rely on a certain measure of complicity on the part of their victims, and
there was certainly very little of that among the *Tisza*'s lower deck, where
the Captain was normally referred to as the "pulykakakas"—Magyar for
turkey-cock—and treated with a sort of weary patience. He might perhaps
have been Ivan the Terrible back at Pola, with all the resources of provost
petty officers and the naval prison to support him; out here though, in
the Hungarian puszta, with only himself to rely upon, his threats were
largely ignored.

In Poltl's eyes the ratings were no more than a rabble of untrust-
worthy and ignorant Magyar peasants, while as for us young officers, we
were complete fools who knew nothing about ship-handling. However,
his own ideas in this department were peculiar to say the least of it. I
suspect, for example, that most schoolchildren would be able to tell you
that when a river flows around a bend the water on the outside of the
curve has to move a good deal faster than that on the inside, like a column
of soldiers turning a corner. From this it follows that a ship proceeding
upriver against the current will have a far easier time of it if her pilot
takes her across the inside of bends—provided of course that he watches
out for the shallows and takes care not to run foul of other vessels.
Poltl would have none of this; the rule of the road was that ships should
keep to starboard; so as far as he was concerned the River Danube was a
twin-track railway along which ships ran upstream and downstream, each
on its own pair of rails, all the way from the Sulina Mouth up to Ulm.
The *Tisza*'s engines and boilers were old: she could barely manage eight
knots or sustain this speed for more than an hour, so the watchers on
shore were treated to some curious spectacles; as on that notable spring
morning on the bend just below Petwardein Fortress when S.M.S. *Tisza*
took three hours and consumed thirteen tonnes of coal to steam two
hundred metres upstream, battling desperately against the current while

the boilers groaned ominously and Poltl danced with rage on the bridge, threatening the sweating stokers with public quartering unless they could deliver more pressure. Likewise the man either could not or would not grasp that the correct way to bring a powered vessel—even a rowing skiff—up to a jetty in moving water is not to rush down upon it with the current and try to grapple it as one passes, but to drop down below it and then bring the boat's head round into the current to edge up to the jetty, balancing the current and the boat's own forward motion to achieve a delicacy of contact which, in the hands of a skilled helmsman, could bring a twenty-tonne pinnace up against a hard-boiled egg without cracking it (and I have seen it done, by the way). Poltl had no time for such finicking about. It was full speed ahead with the current every time, and each devastated jetty merely seemed to increase his determination to try it again.

At other times Poltl's exaggerated respect for the rules of the road was constrained by the fact that he seemed totally unable to relate a chart to his surroundings—for him the chart was the reality, not the river which it was supposed to represent—or to recognise the navigation buoys marking the deep-water channel. He would also insist, when we were on the Serbian frontier sections of the Danube below Belgrade, that we were on active service and therefore obliged by regulations to steer the ship from inside the conning tower instead of the little bridge on top of it. This was bad enough in daytime, standing inside the stuffy steel tube and peering out through the narrow vision-slits; at night, we might as well have been steering the ship with our heads inside galvanised buckets. When I was on watch I used to keep a crewman standing beneath the foredeck with his head through a skylight, calling back directions to me. Even so we nearly came to grief one night in mid-March, steaming back down the Sava near Zemlin when we ran down a floating water-mill. There were still quite a few of them on the Danube in those days: built on two barges anchored in the fastest part of the stream with the wheel slung between them and a wooden shed on top for the mill machinery. On this occasion, luckily for the millers, the *Tisza* managed to strike between the barges, smashing the wheel and the shed to matchwood but leaving the two barges afloat with the brutally awakened millers still aboard them, showering us with curses and threats as we disappeared into the darkness. A week later we hit the railway bridge at Ujvidek and then one night at the end of the month we ran aground on the Serbian shore just above one of the Belgrade forts. Luckily for us the night was overcast. Jovanović and I tumbled into a zille and rowed to the Austrian side, where at last we found a customs post with a telephone and called up a tug from Pancsova, which managed to pull us clear just before first light. If it had not then I dread to think what diplomatic complications might have followed. It was fortunate at least that throughout this catalogue of navigational error we were sailing aboard a stoutly built ship with an armoured belt of 5cm steel. At least when we hit something the other party normally came off worse.

You may anyway have concluded from this that, professionally speaking, I could scarcely have found myself in a lower position than that to which I had fallen in the spring of the year 1914: second-in-command to an incurable idiot aboard a floating battery crewed by disaffected Magyars, crawling up and down a marshy river in the heart of Europe. But there was worse, far worse, to come. For on 16 April 1914, while lying at Pancsova, S.M.S. *Tisza* received orders to proceed forthwith to the town of Neugraditz, about forty kilometres downriver. Our orders were to lend support to the local gendarmery and customs authorities in their efforts to prevent smuggling of livestock.

# 7

# THE PIG WAR

THE REASON FOR OUR SUDDEN TRANSFORMATION into surrogate customs men was that the kingdoms of Hungary and Serbia were now engaged in that traditional Central European pastime, a pig war. The breeding and sale of pigs had always meant a great deal to the Serbian peasantry, who would commonly raise at least one piglet a year to sell for cash so that they could pay their taxes. Austria-Hungary was a great consumer of pork, so in normal times there would be a brisk trade in livestock across the Danube and the Sava, squealing herds and trainloads of Serbian pigs making their one-way journey to the slaughterhouses and sausage factories of the Dual Monarchy. The corollary of this, however, was that if Austria-Hungary wished to apply pressure to its troublesome southern neighbour, all it needed to do was to ban the import of pigs for a while on one pretext or other—usually an alleged outbreak of swine fever. The most vicious and prolonged pig war had been back in 1908, after Austria had annexed Bosnia and Herzegovina, when the Serbian economy had been all but strangled by the embargo. That had all blown over in the end. But Serbia had done well out of the Balkan War of 1913, Budapest was alarmed about possible unrest (most of the people of southern Hungary were in fact ethnic Serbs), and a partial pig blockade was now in force, applying only to the Serbian frontier with the Kingdom of Hungary.

S.M.S. *Tisza* was now embroiled in all this because the pig dealers of Serbia and the sausage-factory owners of Hungary, still anxious to trade with one another despite the closing of the frontier, had taken of late to running their livestock across the Danube in boats under cover of darkness. The customs and gendarmery were trying to stop them, and the k.u.k. Kriegsmarine was there to show the flag and provide military support if the pig-smuggling gangs (who were reported to be armed and well-organised) started getting rough. It looked like being great fun for us all.

We moored at—or to be more precise, hit—the pier at Neugraditz (or Novi Gradic in Serb) on the afternoon of 17 April. This was to be our base until further notice. A heap of bunker coal had already been left there for us, supplies would be sent each week by river steamer from Pancsova, and in the mean time if there was anything that we required would we please be so good as to go and hang ourselves? Seifert and I stood together on the *Tisza*'s bridge once we had tied up. We looked about us, silent. Pancsova had been remote enough, but this . . . We might as well have been on the banks of the Congo. Apart from the landing stage where we lay, the only sign of man's presence had been the old Turkish border-fortress of Semandria on the Serbian bank about twelve kilometres upstream, its long walls and multiple turrets crowning a low bluff above the shore out of the reach of the floods. Here, though, there was nothing: not a house nor a boat nor even the smoke of a cottage chimney, only water and sky and low, wooded islands as far as the eye could reach.

"My God," said Seifert, "desolation . . . Utter desolation . . ."

As soon as we came off duty and were able to escape from under the bulging eye of our beloved Captain, Seifert and I resolved to go exploring. We put on our best walking-out dress, complete with swords and black-and-yellow silk sword-belts as per regulation, and then set off in search of what Seifert referred to optimistically as "civilisation." Our only navigational aid in this quest was a wooden sign on the landing stage which said simply To The Town and pointed along a rutted trackway which led inland across the water meadows. We set out to follow it. Half an hour passed, then an hour, and still no sign of humanity. I knew that towns along the Danube were generally set well back from the river, because of the floods, but surely . . . At last, in a field of beans, we saw a peasant woman at work with a hoe, her head wrapped in the characteristic white scarf of the Serbian countryside. I was fluent in Croat, which is almost the same as Serb except for being written in Latin script, so I hailed her:

"*Dobar dan gospodja*. Please could you tell us the way to Novi Gradic?"

She stood and regarded us for a while in silence, then turned, bent down and lifted her skirts to reveal a pallid, dimpled backside. She slapped this with the words "Kiss my arse where it isn't sunburnt," then resumed her work as demurely as if nothing had happened.

"Well," said Seifert, "are we to assume from this that the civil populace in these parts is not well disposed towards the Imperial and Royal armed forces?"

We resumed our weary march. After another twenty minutes however the land began to rise gently, then we saw a factory chimney in the distance above the poplar trees, then the dome of a church. "Ah, this must be it," said Seifert, "human habitation at last." At length we came upon a freshly painted sign beside the road. It had a red, white and green border and bore the legend SZEKÉRESFELEGYHÁZA in bold black letters. We stood staring at it in bewilderment.

"Funny," said Seifert, scratching his head, "surely we can't have got that far off course. So where's Neugraditz or Novi Gradic or whatever they call it then? That looks like a Magyar name to me." However, we were obviously on the edge of a settlement of some kind, so we determined to go in and ask for directions.

The town-village that we entered stood in roughly the same relation to Pancsova as Addis Ababa does to Paris. In fact I think that even in Poland I never saw a more squalid, tumbledown collection of hovels masquerading as a town. We picked our way between the evil-smelling puddles and heaps of rubbish along the filthy slough that passed for a main street. The only amenities were a dilapidated Serbian Orthodox church, a two-storey building (closed) which might have been government offices, and a couple of "cafés" which were in fact slivovica shops of the lowest and most sordid kind. One of these had (I remember) a sign in Latin script as well as in Cyrillic. It read CAFÉ METROPOLE. Beneath it a fight was taking place among a number of the café's patrons, Serb peasants black-faced with alcohol and laying into one another with spades and pick-handles. One of them already lay in the mud with an ear and half his face dislodged by a blow from a shovel. Then the brawlers spotted us and the fight died away. Various main-street loafers—many of them obviously cretinous or destroyed by drink and disease—had noticed our arrival in town and were now sidling towards us in a sinister fashion. I sensed trouble.

"Seifert, let's get out of here. They're going . . ." Seifert suddenly fell over, knocked off his feet by the impact of what I thought was a football, but which was in fact a decaying pig's head flung by one of the gathering mob. He got to his feet and we both made off, stones and assorted filth showering around us as we ran. We had our swords, but I saw that any attempt to stand and fight would merely lead to our being lynched. We had no idea where we were running to, so long as it led away from our baying pursuers. Suddenly an open gate-arch lay before us, leading off the street. Instinctively we dodged into it—and found ourselves facing a sizeable and comparatively well-kept house, behind which lay the factory whose chimney we had seen earlier. Its front door was open, so we dashed into it and slammed it shut behind us, then stood panting in the cool-tiled entrance hall.

I had hitherto considered the Heir-Apparent's residence at Schloss Konopischt to be the most vulgarly over-furnished dwelling that I had ever come across. But Konopischt was a model of austerity compared with the house in which we found ourselves now. Statues, pictures, tapestry, suits of armour, gilding, brocade and damask were all packed into that entrance hall with a lack of taste so total, so barbarically ruthless that it almost achieved that rare feat of passing clean through vulgarity and emerging on the other side as a sort of distinction. It took away even such of our breath as remained after our pursuit by the mob. However there was another, even greater surprise in store for me. There was a mighty barking, and two large mastiffs came bounding down the marble stairs from the landing to attack us, snarling and baring their fangs. We stood stock-still with our hands to our sides, giving them no point of attack. A woman's voice called from upstairs.

"Who's there?" Its owner came into sight at the top of the stairs—and we stood speechless for some moments, staring at one another. It was Pani Bożena.

"Ottokar . . . Jezus Maria! Holy Wounds of God! . . . What on earth are you doing here?"

"Bożena . . . I'm sorry, I'll explain . . . Only there's a mob outside . . ."

"For the love of God, get out quick—my husband'll soon be home! He'll kill us both if he finds you here!"

She ran down the stairs and began to bundle us towards the door, then heard the commotion outside as the crowd arrived in the courtyard. She flung the window open and shouted in Serb. "Be off with you, you louse-ridden scum!"

"Stuff yourself, Polish whore!"

"Away with you or I'll . . ." The sentence was left unfinished as a volley of shots crashed in the street outside. The crowd scrambled out of the courtyard and ran as nine or ten Royal Hungarian gendarmes appeared, some with smoking rifles, others whacking our erstwhile pursuers with the flats of their sabres. After a minute or so the street had been cleared and peace returned. Bozena pushed us out of the house and slammed the door behind us. The first person we met outside was a young Hungarian gendarmery sergeant. He spoke some German.

"Bug-infested Serb rabble," he said. "I can tell you, we have to manage them with a firm hand in these parts. My apologies to you, *meine Herren,* but I'm afraid that strangers often get a rough reception in this town: particularly when they're in uniform."

"Wachtmeister," I said, "would you be so good as to tell us where we are? We were looking for a place called Neugraditz, or Novi Gradic in Serb, but this town is Szekéresfelegyháza. Could you please direct us on to the right road?"

He laughed. "No need, Herr Leutnant: this is the place you were looking for. I believe that some of the inhabitants still call it Novi Gradic in their crude local dialect. But this is the Kingdom of Hungary and the authorities in Budapest are anxious to raise the cultural level of the district. So now it's Szekéresfelegyháza."

We thanked the sergeant, and he detailed two of his men to escort us to the Café Metropole for refreshments, then back to our ship at the landing stage. While at the café—a leprous mud hut with an earthen floor—I made some enquiries of the depressed-looking Jewish landlord.

"Oh yes," he reported, "you officer gentlemen aren't at all popular around here since the border was closed. Old Grbić's sausage factory up the road was the only employer in this town, so when it had to shut down everyone was thrown out on the street. I tell you, you were lucky to escape with your lives."

"Grbić, you say . . . ?"

"Yes, Trifko Grbić. He's the chief man around here." (He lowered his voice.) "Tightest-fisted old bastard that ever drew breath if you ask me. When his factory's working it stinks the whole town out too. Just a common pig dealer until he got the idea of turning pigs into sausages here instead of in Budapest. Then he made his pile and built the big house up the street and got himself a Polish actress for a wife. Not a bad-looking piece of skirt either, but they fight all the time and she can't stand Serbs or gypsies. She's in Vienna or Budapest most of the time spending his money, but when she's back here the only people she talks with are the Magyars."

"Are there a lot of Magyars round here then?"

He found this hugely funny. "Not enough to fill a chicken-house. There's only officials and gendarmes and customs people. But I tell you the swine are squeezing the life out of the rest of us, what with their 'Szekéresfelegyháza,' may it choke them. Even the kids in junior school have to learn their horrible language now." He spat on the floor. "May the pox take them all."

We returned to the ship, where Seifert got a fortnight's board-arrest for the stains left on his uniform by the impact of the pig's head. But at least we had learnt that Neugraditz/Novi Gradic/Szekéresfelegyháza was a good place to avoid. Bozena though . . . My mind was whirling. What on earth ought I to do?

Back aboard the *Tisza,* I soon had the normal concerns of shipboard existence to distract my mind from the complications of my private life. And these problems, bad enough even before, were now all the worse once the town had been placed out of bounds to the crew for reasons of their own safety. For if the amenities of Pancsova had been minimal, those of the riverbank at Neugraditz were entirely non-existent. The prospect of action looked remote—pig-smuggling was going through a quiet phase that month—so we soon had a serious problem of morale on our hands. The crew, previously sticky and uncommunicative, were rapidly becoming sullen to the point where I feared that a mutiny might break out, perhaps as a result of one of the Captain's frequent disciplinary razzias. Poltl had recently discovered that paragraph 273 of Volume 4 of the *K.u.K. Dienstreglement* ("Permissible off-duty amusements aboard Imperial and Royal warships"), as well as forbidding whistling and card games for money, sanctioned only "respectable music and dancing." Now, one of the very few pleasures of having a ship's crew made up largely of Magyars was that one could sit in one's cabin with the skylight open in the evening dusk, as the insects chirped along the darkening riverbank, and listen to the fiery melancholy of the csárdás being danced on the foredeck to the wail of violin and accordion, the incomprehensible words sung against an intricate background of hand-clapping. For the lower deck it was one of the very few outlets permitted; and now here was Poltl announcing one morning at Divisions that from now on the csárdás—"a beastly convulsion more fit for animals than for sailors of a German-speaking navy" as he put it—would be strictly forbidden as not falling within the limits of musical respectability laid down in the service regulations. This, I feared, might prove to be the last straw. Commands in German which had previously evoked a slow and unwilling compliance now produced, as often as not, a blank stare and a reply in Magyar. On one occasion I even saw Poltl himself screaming at a rating on Captain's Report and the man turning casually to his neighbour, with the patient air of a male nurse in a mental asylum, to enquire, "What's the silly old fool on about now?"

It was Seifert who eventually solved the command problem with a stroke of genius so astounding that even now I still whistle inwardly with awe when I think of it. It happened one morning about 7 a.m. as we sat at breakfast in our little steel cubicle of a wardroom. The skylights were all open and there was still a light early-morning mist on the river, but the sun was climbing in the sky and it was starting to get stuffy below decks. Breakfast was nasty as usual: our cook Barcsai in his furnace of a galley seemed to take a sadistic delight in providing horrible meals for the officers. Suddenly Seifert stood up and stuck his head through the skylight to look around on deck and make sure that we were not overheard. Then he sat down again.

"I know what we'll do, Prohaska. We'll run the ship in English."

I choked on my coffee, then stared at him speechless. Had he started going mad like his predecessors? "Seifert, are you off your head? What do you mean, run the ship in English?"

"What I say: use English as the language of command aboard this vessel instead of German—except when the Old Man's about of course."

"But . . . how?"

"Look, we both went through the Marine Academy so we both speak fluent English, right? Well, I've been taking soundings on the lower deck these past few days and I find that nearly all the ratings speak it as well, or at least understand it. There's been quite a vogue in Hungary for emigration to America these past few years—and when I look at dumps like Neugraditz I don't wonder at it—so every one-eyed little village now runs evening classes for would-be emigrants. And as for Jovanović, I believe that he speaks it quite well from having spent two years as a deckhand aboard a British sailing barque before he joined the Navy. I ask you, what could be simpler? Let's try it: at least it couldn't possibly work worse than the present arrangement."

So Seifert and I and Jovanović and the crew now embarked on a secret operation whereby—when the Captain was not around at any rate—His Imperial, Royal and Catholic Majesty's river monitor *Tisza* became unofficially an English-speaking ship. I was sceptical of the experiment at first, but to my surprise it seemed to work rather well. The English used of course was not that of Shaw or Galsworthy or a *Times* editorial, much less that of Shakespeare. But it was a neutral language, and for Magyars possessed none of the bitter connotations of German, with its echoes of 1849 and Haynau's executioners flogging women to ribbons on the ramparts of Arád Fortress. Also, once the ratings had got over their initial surprise, the exercise seemed to appeal by its very absurdity to the rather dark Magyar sense of humour. As the weeks passed, it became clear that the whole preposterous experiment was working. In fact, I even began to notice a certain degree of comradeship and affection developing between the crew on the one hand and Seifert and myself on the other; that we who had formerly been alien impositions as well as officers were now seen in some measure by the lower deck as two young men not very

different from themselves, and engaged with them in a common conspiracy to bamboozle our despised commanding officer.

I suppose that the strangest manifestation of this new spirit aboard
came early in May when Seifert announced one morning at Divisions
that since the summer was now nearly upon us—and since we were all
perishing of boredom on this desolate riverbank—he would personally
tutor the ship in the great English national game of cricket, a sport of
which he claimed an intimate knowledge on the strength of several sum-
mers spent staying with cousins by marriage in a village near Malvern in
Worcestershire. The ratings stared at him in bewilderment as he produced
a ball, a set of stumps and two bats carved for him from riverside willow
by the ship's carpenter. Then tuition began in a flat meadow beside the
landing stage, with the lower deck divided into four teams of eleven men
and myself as umpire. Practice was noisy and chaotic at first: Seifert's own
grasp of the rules of cricket was—I suspect—highly impressionistic, while
as for myself, I frankly made it up as I went along. I doubt whether much
of the game would have been at all recognisable to the committee of the
MCC, but I have to admit that it was all great fun, and a splendid way of
passing the time. The Magyars also seemed to enjoy it and became—in
their own terms at any rate—pretty proficient cricketers after a week or
two. In the end quite considerable sums were being secretly wagered on
the outcome of matches, and bribery used in an attempt to lure players to
one side or another. I often wonder whether cricket would have caught on
in Hungary if the World War had not intervened.

At any rate, by the middle of May discipline and morale aboard S.M.S.
*Tisza* had improved beyond recognition. The crew were smart about their
duties and seemed to take a pride in their ship, while even cook Barcsai's food
had become edible. The three of us—the Captain, Seifert and I—sat at dinner one day in the wardroom, eating a quite creditable goulash. Poltl spoke.

"A firm hand, the *K.u.K. Dienstreglement* and plenty of Old Austrian
discipline, that's what you need with these insubordinate Magyar pigs:
show the subversive scum that the Teuton is on top and intends staying
there. Why, just crack the whip hard and enforce discipline more strictly
and even Barcsai's cooking becomes better."

It was a good thing that he was not on the bridge to hear us an hour or so later.

"Ten degrees port, helmsman, then keep her steady."

"Tain dikrees poart, Sir-Leutnant, zen kip hair staidy."

Seifert turned to me. "Y'know, Prohaska old bean, these chappies might be Magyars and all that, but they're not at all bad fellows once you get to know 'em."

"Not half," I replied, "don't y'know?"


Soon though I was to have preoccupations of a more personal nature. It happened one evening beside the landing stage at Neugraditz. I was standing in the gathering dusk smoking a cigar. It was still only early May but the mosquitoes of the Danubian marshes were already active—great brutes the size of a crane-fly with a bite like a jab with a darning needle. At least the smoke helped to keep them at a distance. Suddenly I heard a scuffle in the bushes by the pathway.

"Pssst! Ottokar!" I turned around. It was Pani Bozena. "Quick, come here. I have to talk with you." I looked around to make sure that we were unobserved, then slipped over to join her behind the wooden shed which served as a ticket office when the river steamers called.

"Bozena, what on earth . . . ?"

She flung her arms around me. "Oh Ottokar, my dearest sweet love. That you should come so far for your little Bozeneczka. How long did it take you to find out where I was?"

"I . . . well . . . you see, it's . . ."

"Darling one—I'm sorry that I had to throw you out when you came to the house looking for me, but if my pig of a husband knew you were here he'd kill the pair of us. He's shot one man already for looking at me. But for the moment he suspects nothing, so if we are careful . . ." She squeezed me hard. She was a strong woman and my ribs creaked audibly. "Ah, my poor dear brave Herr Leutnant: how many lonely nights has your little Bozena spent these last months longing to be in your arms, yearning for you to lie between her breasts and kiss . . ."

"Bozena, I'm sorry, but I can't."

She started back, surprised, and looked at me for a moment or two in puzzlement.

"What do you mean, you can't. You always could before."

"No, it's not that. I still can. I mean . . . I mean that, well, things are not as before . . ."

"What on earth are you talking about? Have you come all the way from Vienna just to tell me that?"

"I mean—I didn't really come here to see you at all, you see . . . No, I mean that I'm glad to see you and all that, but . . ."

Her face fell in dismay. Trouble was coming. "What? You mean . . . you mean you do not love your little Boźena any more . . . ?" She was gathering breath for a bout of hysterics, like a swimmer about to dive. It began as a low wail. "Ohhhh! He does not love me any more . . . Oh Jezus Maria . . . Wounds of God . . . For what sins, oh, for what sins? . . . Oh, who would be a woman?" She fell to sobbing uncontrollably. "Oh you wretched men, you're all alike: you use our bodies for your pleasure, then throw us away like old floor-cloths . . ." Her voice rose to a shriek. "Like old floor-cloths! Wretch! Serpent! Hypocrite! You are as base and vile as the rest of them . . ." Her sturdy frame shook with grief.

I might perhaps have observed at this point, had I been callous enough, that if I had used her body for my pleasure she had certainly obtained pretty good value from mine. But I was frightened that her sobs would attract attention aboard the ship; and anyway I have always been distressed by the sight of a woman in tears. So, with a disagreeable feeling that I was landing myself even further in trouble, I took her in my arms and pressed her head to my breast to comfort her—no easy feat, I might add, since she was as tall as I was.

"There, there, my dear. I'm sorry, I didn't mean it. I can explain everything if you just listen a moment or two."

"Beast! Rotter! Deceiver!"

"No really, Boźena, just calm down and I'll explain. I'm here on duty, because the Navy sent my ship here."

"The devil take your duty. What do I care about your miserable navy?"

"No, please be sensible. We can meet . . ." (my heart sank at these words, though I was not quite sure why) "... but we'll have to be discreet about it. I can't come to visit you in Neugraditz because of your husband and the townspeople, and you can't visit me here because we are on active service and our Captain forbids us to have civilians aboard, or even to let them near the landing stage ..." She looked up, tearful but smiling slightly. Her face brightened.

"Good then. I know what: meet me tomorrow morning at ten at the little jetty just upriver—you can't see it from here but it's just around the next bend—and we'll row across in a skiff to an island I know out in the river. It's really lovely. I often go swimming there." She looked at me archly. "Sometimes I forget to take my bathing costume. Of course I shall have to be a good girl and remember it tomorrow, and I hope that you'll remember to bring yours as well. But if you don't it doesn't really matter: no one can see us out there. Until tomorrow then, dear Ottokar, *au revoir.*"

We met the next morning and rowed out to the island as arranged. I had a day's leave booked anyway, so there was no trouble with the Captain. I told him that I was going away for the day to study Volume 6 of the *K.u.K. Dienstreglement* in solitude. He was visibly pleased.

"Splendid, Prohaska, excellent. Best possible reading matter for a young officer like yourself." He swelled up. "I venture to say that I am what I am today through diligent study of the service regulations. See to it that you are properly dressed though."

My uniform was in impeccable order when I set out. It was still fairly *korrekt* when we bumped the skiff into a secluded little creek on the side of the wooded, grassy islet which lay away from the land. But it did not stay in that condition for long afterwards. I suppose, looking back on it, that one of the few benefits of being an officer of the Noble House of Austria and spending one's entire waking existence encased in the Emperor's Coloured Coat was that it made it doubly blissful to remove the thing—like being born again as someone else. But it was all folded carefully enough, and wrapped around Volume 6 of the service regulations before we went to swim from the sandy little beach. And afterwards it made a convenient pillow beneath her head as we embraced on the sun-dappled grass of the glade, while the birds sang and the whistles of the river steamers sounded faintly in the distance.

It was a marvellous day, all cares cast aside along with our clothing. When I returned in the evening Poltl enquired how I had progressed in my study of Volume 6 of the service regulations. I most obediently replied that I had found it to be very useful. He bulged inside his tunic, and almost purred with satisfaction.

"Excellent. I always say that the *K.u.K. Dienstreglement* will be of use in any conceivable situation in which an Austrian officer can find himself."

We met almost every other day over the next couple of weeks, she and I, and for the moment at any rate she seemed quite equable: none of the constant, exhausting emotional roller-coaster ride which had so worn me out in Vienna. Seifert was fascinated. He finally tackled me at breakfast one morning, when Poltl was in his cabin.

"Well Prohaska, you're a deep one and no mistake. Every free hour you're off somewhere on your own. And these funny little notes the village urchins keep bringing you. I'll tell you what I think, my dear Prohaska: I think you've found yourself a village doxy somewhere and are tumbling her secretly in the hay-ricks."

I swallowed a little. "Well Seifert, what would it be to you if I were?"

"Nothing at all," he said, laughing, "I'm quite sure that in fact you're living a life of monastic self-denial and sleeping in boxing gloves while you confine yourself to reverent thoughts of Our Lady. But if it were perhaps true, I was just wondering whether she might have a sister or two? The town's out of bounds of course, but even if it wasn't they tell me that the local knocking shop is expensive and quite exceptionally disease-ridden. Tell me Prohaska, is she dark or fair?"

"Blonde . . . Oh shut up, damn you. It's not like that at all . . . I mean . . . Go on, away with you!"

A further tryst with Pani Bozena was scheduled for the following Wednesday, when I had an afternoon's leave. But just as I was about to come off duty a bicycle bell tinkled on the landing stage. It was a postman with a telegram from Marine Station Pancsova. We were to stand by to assist the local customs and gendarmery that very same night. They had received intelligence that a smuggling gang was going to try to move a large herd of swine across the river about eight kilometres downstream from Neugraditz. The pigs, it appeared, were going to be herded down to the Serbian bank just before dusk, then loaded into lighters which would drop down with the current and moor at Grahovski Otok, a low-lying wooded islet in mid-stream, before proceeding across to the Austrian shore in the early hours of the morning. The island had been chosen partly because its dense undergrowth gave excellent cover and partly because it was not certain whether it was Austrian or Serbian territory, the river having changed course a good deal since the eighteenth century, when it had been the frontier between Austria and the Ottoman Empire. The plan was clearly to hoodwink the customs into thinking, once they saw the pigs gathering on the Serbian shore, that the animals would be landed directly opposite.

The authorities planned to ambush the smuggling gang on the island, and our part in this operation was to lend armed support in case they cut up rough. S.M.S. *Tisza* would raise steam at once and proceed upstream towards Pancsova, in order to deceive the smugglers. Then, once darkness had fallen, she would return to a point some way below Neugraditz where she would anchor between two islands. Two boatloads of armed sailors, one commanded by Seifert and one by myself, would then row down to Grahovski Otok with muffled oars and wait for a signal from the gendarmery. Altogether it looked like being quite a lark: a long-overdue diversion from shipboard routine, with just enough danger and secrecy involved to raise it above the level of a nocturnal landing exercise.

We made our preparations. This was 1914, of course: white tunics and gold braid on the battlefield were a recent memory, while commando raids were still well into the future. But we realised that darkness and silence and surprise were our most useful weapons, so we did a thorough job of getting ourselves ready for this unusual little operation. The men—sixteen ratings in all—put aside their smart blue-and-white square rig in favour of overalls, old army tunics and so forth. Boots were replaced by rubber plimsolls or several pairs of old woollen stockings. Faces were a problem, however, until Jovanović had the bright idea of mixing soot from the funnel with linseed oil. My own outfit consisted of plimsolls, old Navy trousers, a fisherman's dark-blue jersey which I had once bought in England and a woollen cap. I was armed with my Steyr pistol and a belaying pin, while as for the men, half carried Mannlicher rifles and the other half pistols and entrenching-tool handles.

I must say that we looked a splendidly piratical lot as we assembled there on the *Tisza*'s quarterdeck beneath the fleeting half-light of the cloud-veiled moon: sixteen young Hungarian sailors transformed from smart naval seamen into fair replicas of the villainous hajduks and betyárs who had been their ancestors. There was an almost palpable tingle of expectation in the air. Life at Neugraditz had been unspeakably boring, despite the cricket matches, and any diversion would be welcome. Also I sensed from the broad grins of anticipation that the prospect of cracking a few local heads was by no means unwelcome to them. There has never been much love lost between Magyars and Serbs.

The Captain had been strangely absent throughout these preparations. He had retired to his cabin about dusk, as we prepared to go about and run downstream, and had remained there ever since, presumably combing the *K.u.K. Dienstreglement* for instructions on how to organise nocturnal assaults on gangs of pig smugglers. If this was what he was doing, then it appeared that he was not having a great deal of luck. So much the better, I thought; at least it keeps the old fool out of the way. Then about 1 a.m., just as we were preparing to board the two zilles, he emerged on deck—and goggled in utter disbelief at the scene which confronted him in the light of a shaded hurricane lamp.

"Gu . . . guu . . . gu . . . gwur . . ." Finally he found his voice. "HIMMELHERRGOTTSAKRA JEZUS MARIA DONNER-WETTER!" he screamed. "Herr Schiffsleutnant—what in the thrice-sacred name of God and the Holy Virgin is THIS? Who are these filthy black-faced bastards? What is the meaning of this outrage? Prohaska—Seifert . . . which one of you is Seifert? . . . I'll have the pair of you court-martialled!" I stepped forward and saluted as nonchalantly as I was able.

"Obediently report the landing party present and correct, Herr Kommandant." I thought that he was going to have a seizure.

"PRESENT AND CORRECT? What do you mean, present and correct? I've never seen a group of men less present and correct in my entire life! You know the *Adjustierungsvorschrift* for landing operations in the temperate zone as well as I do, you insolent pig! Square rig with gaiters and knapsacks and light marching order; water bottle and bayonet to be worn on left hip; entrenching tool on right; two hundred rounds ready ammunition in cartridge pouches; officers and NCOs to wear swords respectively side-arms; parties of over ten to be preceded by bugler and standard-bearer . . . where is the standard-bearer . . . answer me, WHERE IS THE STANDARD-BEARER? Prohaska, I swear I'll have you court-martialled for this outrage. Now get these men below at once and don't return until they're dressed like sailors and not chimney-sweeps! You'll get five years with hard labour in a prison-fortress for this or my name's not von Poltl . . ."

Well, an order is an order, especially when it comes from a ship's captain. Something had to be done quickly or this insufferable buffoon would abort the entire operation for us. Suddenly a mad, irresponsible impulse took hold of me, a feeling that now was all that mattered and that tomorrow could look after itself. I answered him in English.

"I'm sorry, Captain, but I don't understand you." He fell silent and stared at me in puzzlement: as I suspected, he knew only German. When he answered it was but weakly, disjointedly, in the tone of a man who knows that this is really all a bad dream.

"*Was bedeutet* 'Hai doan unnerstand'? *Prohaska, bist du ganz verrückt oder so . . . ?*"

"I said, I'm sorry but I don't understand: I have forgotten how to speak German, and anyway we use English aboard this ship, don't we?" I turned to the assembled raiding party, who were evidently enjoying all this enormously. Sixteen white grins split the mosquito-humming riverine darkness as they chorused, "No, we don' understand too—we all good Magyar boys: not spik Teutsch at all!"

"Sorry Captain," said Seifert, "we'll just have to get an interpreter, don't y'know. Anyway, Prohaska old chap, time to be off, what?"

"You bet. Landing party—stand by to man the boats!"

Poltl stood by helplessly, bubbling and gurgling like a man who has just suffered a stroke. All that he could do as the landing party clambered down into the two zilles was to mumble disarticulated phrases to himself, like someone fingering the rosary beads.

"Arrest . . . prisoner's escort . . . leg-irons . . . take these men away and lock them up . . ." We ignored him. I knew that there would be the devil to pay next day as the mechanisms of naval discipline reasserted themselves: at the very least a court martial and official enquiry. But for the moment I cared not at all: the task in hand was all that mattered.

We drifted down towards Grahovski Otok in silence and near-darkness: there was a moon that night, but thin cloud obscured it most of the time. The oars worked noiselessly to steer us in the current, muffled by wads of oakum in the rowlocks. About 2:30 we heard a sound in the distance: the unmistakable squealing of pigs. I turned to Jovanović, who was steering our boat.

"It looks as if the customs were right," I whispered. "Tell the men to get ready—the island's about a hundred metres ahead." The moon emerged from behind the clouds to reveal the dim, wooded shape looming ahead. Then I heard a faint splashing from astern. I turned. It was a small boat trying to catch up with us. Well, I thought, land the men, then deal with him, whoever he is. Our boat bumped gently against the bank at the upstream tip of the island.

"All right men," I said softly, "get ashore quietly and wait, then follow me. Don't use firearms unless you have to." I turned back and drew my pistol. The small boat was almost upon us now, its occupant splashing erratically with a paddle and panting loudly.

"Halt or I fire," I said, as quietly as I was able. The boat kept on until it bumped alongside ours. It was our canoe—and the paddler was Poltl. He stood up and shouted:

"This is your captain, men. I'm going to lead you . . ." He tried to jump ashore ahead of them, and missed, landing up to his waist in the river with a great splash. Nothing daunted, he struggled up the bank, pistol in hand, streaming water and stumbling over alder roots. "Come on my men, follow me I say!"

I gazed in horror. "Jovanović, for God's sake stop the man! They'll hear us. The silly old fool's going to ruin the whole thing!" We scrambled ashore and followed him, intending to seize and gag him if necessary. He turned once more to us.

"Come on I say, follow me, you cowardly Magyar dogs!" I noticed that his white shirt-front stood out with livid clarity in the faint moonlight. So, evidently, did someone else. There was a loud bang and a flash from some way ahead in the trees, and Poltl stumbled and fell, clutching his chest. With that, shouts and the noise of fighting broke out further down the island. Seifert shouted, "Come on!" and the *Tisza* landing party rushed forward into the undergrowth, cheering loudly. There were yells, then shots were exchanged. Meanwhile pigs were squealing in panic somewhere near by as Jovanović and I attended to the Captain.

"Herr Kommandant, are you all right? How bad is it?"

He tried to rise.

"My legs . . . my legs won't work . . . I can't feel anything . . ."

"What's the matter, Herr Leutnant?"

"He's been shot through the spine I think Jovanović. Here . . ." I unbuttoned his jacket and felt around his back. My hand was sticky with blood when I withdrew it. "Come on, let's get him out of the way—find somewhere flat to lie him down." The ground was wet underfoot and humped with tree-roots. Then Jovanović called to me:

"Over here, Herr Leutnant. There's a lighter full of pigs. They must have moored it under the trees."

I ran over to look. It was difficult to see by the light of a shaded torch, but it was a wooden barge with perhaps twenty or thirty jostling, grunting swine aboard. It seemed to have a sort of low wooden steering platform above the pigs, near the stern. At least it was somewhere flat and dry. So we dragged Poltl across, legs trailing behind him like a pair of old trousers stuffed with newspaper, and made him as comfortable as we could, assuring him that we would be back in a few minutes with a stretcher. Then we ran forward to join the landing party.

It had been about five minutes' work in all for Seifert's men and the gendarmes. Of the smuggling gang, who had numbered about twenty, twelve had been captured and one shot dead. Casualties on our side, apart from Poltl, were one rating with a revolver bullet through his thigh and a couple of cracked heads. I bandaged the wounded man, then we set off with Jovanović and two ratings carrying a stretcher to collect the Captain. We splashed and stumbled back to the head of the island where the lighter had been. But when we got there we were quite unable to find it. Slowly it dawned upon us: the smugglers had cast it loose before they fled and the current had borne it away.

We rowed back and forth for the rest of that night and most of the next day, searching every creek and backwater. We even called a motor boat down from Pancsova to help us. But it was not until four days later that we finally found the lighter, as we edged into a creek on a small island about six kilometres downstream. Jovanović suddenly turned: "Herr Leutnant. I heard a pig squeal."

We stopped rowing and listened, then craned our necks to look over the low bank, peering through the rushes and willows into a swampy clearing. There were seven or eight of them, grunting blissfully as they wallowed in the wet, black earth around the alder trunks, condemned prisoners not only reprieved at the foot of the gallows but set free in a porcine version of the Garden of Eden. We rowed further down the channel, pushing ourselves along by overhanging branches when it became too narrow for oars. Then we saw the lighter, canted over slightly against some fallen trees but still afloat. Jovanović and I scrambled on to the marshy bank and squelched towards the lighter while our men tied up the zille and landed to search the undergrowth. He had been paralysed when we left him, but might have recovered sufficiently to crawl into the bushes. Certainly there was no sign of him aboard the vessel. I set off to join the rest of the men when a shout from Jovanović called me back to the lighter. He was standing on the bottom boards among a welter of pig-dung, broken branches and other litter. Grimly, he held out a shoe for me to inspect. It was only when I took it from him that I realised with disgust that it still had a foot in it, chewed off at the ankle-bone. I dropped it with a shudder of distaste. Jovanović nodded down grimly towards the floor of the lighter. Among the ordure and refuse lay some rags of navy blue cloth, and a human hand

and part of a spinal column, both gnawed like bones in a dog kennel. We stood silent for some time.

"Holy Mother of God, surely not . . ."

"Afraid so, Herr Leutnant. They must have been drifting a couple of days before they ran aground here, and they just . . . ate him."

"But . . . how?"

"Herr Leutnant, I'm a farmer's son. There's no animal of its size with jaws as powerful as a pig's. Give them the chance and they'll crunch their way through a heap of bricks." He gazed down. "Stupid old sod he was, begging your pardon, Herr Leutnant. I make no secret that I didn't care for him at all. But to die like that . . . What a rotten way to go."

The funeral took place next day in the Catholic cemetery at Pancsova. In its way it was quite an impressive affair I suppose. The entire town turned out to line the route as the crew of S.M.S. *Tisza* slow-marched in immaculate order behind the flag-draped gun-carriage and the band of the local garrison, then stood by the graveside with their rifles slung, saluting the deceased with the left hand as was the custom in the Austrian service. The coffin had felt unexpectedly heavy as I and three other officers had lifted it on to the gun-carriage at the start of the journey. As we followed it on foot, heads bowed, I managed to whisper to Jovanović, who was walking beside me, "Bos'un, what did you put in the coffin to weigh it down? There can't have been more than half a bucketful of him left."

"No, Herr Leutnant. But I reasoned it out that what with three days passing, the pig-dung in the bottom of the lighter must have been mostly old Poltl. So I told the men to shovel it in with the rest."

I was a trifle perturbed by this news. I must say, especially when the priest sprinkled holy water over the coffin and blessed it *in nomine patri, filii et spiritu sancti*. It was a hot afternoon, and I noticed that his expression became rather strained while he read the Office of Burial; also that he took good care to stand upwind of the coffin during the interment.

We arrived back at Neugraditz just as it was getting dark, having travelled up to Pancsova by river steamer since the *Tisza* was having boiler trouble. The first person to greet me was cook Barcsai, who had not been part of the burial detachment. He obediently reported that while I had been away, a group of Serbs led by a large man with a black moustache had come to the landing stage enquiring after me and wishing to speak with me in private on a matter of some importance. Barcsai had fobbed them off with a story about my going up to Petwardein for a week, but he and I both sensed that they would be back tomorrow. So I felt that in the circumstances, tomorrow might be a good day to take the leave owing to me from the previous week. Barcsai promised to make me a packed lunch to take with me when I set off early next morning to do some exploring by canoe.

I left the *Tisza* at five bells the next morning while the river was still shrouded in mist. I paddled out into the stream then set off slowly, fighting against the current, to the island where Bożena and I used to meet. It was a very secluded place and no one would think of looking for me there. Somehow I felt a need to sit quietly for a day and think things over. Not only were there the growing complications with Pani Bożena, who might now be about to prove a femme fatale in the most literal sense of the term; there was also the death of old Poltl, and the grotesque manner in which he had met it—and the official enquiry which would soon follow. It all seemed so unnecesarily complicated . . . I arrived at the island just as the sunlight was beginning to suffuse the gauze curtains of mist. I lit a fire and ate some breakfast—no danger of smoke being seen in this fog—then lay down on the grass to read awhile as the sun rose in the sky. It was Conrad I think: I was going through a very English-literature phase at that time. I dozed awhile, then read again, then lay thinking as the birds sang in the willow thickets and the fish splashed out in the great river. The mist had almost cleared. The mighty Danube was now a slowly moving sheet of pale-blue glass in the morning sunlight, the only sign of human presence a smudge of smoke away towards the Serbian shore where a steamer was making its way upriver. It disappeared after a while, and I was alone again. Surely peace as profound as this could never be disturbed.

Towards eleven it had become quite hot. Why not go for a dip, I thought? The exercise will get some of the stiffness out of your leg. So I undressed and lowered myself into the cool river, then swam across to another islet a few hundred metres away. I rested there a while, then swam back, aiming well upstream because of the current, which must have been two or three knots. I reached my point of departure after five minutes or so and hauled myself up on to the sandy bank, then walked back to the clearing where my clothes lay. A surprise awaited me: Pani Bozena, standing there without a stitch of clothing. She seemed not at all surprised to see me, but still shrieked in feigned terror and flung one hand across her breasts, the other across her loins, in the manner of "Diana and her Nymphs Surprised by Acteon," that popular subject for Viennese allegorical painters of the more lubricious kind.

"Ooh!" she squealed, "a man! And in a completely unclothed state as well! Oh, what on earth shall I do? A poor innocent maiden out for a swim and surprised by this horrible, hairy, virile male person! What shall I do if he chooses to hurl himself upon me and deprive me of my virtue? Ah me! Who will hear my screams for help in this remote spot and come to my aid?"

"Bozena, stop playing the idiot. What on earth are you doing here?"

She sniffed and looked at me disdainfully. "As far as I was aware, the islands of the River Danube are open to the general public." She craned her neck. "And I must have failed to see the notices prohibiting mixed bathing. Oh, but perhaps the Herr Leutnant has recently purchased this island out of his salary? How stupid of me not to have realised: I shall apologise and leave."

"Shut up and listen, you silly woman. Your husband was at the landing stage yesterday when I was up at Pancsova. He had a gang of ruffians with him and was asking to speak with me. Luckily I was away but he must suspect . . ."

She snorted. "Of course he does, the lout. I came home with damp hair last week and had to spin him some tale about being caught out in a rainstorm. But what does it matter?" She stepped across and wrapped her arms around me. "There's only the two of us here now, just as we were before . . ."

"But your husband?"

"Don't worry: he's gone to Temesvár for two days; something about the bank foreclosing the mortgage on the sausage factory. But come now, my dear Ottokar; won't you please your little Bozenka again—and allow her to please you?"

"Bożena . . . be sensible . . . this is not wise . . ." She dragged me down on to the grass of the glade beside her.

"Oh come on you silly boy, don't you love me any more?" She lay back, smiling. "Be good to your little Polish girl, just this once. I may have to invent some urgent family business back in Gródek and leave for a while . . ."

My resistance drained away like tepid water from a punctured hot-water bottle, and soon we were engaged in a passionate session of physiotherapy, flattening the grass beneath us as we urged one another on. At length her eyes dilated to about twice their normal width and she emitted a shriek like a steamer-whistle. Bożena had always been unrestrained in her love-making, but I had never known her to act like this before. Then suddenly she was pushing me away from her and trying frantically to struggle to her feet. Powerful hands seized me and dragged me away from her amid a pandemonium of shouts and screams and barking dogs. I struggled, and launched a kick with my heel at a figure behind me. The reply was a punch in the stomach which knocked the breath out of me and set my ears singing. When the fog of pain cleared I was pinioned from behind by four or five men as the pair of mastiffs strained to get at me, snarling furiously. I found myself looking into a large, florid, black-moustachioed face. It was Grbić. He held a wickedly sharp-looking butcher's knife which he brandished a few millimetres from the tip of my nose. Bożena was opposite me, struggling desperately in the grip of three large men. One of them was holding a cloth around her mouth as a gag.

"So, Herr Leutnant," he said in his guttural Serb-German, "first you reduce me to beggary with your meddling in trade, then you make a cuckold of me for good measure. Well, you will shortly find out what it means to cross a Serb. Do you see these fine lads of mine here? They are my slaughter-men—or rather were, until your cursed embargo put them out of work, along with the whole town besides. But you'll soon see how skilful they still are with the knife—because you will be watching as my dogs eat your liver! As for you, my Polish mare, you can look on as we make a gelding of your fine Bohemian stallion. Then I shall decide what to do with you, you miserable slut!"

I am still not entirely clear what happened at this point. Three or four of Grbić's henchmen had guns—heavy fowling-pieces mostly—and I think that one of them was trying to hold his gun with one hand while restraining Božena (who was struggling ferociously) with the other. At any rate, there was a flash and a loud bang, then smoke and barking as the dogs, thinking that their master was being attacked, broke loose and ran about biting at random. I struggled with the men holding me and in their momentary surprise their grip on my wet body loosened. I was away like a hare, running for my life, sprinting blindly ahead with the whole mob of men and dogs howling in pursuit. Running naked, I had a slight edge over Grbić's ruffians in their heavy boots. But the mastiffs were gaining on me. I crashed through the undergrowth, floundered through reed beds, struggled blindly through thickets with the whole wild hunt in full cry behind me. The breath sobbed in my lungs as I ran, propelled by the desperate, blind urge to survive. Soon the whole world had contracted to a throbbing red-walled tunnel as I slithered on the wet ground and tripped over tree-roots and was torn by the rushing branches. At one point one of the dogs managed to snap at my calf. But luckily at that moment one of Grbić's men fired at me. I heard a yelp of pain as some of the pellets hit the dog, and the beast let go of me. I crashed over a willow-root, but got up and struggled on. If only I could reach the river . . . perhaps I could leap in and swim clear of them . . . I was splashing through reeds now. Another charge of shot sang over my head. I plunged on, near to collapse—then tripped and fell and cracked my head against something hard. I lay dazed for a few moments, then tried groggily to get up. But as the stars cleared I saw a cruel, brown face above me and a pair of black eyes looking down at me, felt a chill edge of steel at my throat. The game was up.

"What is your name?" said the face. He spoke in Serb. Well there was no point being polite now: the end was at hand and I might as well go defiantly.

"Prohaska," I gasped. "Are people asking?"

The man turned. "Row away!" I heard the creak of oars in rowlocks and a grunt of effort as the rowers strained against the foot-rests, felt the sudden sway as the skiff shot out from among the reeds and into the main stream of the Danube.

# 8

# UNION OR DEATH

MY RESCUERS LUGGED AT THE OARS to shoot us along downstream with the current. But Grbić and his accomplices had no intention of letting me escape so easily. We were not twenty seconds out of the reed-bed before they came into sight astern of us: Grbić himself and two of his slaughter-men, paddling furiously in my own canoe, which I had left tied up in a creek when I arrived at the fateful island that morning. They were shouting at us to stop, and were gaining on us. Grbić levelled his gun and fired. But firing a shotgun from a canoe is not easy, and the shot whistled harmlessly over our heads. My rescuer, the swarthy man who had held a knife to my throat when I tumbled into the skiff, signalled to his two rowers to slow down, then took his own gun—a heavy fowling-weapon—and lay down on the bottom boards, resting the piece in the sculling notch at the stern. Grbić and his men came to within ten metres or so before he fired. It was beautifully placed: the charge of swan-shot smashed in an area of the flimsy cedar planking about the size of a dinner plate, right on the canoe's waterline. The boat stayed upright for a moment or two under its own momentum, then dipped by the bow and capsized, tipping its howling occupants into the river. We left them in our wake, clinging to the upturned canoe and treating us to the Serbian language's entire rich treasury of blasphemy and obscenity.

The immediate danger past, my mysterious benefactor turned back to me, still lying breathless and half-stunned, propped against a thwart.

"Well, Prohaska, you certainly took your time about it. Naked as a frog and with all that lot on your heels as well. Looks as if their border guards are starting to wear plain clothes, the bastards. Did you have to swim for it?"

It seemed better to agree with him, so I nodded in as noncommittal a fashion as possible. "Anyway my friend," he laughed, "good job that you answered as quickly as you did. Any hesitation and I'd have slit your throat for you."

I looked at him. He was a short but powerful-looking man with a hooked nose, more Turkish than Serb in appearance. Something about him told me that his remark about slitting my throat was no idle figure of speech. But who were these people? And more to the point, who was I supposed to be? All that I had been able to gather about them so far was that they had been waiting to pick up someone called Prohaska. Well, Prohaska is a common enough Czech name. But Bohemia was hundreds of kilometres away from southern Hungary. Was it thus reasonable to deduce that this was an assumed name for someone else; also that by answering "Are people asking?" I had inadvertently given some kind of password to these desperadoes? I guessed that they must be pig smugglers who had perhaps been reconnoitring the island with a view to another nocturnal crossing like the one which we had frustrated at Grahovski Otok a few days before. That would at least explain why they had found nothing odd in my being chased by a gang of armed men. Perhaps they thought that an Austrian undercover border patrol had taken after me, or maybe that I was being pursued by rival criminals. Only the previous week a gendarmery officer had told me that the Serb pig-smuggling gangs were not above fighting one another for a larger share of this profitable trade. I decided to keep quiet and find out all I could. It looked as though I had stumbled by chance into a highly organised gang. These ruffians would certainly kill me if I tried to escape now, so for the moment it was perhaps best to swim with the current and see what they were up to. The first necessity though was to find out who I was supposed to be. My rescuer, who had been gazing astern towards the Austrian shore, turned back to me. "How is the Falcon, then?"

I decided to be vague: "the Falcon" was clearly an alias for some smuggler chief on our side of the river. "Well enough, thank you."

"And what does he say, to go ahead or wait?" This was more difficult. My mind raced: I had to give a yes or no. At last I decided that, since I was now trying to uncover the plans of these criminals, setting them in motion would be better than delaying them. So, feeling rather as if I were placing a pistol to my head without knowing whether it was loaded or empty, I answered:

"The Falcon says to go ahead."

We lay up for a day on an island just off the Serbian shore, the three men and I, then crossed to the mainland just before dawn the next day. I had been given some bread and sheep's-milk cheese to eat and a swig or two of slivovica (which I detested) and provided with clothes: an ill-fitting old three-piece suit, a felt hat and a tieless, collarless workman's shirt. It was then, as we made our way along a rough country road to the railway station at Požarevac, that I first began to wonder what these men were really about, for it seemed from the elaborate caution with which we proceeded—tumbling into a ditch to hide when we saw a customs man, for instance—that they were quite as anxious to avoid the Serbian authorities as the Austrian. Likewise when we got to Požarevac we bought our tickets singly and sat in different compartments of the train. And why were we going to Belgrade instead of one or other of the riverside villages which were the bases of the smuggling business? I must have stumbled into the very nerve centre of the whole operation.

Two evenings after my escape from dismemberment by Grbić and his henchmen I was sitting over a tiny, sweet cup of Turkish coffee in an upper room of the café Pod Zlatna Grana—The Golden Branch—in the old Turkish quarter of the Serbian capital. Belgrade in those days was a town more appropriate to Syria than to the centre of Europe: within sight of Austria-Hungary on the other bank of the Danube, but otherwise more like a souk in Aleppo than the capital of a European state. It was not difficult to see that for four centuries Belgrade had been a frontier fortress of the Ottoman Empire. The quarter of the town in which I now found myself lay just below the citadel of the Kalamegdan, a dilapidated area of low, oriental-looking houses with wooden balconies and fretted wooden shutters amid a warren of narrow, evil-smelling alleyways where the open drains ran down the middle of the street and stray dogs scratched their sores in the gutter, a milieu of rooming-houses and bordellos and small café-taverns where the clientele would sit all day over a glass of slivovica or a succession of tiny, thimble-like cups of coffee.

I had had nearly two days now in which to think over my predicament; two days of straining all five senses to try and pick up information about my erstwhile rescuers and about my new, fortuitous identity. One thing had emerged beyond any possible doubt: that whoever these people were, they were no common criminals. For one thing they were plainly too secretive and too well organised to be anything but the very aristocracy of crime—perhaps (I thought) some local version of the Sicilian Camorra, involved in God alone knew what elaborate villainies. For another, the speech and bearing of the five or six of them whom I had so far encountered was not that of what used to be called the criminal classes. These were clearly educated men, and their whole demeanour was that of people engaged in some higher enterprise than mere smuggling and extortion. In fact it was beginning to occur to me, as a career officer myself, that they were part of some military-style organisation, to judge by the calm way in which they gave and received orders, quite unlike the mutual snarling and cursing which is supposed to characterise the relations of common brigands. But it was also plain that whatever this organisation was, it was keen not to attract the attention of the Serbian police or military—at any rate to judge by the elaborate secrecy with which we had travelled to Belgrade and the rigmarole of passwords and shuttered rooms once we arrived.

Who was I supposed to be, though? This was still a mystery. But at least I had put my time to good use in concocting an identity for myself. These people thought I was a fellow-Serb, that much was plain, and I should have little difficulty in keeping up that fiction. Nearly fifteen years in the k.u.k Kriegsmarine had made me perfectly fluent in Serbo-Croat— which is anyway quite intelligible to a Czech—and I had been stationed several years before on the Gulf of Cattaro, where the local populace are mostly Montenegrin Serbs. Also they thought that I was some kind of emissary from the Austrian side: perhaps an army officer, to judge from a couple of allusions they had made. So I had decided to make myself into an Oberleutnant Ante Radić of the 5th Field Artillery Regiment, a native of Castellnuovo on the Gulf of Cattaro. This coastal provenance would (I hoped) at least explain why I spoke Serb with a slight Croat accent.

But who in the devil's name was the Falcon? And what news or instructions was I supposed to be bringing from him? Well, one way or the other I would soon find out, when my interviewer arrived. As I sat there in that room above the shabby little café, I weighed the alternatives in my mind. I was in deadly peril if I went ahead, that much was clear: for whoever these men were they meant business and would certainly not hesitate to kill anyone they suspected of being an imposter. But then, I was in equally great—perhaps even worse—danger if I tried to escape. The café was closely watched by their sentries, I knew; and even if I managed to evade them I still had to get through this unfamiliar town and somehow cross the Danube to the Austrian side. No, what was it they used to tell us at the Marine Academy when we were learning infantry tactics—that in battle, more men are killed running away than going forward? For the moment at any rate retreat looked more dangerous than advance.

But in any case, did not my oath as an officer of the Noble House of Austria oblige me to press on and see how far I could bluff my way? These people were plainly engaged in some high-level conspiracy, apparently with the knowledge and connivance of people on our own side of the frontier. The conspiracy was certainly criminal; it might perhaps even be political. But in either event, given the national mood in Serbia in the year 1914, the target was quite likely to be Austria. No, it was clearly my duty to use my luck in falling among them to find out as much as I possibly could, then—if I survived—escape back to my own side and relate everything I had learnt to the police.

My interlocutor, when he arrived, was anything but a reassuring sight: a powerful, tall, handsome man with a dense black beard amidst which a set of perfect white teeth flashed from time to time like the beam of a lighthouse on a dark night. As he greeted me and shook my hand with a great bone-crushing paw I noticed that he spoke Serb with a pronounced Montenegrin accent.

"Well Prohaska, welcome to Belgrade. Allow me to introduce myself: Major Mirko Draganić, otherwise known as 'the Ant.'" He laughed, and the white teeth gleamed amid the beard. "A good pseudonym, don't you think, for someone as small as I am? I chose it myself for fun—just as I had them call you 'Prohaska' after that jackass of an Austrian consul. Not a bad joke, eh? That's the trouble with these Serbs of Serbia: they're all so solemn about everything." A ray of light dawned here: so I had been given my code-name in honour of Oskar Prohaska (no relation), the Austro-Hungarian Consul at Prizen in Macedonia whose alleged beating-up by Serbian Army officers the previous year had caused the Viennese press to work itself into frenzy of patriotic indignation for a week or so—and had then been as quickly forgotten. "Anyway, Prohaska, what does the Falcon say? Stupanić says that your message tells us to go ahead."

This was the moment I had been dreading: surely further information would be required about the mysterious Falcon. I prepared a non-committal reply, without really believing that it would wash. It was never needed though: luckily for me Major Draganić was a man of an expansive, extrovert—in fact rather theatrical—nature and would generally ask a question only to answer it himself.

"He did," I answered, trying to stop my voice from trembling.

"Splendid. Then we shall act. The Boar will walk into our trap and the hunters will be waiting. Their hands will not tremble."

The Boar, I thought. Was this really pig-smuggling after all? Or was I now involved in a murder plot? The thought suddenly struck me that quite possibly I had blundered not into a Serbian plot against Austria but an Austrian-sponsored conspiracy against the Serbian state: perhaps an assassination plot against their Prime Minister Pasić or even against King Peter himself. This was by no means a fanciful or melodramatic notion: in that turbulent little country conspiracy was a way of life and politics often not much better than organised gang-warfare. Only a few hundred metres from the café Pod Zlatna Grana, back in 1903, the then King Alexander Obrenović and the entire royal family had been casually wiped out: shot and then hacked to pieces in a nocturnal blood-bath by their Karageorgević rivals and dissident army officers. Serbia was still officially a friendly state as far as the Danubian Monarchy was concerned, but relations had been strained for years, and there was nothing inherently unlikely in Vienna secretly supporting one of the many factions. "Major" Draganić though: was the military rank self-awarded, as was so often the case in the Balkans, where grandmothers and lady's maids frequently knew more about infantry warfare than the entire Swedish General Staff? Or was he a real, serving army officer? By the look of him I would have said the latter, for despite his theatrical appearance and decidedly un-staff-college manner he had about him the indefinable air of someone who has heard the bullets fly in earnest. He had been gazing down from the window for a while into the dirty alleyway below, apparently lost in thought. At last he spoke.

"Well then, the 25th of June it shall be. The warriors of the nation have already begun to depart for the field." He turned to me and smiled. "But no doubt the Falcon would like you to take back a report on how we are spending his money, so perhaps we shall go downstairs so that you can meet some of my pupils. Stupanić is bringing two of them for you to see, and after that you can watch the swearing-in. Then tomorrow I shall take you with me through our tunnel. Come!" He slapped me on the shoulder, and nearly knocked me off my feet. It was like being hit with a wet sandbag. Then we made our way down the dark, rickety staircase.

It was evening and the kerosene lamps were being lit in the dim back room of the Pod Zlatna Grana. As we entered, a dense reek of frying, onions, coffee and cheap cigarettes leapt up to meet us like some large, unkempt and smelly dog. As my eyes became accustomed to the dim light I recognised Stupanić and one of his assistants sitting at a table near the back of the room. They were accompanied by two sallow-faced youths of about nineteen or twenty, awkward-looking in their shabby suits and straggly, embryonic moustaches (in those days to be a Serb adult male without a moustache was to be like a Polish teetotaller, only more conspicuous). One of them wore a Muslim fez, the other a grubby straw boater. They stood up to greet us.

"Prohaska," said Draganić with a grin, "permit me to introduce you to our two latest recruits to the cause: Mehemet Dusić and Ilya Kardjejev, both students of the University of Belgrade." I shook hands with them and we sat down.

"Well, my young heroes," said Draganić as glasses of slivovica were brought to us, "are you ready to begin your journey tomorrow?"

It was Dusić the Muslim who replied. "Yes brother Major, I have the honour to report that we are both ready for our sacred appointment with destiny."

"Good, good. Prohaska and I will accompany you for some way through the tunnel while Stupanić goes on ahead, but then we must leave you. I hope that when you arrive you will acquit yourselves as true sons of the nation."

Kardjejev spoke in his piping adolescent's voice, eyes shining. "You may depend upon it, brother Major. We shall discharge our duty like true Serbs when the hour comes. Generations yet unborn shall speak of our deed while the enemies of our people shall mourn the day. We shall bear ourselves like faithful sons of the Serbian motherland, nourished at her breast, and when we fall our blood shall water her sacred soil." It was at this point that I realised exactly why—quite apart from its absurdly melodramatic content—Kardjejev's speech sounded so peculiar to me. It was because he had fallen into speaking in a kind of blank verse, still a frequent habit among the Balkan Slavs in those days and one which, believe me, sounded very odd to the more prosaic ear of a Czech like myself, brought up among the electric tramways and gaslit rationality of northern Moravia. Yet despite the manner of speaking and the high-flown patriotic sentiments, I saw that a group of five or six men playing draughts at the next table took no notice of us whatever.

"Anyway," said Draganić, "have you received the tools for your task?"

I could see that Kardjejev had been waiting for this. Almost before the words were out of the Major's mouth he had reached into his pocket, like a child asked to show an uncle his new toy on Christmas morning. He pulled it out awkwardly and showed it to us, just beneath the edge of the table. It was a Browning automatic pistol, brand new by the looks of it. I noticed that the safety catch had been left off.

"Here," he said, grinning in the lamplight, "see: with this weapon I shall strike such a blow for the nation as—" There was a sudden flash and report, deafening in the confines of the room, and a leg of the table behind us flew into splinters. The table teetered for a moment, then draughts, draughtboard and slivovica glasses all slid with a crash on to the dirty tiled floor. There was an embarrassed, smoke-wreathed silence as the draught-players turned to look at us—not in anger but with the sort of weary reproach one gets from people in the row in front at the theatre if they consider one is whispering too loudly. The landlord came in, pausing in his wiping of a glass with a grubby cloth.

"Right, if I've said it once I've said it a hundred times: no guns in here is the rule of the house. We're a respectable café and if you can't stop yourself from shooting the place up you'd better go somewhere else. And what's more, somebody's going to have to cough up for that table leg or I'll call the police. Students! All the same if you ask me." He went back to the kitchen, wiping the glass and muttering under his breath. Kardjejev was profusely apologetic.

"Really, brother Major . . . It just went off in my hand . . . I didn't . . ."

Draganić waved aside his protestations. "All right, all right, it's nothing. Better to fire too much than too little. Safety catches never won a battle yet. Anyway, if you'll excuse me I must go and pay the landlord. He meant what he said about calling the police." He rose from the table, bowed slightly and went to the kitchen. As he disappeared Kardjejev whispered to me:

"Here, do you want to see it?"

"See what?"

"This." He dipped into the other pocket of his jacket and produced a rectangular black object, about the size and shape of a small medicine bottle but evidently made from metal. It had a brass cap over the neck and gleamed dully in the lamplight. My blood suddenly ran chill as I realised what it was. "There, isn't it a beauty? Brother Stupanić gave us two each. It works like this: you take it in your hand and bang the cap hard like this . . ." He raised his arm above the table. I yelled, "No!" and caught his wrist in mid-descent, sweating with fright. "No, for God's sake not here! Be sensible and put the thing back in your pocket until you need it. There might be plain-clothes police about . . ."

"Anyway," he said peevishly, slipping it back into his pocket, "You have eight seconds to throw it and the Major says it'll kill anyone within ten metres."

"Yes, yes, I'm sure the Major's right. But not here for heaven's sake . . ." It had occurred to me that, quite apart from the strong likelihood of being shot or blown to pieces by these juvenile zealots before the evening was out, there was also a remarkably good chance of us all being run in by the police. In which case I might have some difficulty explaining exactly how it came about that I, a serving Austrian naval officer, came to be arrested wearing civilian clothes in the Serbian capital in the company of an armed gang of terrorists. There already loomed a hazy but none the less unpleasant vision of a fortress wall at dawn, a blindfold and a row of levelled rifles.

Draganić returned meanwhile from compensating the landlord for the gunshot damage. "Well, my friends," he said, "an early night is my prescription for you two young fellows. You've a long day ahead of you tomorrow and I don't want you spending the night boasting and drinking brandy with your student pals. But Stupanić and Prohaska, you can come along with me. We have the oath-taking to witness."

We said our farewells and left the café to make our way through the labyrinth of alleyways. Our destination was a house just under the walls of the fortress. There was an elaborate pantomime of passwords and eyes peering through spyholes in doors, until at length we were admitted to a small, tightly shuttered room lit by a single kerosene lamp. Three youths of about the same age as Dusić and Kardjejev awaited us. They were presided over by an angular, thinnish, balding man in his early forties wearing a steel pince-nez and a sour expression.

"You're late, Draganić," he snapped. "Where have you been?"

To my surprise Draganić's reply was as meekly apologetic as that of a schoolboy to his headmaster. "Sorry Commander, but I had business at the Pod Zlatna Grana . . ."

"Yes, I can imagine what sort of business as well, drinking and bragging with your cronies. You'll be the undoing of us all with your tongue. Anyway, let's get on with the oath-taking: I've got more important things to occupy my time than sitting here waiting for you to turn up."

He lit two candles on a small table at the end of the room, and the kerosene lamp was extinguished. An expectant hush fell over the room as the candlelight flickered in the nervous eyes of the three young men. Between the two candles something lay covered by a cloth. The Commander took up his position behind the table, and one by one the youths stepped forward to swear loyalty. The affirmations were lengthy, and couched in the most blood-curdling language: pledging lifelong devotion to the society, total obedience to its officers, unconditional readiness to die under torture without revealing the smallest of its secrets, liability to the most extravagantly ferocious punishments for the smallest deviation from its rules. Then the cloth was removed with a flourish. It revealed a human skull, a bomb, a pistol, a dagger and a crucifix. I had to pinch myself to make sure that I was not dreaming, it was all so preposterously theatrical: as if I had accidentally wandered into act two of an operetta about the charcoal-burners of Sicily and the soubrette might enter left at any moment, warbling about being only a simple shepherd girl. The aspirants seemed to take it seriously enough though: each in turn raised his right hand over the stage props on the table and made the affirmation "By the sun that warms me, by the earth that nourishes me, by the blood of my ancestors, on my honour and by my life's blood." They were then congratulated by the Commander on having become probationary members of the patriotic society Zvaz o Smrt—Union or Death. It was only later that I came to know this organisation by the name under which history remembers it: Crna Ruka, or The Black Hand.

We were up early next morning, rising from our bug-infested beds in a cheap lodging-house to make our way to the steamer pier on the River Sava. Our destination, I learnt, was the town of Šabac, where we would board a train to take us up the valley of the River Drina to Loznica. Well, that settled it for me at any rate: Loznica was on the Serbian side of the border with the Austro-Hungarian Empire—or, to be more precise, with its recently annexed provinces of Bosnia and Herzegovina. That meant that whatever conspiracy these bumbling terrorists were involved in, the Monarchy must be its target. Not that there was anything out of the ordinary in that: Bosnia-Herzegovina had been annexed only in

1908—last seedy triumph of Habsburg diplomacy—and since then there had scarcely been a year in which one of the Emperor Franz Joseph's new and unwilling subjects (almost all of them ethnic Serbs) had not taken a pot-shot at the Military Governor or tossed a bomb at some visiting dignitary. Assassination and lying in ambush were anyway as traditional a part of Bosnian life as pigs and plum-trees. Like most Austrians, I had taken as little interest in that remote and poverty-stricken province as most English people nowadays take in events on the streets of Belfast. But I had gathered from cursory reading of newspaper reports that the common feature of all these attentats was their picturesque incompetence, like the attempt on the life of the Emperor at Mostar in 1910, when the assassin managed to get the old man in his sights—then changed his mind for no apparent reason and set off for Agram to try and shoot the Governor of Croatia, being killed himself in the attempt while the Governor escaped unharmed.

From what I could see of my travelling companions as the train steamed out of Šabac railway station, they were fairly and squarely within this tradition of murderous ineptitude. We travelled in pairs in different carriages, and I was with the egregious Kardjejev. And he gave a gala performance as we sat there on the wooden-slatted benches of that grimy third-class compartment, sweating in the oppressive heat of an early-summer noonday as the train clanked and swayed southwards. Our travelling companions were a couple of elderly Serb peasants and a trussed-up piglet which they had just bought in Šabac market. Kardjejev, I could see, was fairly bursting to tell them of our mission, and before long his tongue had anyway been loosened by a swig of slivovica from a bottle which one of the rustics carried in his back pocket. The old man took his gulp from the bottle, then wiped his luxuriant white moustaches with the back of his hand and regarded the student with twinkling black eyes set in a mahogany-coloured, intricately wrinkled face.

"So young sir, do I take it you're bound for Loznica as well?"

"Yes, to Loznica, old father. But . . ." he added darkly, ". . . our journey does not end there, not by a long way I can tell you."

"Are you going on with the train to Zvornik then?"

"No, not to Zvornik: our business takes us far beyond Loznica—but on foot."

A look of childish cunning spread across the old countrymen's faces. "Aha," one of them said, "does that mean that you're in, er . . . trade . . . across the river, so to speak? They say there are many that travel on this train who carry tobacco and brandy across into Bosnia without bothering the customs men."

Kardjejev smiled knowingly, and gazed mysteriously for some moments up at the luggage rack, where there lay a cheap fibre suitcase containing two Browning pistols, sixty rounds of ammunition and four bombs.

"Yes father, you might call it smuggling. But the tobacco we carry is very strong; so strong that, believe me, the Austrians will be sick indeed when they taste of it." The old peasants looked at one another and nodded, visibly impressed. Meanwhile I winced and tried desperately to signal him to shut up. These men could quite well be police informers, and anyway there were customs men on the train and the corridor was full of travellers. But Kardjejev was playing to an appreciative audience. He was well into his stride now, eyes shining in patriotic ecstasy. He leant across to them and his voice sank to a penetrating whisper, "In fact . . ." he looked around him, ". . . in fact, I'm on my way to strike such a blow for the Serbs that all generations will tell of it, and you, my fathers, will count it an honour to be able to tell the folk of your village that you met me."

The two rustics were round-eyed now with wonder and plum brandy. At last one of them spoke. "But how will you return to Serbia when you have . . . done the deed of which you speak? Surely the Austrians will hunt you down like a dog?"

Kardjejev sighed, and cast down his eyes with a look of noble resignation. "Alas, old one, the light of the sun will shine upon me no more after that day. If the Austrians caught me I would die upon the gallows. But they shall not have that satisfaction. Here . . ." he rummaged in his pocket. "What do you think this is?" It was a small glass phial. The two old men gazed at it, goggle-eyed. Kardjejev unscrewed the top a little, and a pungent smell of bitter almonds filled the compartment, submerging for a while even the smells of tobacco and piglet and plum brandy.

"Do you see this, my fathers? This is prussic acid—cyanide. I have only to swallow this and I shall be dead in seconds. No, the oppressors of my people shall not take me alive, I can tell you."

I squirmed in desperation and looked about me. The conductor was only a compartment or two down the corridor. I tried to gauge the train's speed with a view to jumping out if I had to. At length one of the rustics overcame his wonderment sufficiently to speak.

"But where are you going, and what is this deed that you will do when you get there?"

Kardjejev waited some time before speaking, to heighten the dramatic effect.

"Where am I going, my father? Why, to Sarajevo of course. And my errand is the greatest of deeds that the son of a Serbian mother can perform: to kill the Austrian Archduke."

The train slowed and squealed to a halt as we arrived at Loznica. Despite Kardjejev's incontinent tongue we were still miraculously undiscovered, and my mind was racing as I digested the things that I had just learnt. The Noble House of Austria numbered at that time some sixty-three extant archdukes—but there could be no doubt as to which one was the target of this plot. I remembered now how my brother Anton, when we had met for the weekend in Ujvidek at the beginning of May, had mentioned that the Adjutant of the 26th Jäger Regiment was already getting into a flap because the Heir-Apparent was attending the summer manoeuvres to be held in Bosnia late in June. Presumably he was to visit the provincial capital, the society Union or Death had got wind of it and these young men were now being despatched there to provide an unofficial welcoming committee. Well, that was good to know: the pieces of the jigsaw were now beginning to fit together. Of course—the Boar: with those moustaches and the character that went with them I had to admit that it was an aptly chosen code-name. The train stopped, and soon we were assembling outside the station to begin the next stage of our journey, through Major Draganić's much-vaunted tunnel.

Looking back on it afterwards, I imagine that it could only have been thirty-six hours or so. It merely seemed like thirty-six days, passing through the tunnel from Serbia across the River Drina to Austrian territory, then over the wooded hills to the small town of Obrenica. In fact I think that as the swallow flies it could have been no more than about twenty kilometres from our crossing point near Loznica to our first rendezvous inside Bosnia. To us on the ground though it seemed like crossing the Andes and the Amazon jungle simultaneously. The trouble was that we had to evade Serbian as well as Austrian border patrols, since Zvaz o Smrt was evidently viewed with scarcely more favour by its own government than by mine. This meant that our party—Draganić, myself, the two juvenile patriots and a local guide whose name I never learnt—had to travel pretty well the entire distance wriggling along ditches, struggling through riverside thickets and stumbling across ploughed fields to escape detection: and most of the time under cover of darkness as well.

Our crossing of the Drina was the first problem. A boat of sorts—a half-rotten duck punt—had been provided, but we had to spend most of the first day lying concealed in the reed-beds, waiting for the summer dusk to fall. And when we finally pushed ourselves out into the river we found that the current was stronger than expected, since it had been a wet spring in those parts. In consequence, we drifted downstream a good way below our intended landfall on the Austrian bank. By the time we struggled ashore we were wet through and filthy from our sojourn in the reed-bed. But it mattered little, since it soon began to drizzle; and drizzled with monotonous, unvarying intensity for the next two days. We struggled on through the riverside marshes, then through alder woods and water meadows, then across fields of dripping, rustling maize. It was pure purgatory for me, struggling along through mud and rain with a suitcase in my hand, wearing an ill-fitting suit and cheap town shoes; a dreary, unremitting assault course made all the worse by the fact that only the guide knew the way and only Draganić knew where we were bound for, so that we had to follow them blindly up hill and down dale, hour after hour, without the slightest idea of how long this ordeal would last.

To make matters worse, my injured leg began to ache, protesting at the unreasonable demands being placed upon it. But a far worse ache was the realisation that I was now back on Austrian territory, five days absent without leave from my ship, in civilian dress and re-entering the country illegally in the company of a band of desperadoes intent on killing its heir to the throne. If we were caught I would have some explaining to do which might, on balance, be even more awkward than that which would have been necessary if the Serbian police had arrested us all at the Pod Zlatna Grana.

It very nearly came to that at one point the next morning as we were making our way in single file around the edge of a field of beans. Draganić stopped suddenly and crouched down, motioning us to do the same. I caught a glimpse of five or six figures on the trackway which led across the end of the field. Two of them were in dark blue, the rest in field grey with rifles slung at their shoulders: doubtless Austrian customs men escorted by soldiers and returning from a night's anti-smuggling patrol. Luckily for us they were as tired and wet as ourselves, anxious to get to the next village and tea laced with rum in the local café. They passed by without catching sight of us, and when they were gone we rose achingly to our feet and trudged on once more.

We did not make Obrenica until early the next morning, after a night during which we had twice got lost in the sodden pine forests to the east of the town. All we had managed to eat in the whole miserable day and a half of our journey was a slice or two of wet bread and a couple of sugar lumps, so bean stew and hot coffee never tasted better to me than there in that back room of the town's newly opened cinema—the Bioskop—whose proprietor was a secret member of Zvaz o Smrt. Even Kardjejev and Dusić were in low spirits; for, as we had tramped wearily through the back streets of the little town in the drizzle, a horribly conspicuous group of oddly dressed and mud-besmeared strangers, the fibre suitcase which contained the party's weapons had finally given up the ghost and fallen to pieces, allowing pistols, bombs and ammunition to clatter on to the cobblestones just after a rural gendarme had ambled past us on his early-morning beat. White-faced, we scooped everything together as best we could and dived for cover in the cinema.

Once we had breakfasted and dried ourselves out a little in the back room of the Bioskop, Major Draganić and I bade the rest farewell. The guide and the two would-be assassins were to make their way to Tuzla and thence by rail to Sarajevo. As for us, it appeared that we would head southwards for eighty kilometres or so across Austrian territory to the border with Montenegro, near Foča, where Draganić had some important business to attend to. The reasons for his decision to make this journey across (for him) enemy territory were twofold, he said: firstly that now we had gone to the trouble of getting across the Austro-Serbian border it would be a waste of time to do it again; secondly that the distance to our destination would be much longer if we headed east back into Serbia, since Austrian territory in those days protruded like a wedge into the join between that country and Montenegro. The Austrian-Montenegrin border above Foča, Draganić said, was in mountainous, heavily wooded country and much less rigorously guarded than the frontier we had crossed on the Drina. He added mysteriously that he was too well known to the guards on the Montenegrin frontier with Serbia. I puzzled over this remark and wondered why on earth it should matter, since Draganić was a Montenegrin himself and presumably a subject of King Nikita. As for myself, now that we were across the frontier, well into Austrian territory and rid of Kardjejev, I thought that the remainder of the journey would not be too hazardous. In for a penny, in for a pound, I think you say: well, I had discovered the plot against the Heir-Apparent and there was still over a month to go before he arrived in Bosnia, so I thought that I might as well find out what this "business" was in Montenegro that Draganić was so anxious to attend to. Somehow I doubted whether it would be a bicycle repair shop.

The sun was shining again by the time we left Obrenica, creaking southwards along the roughly metalled road in a horse-drawn trap supplied by the cinema proprietor. Before we left he had insisted on showing the Major and me his latest film-reel, sent him by a cousin in Pittsburgh. It was a ten-minute cowboy story featuring Tom Mix. It was the first Western film I ever saw, and very interesting—*Brett of the Badlands,* if I remember rightly. Draganić was fascinated, and later that day, when we were resting in the forest, I saw him practising quick draws with his revolver.

Otherwise the two-day journey towards the Montenegrin frontier passed without incident. The countryside became increasingly wild and thinly populated as we climbed up into the mountains. Wayfarers were few, while as for the military or gendarmes we met not a single one. Draganić was in a jovial mood. His tunnel had worked well, despite the rigours involved in passing through it, and the weather had now turned fine and warm to dry our clothes out. He passed the time as we ambled southwards by regaling me with a string of luridly coloured but (I have to admit) highly entertaining yarns about his recent exploits in the two Balkan wars as leader of a band of Comitadjis: those murderously brave semi-regular troops who had fought with such ferocity in the first war to drive the Turks out of Europe—and had then fallen upon one another with even greater ferocity a few months later when the Balkan states began quarrelling over the spoils. The Major's stories undoubtedly contained a good measure of heroic exaggeration, the artistic licence natural to a man from a country where, even in the early years of this century, the two chief male occupations were still warfare and composing epic poetry. But I think that even then I recognised a braggart when I saw one, and his tales certainly had for me the ring of truth. The Serbs, after all, were courageous and highly competent soldiers—as they were to prove on a number of occasions before 1914 was out—and no branch of the Serb nation was more warlike than its Montenegrin offshoot, a tribal society which had supplied Europe with its surplus warriors for centuries past. Most of his yarns sounded plausible, even the one about how, back in 1912, armed only with a rifle and bayonet, he had held the bridge at Strumitsa single-handed, like Horatius of old, against a battalion of Turks while the Serbian sappers laid dynamite behind him to demolish it; and how, after receiving fifteen wounds, he had leapt over the parapet and dived forty metres into the river below while the charges went off and the bridge collapsed about him.

But quite apart from their entertainment value—which was considerable—I had another reason for getting Draganić to tell me these tales. For the longer he kept talking the less time there was for him to ask me embarrassing questions. I had my story ready about being Artillerie Oberleutnant

Radić from Castellnuovo, but I was far from confident that it would stand up for long under cross-examination. We were on our own now, far from human habitation. Draganić was armed; I was not; and despite his jovial manner I knew that he would kill me without the slightest compunction if he began to suspect anything. I fully intended giving him the slip as soon as I had found out all that I wanted to know—but only when the safety of an Austrian gendarmery post was within easy reach. Draganić had a rifle concealed in the back of the cart as well as his revolver, and I knew that if I suddenly made a run for it he would shoot me dead before I had gone a hundred metres.

In the event it was he who did the talking for most of the journey. In fact it was not until the afternoon of the second day, as we neared the Montenegrin border, that he asked me anything at all. It was a warm mid-afternoon as we lay beside a mountain stream in a forest clearing just off the trackway. The horse was cropping the grass nearby and Draganić lay on his back with a straw in his mouth, gazing into the sky. He had been uncharacteristically silent for some time, as if deciding whether or not to take me into his confidence. At last he spoke.

"Tell me, Prohaska, as one Montenegrin to another: what do you think of my warriors of the nation, eh?"

I sensed from the faint note of irony in his voice that the reply expected was not the formal compliment that courtesy demanded. But still I tried to dodge the question.

"Whom do you mean, brother Major?"

His white teeth flashed in the thicket of his beard. "My fine boys, of course, who by now will have arrived in Sarajevo. Are they not fighters such as any nation might be proud of?"

"Since you ask I must say . . ."

"That you think they are a pathetic lot of half-wits, yes? Is that what you wish to say?"

I tried to remain neutral. "Well, I did think . . ."

He laughed. "Of course you do. And I couldn't agree with you more: a total waste of our time and your money, and you will doubtless report as much to your superiors when you get back. But do you know why this is?

I will tell you: because I, Major Mirko Draganić, deliberately chose them so! But I'll tell you one thing, Prohaska: count yourself lucky that you didn't meet the advance party we sent to Sarajevo last week, because if anything they were worse. One of them, Čabrinović, was nearly as great a blabber-mouth as our friend Kardjejev, while as for his companion—whose name I don't even remember—he was a scrawny little consumptive of about eighteen who could scarcely lift his pistol, let alone fire it. I took him out to test his markmanship before we signed him up and, honestly, I nearly pissed myself laughing. He fired ten shots at the side of a barn at twenty-five paces—and missed each time." He paused. "So, you will doubtless ask yourself why I, the Ant, should select such a miserable gang of schoolboys to do my work when I have only to snap my fingers to get a score of battle-hardened Comitadjis, warriors of the finest quality and unconditionally willing to give their lives for the Serb nation. And I will tell you why: be-cause I want the operation in Sarajevo to be as big a failure as possible."

I stared at him. "But why on earth, after going to all this trouble...?"

"Because I have a head on my shoulders. Do you know what the operation in Sarajevo is?"

I knew of course, because Kardjejev had told me. I thought it best at first to feign ignorance, but then I remembered that I was supposed to be an emissary from the mysterious Falcon, and therefore fully aware of what the aim of the conspiracy was.

"Of course: to kill the Archduke Franz Ferdinand."

He looked at me, then burst into laughter. "Well, my Prohaska, that shows how little they have told you back in Austria. But then the gentle-men in Vienna don't really want your Archduke dead either, as far as I can make out. When they first approached us I thought they did, but now I realise what the game is. You see, Major Draganić may be a fighting sol-dier—which by your leave is a good deal more than can be said of anyone in your k.u.k. Armee—but he still has a head on his shoulders. If you ask me, I think that they just want him to get a bad fright so that they can have an excuse for a war with Serbia. And for my part I am content to play along with this game. Because I too have other plans."

"I'm sorry, but I don't understand."

"Your generals—Conrad and Governor Potiorek in Sarajevo and the rest—have long wanted a war to crush Serbia once and for all. But, from what I hear, your old Emperor has always refused to give his permission, while your Archduke swings to and fro like a leaf in the wind: sometimes for war, sometimes against. The one thing that would force their hand is an attack by our fighters on the old man or his Heir-Apparent—provided Vienna can prove that these timorous dogs of a government of ours in Belgrade were behind it."

"Yes, I understand: they would like an attempt to murder the Archduke, but an unsuccessful one. But why should you also wish it to fail?"

"Prohaska, I am a Montenegrin like yourself, not a Serb of Serbia. I have my own plans. I have selected the greatest cretins I could find for this operation because I want it not only to fail, but to fail abjectly. You saw Kardjejev and Dusić and I have seen the rest of them—six in all. And I assure you they're all utterly worthless. In fact I doubt whether they'll even get near the Archduke, because the Austrian police will have rounded them all up days before. With tongues as loose as Kardjejev's and Cabrinović's the lot of them are probably in the police cells already. No, I want them to get caught, because as soon as your Austrian detectives start to squeeze them a little our young heroes will all start blubbering for their mummies and spill the nice uncle police interrogators all the horse-shit I've fed to them these past few weeks: about getting personal orders from old fat-belly Dmitrević on the governing council and perhaps even from that cowardly rat Pasić himself. With evidence like that Conrad and the war-party in Vienna will have everything they need. Tell me Prohaska, did that idiot Kardjejev show you his suicide phial on the train to Loznica?"

"He even unscrewed the top to let us smell it: cyanide of potassium I believe."

He laughed uproariously. "Cyanide of my backside: I bought it myself in a Belgrade grocer's shop. It's almond essence for cakes. The young fool is just going to have the bellyache and smell like a sugared plum in marzipan for a few days after he swallows it, that's all."

"But surely, isn't that . . . rather ruthless of you, to send those poor youths unsuspecting into such a trap?"

"Ruthless, my dear Prohaska? Where the interests of the nation are concerned, no such considerations can apply. Our young friends volunteered to give their lives for Serbia, so as far as I'm concerned it doesn't really matter how they give them. Whether they die on the battlefield or on an Austrian gallows, the sacrifice is the same. The nation is everything, the individual nothing. This is war, and in war it will often be necessary to expend lives in a feigned attack in order to draw the enemy away from the main thrust."

"So the operation at Sarajevo is just a decoy then?"

"Precisely." He paused impressively, like a master artist about to unveil his *chef d'oeuvre*. "My main intention, Prohaska, is to make sure that even if our friends Conrad and Potiorek get their war with Serbia at last, they don't live long to enjoy their success. You see, your Austrian masters have a pretty poor opinion of our national intelligence. They think that we Serbs are only half-witted peasants who play at conspiracy; and I hope that the fiasco in Sarajevo will confirm them in that mistaken view, that we are too stupid to set up more than one plot at a time. No, once the Austrian police have uncovered the conspiracy they will smile and congratulate themselves and buy one another cream cakes in the Konditorei—and leave your Chief of Staff and the Governor to travel on to Foča and fall into my trap. You see, I have information that on the 26th of June, when the manoeuvres end, Conrad and Potiorek will be there to attend a demonstration of a new mountain artillery gun, within sight of the Montenegrin frontier. Well, I have arranged a little demonstration of my own: fifty of my finest Comitadjis armed to the teeth and lying in wait in the forest. None of my men will survive, they know that; but our two military friends will certainly die with them."

"But that means war for certain between Austria and Serbia. How can you hope to win?"

"Not between Austria and Serbia alone, but with Montenegro as well. Hah! I and everyone else knows that the miserable old dog Nikita in Cetinje is getting a secret subsidy from Vienna. But the killing of Conrad and the Governor of Bosnia from Montenegrin territory is something which not even that old fox will be able to explain away. I have my plans for King Nikita Petrović-Njegus as well, I can assure you. Perhaps a month from now it will be King Mirko, since my clan's claim to the throne is quite as good as that of the Petrovici. No, with Montenegro and Serbia in alliance—and with your two best generals dead—we shall certainly win. Perhaps a million Serbs will die, but we shall certainly win."

"Tell me something though, Draganić. Why do you not wish to kill the Archduke? Surely if he ended up dead it would make no difference to you."

He shook his head sadly. "Prohaska, Prohaska, you are really a disgrace to Montenegro. Service with the Austrians has made you as dimwitted as they are. When the Archduke comes to Sarajevo I suspect that your police and military will not be over-zealous about protecting the poor man. However, I have my own men there already, and on the day they will stand next to our young patriots in the crowd just to make sure that no harm befalls him. You may not believe it, but Franz Ferdinand has no more diligent guardian angel in the world than myself at present. My intention is that when he comes to Sarajevo he will be as safe as if he were in his bed at home."

"Why, for goodness' sake? Aren't the Habsburgs the oppressors of all the South Slavs?"

"Maybe they are. But has it ever occurred to you that perhaps the Croats and the Slovenes—even some of the so-called Serbs in Bosnia—perhaps rather like being oppressed, provided that it's their precious Austrian archdukes and their fat Catholic priests who are doing it? I tell you, Prohaska, they talk now of the South Slav nation—Jugoslavia or some such drivel—but I wouldn't give you the pickings of my nose for it. We Serbs are an eastern people like the Russians. What do we want with the filthy Latin-mumbling Croats? No, our future lies to the east: the union of all the Serbs, then one day perhaps Constantinople, the Empire of Stefan Dušan come back to life. I tell you, Prohaska, you may yet one day see the Emperor Mirko of Greater Serbia celebrating Eastertide in the cathedral of Haghia Sophia. As for the wretched Croats and Slovenes, Austria is welcome to them. They can keep Franz Ferdinand and he them since they love one another so much. He will become Emperor in Vienna before long, when the old man in the Schönbrunn dies at last, and all the little Croats and Slovenes will bow and scrape and put on folk-costumes and attend thanksgiving masses and live happily ever after in the land of Edelweiss and potato dumplings. What could be neater? Long live the Emperor Franz Ferdinand! There's certainly no one who wishes him a longer and more auspicious reign than Major Mirko Draganić!"

It was early on the morning of the third day out from Obrenica that we reached the Montenegrin frontier. Not that there was anything to mark the boundary between the two countries, here in this mountainous land where tracts of pine forest alternated with bare limestone screes. The border, Draganić said, ran along a small but very fast river which rushed down a steep-sided valley. Our intended crossing point was an old, high-arched Turkish bridge which carried the rough trackway over the stream into the realms of King Nikita. We were on foot when we reached it, having left the horse and trap in the village where we had spent the night. Draganić was now carrying the rifle quite openly, slung at his shoulder. This, after all, was almost Montenegro and there were wolves and bears in the forests—and anyway, everyone knew that a rifle was part of Montenegrin national costume. No border formalities were anticipated in this wild, remote, thinly populated region. So it was something of a shock for us, descending through the woods towards the bridge, when we saw that it was barred with a red-and-white-striped pole—and that the pole was guarded by an Austrian soldier with rifle and fixed bayonet, dressed in a baggy infantry uniform and shivering in the early-morning chill. He was surreptitiously smoking a cigarette in his cupped hands and, even at this distance, was quite evidently drained as grey as his uniform with boredom.

"Damn it," said Draganić under his breath, "they're posting sentries at the crossings."

"Why? Do you think they've got wind of us?"

"No, it looks like they're after smugglers. There's a lot of it goes on around here, what with the Austrian tobacco duty being so high."

"What are we going to do? Can we wade across the river further up?"

"I wouldn't advise it; it's deeper than it looks and the current's very fast. No, I think I shall merely give our Austrian friend down there the benefit of my personal attention . . ." Smiling grimly to himself, he drew his knife from its sheath and tested the edge with his thumb.

"But Draganić, for God's sake! Surely you don't propose . . ."

"Why not? We'll be at war with Austria within the month. So if one of them gets killed a little early, what does it matter? It keeps them on their toes, and cutting the odd throat from time to time keeps me in practice: I haven't killed a man now for at least six months. And anyway, that slovenly bastard down there deserves death for his unsoldierly bearing. If he was one of my own men I'd have killed him already . . . Hello, what's this?"

As we watched, the soldier at the bridge quickly discarded his cigarette and snapped to attention. An officer was walking up the trackway which ran above the river. He saluted, and they talked for some time. We could hear their voices, but it was too far to make out what they were saying.

"Well," said Draganić, unslinging his rifle, "two will do as nicely as one. Watch this—I bet you'll never have seen markmanship like it. Take the field glasses and look on if you like. I'll just wait until they're in line, then drop the pair of them. What will you bet me that the second one'll be dead before the first hits the ground?" I peered desperately through the field glasses, sickened, as Draganić nestled down and adjusted the butt against his shoulder, then worked the bolt—slowly, so as not to make any noise. The officer had his back to us. He turned—and the floor of my stomach seemed to give way. It was my brother Anton.

# 9

# ACROSS THE BLACK MOUNTAIN

Major Draganić was squinting along the barrel of his rifle. Down by the bridge my brother and the soldier were laughing together, unaware of Death's dry wings rattling above them. I had to act fast. With a sudden scream I leapt and knocked the rifle aside, just as Draganić fired. Anton and the soldier turned, startled. Then my brother drew his pistol and the soldier unslung his rifle as they dived for cover in the undergrowth. That was the last I saw of them, because I was now trying to save my own neck by feigning an epileptic fit, rolling on the ground groaning and twitching as realistically as I could manage. Draganić kicked me, then made for the depths of the forest, dragging me along with him by the collar. When he thought we were safe he propped me up against a tree and dealt me a few heavy slaps about the face.

"In God's name, imbecile! What did you do that for? You'll have the whole Austrian Army after us!"

"Uuh . . . urgh . . . Where am I? . . . What happened? . . . Everything went black . . ."

We lay for some time, expecting pursuit, but after a while we realised that instead of trying to deal with the invisible sniper on their own, Anton and the soldier had wisely gone for assistance. This meant that the bridge across the river was now ours to cross unhindered. Once we were safely on the Montenegrin side I tried to explain as convincingly as I could.

"Sorry . . . I don't feel at all well. It's these fits: I get them sometimes during moments of great nervous tension."

Draganić eyed me suspiciously. "Last time I ever take you with me on active service. In fact if you were a Comitadji you would've been shot by now. Sick men ought not to play at soldiers."

If passport and customs formalities on the Austrian side of the frontier were sketchy, on the Montenegrin side they were entirely non-existent. The Kingdom of Montenegro was a figment of the diplomatic imagination, not a coherent state. The authority of King Nikita barely extended beyond the walls of his palace in Cetinje, far away to the south, while over the rest of his realms his subjects pursued their time-hallowed pastimes of banditry and tribal vendetta pretty well unhindered by central authority. In Bosnia the agents of the law had been our foes; but from now on lawlessness would be the greater enemy.

We made our rendezvous in a forest clearing about five kilometres inside Montenegrin territory. Twelve men awaited us, mounted on mules. Stupanić, my rescuer on the Danube, was there in civilian clothing, as was the bespectacled eminence whom I had already met in Belgrade and whom the others referred to as "the Commander." The rest of the party were plainly locals, barely less ferocious-looking than their fellow-countryman Draganić, festooned with weapons and all wearing the little pillbox cap which was the universal headgear of the Montenegrins: black around the sides and with a red top with five concentric half-circles of gold thread worked into its edge. Mules were provided for Draganić and myself—a great relief to me since my injured leg was aching—and we set off. The Commander rode beside us.

"Well Draganić, you made it after all. We heard a shot about an hour ago. Was that you?"

"I fired at an Austrian sentry on the border."

"Lunatic! Do you want to get us into a war with the Austrians now, before we're ready? Be more careful in future and try thinking more with your brains instead of your testicles."

The trackway wound upwards through the pine forests. Draganić and I were riding near the head of the column as the Commander plied me with questions about our experiences in Bosnia and my contacts in Austria. For my part I tried to answer as neutrally as possible on the last point, but also to find out as much as I could from the questions he asked me. I knew a good deal already about the plot, thanks to Draganić's incurable tendency to melodrama, and I was keen to learn as much as I could about the other operations of Zvaz o Smrt before I finally bade my hosts *adieu*. If these conspiracies were receiving support from Vienna or—more likely—from Budapest, then the more that I could report back to Austrian military intelligence the greater would be my chances of escaping court martial for being absent without leave, perhaps even of getting an "Expression of the All-Highest's Satisfaction" instead.

We were passing now through a region of boulders and stunted pine trees. Suddenly there was a commotion at the rear of the column. Mules were wheeled about, snorting in alarm, and rifle bolts rattled. We halted, waiting. There was an uneasy silence; then I became clammily aware that the tumbled boulders above the trackway contained men crouching among them, pointing their rifles down at us. No one moved. After some time a mounted figure emerged on to the trackway about fifty metres ahead and ambled slowly down towards us, rifle resting casually across the pommel of the mule's saddle. As the mysterious figure came nearer and halted before us I saw to my surprise that it was a young woman with sandy-coloured curly hair. She was dressed like a Montenegrin man, with curl-toed slippers and breeches tight to the calf but baggy from the knee upwards. She wore a waistcoat covered in a sort of mail of silver coins held together by chain, and a sash in which she carried a long-barrelled revolver and a yatagan, the graceful double-curved fighting knife much favoured in those parts. In fact the only difference between her outfit and that of our own Montenegrins was that her red-and-black cap had a veil covering her neck. She surveyed us for a while with haughty contempt before she spoke, her clear girlish voice sounding odd in such a tense situation.

"So, Mirko of the accursed tribe of the Draganici. I see that you have strangers with you. Count yourself fortunate then, for otherwise your carcass would now be lying riddled in the dust. What a poltroon you are, though, to ride straight into an ambush like that. You should be a goose-herd and not a warrior."

Draganić had recovered from his surprise. He roared with laughter.

"Away with you, Zaga Danilović. Go play with your dolls like the other girls and leave fighting to men, or Mirko Draganić will put you across his knee and give you a sound spanking. My father killed your father and I killed your brothers, but I would hate to have to kill a woman as well. You and your oath of virginity though: with a face as ugly as yours I can't see why you bothered."

The girl flushed and her eyes blazed with anger: it was true that she was not a particularly well-favoured young woman. "Handsome is as handsome does, Major Mirko. Have you ever considered how uncommonly well that beautiful head of yours would look stuck on a pole outside our house? I hope to see it there one day, drying in the sun as my father's and brothers' heads once dried outside yours. Anyway, dog-filth and spawn of the Turk, go on your way now in peace. I hope that we shall meet again when you have no guests to hide behind." With that she turned and rode away into the forest, and our column moved forward once more. When we were beyond rifle-range the Commander gave Draganić his views on the incident.

"You damned Montenegrins and your precious četa—you were nearly the death of us all back there. Are you all completely insane or what? Two wars with Turkey in as many years and now perhaps a war with Austria as well, yet you still pour away good Serb blood like water in your idiotic tribal feuds. Save your bullets for your nation's enemies. God only knows there are enough of them!"

I had fallen back in the column and was riding beside Stupanić. "But Stupanić," I said, "I thought that the četa had been outlawed years ago. How did this come about?"

He found this hugely amusing. "Outlawed? Oh yes, of course: send a policeman up here and have them arrested for a breach of the peace. Blessed trinity and the saints, man, look around you: not a metalled road or a school or a railway in this whole terrible little country, only a hundred thousand proud savages like Draganić. Četa outlawed you say? My God, if only you knew! That was no idle talk about heads on poles back there, by the way: they still collect skulls up here the way people in Belgrade collect postage stamps."

"But what's this feud about?"

"The Draganići and the Danilovići? God alone knows—or more

likely he once knew but he's long since forgotten. They say it's been going on for so long that it's just about itself now. The Draganici were once Turkish mercenaries, before they changed sides. If you ask me that's why our Major is such a patriot. The Gospodarijca Zaga's father Njegus Danilović was killed by Draganić's father at Kolašin during the 1912 war. Her brother Slavko killed Draganić's father a few days later, then Draganić and his men shot her two eldest brothers down in an ambush in the 1913 war. Her remaining brother died of cholera at Monastir, so she took an oath of virginity for five years and became a man to carry on the četa and avenge her people. They say she's quite as fierce as any of their warriors and fights in the battle-line with the best of them."

We were nearing our destination now: an isolated farmstead on a barren, stony ridge. Like many farms and villages in these parts it was built like a miniature fortress, designed for defence in the days when this was Turkish territory and the Ottoman Department of Inland Revenue would come round every few years on a tax-collecting expedition, leaving the tree-branches in its wake festooned with the severed limbs of defaulters. The flat-roofed buildings were grouped around a central courtyard, loopholed for musketry and constructed of limestone masonry so solid that it would resist at least field-calibre artillery. We clattered through the gate into the stone-flagged farmyard, occupied on one side by a dung-hill of prodigious size and antiquity. We had arrived at the operational headquarters for the attempt on the lives of the Austro-Hungarian Chief of Staff and the Military Governor of Bosnia-Herzegovina.

A fire was lit in the kitchen, a couple of sheep were killed and dinner was prepared. Just as we were finishing the meal, a sentry came rushing in.

"Commander, Major, there are three horsemen at the gate!"

"What do they want? Who are they?"

"Brothers from Belgrade, Commander. They say that they wish to speak with you urgently."

"Very well, bring them in."

Three weary, dust-caked men entered. They were so covered in the grime of hard riding that it took me several moments to realise with horrified disbelief that I knew one of them already; that in fact it was none other than my one-time room-mate on the Heir-Apparent's staff in Vienna, the enigmatic Hauptmann Belcredi! It also took him quite some time to recognise me. We stared at one another incredulously. He was in civilian clothes: a Norfolk jacket and riding breeches. One of his guides broke the astonished silence.

"Commander, allow me to present the emissary from our friends across the Austrian frontier, Herr Prohaska. He apologises for the delay in getting to you."

I looked around me—and saw that men were already moving discreetly to cut off my line of escape to the door. The Commander spoke.

"But . . . we already have Prohaska with us . . . You can't both be Prohaska."

Belcredi spoke in German. "Commander, Major—I am the man you have named Prohaska and this man is an impostor. He is also called Prohaska as it happens, but that's because it's his real name: Linienschiffsleutnant Otto Prohaska of the Austro-Hungarian Navy. I know, because we once worked together in Vienna. The man is clearly among you as a spy sent by Austrian military intelligence. But I also have the duty of bringing you an urgent message from your people in Belgrade." He drew a white envelope from inside his jacket and handed it to the Commander.

He tore the envelope open and pulled out the letter, then read it in evident disbelief. At last he looked up. "Seize them!" he yelled, "the Austrian and the dog Stupanić! Away with them to the lock up until we've sorted this out! Draganić, you are a thrice-distilled fool, do you know that? You not only allow an Austrian spy to penetrate to the very heart of the society, you sit by while one of your closest associates works for the King of Bulgaria. I assure you, my dear Major, that I shall have your tripes for this when we get back to Belgrade. You are not fit to be a waiter in a coffeehouse, do you understand?"

That was the last I heard of the Commander's remarks, because Stupanić and I were being roughly bundled along a dark stone passageway, Stupanić protesting his innocence and blaming it all on me. We were flung into a small store-room and the great oaken door slammed shut behind us. As the door-bar fell into place outside, Stupanić hammered on the indifferent planks with his fists. His face was the colour of uncooked dough and he was fairly shaking with terror. "It's not true! Listen to me, I tell you it's not true . . . !" He ceased pounding the door and sank to his knees, holding his face in his hands. "Oh Blessed Virgin what will happen to me . . . ?" It was evening now and the sky was darkening in the small barred window set high up in the stone wall. He turned to me. "May Satan dry you up in the flames of hell for this . . . How did you know where to be that morning? How did you know the passwords? Why did I ever pick you up? . . . Oh God, oh God . . ." He fell to sobbing. For myself I sat down on some sacks, and waited. There seemed little else to be done, while as for Stupanić I doubted whether there was much comfort that I could offer him in his present predicament. After about half an hour we heard feet and voices in the passageway outside, then the noise of the door-bar being lifted. The massive door creaked open to reveal Major Draganić and six or seven warriors. The Major was clearly not in a benevolent mood.

"Take him!" he yelled, indicating the wretched Stupanić, who tried to shelter behind me. The ruffians knocked me aside and laid hold of him to drag him, shrieking with terror, out into the passageway. "Good. Take him away then, the filthy traitor, and let's see what he has to say for himself. Is the brazier burning well?"

Begging for mercy, Stupanić was hustled away into the darkness as the door was closed and barred once more, leaving me on my own. I heard shouts and curses, and Stupanić's voice among them.

"No! No! . . . It's not true . . . I can explain . . . No, Mirko . . . No!" Then there was a terrible, prolonged scream, echoing in the stone walls, the agonised howl of some wounded animal. It died away amid a great shout of laughter—and was followed by a shriek even more piercing than the first. I tried to stop my ears to keep out the noise. But I could not block my nostrils as well, to shut out the horrid stink of burning hair which soon penetrated even into my remote prison-cell. The screams rose to a crescendo, then diminished into a sort of crazed, babbling moan punctuated by curses and roars of laughter. It must have gone on for a good hour or so. At length I heard the sound of spades working out in the courtyard, and then Draganić's voice.

"Right then, my men—away to the dung-hill with him! Let every one of you see this and remember that this is how the society Zvaz o Smrt repays treachery." I heard Stupanić's voice for the last time, barely recognisable, still pleading for mercy. There was the sound of many feet and of something being dragged into the courtyard, then one last scream—and the noise of shovelling. At last there was a great cheer, like the howling of a troop of demons. Stupanić had been dealt with; it was my turn now.

The door swung open. Draganić and his assistants entered bearing pine-torches. The Major was swaying slightly from the combined effects of exertion and slivovica. He carried a pair of bloody dental pliers in his huge fist. Two of his attendents laid hold of me, one on each side, pinioning my arms behind my back. I made no resistance: what was the point? The game was up now and all I could hope for was as quick an end as possible. Draganić came up to me and held his great bearded face close to mine. His breath was like an acetylene bicycle lamp.

"Well, my friend Prohaska, let's go and have a little amusement with you, shall we? We shall try and do something about your epilepsy, I think. You heard the song that Brother Stupanić sang for us just now? Well, I hope that you are in good voice as well. Away with him!" The warriors started to drag me towards the door. Then Draganić turned, smiling. "No. Major Mirko Draganić has changed his mind: leave him until morning. The hour is late and we've had good enough sport tonight—and anyway I have had too much to drink. I want a clear head to question this one in the morning." He came back to me and gazed into my eyes with his great bloodshot orbs, like those of an ox's head in the window of a butcher's shop. "Oh, you are an artful one and no mistake, my Prohaska. For seven days you deceived even me. You're as slippery as a frog in a bowl of oil. But not slippery enough to escape Major Draganić this time." He waved the pliers under my nose. "Sniff these, my Prohaska. No doubt you will be able to tell me many interesting things tomorrow about the operations of your intelligence service in Serbia." He suddenly thrust his face close to mine, teeth bared. "But I warn you, don't try to fill my ears with your lies. Because even if I don't know everything about Austria's spying in our country, I know enough to tell when you're feeding me nonsense. Better to tell the truth and die quickly. Because I swear by the Holy Trinity I'll drag it from you piece by piece if it takes me all day to do it. Here, try this little sample . . ." He seized a tuft of my moustache with the pliers—and ripped it out, along with the skin behind it. God, how it hurt! I never imagined that such a small injury could cause such pain. I still have a faint scar on my lip to this day. My eyes watered, but I managed to stay silent and not flinch.

"A little foretaste of what awaits you tomorrow if you try to make a monkey out of me again." He paused, then laughed and slapped my shoulder with his great paw. "But I promise you one thing: you may die under questioning tomorrow or we may kill you once we have squeezed what we want out of you—that depends largely on you—but if you are alive once we have finished with you, then you will die honourably. We buried the dog Stupanić in the dung-hill where he belongs. But you, my Prohaska, who pretended to be a Montenegrin, will meet your end as befits a warrior of our people: from powder and shot, standing on your feet with your face towards the enemy. I, Mirko Draganić, promise this. For it seems to me that he who willingly places himself within the grasp of the Black Hand must be either a very brave man or a very great fool, perhaps both. Anyway, my Prohaska, I bid you good-night." He turned to leave. "You've a hard day ahead of you tomorrow, so I advise you to get some rest while you can. *Dobro spavate!*"

I was left alone in the makeshift prison—alone with thoughts which were the very opposite of agreeable. I had not the slightest reason to doubt, having heard the terrible last hour of Stupanić's life, that they would use every torment in their repertoire to extract information from me tomorrow. The only trouble was that I really had nothing to offer them to avert the pliers and red-hot irons. Draganić was probably telling no less than the truth when he said that he knew enough already about Austrian operations in Serbia to detect whether or not I was lying. I tried to gather my thoughts. It was not just the prolonged and painful end that I faced; it was the very idea of it. For these were the first days of June 1914. The civilised nineteenth century still had a few weeks left to run, and to most people in Europe in those days—even in backward Russia—the idea of torture was scarcely less repugnant than that of cannibalism. That would change in a very few years, as the standards of the Balkans spread to infect the most powerful and advanced nations on earth; but for the moment the very thought was horrifying. I rummaged desperately in the recesses of my mind for all the stories of the Christian martyrs, torn with hooks and roasted on gridirons, and wondered how I would face the ordeal.

But somehow the patient resignation of the martyr has never been part of my make-up. I looked about the store-room, and up at the window. Then I saw what I was looking for: an iron nail protruding from one of the rafters of the low, flat roof. Standing on an empty barrel, I worked it loose after an infinity of effort, then climbed up to the window to begin picking at the mortar which held in the single, vertical iron bar in its middle. The aperture was small, but I might just manage to squeeze through . . . I worked at the mortar for two hours or more, and though my fingers ached and bled I managed to pick about half of it loose. But my spirits sagged as I saw that the bar was no afterthought: the wall had been built around it and it was deeply recessed into the two massive limestone blocks which formed the lintel and sill. To extract it I would need to dismantle the wall around it stone by stone. Exhausted and miserable, I climbed down again and sat on a pile of sacks. I stared at the wall. Perhaps I could pick loose the mortar around a stone . . . Perhaps . . . Perhaps it would be better than sitting here waiting for them to come for me. The square of sky beyond the window was getting light now and the stars were fading. Hopelessly, I sat and stared at the wall. It was at least a metre and a half thick, built of finely cut and well-mortared stone. No, I thought, no use: even a direct hit from a field howitzer would scarcely scratch it.

I believe that I was not too far out there, in my guess about a field-howitzer shell. At any rate, I learnt later that the demolition charge consisted of nearly forty kilograms of dynamite in two knapsacks. Seen from my side of the wall, the effect was certainly dramatic. In fact I am sure that if the masonry had been less solid I would not be here to tell you this. The wall seemed to leap in at me and the floor heaved beneath my feet as a tremendous crash smote the building. I remember little of what happened after this, only of coming round to find myself buried under fallen masonry and roof-timbers and choking with smoke and dust. Only my head, a shoulder and an arm protruded from the rubble as yelling figures ran over me and pistols cracked in the swirling fog. They were attacking in the Montenegrin fashion, charging in line with a yatagan in one hand and in the other a heavy, long-barrelled revolver which fired black-powder cartridges to make the greatest possible flash and smoke. Suddenly a pair of large, slippered feet straddled me as a figure loomed out of the murk. The man above me cursed and fired, then swiped at his assailant with his rifle-butt. He missed and lost his footing. There was a bang, he bellowed and staggered, then collapsed on top of me, nearly crushing out such life as remained in me.

I must have fainted, for when I came to the sun was shining weakly through the thinning smoke and the din of battle had died away. The body was dragged off me—then a hand seized my hair. My head was yanked back and I felt the edge of a knife presented to my throat.

"Gospodarijca, there's one here still alive. Shall I finish him off?"

A familiar voice answered. "Let me see. Oh heavens, no! He's one of their guests. Quick, let's get the poor man out. Help me." Hands scrabbled about me to drag aside the rafters and the ruins of the wall. A few minutes later I was standing unsteadily before my benefactress, cut and bruised and tattered but otherwise unhurt. The Gospodarijca Zaga was weary and powder-stained, but clearly very happy. She was wiping her blood-smeared knife on a rag.

"Here, catch!" she said, and threw something to me. Without think-ing, I caught it. I had never before imagined that a human head would weigh so much. I stood for a moment, staring in horror at the ghastly thing: at Draganić's bloodshot, rolled-up eyes and the white teeth clenched in the rictus of death. Then nausea welled up inside me and I dropped it in disgust.

"Oh do be careful," she said, "don't drop it like that or you'll bruise it. I want it to be in good condition for my mother. Lord though, what a tough neck the dog had. I've quite taken the edge off my knife." Draganić's headless corpse lay nearby. He had been shot through the heart by a bullet from the Gospodarijca's revolver. "Anyway," she said, "who are you and where do you come from?"

Uncertain of what the Danilovici would do to me if they learnt my true identity, I tried to explain as best I could how I came to be here without saying who I really was. It appeared that I was the only survivor from the party in the farmhouse. The Commander and Hauptmann Belcredi had left the previous evening, while of the remainder, all had either been killed or had fled. To my surprise though, my reasons for being here—the society Zvaz o Smrt and the rest—seemed to interest the Gospodarijca not one bit.

"Well, Radić, you can't stay around here, that's for sure. This is Draganić country and they'll be after us like a nest of hornets once they hear of our deeds here today. We shall burn the farmstead and then scatter into the mountains. You had better come with me: you were their guest and they are no more, so as a stranger you now fall under the protection of my clan. You say you come from the Bay of Cattaro?"

"Yes, from Castellnuovo."

"Then we had better get you back there as soon as we can. The whole country north of the Morača will be up in arms against us once they learn of this, and our quarrels are no affair of yours."

"Thank you for your concern, Gospodarijca, but why should you trouble yourselves to protect me?"

"It's the custom. But tell me, are you hurt? Are you able to walk?"

"Just a bit bruised and shaken, thank you, and my leg aches a little from an old wound. I can still walk though."

"Good. But we shall have mules to take us to my family's house this day even if we have to walk from there onwards."

"We . . . ?"

"Yes, I shall be your guide myself. I know the whole of the country to the Morača. You would only get lost in the mountains and perish. Once I get you to the river I can hand you over to relatives of mine who will escort you to Cetinje. Anyway, let's fire the buildings and get moving."

Torches were applied to the wooden roofs of the farmstead, and before long a column of smoke and sparks was rising into the clear blue morning sky. We only lost sight of it as we climbed over the ridge of the mountain.

Until then I had never appreciated how glorious a place inland Montenegro is. As a sailor my acquaintance with the land of the Black Mountain— Crna Gora—had been limited to its seaward side, that desolate coastal range of limestone karst-mountains—treeless, waterless, eroded, seemingly cursed by God at the creation of the world to perpetual barrenness. Here, though, in the north-western part of the little mountain-kingdom, the scenery was quite different. The mountains were just as precipitous and even higher than the Lovčen range above the town of Cattaro, but here they were decently clad in forest: chestnut and oak on the lower slopes; tall, graceful black pines on the higher faces. Sparkling streams cascaded along the narrow valleys through meadows of vivid green, densely sprinkled with flowers of every kind. The streambeds, I noticed, were a peculiar bright turquoise colour—I suppose from some copper salt or other that had stained the limestone. It was a landscape that sometimes recalled Switzerland, sometimes the Atlas Mountains in Morocco. The only disturbing thing about this demi-paradise was that no one appeared to live there. We saw not a house nor a hut in all that day of riding, while the only other human being we encountered was a charcoal-burner in the forest. I imagine that four centuries of occupation by the Turks—not to speak of the četa—had done much to keep down the population level.

We rode up to the Danilović homestead early that evening. It was a circular wall of dry stones topped with a wooden palisade and surrounding a single, long, steep-roofed wooden hall rather like a ship turned upside-down. It was a noble enough building from the outside, but furnished inside as austerely as a cowshed. As we made our way up the trackway towards the gate I noticed a number of poles fixed at intervals on the palisade with round objects on the tops of them. It was some moments before I realised with a shudder what these were. Some, I saw on closer inspection, were mere skulls, bleached clean by years of sun and rain and frost, though one of them wore a Turkish fez which seemed quite new.

Others—evidently the more recent additions—were horribly shrivelled black things. I knew that soon another head would be put on display there: the head of Major Draganić, which bounced in a sack hanging at the Gospodarijca Zaga's saddle. We stopped in the courtyard amid an excited crowd of relatives and retainers. Prominent among them was a wrinkled but still straight-backed old woman of (I thought) about seventy. This was the Gospodarijca's mother who—I later learnt—was barely forty years of age. Zaga rummaged in the sack, and there was a great cheer as she triumphantly held up the head of Draganić by its black hair. She tossed it to her mother.

"A present for you, Mama."

"Thank you my dear. My, isn't he a beauty? He shall have the place of honour at our feast this evening."

The celebratory dinner consisted of roast mutton and flat Turkish bread followed by curious little honey-flavoured doughnuts, and an unspeakably nasty drink called "loza," a sort of brandy made from the residue after grape-pressing and which united perfectly the flavours of benzine and that horrid bitter taste one gets from inadvertently crunching a grape-pip. I had once thought that slivovica must be the foulest drink on earth, but even the rawest of Serbian plum brandies was nectar compared with this fluid. I downed a thimble-sized glass for courtesy's sake. The Gospodarijca smiled.

"How do you like our native drink then? We say here that after three glasses you will be able to speak all the languages of the world, while after four you will not even be able to speak your own language."

But at least a glass of loza, vile as it was, helped me to avoid looking at Major Draganić's bloody head, reposing in a basket in the middle of the table and already turning a mottled blue.

After the meal, in honour of that morning's successful raid, we were entertained by a wandering poet, a guslar, who had arrived at the homestead a few days before. He was blind, and his assistant, a young boy, led him into the hall to sit by the fire. Then he began to sing. I think that I had never heard such a strange sound: so uncouth yet so oddly moving, as if I had suddenly stepped back three millenia to the halls of Menelaos.

It was an unearthly, wailing lament in archaic Serb, accompanied on the gusle, a kind of primitive one-string fiddle which gave out a note somewhere between that of a hurdy-gurdy and a man blowing across the top of an empty bottle. To an ear brought up on Brahms and Smetena it was barely recognisable as music at all, without apparent melody or form or metre. Yet as it progressed there was a strange hypnotic quality about it, and pattern began to emerge as stanza succeeded stanza. It told of the battle at a place called Kragujevo Polje in 1877 or thereabouts, when the Gospodarijca Zaga's grandfather and his warriors had wiped out a Turkish army led by the villainous Bey of Novipazar. Verse after verse the song wound on, each word seeming to tear its way out of the old man's breast as he told of the valour of the Montenegrins and the deeds each of them had performed that day. Each stanza ended with the refrain "And never feasted the crows so well as there upon Kragujevo's field."

Zaga and I set out before dawn the next morning, on foot this time. We carried a leather knapsack full of smoked mutton and bread for provisions, a water bottle, and a revolver and a yatagan each stuck in our sashes. There were no mirrors in these parts, but I must have looked a grotesque figure as we left the Danilović homestead to start our journey. I was still wearing the remains of the three-piece suit and felt hat which Stupanić had given me that day when he had rescued me stark naked on the banks of the Danube. But I now had a red sash to carry my weapons and—since my cheap shoes had long since fallen to pieces—a pair of Montenegrin cloth-boots. These were made by winding my legs and feet in strips of cloth until I looked like an old man at Marienbad with gout in both legs. Then bull-hide slippers were tied on over these clumsy leggings with leather thongs. The effect was anything but graceful to look at, but the Gospodarijca assured me that this footwear gave an unrivalled grip for rock-climbing.

This was certainly going to be needed over the next few days; that much became clear after the first few kilometres of our journey. Our route lay along the bottom of the deep, wooded canyon of the River Tara. We were to head upstream, south-eastwards, for about thirty kilometres, then cross the mountains into the valley of the Morača and head southwards towards Cetinje. In these early stages of the journey the Gospodarijca made us cross the rushing, foaming torrent wherever we could so that our footprints and scent would be lost to any pursuers. Word of the previous day's events would have got around by now, she said, and Draganić's kinsmen would certainly be out hunting for us. This went on for most of the first day. I found it heavy going, clambering over the boulders along the bottom of the canyon. My leg hurt, and when we stopped for a rest at midday and I had a chance to remove my leg-windings, I discovered a painful, hard lump forming on the side of the calf. It looked as if the Freiherr von Eiselberg had been right after all about the bone splinter. It would take about eighteen months to work to the surface, he had said, and we were now nearly eighteen months after my accident.

We camped out that night in a high forest, then set off again next morning at first light. My leg was making me limp now as we trudged along the barely discernible trackway that passed for a road. But at least I had the Gospodarijca Zaga's company to divert me, for despite her regrettable choice of hobbies she was undeniably a lively and talkative young woman. I soon discovered also that there was more to her than I had at first supposed. Certainly Draganić's fatal jibe about her looks had a good deal of point to it. Slightly built and of medium height, she had sandy-coloured curly hair, protruding teeth and curious eyes, set slightly too far apart and slightly too high up in her face, which gave her the look of a sheep. And this plainness was all the more apparent because the Montenegrins were in general a remarkably fine-looking people: Serb in language and sentiment, but not in the least Slavic in appearance, being tall and slender with straight black hair and ivory complexions and marvellous high-arched noses like eagles' beaks. The women, I remember, were particularly splendid creatures, endowed with a nobility and easy grace of carriage that made the world's queens and empresses look like washerwomen. In the coastal towns they would dress from head to foot in black, so that the streets of Cattaro on market day always seemed to have become the venue for some vast royal funeral. But it has to be said that if they had the bearing of royalty, they also shared much of its intellectual nullity. I had been stationed on the Gulf of Cattaro back in 1910 and had become very much enamoured, as young men will, of a certain Jadranka Menotti, wife of a wine merchant in Castellnuovo. I had pressed my attentions upon her and eventually got her to bed one afternoon when her husband was away. I well remember how, when she finally admitted me to her favours, it was with the distant air of a duchess at a garden party offering two gloved fingers to be shaken. And how, as I neared the summit of my endeavours, she suddenly asked, apropos of nothing, "And is it your opinion, Capitano, that we shall have a good crop of damsons this year?" Young and foolish as I was, I had still to learn that not every sphinx has a riddle and that not every sheet of ice covers hidden depths.

But then, Montenegrins of the male sex were not a great deal better as far as I could make out: brave as tigers, no question of that, and honourable in their way, but indolent, vain, cruel and generally rather empty-headed. A few months after these events (I was later told) the Montenegrin division fighting alongside the Serbs at Cer Mountain was comprehensively destroyed in a few minutes by our artillery because its soldiers had refused to dig themselves in, holding it to be beneath the dignity of warriors to skulk in holes in the ground.

Anyway, perhaps as a result of her lack of looks to carry her through life, Zaga Danilović seemed to have a lot more going on in her attic rooms than the rest of her fellow-countrymen. By the standards of civilised Europe pre-1914 she was unquestionably a bloodthirsty savage. I was a serving officer, but I doubt whether I would have charged an enemy position with quite such reckless dash—or had the stomach to hack a dead enemy's head off afterwards. Yet I found that she was not only well-informed about the rest of the world, but also literate—quite extraordinary in a country with only one school and where women were commonly treated as draught-animals. She chatted gaily as we trudged onwards, making the mountain slopes less steep and the knapsack lighter with her high spirits. But the greatest surprise was yet to come. We talked in Serb, but at one point, being unable to remember the correct expression, I used a Viennese-French one instead—*"das ist mir tout égal"* or some such. This seemed to flick a switch. Her eyes lit up with delight.

*"Ah m'sieur, donc vous parlez français? Mais quel plaisir!"*

There followed a stream of perfect idiomatic French, so far as I could tell without any trace of accent. I tried my best to keep up with her, but the strain on my starch-collared naval-diplomatic French was severe, reeking as it did of the schoolroom and official receptions aboard visiting warships. For not only did she speak with perfect fluency, she also appeared to be well acquainted not only with the classics of French literature (which she automatically assumed I must also have read) and music and painting, but also with writers like Mauriac and Anatole France who were in those days so avant-garde as to be barely discernible on the horizons of an Austrian naval lieutenant. At last I managed to ask her:

"But Gospodarijca, tell me if you will: how is it that you speak such excellent French?"

"Oh, I spent two years in the Lyceum for the Daughters of the Nobility in Cetinje. Ugh! I hated it—having to wear silly long dresses and a hat and white gloves and not being able to spit or pick my teeth. But at least I learnt French and German and Russian while I was there."

"Why did you leave?"

"I ran away."

"But how did you carry on your study of French?"

"My teacher ran away with me: Mademoiselle Lannette from Tours. She hated it there as well, so she came to live with my clan. She wore men's clothes and after a while she could shoot and use a knife as well as any Montenegrin. She was killed in a skirmish with the Draganici. But I think that France must be the most wonderful country in the world, and Paris the noblest of cities. Mademoiselle Lannette used to say that it's even bigger than Cetinje. My own country has many poets and philosophers too, and our bravery in warfare is without equal; but I am afraid that my people is ethically underdeveloped and backward in the arts of civilisation." She paused for a few moments, wondering whether to take me into her confidence. Then she spoke. "Lieutenant Radić, I will tell you this because I think that you are now my friend as well as the guest of my family. I have long had a dream in my heart that one day, when I am a little older and the četa with the Draganici is over, I shall go to France to study in Paris, and then come back here one day to devote myself to raising the philosophical and cultural level of my people. And now of course I can! Draganić is dead, so the blood-debt of my father and brothers is wiped out. That is why I have chattered and sung like a lark these two days, because I am so happy. Here" (she rummaged inside her blouse), "here, I shall show you something that I have never shown to anyone else." She fumbled and drew out a grubby, dog-eared wad of paper, stained and damp with sweat. She handed it to me to examine. It was a folded map: "Carte de la Ville de Paris et ses Environs—Editions Hachette 1906."

"There," she said, "I have worn it next to my heart these past two years because I know that one day I shall go there. I have memorised every street now. Tell me, dear Lieutenant, have you ever been there?" As it happened I had: for two days in 1907 when I was on my way to London to begin a six-month posting with the Royal Navy. She turned to gaze at me as if I were some walking holy relic. "Oh Lieutenant, how marvellous! And do the painters all live about Montmartre? I long to meet them all. Tell me, did you speak with Ravel while you were there? One day I shall go there, I know it."

Midday passed. We had climbed above the treeline and were now traversing an arid patch of tumbled limestone boulders and scrub, an outlier of the coastal karst-fields. The heat shimmered from the pale-grey rock as we made our way along a shallow defile. Suddenly my eye was caught by something beside the trackway. It was a human skull, lying like a discarded milk jug as its empty eye-sockets gazed forlornly up at us. Then there was another, then a rib-cage, then a near-complete skeleton. Soon the ground all around us was littered with bones and rusted weapons and age-rotted fragments of military equipment. And everywhere, strewn among the rocks, lay thousands of brass cartridge cases. The remains of a wooden cart lay beside the track, drawn by two skeletal oxen permanently yoked together in death. Whatever had taken place here had quite obviously happened a long time ago, to judge from the few tatters of faded cloth which still fluttered among the heaped-up bones lying in the gullies in the rock.

"Whose remains are these?" I enquired of the Gospodarijca, who seemed not to consider the bones worthy of any special remark.

"Oh, these? This is the Kragujevo field of which the guslar sang. My grandfather defeated an army of Turks here once, many years ago."

"And do your grandfather's bones lie here as well?"

She flushed. "Goodness no—what an idea! No, we gathered up our own dead and took them down into the valley for burial. But the Turk we left here for the buzzards and foxes."

"Did your grandfather's men take many prisoners?"

"Only one: the Bey of Novipazar himself. All the others we put to the sword. But him we kept so that we could repay him for his villainies."

"What had he done?"

"Done? His cruelties and oppressions were a byword even among the Turks. The year before, his men had captured my great uncle Milan alive. They hanged him from a gibbet in Kolašin marketplace with an iron hook through his ribs. He took three days to die, but they say he passed as a warrior should, cursing the Bey and his men to the end. So my grandfather's men ambushed a column of Turks in the Tara gorge and killed them all, except for one man whom they sent back to Novipazar with a letter to the Bey nailed to his head. Then the Bey and his men raided Mohačko at the Epiphany feast and killed a thousand people and took my great uncle Dušan and his wife and daughters prisoner. They impaled the women on stakes on the battlements of Novipazar. They made Dušan watch and had a brazier and irons ready to blind him so that their agony would be the last thing he saw. But he had the better of them. He was a strong man even for a Montenegrin and he tore his chains from the wall, smashed the executioner's head with them and then flung himself off the walls on to the rocks in the riverbed below." She smiled. "Yes, he died like a warrior."

"And the Bey of Novipazar?"

"Oh, when my grandfather's men caught him they treated him like the dog he was: cut his balls off and roasted them on skewers and made him eat them, then skinned him alive. They say his screams were heard in Kolašin. My grandfather had his head fixed up over our gate and gave orders that a new fez should be fixed to it each year in memory. As for his skin, they tanned it and made it into a mat. I used to play on it when I was little," she added brightly.

I was silent for some time after this. Not only had the melancholy sights of the old battlefield made a deep impression on me, but I was also left feeling rather unwell by the fearful catalogue of atrocity and counter-atrocity recited by the Gospodarijca—and by the cheerful tone of voice in which she had recounted it, as if she were reporting the results of a badminton tournament at one of Vienna's more select girls' schools. I slept badly that night. It was cold and my leg hurt even worse than the previous day, and I was troubled by disturbingly vivid dreams: dreams in which Rimbaud roasted Debussy over a slow fire and armies of skeletal warriors in fezzes stormed barricades of painters' easels on the slopes of the Butte de Montmartre while the guslar's haunting wail echoed through the streets: "Never feasted the crows so well as there in the Parc Monceau."

# 10

# FUGITIVES

W E WERE OFF AGAIN AT FIRST LIGHT THE NEXT MORNING, descending through the forests into the valley of the River Morača. Along this ran one of the Kingdom of Montenegro's two (more or less) metalled roads. Our plan was to follow this southwards until we came to the town of Podgorica, where the valley opened out into a plain, then turn north-westwards to climb up to the Montenegrin capital, the town of Cetinje.

The problem was that my leg was plainly not going to carry me that far. The swelling caused by the bone splinter attempting to surface had got worse in the night, and by mid-morning I could barely hobble along on a stick. At length Zaga took me aside into the pine forest and laid me down on a bank of moss. She unwrapped the leg-winding to examine the hard, blue-black lump.

"This looks bad," she said. "I shall have to cut it open and dig the splinter out." My hair fairly stood on end at this.

"Are you mad, Gospodarijca? Cut it open? It'll turn gangrenous. And what will you cut it with?"

She drew her yatagan. "With this. I'll bet that I've treated more wounds in my time than you're ever likely to see. There are no doctors or surgeons where I come from."

"But the risk of infection . . ." I thought with distaste of the things I had seen her use her knife for during the past five days: as a weapon, for eating at table and for removing people's heads. She laughed at my fears.

"There," she said, flicking the blade with her thumbnail so that it rang, "do you hear that? The very finest steel. This knife has been mine all my life: they even cut the cord with it when I was born. How could steel as noble as this cause an infection, I ask you? I never heard such nonsense in my life. But wait, I must make some liniment." She took a small pottery flask of the villainous loza from our knapsack and disappeared into the trees for ten minutes or so, leaving me to wonder desperately what I had let myself in for. When she returned she was shaking the flask vigorously. "Resin of the black pine dissolved in loza—the very best embrocation for open wounds, better than all the doctor's medicines."

I shut my eyes tight and clenched a leather strap between my teeth as she got to work with the tip of the yatagan. It was only a minute or so, I think, but still the longest minute of my life. I tried not to whimper, but at the very end I could not hold back a yelp of pain as she pulled out the splinter. I opened my eyes as she held it up for my inspection: a blood-streaked white fragment the size and shape of a dog's tooth.

"There now—so much noise and about so little. You call yourself a Serb and a soldier: what sort of warriors must the Emperor of Austria's men be when they make so much fuss about such a trifle? There are far worse things, I can tell you." She was quite right there: the operation itself might have been agony, but it was the sweetest of caresses compared with the application of the loza-and-resin dressing, which caused me to let out a howl of pain that rang across the valley and came echoing back from the mountainside opposite. "There," she said cheerfully, "it stings, doesn't it? But it keeps wounds clean like magic."

She was right, oddly enough: the swelling decreased as the day wore on and the primitive ointment did indeed seem to soothe the inflammation once the initial searing agony was past. It was plain though to both of us that I would not be able to walk much further, once we had reached the road in the valley bottom. We sat by the roadside and wondered what to do next. But as we debated whether to ask for help at the next farm—even though the farmer might be a kinsman of the Draganici—or make for the Morača monastery and seek refuge with the monks, my ear caught a distant sound—familiar, but wildly incongruous in this primitive little country. Surely it couldn't be? Not in this enclave of Afghanistan in Europe? But it was: the honking of a motor-car horn. Before long the source of the noise hove into sight, lurching along the potholed trackway which passed for a made-up road in these parts. It was a large and extremely battered Panhard motor car of the Royal Montenegrin Postal Service, carrying the week's mailbags from Kolašin down to the sorting office at Podgorica. The driver was a genial young man and also—more to the point—a distant kinsman of the Gospodarijca. So we climbed on top of the mail-sacks, the two of us, and set off down the winding valley road. No questions had been asked about why two dishevelled, armed wayfarers, one of them quite obviously injured, should be so anxious to make their way southwards. Blood feuds and tribal warfare were clearly such normal features of life in this strange land that any prying into other people's business would be regarded as the height of bad form.

I thought that I had been through enough hair-raising experiences over the previous two weeks to last most people a lifetime. But those thirty kilometres in the post-car along the road from Kolašin to Podgorica surpassed the lot of them in sheer, stark terror. The vehicle itself, though less than two years old to judge by its bonnet-marque, was in the last stages of decrepitude, to a degree where it was nothing short of miraculous that the thing moved at all. The exhaust manifold had long since gone by the board, so the eight cylinders all blasted deafeningly into the air. The rust-eaten bodywork and running boards were so caked with mud and dust that they seemed to have grown out of the earth, and were lashed together by a network of old rope and lengths of wire. In several places I saw the unmistakable holes left by rifle bullets. As for the gearbox, I doubt whether it any longer contained a single drop of oil. The gears ground and screeched with a noise that was a torment to hear, while the driver would assist the lever from second gear into third with a hammer which lay on the floorboards. And as for the brakes, they had long since given up the ghost: the driver would stop the car by running it up a convenient slope, then jump out to wedge a baulk of timber under the back wheels.

This was bad enough, but our chauffeur's driving style was infinitely worse. In truth, it would have been alarming enough in the middle of a smooth plain. But here, lurching along the narrow, winding trackway cut into the walls of the Morača gorge, with the torrent rushing along a hundred metres below, it was one of the severest moral tests that I ever had to endure. All that I could do was brace myself atop the mailbags, squeeze my eyes shut and repeat in my mind, like the decades of the rosary, "Hail Mary, full of grace; this man has no more wish to die than I have; this man knows what he is doing and has travelled this road many times before; this man has a wife and children whom he loves dearly waiting for him at home."

At last the Morača canyon began to broaden out while the mountains on either side became lower and more devoid of vegetation. We were leaving inland Montenegro and entering the desolate karsts of the region along the coast, the Kameno More as the Serbs called it—the Sea of Stone. We would soon be in Podgorica and would then take the road westwards up into the mountains once more, towards the country's village-capital of Cetinje. It would be about a day's journey, I thought. Once there I would make straight for the Austro-Hungarian Legation and get them to telegraph directly to Vienna with the news of the double assassination plot. We still had time. I was not exactly sure of the date, so much had happened over the past two weeks; but by counting back I worked out that today was probably 10 June. The Heir-Apparent and Field Marshal Conrad were not due to attend the Bosnian manoeuvres until the last week of the month; and in any case, for all I knew the attack near Foča had already been called off after the death of Major Draganić. If the main threat was now in Sarajevo, then two weeks should be ample time for our police to round up the plotters—that is, if Kardjejev had not already landed them all in jail—and to arrest Hauptmann Belcredi when he reappeared on Austrian territory.

Our car lurched to a sudden, groaning, shuddering halt, nearly tipping the Gospodarijca and me into the dust as the driver ran its front wheels up the roadside bank to stop it. We had been waved down by an elderly countryman with white moustaches and a rifle slung across his back, mounted on a donkey while his black-clad wife trudged behind, bent double beneath an enormous bundle of firewood. Our driver leant out.

"What is it, little father?" he asked pleasantly. "Has there been another landslide further down?"

"No, my son, there are soldiers a rifle-shot further along, around the next bend. They are barring the road because they seek a woman of our people, and a stranger . . ." He looked at me with his bright eyes " . . . a stranger in foreign dress with a lame leg. I talked with them and they spoke of treasonable plots against King Nikola and the House of Petrović-Njegus; also of an Austrian spy."

The driver turned to us. "Well, my friends, I must not carry passengers anyway, they tell me, so I must drop you here. God speed you both to wherever you wish to be."

"May God and all his saints reward you for the ride," said Zaga. (I would have muttered, "The Devil and all his imps," but it would have been ungrateful.) We waved goodbye as the wreck of a car rattled away down the road like the stock of an ironmonger's shop being rolled along in an oildrum. We wondered what to do next. But the old man and his wife seemed to share in the general Montenegrin sympathy for people on the run. Zaga asked him how he thought we might evade the road-block to reach Podgorica. He stroked his moustaches for ten minutes or so (time clearly meant very little in these parts) then spoke.

"There is a fisherman's hut down there by the river, little daughter. One Milan Milanković owns it. He has several boats, and he would certainly let you borrow one to paddle down to Podgorica, provided you left it there for him to collect."

"But is the river navigable? It looks very fast from up here."

"God alone can say. At this time of year it usually is."

We scrambled down the rocky sides of the valley to the fisherman Milanković's hut, which lay just above a small, stony beach. Four or five of the local skiffs were drawn up in front of it—curious little craft with pointed, turned-up stems and sterns, each of them made from a hollowed-out tree-trunk with sides of planking. Milanković was amenable—needless to say, he too was a distant relative of Zaga's clan—so we decided to chance it. Soon we were hurtling down the River Morača at terrifying speed, paddling desperately to avoid the giant boulders that loomed ahead of us every few dozen metres. We just had time to look up and see the soldiers and their road-block on the cliffs above. Luckily for us, we saw them before they caught sight of us. We were almost around the next bend in the river before the bullets began splashing around us and whining off the rocks.

About five kilometres down towards Podgorica the river, though still very fast, became broader and less liberally scattered with boulders. It was beginning to get dark as we passed under the first of the bridges above the town. We negotiated the first three without incident, but as we neared the fourth and last, on a stretch where the river was slow enough to have reed-beds along its banks, some instinct made us slow down. There was just enough light to see the sentry with rifle and bayonet pacing up and down on the bridge. We pulled in to the bank, half hidden by the reeds. He seemed alert, the bridge was low and I very much doubted whether we would be able to slip beneath it without being fired upon. But before I could decide what to do the Gospodarijca had made her own decision. Silent and agile as a cat, she sprang ashore, then drew her knife and began to creep through the undergrowth. I waited with my heart pounding. At length there was a brief scuffle on the bridge, a muffled "Ooof!" then a splash as something fell into the water. I felt desperately sick, Zaga returned, wiping her yatagan as casually as if she had just killed a chicken. We pushed off and paddled cautiously downstream once more. We had to keep silent. But there was nothing that I could have said anyway to express my feelings.

Some hours later we were in difficulties again. It was dark now. Rags of cloud were beginning to drift across the moon as we glided through the marshes that fringed the shallow Scutari Lake, threading our way along the shallow channels among the banks of silt and beds of reeds and water-lilies where the River Morača formed a miniature delta. The problem now was quite simply that we were lost. I had never before seen the lake—the Bojanasee as we used to call it—except from the air, while as for the Gospodarijca, her knowledge of her country's geography, though intimate, seemed to be very local. All I knew was that on the other side of the lake was a village called Virpazar which formed the terminus of a narrow-gauge mountain railway up from the Montenegrin coast at Antivari. Whether it was still working I could not say, since I knew that it had been damaged by the Turks during the 1912 war. Still, it was worth a try.

Cetinje was out of the question, now that the Montenegrin Army was after us as well as the Draganić clan, and my leg was in no condition for nocturnal mountaineering. We paddled onwards, trusting to our sense of direction and the sluggish, barely detectable current to lead us out on to the lake. Every now and then we would paddle into a flock of roosting waterfowl and send them flapping and screaming into the air.

At last we saw a light on the opposite shore. The black mountains loomed ahead of us, so we must be on the right course. And as it happened we were, for half an hour later we were tying our skiff up to a small wooden jetty on the edge of Virpazar. We made for the railway station, a simple wooden shed. There was no sign of life, except for one paraffin lamp, and grass grew between the rusty nails. We called, "Anyone there?" After some time a figure appeared with a hurricane lamp.

"What d'you want at this hour?" It was the station master.

"We're two travellers who want to get to Antivari. What time is the next train?"

He looked at us in amazement. "Where have you been living, then? There hasn't been a train here for the past eighteen months. The Turks dynamited the line during the war, God rot them, and no one's got around to repairing it yet. But who are you anyway? . . ." We mumbled some apologies and set off back to the jetty as fast as we could. The only course open to us now was to head southward down the lake towards the end where the River Bojana debouched into the Adriatic Sea. I knew that the Austro-Lloyd line ran a weekly steamer service up into the lake, but when exactly it ran I was unable to say. Tired out and aching, we cast off our skiff and paddled out into the lake once more. It was beginning to rain. We paddled for an hour or more—until we stopped and strained our ears. It was the put-put-put of a motor boat—coming in our direction. We altered course for the bushes along the shore, but too late. A spotlight beam swung round to see us and a distant voice shouted, "There they are!" Before we had time to think, bullets were plopping about us in the water. In the event we just beat them to the shore, abandoned the skiff and scrambled into the trees as a machine gun clattered in the darkness and bullets thwacked through the tree-branches above us. The motor boat followed us in. Soon we could hear men scrambling ashore. We had no choice now. Leg or no leg, it was over the mountains or die.

That nocturnal crossing of the Rumija Mountains stands out in my memory even now as one of the worst nights of my life. The range is not wide—no more than ten or twelve kilometres I should think—but is precipitous in the extreme, rising almost sheer to two thousand metres from the Scutari Lake and then falling again with equal abruptness to the Adriatic shore on the other side. I had often seen it from the decks of ships as we passed along the coast, its grey, bare limestone ramparts as jagged and forbidding as the mountains of some long-dead planet. But that was not the worst of it, for over much of its lower slopes the Rumija massif was covered in the typical undergrowth of the karst country, what the French call *maquis:* a tightly matted, impenetrable scrub of dwarf oak and pine and myrtle and oleander and gorse mixed with sharp-edged shards of limestone like fragments of broken glass in a scouring pad, heaven to smell in May and June, but hell on earth to try and negotiate. My mind went back to a morning years before when I had been a cadet in charge of a landing party trying to capture a small fort on Brazza Island, and we had taken five hours to cover two hundred metres through the tangled scrub, arriving only when the exercise was already long over and the umpires had given Landungsdetachement Prohaska up for dead. But at least that had been in daylight and in good weather, and I had not been exhausted and dragging an injured leg—or had armed men behind me seeking my life. Several times that terrible night I fell, and begged the Gospodarijca to leave me and save herself. But always she dragged me up by my collar and struggled on, giving me her shoulder to lean on and hauling me over the great tumbled boulders. In the end our salvation was a goat-track, otherwise I should not be here now telling you this. This allowed us to make better speed upwards and shake off our pursuers for the moment. We heard voices and the occasional shot behind us, but these grew fainter and fewer as the scrub and the drizzling low cloud slowed them down. We were left to carry on our torturing climb through the scratching, tearing undergrowth and then, when that thinned out, across the crags and boulder-screes. It seemed to go on for ever. Then we noticed that the slopes were becoming less steep; eventually that they were beginning to slope the other way.

The climb to the top of the Rumija range was pure torment; but I found that on balance the descent of the other side in the early morning wet and darkness was even worse, picking our way among the bone-jarring jumble of rocks and down precipices—then once more into the hateful *maquis*. We followed what seemed to be a faint path, but soon it petered out among a patch of scrub so densely matted that not all the buffaloes and rhinoceroses in the world could have battered a path through it. I had not the remotest idea where we were, none at all; and by now I cared even less.

"Gospodarijca . . . we can't go on . . . not any more . . ." She nodded, utterly spent.

"No . . . not any more . . . neither can I. Let's just lie here . . . At least we'll be safe until morning here in the undergrowth."

So we lay down, exhausted, wet and scratched to ribbons, and huddled together for what warmth we could find in the chill drizzle. But as we were falling into the dead sleep of bone-weariness, my ears caught a faint sound. At first I wondered whether it was some ringing in my ears brought on by exhaustion. But no, there could be no doubt about it: it was the gentle lapping of waves on a beach.

When we awoke, stiff and cold, it was just after dawn. The rain had cleared, but the sun had still a long way to rise before its warming rays would shine over the great towering range of cliffs above us. As I gazed up at them from the scrub it was barely credible that we should have been able to descend them in daylight and clear weather, let alone in darkness and low cloud. Then I tried to move—and groaned in pain. Each joint seemed to have been expertly dislocated by some Chinese master-torturer, my body to have shrunk until my skin was several sizes too large for it. Zaga stirred. She looked quite as awful as I felt—barely human after our night's journey. She yawned and stretched.

"Well," she said, "I'm starving and so must you be. I must go and forage something to eat before we stir another arm's length."

"But where . . . ?"

"I heard goat-bells just now. That means that there must be a hut nearby. Wait here until I come back." She disappeared into the undergrowth. '

I lifted myself up, creaking like an old chair from my multitude of aches, and looked out over the shoulder-high carpet of *maquis*. Then my heart leapt in my breast for joy as I gazed about me: I knew where we were! We had spent the night on a low, scrub-covered ridge of limestone just above the pebbly shore of a wide, shallow bay. A few kilometres to southward, scattered over a spur of the mountainside, I could make out a group of white buildings which I knew must be the town of Antivari. At the other extremity of the bay, about seven or eight kilometres to north-westward, was a group of rocky headlands. Behind these lay two conical mountain peaks. The smaller, more eastern of these was crowned with ruins which I recognised as the old Venetian fortress of Haj-Nehaj. And just south of this, I knew, lay the village of Spizza, latitude 42 08' North.

"There," you will doubtless say to yourselves at this point, "we have caught the old liar out at last. How could anyone possibly remember a detail like that after nearly three-quarters of a century?" But understand if you will that the precise position of Spizza had been indelibly branded on to my adolescent consciousness in my very earliest days at the k.u.k. Marine Akademie. For Spizza was the very southernmost point of the Austro-Hungarian Monarchy, and its latitude was known throughout the Imperial and Royal Fleet as "the Golden Line," since warships operating south of it were deemed to be on foreign service, in respect of which their crews received their pay and allowances in gold coin. Well, that settled the matter: the Austrian frontier with Montenegro ran along a nameless mountain brook no more than a couple of kilometres to the north of where I lay. In fact, if we had been a little further to the north last night we would now be safe and sound on friendly territory. But the difference scarcely mattered, for all that we had to do now was to eat something to re-gain our strength, then limp the short distance to the border—which was almost certainly unguarded except for a customs post on the bridge—and slip unobtrusively across into the domains of the Emperor Franz Joseph.

Already dog-weariness was being driven from my early-morning mind by a series of gratifying visions of what would happen when we got there. I would report to the gendarmery post in Spizza and demand to use their telephone to contact the naval headquarters at Teodo, who would doubtless send a motor car for us once they knew the momentous nature of the intelligence I was bringing with me. I would make my report in detail, and would be officially ticked off by the Port Admiral—no doubt in a fairly indulgent manner—for my escapade. I would then get a desperately needed bath and shave and change of clothes, and arrange the same for the Gospodarijca. Then perhaps, a few days later, the scene would change to an antechamber in the Schönbrunn Palace, with myself in best Flottenrock with sword-belt and gold epaulettes, while the Old Gentleman in the pale-blue tunic would press my hand with some such words as "We are truly grateful, Prohaska, that you have averted this dastardly plot against our Imperial House and High Command. Be pleased to accept this small token of our undying gratitude . . ." And there was also the Gospodarijca Zaga's future to be thought of. She could lodge in Cattaro of course until things had quietened down sufficiently at home for her to rejoin her family. Or (I thought) perhaps not. I was only a humble Linienschiffsleutnant, but I would move heaven and earth to see that she was rewarded for her selfless protection of me during these wild adventures. Who knew? Perhaps if the reward was sufficiently large it might fund the longed-for visit to Paris. I was already making plans for lodging her with my Aunt Aleksia in Vienna to acquire a little civilised polish when these agreeable daydreams were interrupted by the return of the Gospodarijca herself. There was a rustling in the scrub, and she reappeared holding a loaf of bread and a lump of pallid white sheep's-milk cheese. She brought bad news.

"I got the bread from an old woman in a hut down by the brook. She says that the soldiers have been out since dawn and passed by just before I got there." She paused, and started to hack the loaf in two with her knife. Her eyes avoided mine as she went. "She says they're offering a large reward for the heads of a notorious Austrian secret agent called Prohaska, alias Radić, involved in plots against the state with the late Major Mirko Draganić—and of his female accomplice the Gospodarijca

Zaga Danilović. They know more or less where we are, and it seems that as soon as it gets properly light they'll begin beating the scrub to drive us out."

"Let's try for the border then: it's only a couple of kilometers north of here."

She sighed and looked up at me. "No good I'm afraid: the soldiers are lining the frontier where it's flat enough to cross; and as for trying the mountains again with your leg . . ." The sentence was left unfinished. We both knew the game was up. After what I had seen of Montenegro I had not the slightest reason to doubt that in this country, a reward for someone's head meant exactly that. Mine already felt insecurely fastened to my shoulders.

"Gospodarijca, tell me one thing."

"Yes?"

"Did you know I was an Austrian, even if I am not really the spy and conspirator they say I am?"

She nodded. "Yes."

"So why have you come with me all this way, probably to your own death as well?"

She shrugged. "What would you? It's the custom. You are under the protection of my clan and I am therefore obliged to protect you even if you were the Devil himself or the Turkish Sultan. If I had abandoned you I would have been accursed of God and a dishonour to my family's name. That's all there is to be said about it. Anyway, eat some bread and cheese." She proceeded to tear ravenously at her half-loaf. But I had no appetite for mine now. She saw this, and smiled. "Come on, Prohaska, eat your bread. We have a saying, that it's not healthy to die on an empty stomach."

I took my share of the bread and the sour white cheese and sat munching it apathetically, gazing out to sea. A large ship had just come into view beyond the headlands at the northern edge of the bay. She was some way off, heading down the coast close inshore, but I could see that she was a two-funnelled passenger liner. Strange, I thought to myself: talk about different worlds. Out there are six hundred people cruising southwards amid every luxury that the twentieth century can offer: electric light, central heating, lifts between the decks and hot and cold running water in every cabin. The saloons will soon be open for breakfast and the passengers will rise from their interior-sprung mattresses to wash and shave and dress; then make their way down to be served their hot rolls, coffee, boiled eggs and confiture by silken-silent, white-jacketed waiters. Then it will be an arduous day of deciding whether or not to play deck quoits before the stewards bring round the beef-tea and biscuits at eleven; or of selecting a suitably undemanding novel from the ship's library; or of summoning up the energy to try flirting a little with the pretty girl in the next deck-chair but one while her mamma's back is turned. Yet here are we, not four kilometres away: two filthy vagabonds on the edge of this savage, Bronze Age little country, waiting to be hunted down like hares in a cornfield and have our heads hacked off as soon as the sun gets up.

I watched idly as the ship drew broadside-on to us. She was well inshore I thought, even though the sea bottom falls away steeply on this coast. I could not quite read her name, but I could see that she was an Austro-Lloyd liner. The company crest was clearly visible on the dark-blue, almost black funnels, and the red-white-green Austro-Hungarian merchant flag with its two badges waved at the stern. Then, as I looked on in disbelief, the impossible happened: the ship started to slow down, then once she was three or so kilometres beyond us, ran her engines astern to stop. She did not drop anchor, but a motor launch was lowered and purred away towards the shore below Antivari. Clearly they were picking up mailbags or passengers. But they would not be staying long: half an hour at most. There was no time to be lost: she was about a kilometre and a half off shore, so we might just make it . . .

"Gospodarijca, quick, down to the beach! If we can find a boat of some kind . . ." She did not ask questions, only tumbled after me through the scrub down on to the shingle. There were no soldiers here yet—and there was a fisherman's shed with two boats. We ran to them. One was sound, but too heavy for us to move unaided. The other was a rotten little scow, but light enough to be dragged to the water. It also had two oars. I started to lug at it desperately. But Zaga paused, deep in thought.

"Come on woman, for God's sake . . . we haven't got all day! What's the matter?" She took her knife, and hacked off four or five of the silver coins from her bodice. "What are you playing at, you idiot? Come on!"

"I can't be a thief: I must leave payment for the boat."

"But, woman . . . last night you killed one of your own countrymen in cold blood . . ."

"I know: to kill a man is nothing. But to be a thief is despicable. In Montenegro you could leave a bag of gold by the roadside and come back the next year to collect it . . ."

"COME ON!"

Soon we were paddling like maniacs to propel the skiff towards the waiting liner. Already I could see the launch starting out from the jetty at Antivari. It was now a race between us and them.

I never thought that we would make it. Yet it was a neck-and-neck finish as we came up to the foot of the liner's gangway. The black sides of the S.S. *Gorzkowski,* 8,500 tonnes, registered in Trieste, towered above our tiny craft as we yelled to attract the attention of the Second Mate, who was supervising the embarcation of a family party of first-class passengers and their luggage. There were six of them: white-clad parents (father with panama hat and monocle) and four children in sailor suits, all staring goggle-eyed with incredulity at the two filthy, dishevelled apparitions who were trying to reach the gangway ahead of their launch. I shouted in German to the officer and two sailors who were standing ready with boat-hooks to pull the launch alongside.

"Ahoy there! Quick—take us aboard. I am an Austrian naval lieutenant and I must speak urgently with your Captain on a matter of the greatest importance to the state!" The Second Mate stared at us, then called back:

"Bugger off! This isn't Port Said and we don't want any bumboats hanging around! Get lost!"

"You don't understand—I must speak with your Captain! The life of the heir to the throne is at stake!" There was a whispered conference, then one of the sailors made his way up the gangway. Meanwhile the family disembarked from the launch, glancing fearfully at us over their shoulders as if we were Chinese pirates. At last the sailor reappeared and handed a note to the officer. He read it, and then looked at us.

"Right—come aboard one at a time and don't try any funny business or you're dead meat." I saw that the messenger had brought him a revolver as well as the note. Five minutes later the Gospodarijca and I were standing on the poop deck trying to explain ourselves to the Captain and First Mate while a crowd of passengers stood at the railings trying to get a good look at us and to hear what was being said. I told my story as succinctly as I could, and since I saw that the ship had wireless aerials, demanded to send a wireless telegram to Cattaro. The Captain was not amused.

"Wireless message?" he fumed. "You must be out of your mind. In fact I am quite sure anyway that the pair of you are escaped lunatics . . ."

After some time the wireless operator came up to the Captain and handed him a slip of paper. He read it, looked at us, then turned to the five or six burly deckhands loitering near by. "Very well. Take them both below to the lock-up!"

The sailors moved to lay hold of us. The Gospodarijca screamed and reached for her knife. She lunged at the Captain, but was too late. Three sailors overpowered her.

"Over the side with that mad savage!" the Captain shouted, "cold-water baths are the best treatment for the insane!" and before my horrified gaze they picked her up, struggling and kicking and biting like an enraged cat, and tossed her casually over the rail into the sea. I broke free of them and ran to the rail. I had a horrible apprehension that she would be chopped to pieces by the propellers, since the ship was now getting under way. But I saw her bobbing astern, and striking out for the skiff, which had been cast loose to drift in the liner's wake. She paused for a moment, treading water, and waved to me in farewell. That was the last I ever saw of her. In fact it was the last I saw of anything for quite some time. Large hands grabbed me, a voice behind me said "Sorry, but . . ." and there was a vivid white flash. I had a momentary glimpse of the deck-planks rushing up to meet me. Then all was blackness.

## 11

# THE LAST SUNDAY OF SUMMER

I AWOKE FROM ONE BLACKNESS TO ANOTHER blackness, so profound that my first thought was that I had lost my sight. My head throbbed and my tongue felt dry and withered like an old leather glove. Then, slowly, I began to separate the darkness inside my aching skull from that around it; to disentangle the pounding and queasy swaying of my own brain from the rhythmical thump of engines and the slow, steady rise and fall of a ship steaming at speed on the open sea. I realised that I was lying in some sort of cell, well down in the lower recesses of the ship to judge by the noise, the clammy warmth and the smells of lubricating oil and coal dust. I tried to rise from my foam-rubber mattress—and found that my arms were immobile, pinioned to my sides by the sleeves of some harsh canvas garment. I gave up the attempt as sparks flashed and crackled behind my eyes, then lay still and went back to sleep for a while.

I must have lain like that for an hour or so until, with sudden, searing brightness, a naked light bulb came on behind a steel grille in the bulk-head. As I winced in pain and turned away, a spyhole in the door grated open and a pair of eyes peeped in. A key rattled in the lock and the door swung open to admit a steward carrying a tray with a bread roll and a beaker of hot milk. He was followed by a large seaman with a belaying pin in his hand. The steward proceeded to feed me the bread and milk, as one feeds a small child, while the sailor stood behind him eyeing me with no very evident liking and eloquently whacking the makeshift cosh into the palm of his hand every time I tried to speak. I noticed with some surprise that he was wearing naval rig and not the uniform of an Austro-Lloyd seaman. They finished feeding me and left, having neither of them said a single word during the whole process. The light went out again and, weary beyond all knowing, I lay down on my mattress and fell back into a dead, dreamless slumber.

I was awakened some hours later by the light coming on once more and the door opening. This time it was a man wearing the shoulder-boards of an Austro-Lloyd ship's doctor. He was accompanied by two sick-bay attendants and the same large, grim-faced naval rating as before. Before I knew what was happening I had been hauled to my feet by one of the attendants, still trussed up in the strait-jacket, and held up against the bulkhead while the other produced a tape measure. The doctor had a clipboard and ticked off one item after another as if he were carrying out an inventory of stores.

"Height: metre seventy-five—yes. Build: medium—yes. Hair: dark brown, moustache ditto—yes. Eyes: grey—yes . . ." He paused and looked down.

"Complicated recent post-operative scar pattern on right shin—yes. Well. I think that settles it." He turned to me as if I had just won the faculty of speech in a competition. "Well. Prohaska, you've got a nasty little open wound on your leg there. How did you get it, if I might ask?"

"It was a bone fragment left over from my aeroplane crash last year. It worked to the surface and had to be removed."

"But how did you get it out? Normally it requires an operation under anaesthetic."

"My travelling companion the Gospodarijca Zaga Danilović—the woman whom your Captain has just tried to drown—cut it out with the point of a fighting knife."

He shuddered. "*Du lieber Gott* . . . well, we must dress it right away. It's a wonder it hasn't become infected already. But you'd better get a wash and shave first and we must find you some clothes. We had to burn the rags you came aboard in."

I was escorted to the stokers' bathroom and felt for the first time in two weeks the luxury of soap and hot water. They brought the ship's barber down to shave me, and they gave me a seaman's duck trousers and striped vest. Then the doctor cleaned and bound up the hole in my leg left by the extraction of the bone splinter, and dressed a number of other small cuts and contusions which I had received during the previous night's mad scramble across the Rumija Mountains.

The afternoon audience in my prison in the ship's hold was a more formal affair. The delegation consisted of the ship's Captain accompanied by a stenographer, an elderly Korvettenkapitän of the k.u.k. Kriegsmarine, and the elegant monocled civilian who had been boarding the *Gorzkowski* with his family that morning when the Gospodarijca and I had come alongside in our decaying skiff. Chairs were brought in for them while I sat on the edge of my bunk, but it was still quite a squeeze, and hellishly stuffy in the little cell. I stood to salute the naval officer and was bade sit down. Then the unofficial enquiry began.

First of all I recounted everything that had happened to me, from my leaving the *Tisza* at Neugraditz landing stage that fateful morning to the moment a few hours before when a smart whack behind the ear had brought my adventures to a close. The stenographer noted down every particular, frequently stopping to ask me how the Serb names were spelt. By the time I had finished I reckoned that I had given a pretty comprehensive account of what had taken place during my time with the patriotic society Zvaz o Smrt, alias the Black Hand. I obediently requested in conclusion that my report should be communicated forthwith by wireless to the Naval Defence Commander at Cattaro and the War Ministry in Vienna. To my surprise the naval officer snorted in derision.

"Yes Prohaska, this is all very fine I'm sure. But tell me, have you been out in the sun at all recently?"

"Not to excess, Herr Kapitän. But might I please enquire why you ask?"

"Because, quite frankly, I have never heard such a farrago of nonsense in my entire career."

"But with respect, Herr Kapitän, what can you mean? There is a serious conspiracy afoot to murder the Chief of Staff and the Governor of Bosnia, and also perhaps the Heir-Apparent . . ." The civilian intervened, silkily, condescendingly polite like the professional diplomat I had somehow guessed him to be.

"Yes, my dear Herr Leutnant, of course. The Captain did not intend to question your sanity or your veracity. But we have to face the fact that your story as you have just related it to us does—well—sound wildly far-fetched to say the least of it; so much so in fact that I doubt whether, if it were written up into a novelette, anyone would regard it as being anything other than ridiculously implausible."

"But I assure you, it all happened. To my certain knowledge there are at least eight armed assassins waiting in Sarajevo for the Heir-Apparent's visit, and quite possibly a band of Comitadjis on the Montenegrin border preparing an ambush for Field Marshal Conrad von Hötzendorf and General Potiorek. I am sorry if it sounds incredible, but these are the facts. The Balkans are a melodramatic part of the world I'm afraid."

The diplomat removed his monocle and polished the lens with a silk handkerchief. "Yes, yes, I don't question for one moment that you witnessed everything you say—or had people tell you about the things you didn't personally see. But with respect, I scarcely need you to tell me about the Balkans. You see, I have just finished a five-year posting as Second Secretary in the legation in Cetinje. And believe me, plots are two a penny in those regions; the whole country is as alive with conspiracies and secret societies as a warren is with rabbits. The fundamental trouble with all the Balkan peoples, you see, is that they are children with the bodies of grown men: murderous and cruel and devious, as you have seen, but also fathomlessly incompetent, prone to the most elaborate fantasies and quite incapable of secrecy. In fact I doubt whether any of these Serbian des-peradoes could rob a match seller without first taking out a half-page announcement in the newspapers. As you yourself have observed in your report, the standard of the would-be assassins allegedly despatched to Sarajevo by your Major Draganić was wretchedly low; that much at least of your story I believe. In fact to go by your reports of him I would be prepared to wager that the major himself was an impostor of some kind—probably most of all in regard to himself. He sounds a complete buffoon, and certainly I met a good many like him when I was in Cetinje, conspira-tors whom I personally would not trust to buy a postage stamp."

"But surely, Zvaz o Smrt, and the Black Hand: surely no one can deny their existence."

He smiled wearily. "We went to great trouble and expense today, Prohaska, and monopolised the wireless cabin for several hours in an attempt to verify what you told the Captain when you came aboard. We contacted the Foreign Ministry in Vienna, and they even took the trouble to telegraph the k.u.k. Legation in Belgrade. But with regard to your Union or Death and Black Hand—splendid titles by the way, pure operetta—we drew a complete blank. Neither our intelligence service nor the experts in Balkan terrorist organisations in Belgrade had ever heard of either society. In fact the Foreign Ministry told us off in no uncertain terms for wasting their time."

"But Herr—"

"Baron, Prohaska: Baron Erdelyi von Erdelyháza."

"But Herr Baron, Austrians are involved; I saw at least one of them with my own eyes: Hauptmann Belcredi, with whom I once shared an office in Vienna. He was the emissary they were expecting, the real 'Prohaska.'"

The baron sighed, produced a sheet of paper and replaced the monocle in his eye. "Here, Herr Leutnant. The Marine Section of the War Ministry actually went so far as to telegraph us an extract from your service dossier. Shall I read it out to you? 'A zealous and highly competent young officer, but inclined to be rash in his judgements and to embark upon enterprises without regard to the operation as a whole.' Had it perhaps not occurred to you, Prohaska, even as a remote possibility, that Hauptmann Belcredi—if indeed it was him you saw—was among these ruffians because we *wanted* him to be there? Or that if your band of juvenile conspirators was allowed to enter Austrian territory and is now at large in Sarajevo, they might still be at liberty because the Austrian police wish it to be so? Really, Prohaska, you are reputed to be an intelligent man, and I would have thought that it might perhaps have dawned upon you that one method of combating political terrorism is to infiltrate one's own men into the terrorist gangs and to allow conspiracies to ripen, much as the best way of treating a boil is sometimes to let it grow a little before lancing it?"

"In other words, infiltrating men into societies which you have just assured me don't even exist . . ."

He gave me a hard stare. "I am not saying that they do not exist, even if we have not come across the names before: Serbian political terrorism, alas, is always with us. But in all probability they are no more than minuscule factions which have broken away from the main group, the Narodna Obrana. Really, Herr Leutnant, I assure you that in the great majority of cases the titles are the most impressive things about these organisations. In the legation in Cetinje we had whole filing cabinets full of index cards with their names—the Union of Blood, the Bearded Avengers of St Vitus—and usually no more than that. No, Prohaska, your solicitude for the welfare of the Chief of Staff and the Heir-Apparent is most commendable in such a junior officer, but I think that you can rest assured that they will be well looked after by the competent authorities. Austria has had three centuries' experience of Balkan politics, while since the days of Prince Metternich her political intelligence service has been second to none. I am confident that everything is well under control." He shuffled his papers. "Anyway, that concludes what I have to say, so I shall now leave the matter to be dealt with through the appropriate service channels. Herr Korvettenkapitän?"

"Hmmm? What? Oh yes, thank you, Herr Baron. Well Prohaska, it's like this: the Marineoberkommando has decided in its wisdom that since I am the nearest senior naval officer to hand, I shall become your commanding officer for the time being and take on the job of clearing up the mess after this escapade of yours. Now, I'll be blunt with you: you have a choice."

"A choice, Herr Kommandant? I'm sorry, but I don't understand."

Baron Erdelyi intervened. "What the Herr Korvettenkapitän wishes to convey to you, Prohaska, is that you now have a choice between two possible courses of action."

"And what are those, Herr Baron?"

"Either you press ahead with these extraordinary claims of yours concerning plots to murder the Chief of Staff and Heir-Apparent—even the President of France for all I know—in which case you will be landed at our next port of call and sent back to Pola under close escort to face a court of enquiry . . ."

"Then certainly I shall do that."

"Please Herr Leutnant, please don't be so hasty. Hear me out, I beseech you, and bear in mind the possible consequences."

"Consequences, Herr Baron? For whom?"

"For yourself, my dear fellow. Please try to understand how all this might look in front of what would effectively be a court martial. You have been thirteen days absent from your ship without leave, by your own admission in consequence of an illicit affair with a local woman; you spent most of that time in the company of armed enemies of the Dual Monarchy; you repeatedly left and re-entered Austrian territory without permission, in civilian clothing and without going through border formalities; and when you finally resurfaced at Antivari this morning you were once more in the company of a young woman, this time bristling with weapons. Really Prohaska, be sensible and just consider how all that could be made to look by a skilled prosecuting counsel. Surely I don't have to remind you that, while you are an Austrian officer, you are still of Czech descent. For some years now Vienna has been increasingly worried by Pan-Slavist subversion in the Czech-speaking provinces and in the k.u.k. Armee, and I assure you that if the Military Procurator's department thought that they had got their teeth into a nice little Czech-Serb conspiracy within the officer corps, then their investigators would squeeze you until your eyes popped out, even though you were as innocent as a lamb. The Dual Monarchy is a civilised state and doesn't use the death penalty for treason in peacetime; but I am still fairly confident that you would get twenty-five years' hard labour in a prison-fortress. Think my dear fellow, think first I implore you."

"Then might I enquire, what is the alternative course?"

The Korvettenkapitän answered. "The alternative, Prohaska, is that you just quietly resume your career as a naval officer under my command aboard this ship, leaving this foolish escapade to be forgotten. If you do, then the Marineoberkommando assures me that no further action will be taken—except for requiring you to give an undertaking to secrecy."

"Aboard this ship, Herr Kommandant? But with respect, this vessel is a passenger liner . . ."

"I know. I'm in command of a draft of naval reinforcements on its way to join their ship."

"Might I obediently enquire which ship?"

"Certainly: S.M.S. *Kaiserin Elisabeth*. We're due to board her at Shanghai on the 16th of July."

So really I had very little choice: either being landed at Port Said and sent back to Pola by the next ship as a virtual prisoner facing court martial, or a very supernumerary attachment to a draft of forty sailors on their way to the Far East to replace time-expired men aboard the Austro-Hungarian station-ship in those waters, the elderly cruiser *Kaiserin Elisabeth*. But that was several weeks away, and for the time being I led a curious disembodied existence aboard the *Gorzkowski:* given my own cabin and dressed in clothing lent me by my fellow-officers, but otherwise absolutely forbidden to have any contact with the liner's passengers or crew, or to speak with any of the naval detachment except on strictly service matters. I was not even permitted to mess with the other officers, but had my meals brought to me in my cabin by a civilian steward. He was a grave, dignified man in his late forties called Ferdinand Wong, a Trieste Chinese Catholic whose parents had come to that city from Canton in the 1870s and become prominent in its small Chinese community. He was an affable sort of man, very efficient and discreet in his duties and proud of being a Steward First Class with the Austro-Lloyd line. He was not allowed to speak with me a great deal; but, sensing my awkward position aboard, he was very kind to me in a fatherly sort of way, and treated me throughout the voyage rather as if I were an injured cat being nursed back to health in a cardboard box lined with an old blanket.

Otherwise there was little to do except read the books that Wong brought me from the ship's library. But since I was physically and emotionally exhausted by my adventures in the Balkans, the sea voyage did at least allow me to recuperate and heal the wound in my leg. However, I was a naval officer, so my new commanding officer, Korvettenkapitän Julius Fichterle, had to find some employment for me. In the end all that he could come up with was a post as ciphers officer—as you may well imagine, a monstrously boring job aboard a civilian liner in peacetime. Most of the time I just sat in the wireless cabin reading, as before. I was forbidden to speak with the wireless operator except on service business, but that scarcely mattered: wireless telegraphists aboard ship in those days were leased out along with the W/T apparatus by the Marconi Company and were actively discouraged from being part of the ship's company. Known as "the Marconi Men," they wore their own uniform, kept their own watches and generally had as little as possible to do with anyone else aboard.

There was remarkably little to report during those weeks aboard the liner. The *Gorzkowski* ran across the sunlit Mediterranean as smoothly as a train on rails and anchored at Port Said for a few hours as we waited for a northbound convoy—a French cruiser and two troop-ships en route from Saigon to Marseilles—to emerge from the Suez Canal. Then we entered, and glided ghost-like across the moonlit desert on our way to Ismailia and Port Suez. There followed the awful, broiling passage of the Red Sea, with every living thing aboard, down to the last cockroach, clustering on the shaded port side of the ship and the decks being sluiced with water every couple of hours to prevent the planks from curling up and splitting. We arrived at Aden, and stopped for a day to land passengers and mail at that dreary, torrid cinder-heap. Then it was off into the great shining expanse of the Indian Ocean, already rough and swept by sudden rain-squalls as the monsoon built up.

When we arrived at Colombo it was a Sunday morning. As we entered the harbour the bells of the Anglican cathedral rang out above the waving coconut palms to summon the people of Ceylon to matins. We tied up at the wharf and, since a condenser tube had to be replaced, a twenty-four-hour shore-leave was decreed for passengers, crew and naval detachment. All, that is, except for me. I had to remain aboard and send a few piffling telegrams in code to the Marine Section of the War Ministry in Vienna, informing them of Marine Detachment Fichterle's progress around the globe for all the world as if we were engaged on some momentous voyage of discovery. There were also a few official telegrams waiting for us at Colombo, none of them of the slightest importance. The afternoon came—and with it an unexpected invitation delivered by a midshipman sitting in the stern sheets of a smart rowing gig. It came from the Captain of the British battleship H.M.S. *Inexorable,* lying at anchor on the other side of the harbour, an old *Canopus*-class vessel which for some time past had been the Royal Navy's flagship in the Indian Ocean. They had learnt that there was an Austrian naval detachment aboard the *Gorzkowski* and requested the pleasure of our company at a party aboard their ship that evening. So everyone got ready, glad of the break in the monotony of shipboard life. Except, once again, for me. Old Fichterle was apologetic when he came to see me in the wireless cabin, just before they boarded the launch.

"Well Prohaska, sorry that you can't come with us, especially since I hear that your English is pretty good while mine is nonexistent. I suppose that I'll just have to get someone else to interpret for me. Anyway, I've told the Chinese-steward fellow to bring you up an extra special supper from the first-class saloon by way of compensation."

"Thank you for the kind thought, Herr Kommandant."

"Don't mention it." He was silent for some time, looking out from the open door of the wireless cabin over the harbour, towards the gloriously coloured tropical sun already dipping below the dark horizon of the Arabian Sea. "It's a queer old life; in the Navy, I mean. Personally I think they've been far too hard on you. Young officer in a peacetime fleet—what do they expect? Of course you wanted adventure and got yourself mixed up in something silly. Who wouldn't, if they were worth anything at all? It makes me wonder what sort of desk-bound milksops they want running this navy of ours. If that's the kind of officers they're after then they might as well draft in civil servants and have done with it." He paused for a while, deep in thought. "But there—perhaps that is what they need, in a navy that's hardly fired a shot in half a century. Funny thing when you think about it: I'm just taking these men out to Shanghai and then coming back with the returning draft, then it's retirement for old Julius Fichterle. Fifty-three years I served my Emperor, and never once saw action. I was a midshipman aboard the old *Kaiser,* you know, during the Danish war: arrived at Cuxhaven the day the Danes sued for an armistice. Then I was aboard the *Galatea* in 1866—arrived at Lissa just in time to pick up a few dead bodies. Then it was half a century of polishing brasswork and form-filling and giving sailors two days in the brig for being drunk and disorderly. Not much of a life really. And before long it'll be over. I've already got a deposit down on the retirement villa in Graz, and a place in the family vault for myself and Frau Fichterle. Sometimes makes me wonder why I lived at all. I've got two sons, you know: one in medicine and one a lawyer. I told them, whatever you do never go into the armed forces in peacetime: it's living death. But there, Prohaska, mustn't depress you. The launch is leaving now, so you can be officer of the watch in my absence. Look after the ship and see that no one steals it while we're away. *Auf wiedersehen!*"

"Have a pleasant evening, Herr Kommandant."

"Thank you, I'm sure we shall."

I was left alone. Soon it was dark, and the brilliant stars shone above me out on deck as the fireflies hummed in the darkness. Soon the strains of the "Destiny Waltz," very capably executed by a Royal Marine band, came floating across the water from beneath the awnings stretched over the quarterdeck of the *Inexorable*. The sound of laughter and the chink of glasses could be heard faintly in the distance. Evidently a good time was being had by all. I longed to be among them. My English was fluent, and ever since I had spent six months with the Royal Navy in 1907–08 I had retained a certain soft spot for the rather taciturn but kindly and hospitable men who inhabited its wardrooms. To me it always seemed remarkable how their massive, unassailable self-confidence—fruit of a century's unchallenged mastery of the oceans and a professional competence second to none—had somehow made them genial and good-natured, rather than arrogant and overbearing like the Germans or touchy and peevish like the French and the Russians. It was almost as if they were graciously pleased to allow the rest of us to sail on their ocean and genuinely hoped that we would enjoy it, like some duke opening his gardens to the public one Sunday afternoon for charity.

I ate the supper which Steward Wong brought up for me—excellent as promised—then sat and read for a while. But it was difficult to concentrate, now that I was on my own aboard a ship which was near-deserted and silent, apart from the hollow noise of hammering down below where the engineers were at work on the condenser. Somehow I was still trying to sort out inside my head the bewildering succession of events over the past month. And there was anxiety as well, about the two women who had been involved in my wild journey across the Balkans: the one as instigator of the chain of events which got me into it in the first place; the other as the rescuer who had got me out of it alive. The Gospodarijca Zaga was safe, I was reasonably sure of that. I had last seen her swimming for the skiff, and surely she would have had the sense to paddle for Spizza and land on Austrian territory, evading the hunters on the Montenegrin shore. But what about Pani Božena? Had her husband and his accomplices cut her throat and dumped her in the Danube, or had they perhaps mutilated her face as a punishment for her adultery? Grbić had looked capable of any brutality when crossed. As soon as we landed at Shanghai I would send a letter to Seifert aboard the *Tisza,* asking him to find out what had happened to her. He would already know that I was on my way to the Far East: Fichterle had contacted Marine Detachment Pancsova via Vienna and it appeared that I had been posted missing on 28 May, presumed drowned while swimming in the river. My clothes had been discovered on the island, still neatly folded where I had left them, and had come within a couple of days of being auctioned along with my other effects. Bos'un Jovanović was packing them up to send to me at Shanghai by the next steamer.

It was getting late now, but music still floated across from the party aboard the *Inexorable.* Perhaps in our honour, it was a selection from Lehár's *Count of Luxemburg.* Then, about 11 p.m., a steward knocked at the door of the wireless cabin.

"Excuse me, Herr Schiffsleutnant, but there's a native at the foot of the gangway asking to speak with the senior Austrian naval officer aboard. I don't speak much English I'm afraid, so can you come down and see what he wants?"

I went down to the gangway. It was a skinny-legged, bespectacled native telegraphic clerk with a telegram addressed to "k.u.k. Marine Detachment Fichterle, S.S. *Gorzkowski,* lying at Colombo—Most urgent."

I thanked the man, gave him a tip and sent him away on his bicycle into the warm darkness. I took the telegram up to the wireless cabin and opened it—and saw at once that it was gibberish:

THROW FOLD UNDER GAME LINE IN NEUTER MORDENTS AREA

JEWS TOP WHITE RINSE TRACTION IN SEWER WATER

It seemed to be in code, but I could not recognise which one. We used no less than four code-books in the k.u.k. Kriegsmarine in 1914: the official Triple Alliance naval code, the German-Austrian version of the former (made necessary by well-founded doubts about the loyalty of the third partner Italy), the Austro-German diplomatic code and the Imperial and Royal Fleet's internal code. Dreadful muddles resulting from use of the wrong book were a regular feature of the Austro-Hungarian cipher officer's life. I took each book in turn out of the safe, and tried to decipher the mysterious telegram. Each time the result was even greater nonsense than before. Then I looked again at the message—and saw that even if it made no sense, the words were all English or close approximations to it. Perhaps we had received the wrong telegram? I looked at the words, interested. It was rather like making an anagram of someone's name, staring at the letters knowing that there is something amusing in there, but not being quite able to drag it out. "Neuter" and "mordents" seemed promising for starters: perhaps the manager of a local dyeworks would arrive at his office next morning to be the puzzled recipient of an urgent telegram from Vienna informing him that as a result of an amendment to the *K.u.K. Adjustierungsvorschrift* of 1908, ratings would now show four stripes of their vest at the collar of their jersey instead of the three pre-scribed by the previous regulation. Yet surely, "neuter" in English was what one did to nouns or to tom-cats. Was not "neutral" the correct adjec-tive for chemicals? And what about "mordents?" The dictionary said that it should be "mordants." And come to that, where did the Jew's top fit in, and the traction (presumably "traction engine") which was to be rinsed in sewer water? It was complete nonsense, yet curiously fascinating, as if there was a meaning in there struggling to get out. I sat for nearly two hours with a cold glass of beer beside me and the floor around me littered with screwed-up sheets of paper as I tried combination after combination to make sense of it.

At last I heard the noise of the party-goers returning from the *Inexorable,* the ratings filled up to the ears with British beer and rum and the officers with pink gin. I showed the mysterious telegram to Fichterle, who was swaying quite noticeably and hanging on to the rails at the head of the gangway.

"Think nothing of it, Prohaska—someone's slipped up in the telegraph office. If it's important they'll send it again and if it isn't, well, we're better off without it. Anway, I'm turning in. Good-night."

He went to his cabin. Just as the door closed there was a hail from below. I looked over the rail. A four-oared gig was alongside, its oar-blades glowing with phosphorescence. A British lieutenant-commander stood in the stern sheets. I saw that he also was rather unsteady on his feet.

"I say up there, are you the Austrian Navy? Do—you—speak—English?"

"Yes, I suppose that I am. And I do. In what can I perhaps be of assistance to you?"

"Look old chap, sorry to be the bearer of bad tidings and all that, but I'm from the *Inexorable.* Our wireless operator's just picked up a signal from the German station at Dar-es-Salaam, relayed from Nauen. It seems that your Crown Prince or whatever and his wife were both shot dead this morning by anarchists at a place called Sarah-something in the Balkans. My Captain sent me over to tell you and says that we'll send official condolences and lower the ensign to half-mast and all that in the morning. This isn't a naval vessel, but he says there's an Austrian naval detachment aboard so we'll pay our respects as if it were."

"Thank you very much. You are most kind."

"No trouble at all. Well, must be off now, and sorry again to have brought bad news."

I made my way back to the wireless cabin, wrapped in my thoughts. Fichterle was in his bunk now, snoring loudly. There seemed to be no point in waking him to tell him the news from Sarajevo. So it looked as if Major Draganić's juvenile assassins had not been quite such bunglers after all.

I gazed at the telegram lying on the desk. Of course, it made sense now: German in clear as taken down by a Ceylonese native telegraphist, who had then edited and rearranged it into words that he knew:

THRONFOLGER UND GEMAHLIN HEUTE ERMORDERT SARAJEWO

STOP WEITERE INSTRUKTIONEN ZU ERWARTEN.

I slept little that night.

The formal announcement was made by Fichterle to the naval detachment at eight bells next morning and by Captain Martinelli to the passengers at breakfast. A period of mourning was decreed. No one seemed to know exactly how many days an heir to the throne was worth, so we settled for three to be on the safe side. All dances and concert parties and other shipboard jollifications were cancelled until Thursday. But apart from that the mourning was the merest formality. That evening at dinner, I was told, a group of Hungarian passengers in the second-class dining room had ordered champagne and had begun singing and dancing in a noisy mulatság until the Captain walked over and asked them politely to be quiet. But even among the Austrian passengers there was little sign of grief. Franz Ferdinand had never been much liked by the public, and if anything—though of course no one was cruel enough to say so openly—most people were secretly rather relieved that they would not now have to put up with him as their Emperor. The succession had now passed to the young Archduke Karl and his pretty Italian wife Zita, and everyone agreed that he seemed to be—how do you say?—"a good egg": conscientious, thoughtful and reportedly of liberal and forward-looking opinions. Rather like your own Prince Charles, in fact.

For my own part, I said nothing of what I knew about the events in Sarajevo, having sworn to keep silent. But I was sorry that two people had died so unnecessarily, in part at least as a result of my own warnings being disregarded. Evidently the Baron von Erdelyháza's faith in the competence of the Austrian police and intelligence service had been sadly misplaced; and he tacitly acknowledged as much by avoiding my eyes on the few occasions when we met on deck. Either someone had at best made a classic dog's breakfast of things, I thought, or at worst the Archduke and his wife had quite deliberately been allowed to walk in front of armed assassins. But at a more personal level I was very sad that the Duchess of Hohenberg—the saviour of my right leg—had perished as well, leaving the three children orphans. I remembered the holy medallion I had flung away in my anger that evening in the hospital at Fiume. Had they given it back to her afterwards? What had she thought? I would never get the chance now to explain or to thank her.

As for the Heir-Apparent himself, however, although I do not think that being a nasty piece of work should be a death-penalty offence, I must say that my feelings on learning of his violent end were as mixed as those of most other Austrians. I was sad that a man had been killed, and I still think that for the most part his boorish ill-temper and callousness were a result of heredity and the circumstances in which he had been placed. But as for having him as Emperor, I am glad that we escaped at least that. In the years since, I have sometimes heard people—usually aged Catholic baronesses in moth-eaten fox-furs—say that if he had lived the Danubian Monarchy might have survived. I must say however that I don't believe it; because the inescapable truth is that the man was a violent, bigoted, militaristic despot without a single constructive idea in his bullet head. Old Austria was condemned to die, either from slow senile decay without him, or from an attack of rabies with him. I was one of those who lost everything in Austria's collapse: my career, my country, my home, even the woman I loved. But I still think that it was better that way than the much nastier end that we would certainly have come to with Franz Ferdinand of Österreich-Este as our ruler.

After a few days at sea, rolling and pitching across the Bay of Bengal in the first bad weather of our voyage, the affairs of distant Austria seemed even more remote than before. The passengers had mostly taken to their cabins and only a few hardened seafarers stayed on deck to watch the grey waves and the driving, tepid rain and the frequent displays of sheet-lightning as the low monsoon clouds scudded overhead. Wireless reception was atrocious, but very few signals were sent to us anyway: only confirmation of the news from Sarajevo, and an order for official mourning, then a couple of days later a message that diplomatic complications with Serbia were possible, and that any Serbs on board were to be kept under discreet observation. The only Serbian subject aboard was a commercial traveller bound for Canton. He was duly shadowed about the deck—that is, whenever he took a break from being seasick—by a couple of ratings armed with revolvers and with instructions to shoot him if he showed any disposition to take over the ship. We arrived at Penang on 3 July, passed down to Singapore, then steamed through the Straits of Malacca and into the South China Sea. We called at Hong Kong on 12 July. Then at last, on the morning of 16 July, exactly according to the timetable, we edged our way through a grey early-morning mist into the turbid ochre-coloured waters of the Yangtze Estuary. The Bund and the city of Shanghai lay ahead of us. Our journey was over.

Well, almost. As the *Gorzkowski* edged up to the wharf, we scanned the long rows of shipping moored out in the river. Warships were there in plenty: British, American, French, Dutch, even Danish. But nowhere could we make out the familiar squarish silhouette of the *Kaiserin Elisabeth*. Fichterle and I went ashore, to the offices of the Associated East Asia Telegraphic Company Ltd. Sure enough, a telegram awaited us there. S.M.S. *Kaiserin Elisabeth* had not been able to steam down to Shanghai as planned: instead she was currently engaged in coaling at the port of Chefoo, on the north coast of the Shantung Peninsula. Marine Detachment Fichterle would thus proceed by train up to Tsientsin, and thence by coastal steamer to Chefoo to join their ship.

The rail journey northwards to Tsientsin lasted a day and a half: thirty-six hours in which I rapidly got used once more to the flat, water-logged landscape of eastern China and to that characteristic Chinese smell compounded of privy emptyings, frying-oil and cheap tobacco. I also experienced once again that curious and rather disagreeable feeling, vis-à-vis the inhabitants, of having become translucent: not exactly invisible but not quite there either, regarded not with hostility or even disapproval but with a steady, unsettling, detached gaze of scientific curiosity, such as one might assume when studying some exotic beetle through a magnifying lens. For most of our journey though we had little contact with the Chinese people. The railways were foreign concessions and ran across the Celestial Empire like pipelines: long strips of extra-territoriality governed by foreign laws and guarded by foreign troops.

Another such enclave was the Chinese Eastern Railway Hotel in Tsientsin—a capsule of Europe set down in the middle of the dusty, yellow, windswept plain just south of the Great Wall. I recall that it had a notice in the foyer, No Dogs Or Chinese Except By Permission Of The Manager. We officers stopped there overnight (the ratings were billeted in the nearby German barracks) while we waited for our steamer to Chefoo. I went down to dinner at 7:30 and found a pleasant surprise awaiting me. It was Professor Regnitz, who had just arrived by train from Siberia en route for Yokohama. We had not met since he had visited me in hospital the previous summer, so he invited me to dine with him. The invitation was doubly welcome to me, I must confess, because I was very hard-up at the time. My pay had not yet caught up with me and I had been reduced to borrowing money on account from the *Gorzkowski*'s purser. He told me over dinner that since he detested sea voyages, he had travelled here via Moscow and the Trans-Siberian Railway. The reason for his journey was an invitation to give a series of lectures on administrative law at Tokyo University.

"It appears," he said, "that our little Japanese friends have a high regard for the Austro-Hungarian state administration; in which case I can only conclude that they are not half as clever as everyone says they are. True, we have more of it than just about anyone else. But why should that qualify us to be experts on the subject? You might as well have made the late Archduke Otto an authority on syphilis on the grounds that he contracted it more often than anyone else alive."

Because of my undertaking to secrecy I was unable to tell him anything about my adventures with the Black Hand, but the conversation inevitably came around to the Sarajevo assassinations, about the details of which I still knew very little. "It was a Serbian student who fired the shots," he reported, "a fellow by the name of Prinzip, about nineteen years old. But the more that gets into the newspapers the more curious the whole affair seems to be. At the very least our Austrian state machine, so admired by the Japanese, gave a gala display of Schlamperei that morning. In fact people in Vienna were saying just before I left that Potiorek himself deserves to be shot for the way he handled security during the visit. It seems that the murderer and his accomplices—at least five of them—wandered about the place for a good fortnight beforehand telling everyone what they were going to do, but that none of our plain-clothes police picked them up. Then on the morning one of them tossed a bomb at the Heir-Apparent's car and missed. After that Franz Ferdinand and the duchess decided to leave town as soon as possible by a different route, but the chauffeur got his instructions wrong and turned up the wrong street, then tried to reverse down it again—right in front of our young friend Prinzip standing on the kerb with a revolver in his pocket. No troops along the route, only a handful of police, in fact the whole thing so gloriously mismanaged that people are saying the Heir-Apparent was deliberately allowed to walk into a town full of assassins to get rid of him. I don't believe it myself, knowing as I do the heights of incompetence to which our venerable bureaucracy can rise. But I can understand people smelling conspiracy. Just before I left Vienna there was even a story going around that the Serbian Minister in Vienna handed us a warning note a couple of weeks beforehand—but since Bosnia comes under the Ministry of Finances it landed on the desk of that half-witted Polak Biliński, who sat on it until it was too late to do anything."

"All rather amusing in a grim sort of way," I observed. " 'Wien bleibt Wien' and so forth."

He was silent for a while, looking down at his plate. "I wish that I found it funny. I tell you, there's thunder in the air, and a smell of sulphur. When I came across Siberia our train was stopping every few kilometres to let troop-trains pass by—moving westwards. And before that, when I was in Berlin, I stopped off to have lunch with some friends of mine from the Reichstag. They told me that Sani Berchtold and Conrad have been on the telephone to the Wilhelmstrasse every day this past month demanding German backing for a war against Serbia."

"So?" I said, "why not? That nest of bandits and murderers could do with clearing out. They certainly deserve it."

"That would mean war with Russia, which is why we haven't done it long since. But I understand that the German generals—not their politicians, mark you—have now assured Vienna that they'll deal with Russia in the event of any unpleasantness. The Kaiser is flip-flopping like mad as usual, agreeing with whoever last spoke to him, but Tirpitz and the admirals are keen for a war, on the grounds that there's going to be one anyway within the next two years, and the ratio of German to British battleships will never be more favourable, so why not have it now?"

"Perhaps they're right," I ventured. "If there's going to be one, let's get it over with. It'll only last a few weeks anyway, everyone knows that."

He looked pensive. "What makes you so sure of that? No, Prohaska, it looks as if we might soon have a world war, not because anyone really wants it but because everybody believes it to be inevitable and no one in power seems to have the wit to stop it. And if that's the case, what reason do you have for supposing that once we are in a war the creatures who let us slide into it—the Sani Berchtolds and the Kaiser Wilhelms—will suddenly turn into Napoleons and Bismarcks who can run the thing and keep it under control? No, I'm sure myself that if we get into a war it'll be far longer and far messier than anyone ever expected. In fact I'll stick my neck out and say that it might even last as long as a year."

# 12

# OUT AND ABOUT IN NORTH CHINA

THE CRUISER S.M.S. *KAISERIN ELISABETH*—"Alte Liserl"—was not a particularly awe-inspiring sight that July evening as she lay alongside the coaling wharf at Chefoo. Austria-Hungary's only warship on the China Station, she had been out in the Far East without a break since 1906 and was showing her age rather badly. When she was launched in 1890 she had been quite a remarkable design for her day: an attempt to solve the perennial Austrian problem of miserly naval budgets by building a kind of early pocket battleship, with a heavy main battery and thick armour on a cruiser's displacement. The experiment had not been an unqualified success: the ship had always been overgunned, top-heavy and cramped to live aboard. And now in her twilight years the old lady had been disarmed to a point where she was little better than a large gunboat, then sent to the Far East to show the Austrian flag. Year after year, throughout the golden sunset of the Long Peace, she had ambled along at a steady nine knots from Hong Kong to Saigon and from Singapore to Batavia and from Surabaya to Manila and from Yokohama to Tsingtao, displaying the naked might of the Dual Monarchy to an audience of Chinese and Malays and Japanese. What they thought of it can only be guessed at, but one clue had been given (I was told) during a visit to the Japanese base at Sasebo in 1911. A party of Japanese naval officers was shown around the ship, and were very appreciative of everything, hissing with polite admiration like a flock of geese at each new disclosure of k.u.k. naval technology. Doubts arose only at the very end of the visit, as the guests prepared to board their launch to go ashore, when the Japanese rear-admiral heading the party bowed and said through his interpreter,

"And in conclusion, please be so kind as to present our compliments to the curator."

Even then the old ship had been effectively worthless for any serious military operations, and a further three years in the Far East had not improved matters. Since Austria-Hungary had no colonies, her ships in foreign waters were entirely dependent on other powers for coaling and dockyard facilities. Other powers—even our allies the Germans at Tsingtao—required money for the use of their drydocks, so attention to the ship's bottom had been minimal. Likewise her boilers were in a poor state, heavy consumers of coal and incapable of generating enough steam pressure to maintain even twelve knots for much over an hour. The *Elisabeth*'s lower deck were mostly two-year draftees from Europe, glad to do part of their naval service in the Far East, but a high proportion of the officers and NCOs were aged semi-derelicts who had often spent many years out in the east and who were now useless for anything but summer cruises around the China Seas: showing the red-white-red ensign, providing high-quality musical entertainment, giving receptions on board and generally living up to the popular image of Austrians as agreeable chaps but not very serious; in fact, a sort of floating Viennese operetta.

It was this lack of our own coaling stations which had brought the *Elisabeth* to Chefoo. The original intention had been to coal at the German port-colony of Tsingtao and then proceed down to Shanghai to meet the draft from the *Gorzkowski*. However, the Germans had suddenly upped the price of steam coal just as Vienna found that its warship coaling allocation under the 1914 budget was running low. Chefoo coal was wretched stuff, dusty and of poor heating value, but it was cheap because it was dug out with coolie labour almost alongside the dock. But when the cruiser arrived at Chefoo to begin coaling, further difficulties had arisen over payment, in consequence of which the ship had lain alongside the wharf for the past four days waiting for the order to start filling her bunkers. In fact it was not until the morning after our arrival that the loathsome process began.

One of the consolations of service in the Far East in those days— at least for those who did not think too deeply—was that the ragged multitude of coolie labourers clamouring to toil for a couple of Hallers a day meant that coaling ship, though still a filthy chore, was at least not as back-breaking as in European waters, where we not only had to load several hundred tonnes of coal into the bunkers in sacks and baskets, but also then to sluice down the ship and scrub ourselves and our clothes to shreds to get rid of the insidious black grime which worked its way into everything. Even so it was a depressing couple of days, as the ant-like army of labourers filed up the precarious planks from the dockside to tip their baskets of coal into the bunker ports, then went back down another plank for more. Sacking and oakum had been stuffed into every crack and crevice, but still the fine black dust crept stealthily into the cabins and mess decks.

Mid-morning, just as this delightful process was getting into full swing, I was called to the Harbour Master's office by a velvet-polite young Chinese telegraphic clerk. I was now acting ciphers officer aboard the *Elisabeth* until other duties could be arranged. It was a telegram in code from the German Naval East Asiatic Command at Tsingtao. I took it back aboard, opened it and got to work with a pencil and pad and the Triple Alliance naval code-book. Five minutes later I had finished. It read:

*k.u.k. War Ministry Marine Section*
*Vienna 20 July 1914 7:30 P.M.*

STRONG POSSIBILITY POLITICAL COMPLICATIONS RUSSIA FRANCE
REGARDING SERBIA STOP PROCEED AT ECONOMICAL REPEAT
ECONOMICAL SPEED SHANGHAI AND AWAIT FURTHER ORDERS

I took the decoded telegram up to the bridge to show our Captain, Linienschiffskapitän Makovitz. The Captain—a large, rather ponderous German-Croat with heavy black moustaches—read the telegram then turned to me.

"Herr Schiffsleutnant, pray accompany me to the telegraph office and bring the code-books with you. I have one or two things to tell Vienna." I was loath to do this: the regulations stated clearly that code-books must not leave the ship's wireless cabin. "Do as you are damned well told and get the books. I can't waste time on such foolery."

Five minutes later I stood with Makovitz in the Harbour Master's office encoding the message:

TOP SECRET STOP REF YOUR TELEGRAM 20TH INST CANNOT REPEAT CANNOT STEAM SHANGHAI STOP BOILERS DEFECTIVE STOP WILL PROCEED TSINGTAO.

Since we were unable to telegraph Vienna directly—faults on the line, the Chinese telegraphist said—the message was sent to the Austro-Hungarian Legation in Peking with a request for them to relay it via the United States. We waited until 4 p.m. for an acknowledgement. None came. Finally the Captain lost his temper—something which he did very easily—and demanded a telephone line to Peking. It was a hot, sticky north-Chinese summer afternoon with thunder in the air. We got through to Peking at last but the line was poor. It appeared that they had not received our telegram. Then, to my horror, Makovitz read the message out in clear over the telephone, despite the fact that the windows of the Harbour Master's office were all wide open in the heat. He seemed to be having trouble.

"Yes—I said 'top secret.' YES, YOU IMBECILE—TOP SECRET! The text of the message is, CANNOT STEAM SHANGHAI STOP BOILERS DEFECTIVE STOP WILL PROCEED TSINGTAO INSTEAD! YES, TSINGTAO! T-S-I-N-G-T-A-O . . . !"

We arrived at Tsingtao on the evening of 25 July, having steamed down from Chefoo at an economical repeat economical eight knots. And that is how we spent the last few days of our world, lying at anchor in the sunshine off the picturesque mountainous coast of the Shantung Peninsula while far away, on the other side of the globe, the richest and most self-confident civilisation the world had ever seen completed the arrangements for its own suicide, the nations of Europe slithering helplessly towards the precipice like a party of roped-together climbers as the mobilisation timetables took charge, millions of men across an entire continent bidding farewell to their lives as the buff envelopes dropped through letterboxes and the posters went up on the street corners and the cheering crowds gathered in the squares. Yet here, on the eastern coast of China, we felt scarcely a tremor of the mighty earthquake which was convulsing

Europe. A small Japanese coaster had followed the *Elisabeth* down from Chefoo at a polite distance, and a Russian cruiser which we fell in with off the tip of the Shantung Peninsula the previous day had been rather brusque about exchanging the normal seafaring courtesies. But otherwise it was shipboard routine as usual. In fact, after three days or so lying off Tsingtao we began to suspect that the *Kaiserin Elisabeth* had been forgotten. The Captain went ashore twice daily to confer with the German governor of the colony and see whether there were any messages for us from Vienna or Peking, but nothing came. Meanwhile we could see the ships of our German ally hard at work getting themselves on to a war footing: landing all inflammables, putting up black-out, and coating their gleaming tropical white-and-buff paintwork with mobilisation grey. At least they were too busy to think much about it. But aboard the *Elisabeth,* lying idly at anchor in the clammy late-summer heat, an uneasy realisation was beginning to spread through the mess decks that in a few days' time this ungainly old flat-iron, which ever since anyone could remember had been a warship in name only, might be a shattered, blazing hulk filled with dead and dying.

At long last, on the morning of 29 July, we received a wireless message relayed via the Tsingtao station of AEG Telefunken. The Dual Monarchy had declared war on Serbia, and hostilities with Russia were imminent. Further instructions would follow. That is, if anyone remembered about us.

For myself, I was no stranger to the German treaty port of Tsingtao. I had visited the town twice before, and had in fact seen my first performance of *The Merry Widow* in its garrison theatre, back in 1906 or thereabouts. But however many times I had been there the place would have lost none of its strangeness in my eyes: a late-nineteenth-century German provincial town transported miraculously and intact to the shores of the Yellow Sea—Darmstadt or Göttingen tacked with bizarre effect on to the fringes of the Celestial Empire.

The Germans had extorted the place from China about the turn of the century as compensation (they said) for the murder of two German missionaries, and had then set about building a town that would stand for a thousand years as a lighthouse of German Kultur on the shores of East Asia. And in this it has to be said that they had achieved their aim to a quite depressing degree, setting to work with that frightening Prussian combination of technical skill and absolute single-mindedness to construct an almost surrealistically exact microcosm of the Kaiser's Germany on the opposite side of the world. Everything in Tsingtao was unimaginably neat and orderly: Bismarckian Gothic architecture—indigestion made visible—in brown brickwork, so strongly constructed that it would survive to oppress a hundred future generations with its lumbering charmlessness; lime-flanked boulevards crossing at exact right-angles; the Evangelische Kirche and the Katolische Kirche with its monastery; the Hotel Central at the intersection of the Wilhelmstrasse and the Friedrichstrasse; the Cafés Metropol and Dachsal; the Arboretum and the Fürstenhof beer-hall; the Kaiserin Augusta Hospital; the naval and commercial harbours; the Telefunken wireless station; and the Bahnhof at the end of the Shantungbahn railway line. And around it all, crowning the water-colour mountain peaks which had now been renamed Prinz Heinrich and Diedrechs and Bismarck, the squat ferro-concrete forts with their Krupp guns. Since there are some things in this world that not even German diligence can remedy, the climate was still that of coastal north China: sticky and hot in summer, with typhoon-lashed autumns and dry, shrivellingly cold winters when the dust-laden wind moaned down from Manchuria. In all other respects though the place was a frighteningly precise replica of Wilhelmine Germany. Overweight matrons ate cream cakes in the Café Metropol while their crop-headed husbands perspired at their desks in the government offices and the godowns of the trading companies. And out on the immaculate boulevards civilians stepped aside to make way for stiff-necked, monocled army officers. It had all been built to last for ever. Yet the Chinese, inheritors of a civilisation ten times as old and a thousand times more self-satisfied, appeared to take remark-ably little cognisance of it all; rather as a column of wood-ants, when you place a pebble in their accustomed path, will stroke it for a while with their feelers, then divide to pass around the obstacle and carry on their business as if it were not really there. The Germans at Tsingtao were too few to run the whole show themselves, so not only the menial work of the colony but most of the civil administration as well was carried out by native Chinese working under German managers. What the former thought of the latter can only be surmised.

Tsingtao at the end of July 1914 was in a state of some disquiet as it woke up to the fact that with a general war breaking out in Europe it was virtually defenceless apart from its ring of forts, ten thousand miles from Germany and surrounded by enemies, with the Japanese now likely to enter the war on the Allied side. A powerful German naval force was normally based here: Admiral Graf von Spee's East Asiatic Squadron. But they had been away on manoeuvres now for a fortnight, somewhere out in the Pacific, and would clearly be very unwise to try coming back. That left the light cruiser S.M.S. *Emden,* a collection of elderly gunboats and torpedo vessels, quite useless for modern war—and ourselves. Once the *Emden* had slipped away, which she soon did, S.M.S. *Kaiserin Elisabeth* became (for what it was worth) the most powerful naval unit of the Central Powers in Chinese waters. But what were we to do? Austria-Hungary might soon be at war with Russia. But what about Russia's ally France? And France's ally Britain? And Britain's ally Japan? Once again we tried contacting Vienna, a futile task now, since the overland telegraph line passed across Russia while the undersea cables led to British Hong Kong and French Indo-China. All that we got was a signal on the first day of August telling us to immobilise the ship at Tsingtao and then get all personnel back to Austria "by whatever means possible," or failing that to the Austro-Hungarian Legation in Peking.

So we set to work laying up the *Elisabeth* for what might be a pro-longed hibernation. All furniture and wooden partitions and movable fittings were landed and packed away in vacant godowns on one of the commercial wharves. It was a weary business in the moist August heat: sweating human chains passing thousands of the most bizarrely assorted domestic items from hand to hand across the quayside and into the ware-houses. I imagine that you must have noticed too how, when you move house, the contents appear to swell miraculously in volume, so that what once filled a cupboard now fills half a furniture van. Well, it was like that only far, far worse as the accumulated junk of a quarter-century of foreign service was excavated from the *Elisabeth*'s holds: kitbags containing the personal effects of men long since buried at sea; Javanese rice-spoons and bamboo parrot-cages bought on shore-leave and forgotten by midshipmen who were now grey-haired Fregattenkapitäns; complete cleaning kits for calibres of shipboard artillery long ago consigned to the museum. Then came the ammunition from the magazines, and the guns themselves, released from their cradles and plastered with preservative grease—a loathsome task—before being swung ashore by the derricks and packed away. Meanwhile down in the bowels of the ship the engineers and stokers toiled to drain the water from the boilers and wrap the engines in oil-soaked sacking. At last, by the early afternoon of the 2nd, it was all finished and we went aboard to clean off the grime and pack our belongings for the rail journey to Peking. But as we did so a messenger arrived and handed the Captain a telegram. It was from the War Ministry in Vienna. I had the honour of decoding it—and my heart sank into my boots as the words emerged: we were to put the ship back on a war footing immediately and place ourselves under the orders of the Governor of Tsingtao. The Captain announced this to the crew as they stood on the quayside, grimy and almost falling over with exhaustion. It is a curiously moving experience, to hear 350 sailors uttering the words "Oh shit!" in eleven different languages.

None the less, orders are orders, and back it all had to go, the crew cursing under the light of hurricane-lamps as they removed everything from the godowns and loaded it back aboard, then replaced the guns and cleaned the grease off them, then refilled the boilers and removed the oil-soaked sacking from the engines. At the end of it all I saw men so weary that they just lay down to sleep on the stones of the quayside, too tired even to bother slinging their hammocks.

After these futile exertions the next couple of weeks passed uneventfully enough. Austria-Hungary was now officially at war with France and Britain as well as with Russia and Serbia. But this meant little enough to us out here on the coast of China, except that the ship was now on a war footing, with all wooden fittings removed and black-out in force. Our only task was to take turns with the German gunboat *Jaguar* keeping watch off Tsingtao harbour and the entrance to the near-and-locked Bay of Kiaochow. We would steam out to a point about two miles offshore, then anchor in the lee of a reef and sit there for two days until the *Jaguar* came out to relieve us. It was all rather boring and not in the least how I had imagined active service.

This went on until 23 August. On that day Japan finally declared war on Germany—but not on Austria-Hungary. Once more we cabled Vienna for instructions—this time via San Francisco—and once more we received the reply "Immobilise the ship and proceed to Peking." So we docked at Tsingtao harbour and went through the whole wretched process again, laying up the ship and landing everything movable. Then we packed once more to board the train for Tsientsin and the Chinese capital. Only a small care-and-maintenance party was to remain aboard the ship.

Since for reasons of age or alcoholism or mental incapacity the great majority of the *Elisabeth*'s officers and NCOs were militarily useless, only a couple of the younger artillery specialists were to stay in Tsingtao to aid the German garrison. I was young and I was an ex-gunnery officer, but I was not among them; in fact for some inexplicable reason the telegram from the k.u.k. War Ministry had mentioned me by name as one of those who were to go to Peking and—presumably—to internment by the Chinese for the duration of the war. There was little time however to wonder why this should be, because we were now busy organising our train journey to Peking. We would travel in parties of fifty and I would be second-in-command of one such group. It was to be led by none other than Korvettenkapitän Julius Fichterle, who had not in the end been able to return to Europe with the *Gorzkowski* because of the outbreak of war. My assistant was an elderly Viennese petty officer called Florian Kaindel.

I knew Stabstorpedomeister Kaindel already because he had been my division's petty officer when I was a cadet at the turn of the century, aboard the steam corvette *Windischgrätz* as she set off for a training cruise in the South Atlantic in the autumn of 1902. I remembered him well: a grizzled, fox-faced old rogue with thirty years of sea-service behind him even then—and at least one spell in the naval prison for selling brass cartridge cases to civilian scrap-dealers. Guardian of an inexhaustible treasury of cynicism, he had been a constant source of information and advice for us young lads. I well remember him at the tiller of our rowing cutter one hot November afternoon off Madeira as we boys sat behind our oars, cutlasses hanging at our belts since we were supposed to be a landing party, and watched our ship's worn-out old 15cm guns (rifled breech-loaders but still mounted on wheeled carriages) fire a broadside. Kaindel looked on, cap pushed back on head, as the shells emerged from the smoke-cloud, toppling lazily end over end to splash into the sea a couple of hundred metres abeam. He spat into the water, then turned to address us.

"*Na ja, meine junge Herren*—that's why the Navy gives you your wine-ration before a battle: so that if nothing else you can piss on the enemy as he comes alongside."

Kaindel was less than a year off retirement now, but unhappy to be missing the war, which he regarded as a sport that ought not to be reserved for young men. "It's not that I want to get killed, Herr Schiffsleutnant," he confided to me as the train clanked along towards Tsinanfu junction, "but I haven't really got a lot to go back to in Austria once I come out of the Navy, except for a sister in Vienna. And since it's happened I'd like to be in it—especially as they say it's all going to be over in a few weeks."

Korvettenkapitän Fichterle was less enthusiastic. He was glad, I could see, to be escaping to the relative safety of neutral China. His main anxiety was that in his absence Frau Fichterle would be unable to complete the exchange of contracts on the retirement villa in Graz.

We arrived at Tsientsin junction and were ordered to put up until further notice in the German barrack compound there, a grim collection of brick buildings which might well have been somewhere in the Mark of Brandenburg. It began to rain that night—not the European business of a discreet, hazy drizzle then fine again next day but the sudden, determined onset of the north-Chinese autumn: a steady, relentless, monomaniac downpour which soon turned the roads to canals and the fields to mirror-sheets of liquid yellow mud. But even worse was to come, for on the 27th we received two more telegrams. The first was from our legation in Peking, informing us that because of Chinese neutrality—and because the railway to the capital was British-controlled—we would not be able to proceed any further. The second was from Tsingtao, where a wireless message had been received from Vienna. Austria-Hungary was now at war with Japan and S.M.S. *Kaiserin Elisabeth* was to fight alongside the German garrison. All able-bodied crew members were therefore to report back aboard immediately. Everyone groaned and started packing their belongings: this meant another spell of loading ship when we got back. Then, about midday, we were visited by the German Consul in Tsientsin. The Chinese authorities were unlikely to let us return in Austrian naval uniform, he said, so he had organised an emergency collection of civilian clothing from the German and Austrian community in the town. We were to discard our uniforms and travel back to Tsingtao by rail in civilian dress, split up now into parties of twenty or so which, it was hoped, would attract less notice at the railway stations on the way.

Thus it came about that the evening of 27 August 1914 saw k.u.k. Linienschiffsleutnant Ottokar Prohaska arriving at Tsientsin railway station to further serve his Imperial, Royal and Apostolic Majesty, dressed not as per the *Adjustierungsvorschrift* but as follows: one pair loden-cloth plus-fours, at least two sizes too large; woollen stockings and nailed mountaineering boots; a tweed Norfolk jacket, approximately right size; a stiff wing-collar; and a bowler hat one size too small. The rest of my party were dressed in equally strange fashion or worse: a bizarre mixture of German Alpine rig, striped yachting blazers, Homburg hats, straw boaters, cycling caps and even fragments of evening dress. Most of the clothing donated to us had been cut to fit the more than ample frames of middle-aged German railway officials and factory managers, so it hung very ill on the younger and slimmer figures of Austrian naval ratings.

Despite our outré get-up the first stage of our journey passed smoothly enough, a night-time ride to Tsinanfu junction in a third-class carriage full of cheerful, spitting, smoking, dice-throwing Chinese peasants on their way to market with bundles of trussed-up live fowls and pigs lashed to bamboo poles. They were a highly scented lot, it must be said, but genial and friendly and (it seemed) not at all put out at having to share their journey with twenty long-nose devils dressed like something from a circus. We bartered with them for hard-boiled eggs and peanuts and cigarettes, using sign-language. Then a mah-jong set was produced. I was doubtful, but Kaindel sat down to it with a will. The pieces clacked on the board like pistol shots, and by the time dawn broke over the weeping flat fields he had vindicated the honour of the k.u.k. Kriegsmarine by clearing out the entire bank. These Chinese gamblers were "fesch," he reported; but not quite fesch enough for a Viennese petty officer.

Things got worse after Tsinanfu, the junction with the German-owned Shantungbahn. A suave young Chinese police officer climbed aboard and told us in faultless German that we were to be so kind as to leave the train at the next station, Weifang. The reason? Chinese neutrality. And what were we to do then? He shrugged his shoulders. Could we go back to Tsientsin? No, that would not be possible: his orders did not permit it. Could we contact the German consul in Tsientsin by telegraph then? No, that would not be possible either. It seemed that we were to sit on the platform at Weifang and wait until the Chinese decided to intern us. I sensed that a bribe was being fished for, but even if I had been disposed to pay it we had not the means: our pocket money for the journey was nearly exhausted, and even with Kaindel's mah-jong winnings we could barely scrape together a couple of Chinese dollars. I asked the young policeman if we could press ahead on foot from Weifang? He said that this would not be permitted either, but in any case he doubted whether we would get very far since the Japanese had landed west of Tsingtao and were occupying part of the Shantungbahn railway.

We sat all day on the platform at Weifang as the rain poured down, cold, damp, hungry and waiting for nightfall so that we could give the Chinese police the slip and set out along the railway track. We had agreed that we would travel in two parties of ten, just within hailing distance of one another, and trust to luck and the guiding hand of Providence to stop us from bumping up against a Japanese patrol. If we ran into them we would take to the fields and try to work around them to the north. My companions were not disposed to take the Japanese too seriously, regarding them as a comic-opera army of puny, bespectacled primitives. For my part, though, having seen them at work in Manchuria in 1905, I was anxious to give them a wide berth.

We set off along the railway track as darkness fell, and trudged miserably for several hours along the crunching stone ballast in the teeming rain. We were soaked through and very depressed, but somehow we all bore up; all, that is, except Fichterle, who was far too old for this sort of thing. Halts for him to find his breath became more and more frequent as the night wore on. Then about midnight we saw lights ahead of us and heard voices. We dived for cover and lay in the sodden grass of the embankment. There were about twelve of them I think, but from what I could make out of their voices they were Chinese troops rather than Japanese. We let them pass, then got up and wearily resumed our march. The grey dawn came up to find us resting in the lee of the embankment and sharing out our last scraps of food: some wet rice-biscuits and a few boiled sweets which we had bartered for on the train, so virulently coloured that even as famished as we were we hesitated to eat them. Fichterle lolled beside us. He was in a bad way now, grey-faced and panting for breath. But we could not leave him, so we set off down the line once more, half carrying him with us.

Kaindel and I saw them first, about eight hundred metres down the track: a group of fifty or so men clustered about a railway locomotive with steam up. We bade the others lie down and crept forward in the shelter of the embankment to investigate. The men were dressed in khaki, which gave us no help. Then I saw it: a flag fixed to the front of the firebox. It was white with a red disc in the middle. We turned around as discreetly as we could and went back.

There followed a wide detour through the Chinese countryside, splashing our way along waterlogged paths between inundated fields stinking of the night-soil which the Chinese use as field manure. A number of straw-caped Chinese peasants watched us with curiosity as we passed, making no attempt either to help or to hinder us. It was apparent that to them any eccentricity on the part of the round-eyed demons was perfectly normal, even going for country rambles in fancy dress in the middle of the autumn rains. We passed through a hamlet of mud-walled houses, seemingly deserted. We had almost cleared it when, as if by magic, a group of brown-clad little men with rifles appeared from a side-lane. They might well have been Chinese soldiers, but I had no intention of stopping to ask. We ran. Shouts followed us, then the crack of shots. Bullets splashed in the mud as we dived for the cover of a drainage ditch and half ran, half waded along it.

"I can't . . . I can't . . . Please, leave me . . . I can't keep up," Fichterle sobbed as we half-dragged him along with us. He stumbled and fell. His breath was gurgling now and his face almost blue. "Leave me, comrades, leave me be . . . I can't go . . . on." We hauled him into the shelter of a drainage culvert as a great spasm of choking gripped him. We loosened his collar and opened his jacket to pound his chest but it was no use: he was a dying man, victim of a heart attack. I felt his pulse weaken, then stop after a few minutes. We left him there, in that flooded culvert in the flat, waterlogged fields of Shantung province, under the low grey-brown sky and the pitiless rain. I notified his death when we got back, but so far as I know his body was never found. Perhaps the Chinese villagers discovered it and gave him burial; more probably he sank into the evil-smelling yellow mud and lies there still, half a world away from Fran Fichterle in her vault and the little retirement villa outside Graz with the vines around the door.

The rest of us made it back to Tsingtao the last day of August, wet through, starving, exhausted and with two of our party suffering from the early stages of malaria. There was little time to recuperate: the Japanese had now surrounded the port at a distance of about fifteen kilometres and were only waiting for the rains to break before closing in to lay siege. We would soon be in for it. Aboard the *Elisabeth,* though, we were not waiting idly. By some miracle nearly all of the crew had got back from Tsientsin—by rail or on foot, by boat or by water-buffalo or even, in the case of one party, with the aid of Chinese sail-assisted wheelbarrows. The ship was put back on a war footing and all her armament remounted, with the exception of two 15cm guns, which were installed in a redoubt above the town as "Battery Elisabeth." The cruiser's part in the defence of the port would be to steam out into Kiaochow Bay and anchor in a part of it called the Tsanku Deep, sheltered by hills from the Japanese guns. She would then use her own artillery to provide flanking fire as the enemy moved up towards the town.

The only, obvious snag with this of course was that if the Japanese could not see the *Elisabeth,* she could not see them either. And this was how it came about that on 15 September 1914 Torpedomeister Kaindel, two telegraphist ratings and I took up our position in a railway-sleeper-and-bamboo dug-out on the slopes of the Raven Pass above Tsingtao, looking out over the flat countryside to northwards. We were to act until further notice as a forward artillery observation post for our ship.

We were out on the left flank of the German defences, which consisted of a small network of trenches and dug-outs to the right of our position, linked to it by a short communication trench and protected in front by a half-hearted attempt at barbed-wire entanglements. For our own defence in case of a Japanese assault we had only rifles. It looked as though we might not need them for quite some time, however. Through binoculars we could see the Japanese moving their artillery along the flooded roads into the villages below us on the plain; but apart from lobbing the odd shell in our direction they showed no immediate readiness to attack. For our part, since the *Elisabeth*'s stock of ammunition was limited, all that we were required to do was to observe a few ranging shots, listening to our shells as they rumbled overhead then watching them throw up sudden spouts of ochre mud in the fields beneath. Meanwhile the autumn rain still poured down, driven now by a chill, gusting north wind. Apart from telephoning our ship each hour to report "no movement in past hour," there was nothing to do except keep watch, and when not keeping watch to crouch shivering beneath the dripping roof of our dug-out and try to cook our rations over a thin fire of rice-straw in an old petrol tin. So this was war, I thought to myself as I nursed a ripening mouth-ulcer: not white tunics and the blaring of bugles and the flash of sabres but trying to huddle out of the rain in a waterlogged hole in a Chinese hillside. I had no means of knowing that, far away in Europe, millions were making the same depressing discovery.

It all happened with alarming suddenness just after dawn one morning. We were trying to brew coffee over our makeshift stove, wet through and cold as usual but relieved at least that the rain had let up during the night. Kaindel leant on the sandbag parapet trying to light a damp cigarette—then suddenly dropped his match, staring in disbelief.

"Holy Mother of God—they're coming!"

Others had drawn the same conclusion in the adjacent German trenches: petrol tins and shell-cases were clanking in a frenzy to call the defenders to stand to. I stood up and stared in horrified wonder at the sight before me. It was like a football crowd rushing out of a stadium after a match, only a hundred times wider. Up the stony slope they came at the double, hardly slowed at all by our exiguous lines of barbed wire, childlike figures in khaki overcoats and peaked caps, yelling shrilly as they advanced. Officers ran ahead of them with drawn swords. Bugles screamed and rising-sun flags waved above their massed ranks. There was a pause of a few seconds, filled with the noise of rifle-bolts being worked, and of a Maxim machine gun being cocked in the German redoubt. Then it began. The first rank was about five hundred metres away when it went down, all falling like cardboard cut-outs when a string is pulled behind them. But still they came on. There was no time to think, only to work the bolt and fire and work the bolt and fire and fumble a clip into the magazine then work the bolt again and fire until the rifle grew too hot to touch and rounds went off of their own accord in the breech. There was no need to take aim. Yet still the khaki swarm came on, some falling in a convulsion of limbs, others dropping carefully to their knees and laying down their rifles before they toppled over. By now artillery shells from the forts were howling overhead to burst among them, throwing up fountains of earth and rock and human debris. The din was fearful, preventing any thought but to load and fire and load again. Somewhere at the back of my head the Heir-Apparent's words echoed from that day at the shoot in Bohemia: "The best of all is when a fellow kills without knowing he's killing." Then the Maxim gun to our right jammed. Luckily for us it was just as the Japanese attack was breaking, its momentum spent among a field of dead and dying. Yet still a few heroic survivors were carried forward like some last wash of a wave on a beach, to half jump, half fall into our positions. There followed a brief but ferocious brawl with rifle butts and entrenching tools as we fought to drive out the terrible little men.

It was an officer who came for me with his two-handed sword. He was a good head shorter than myself, but if he had not slipped on the wet sandbags he would certainly have evened the difference. The blade sang over my head as I lunged instinctively with rifle and bayonet. The next thing I knew he had dropped his sword and was gazing down in surprise at the blade buried in his abdomen. With a look of mild exasperation, as if a tunic button had just come off, he grasped the bayonet with both hands to try and pull it out. He coughed and fell to his knees as I withdrew the weapon and turned to assist one of my ratings who was desperately trying to parry the bayonet thrusts of a Japanese soldier. Someone shot him for me before I could get to him. Then it was all over: silence, and a sudden feeling of numb emptiness inside.

Too dazed and bewildered to think of anything much, I went back to our post—and found the officer who had tried to kill me and whom I had just bayoneted. He was still alive, but only just. He gazed up at me with his black eyes, and said something which I could not understand. His lips were parted and I noticed how perfect his teeth were. I found an aluminium water canteen and knelt down to press it to his mouth. He drank a little, and said something else which I could not understand. Then he started to sing faintly to himself, a strange rising-falling song which reminded me— I cannot say why—of the guslar's song that evening months before in the mountains of Montenegro. But the song grew weaker as his fingernails turned blue. He shivered a little at last, and it was all over. It haunted me for long afterwards—in fact still haunts me to this day—the insane waste of it all: that two young men from countries which were scarcely aware of one another's existence should have been sent from opposite sides of the world to kill one another. He was not the first man I had killed: I had shot a tribesman with a revolver when we were attacked once by cannibals in New Guinea. But that was a long way off and amid the confusion of battle. This was the first time I had seen one of my victims die close-to. Seventy-odd years on, the least that I can console myself with is the knowledge that he seemed to die happy, conscious of duty performed to the end. I hope that I shall meet him again before long, in a place where there are no barriers of language, and ask his pardon for what I did, explaining that I would have borne him no malice if his footing had been surer and my arms had been shorter and he had killed me instead.

# 13

# STRESS OF WEATHER

S HOULD BE ANY MOMENT NOW . . ." My brother-officer looked at his wristwatch, then at the grey silhouette out on the smooth, sunlit autumn sea. "Ah, there they go! Regular as clockwork!" The distant shape was suddenly blotted out by swelling puffballs of golden fire which started at the stern and raced to the bow before dissolving into clouds of brownish smoke. A few seconds later the air shuddered to a series of mighty concussions, as if a row of giant steel safe-doors in a bank vault had all slammed shut in quick succession. The shells rumbled overhead like a procession of express trains through a tunnel. If you were sharp-eyed you could have looked up into the clear, blue sky to see the projectiles, four black specks hurtling through the air. We turned to watch the mountainside below Fort Hohenzollern, and the ground shook beneath our feet as four miniature volcanoes suddenly erupted with a deafening roar just below the glacis, flinging geysers of earth and pulverised rock a hundred metres into the air. As the dust and smoke settled we were able to see that, although the battleship's salvo had landed short, the line was correct. They must have been increasing the elevation a half-degree at each broadside, as witnessed by the chain of craters which was slowly but surely reaching up the hillside towards the fort. The reason for this accuracy was not far to seek. Up in the sky above us, ridiculously fragile-looking after the recent display of brutal explosive anger, a small white insect was droning about in slow circles, observing the fall of shot. It was a Farman seaplane, and one could clearly see the red discs beneath its wings.

"Do you think they've got wireless?" I enquired of my companion. "Surely not, though. A Farman seaplane can hardly lift a pilot, let alone a transmitter."

"Perhaps not. But their shooting seems to be getting more accurate by the hour now that the Japs have got an aeroplane up there. It can't just be coincidence. But which ship did you say she is?"

"She must be the *Inexorable:* the Britishers have no other *Canopus*-class vessel in the Far East. It's a funny thing, but I was invited to a reception aboard her not three months back at Colombo, and here they are now, trying to kill us as if we'd never been anything but mortal enemies."

"That's war, Prohaska old man. But I'll say this for the English, their gunnery's as regular as the days of the week: a salvo every five minutes on the dot. Why aren't they firing faster though?"

"I suppose they know there's no danger of us getting away, or of anyone coming to help us now, so they can stand out to sea and knock us about at their leisure. I must say though that I'd have expected twelve-inch shells to have more effect. I had a look at some of the craters near Viktoria Luise yesterday. The shells bury themselves in the ground before they go off and just excavate a deep, narrow hole, like a funnel."

"True. But before long one of them's going to find a magazine chamber at the bottom of the hole, then it'll be good-night Fort Hohenzollern."

We made our way back down the path from the headland overlooking the Yellow Sea. It was about a fortnight now since I had helped beat back the Japanese attack. The autumn rains had ceased for the while and the weather was now clear and bright, though colder with each day that passed. But the siege had not lifted, in fact had drawn closer during the past week. Unlike their counterparts in Europe, the Japanese generals had at least learnt from the slaughter at the Raven Pass that, in the age of the machine gun and the bolt-action rifle, massed infantry assaults in broad daylight were a futile and costly business. They had evidently decided for the time being that slow strangulation was the best way of dealing with Tsingtao. For our part, we had pulled back our defences by several kilometres all around in order to have a shorter line to hold. Stocks of food and ammunition were adequate for several more months, but from what little we were able to learn of the progress of the war in Europe it was obvious that no help was going to reach us now. It might be weeks or it might be months, but the German colony of Tsingtao and its four thousand-strong garrison was now doomed to surrender.

The town as we entered it that morning was now very obviously a fortress under siege. Sandbagged emplacements had been built on every corner, hospitals had been set up in disused schools and hardly anyone in civilian dress was to be seen in the streets. All day and most of the night the air shook to the dull bumping of Japanese heavy artillery shelling the forts from landward, and the guns of Allied warships shelling them from seaward. The bombardment had left the town largely untouched, apart from the odd stray shell, for this was only 1914 and deliberate attacks on civilian property were still taboo for civilised nations. But the forts on the mountains around Tsingtao were having an increasingly hard time of it, especially now that the British had brought up a battleship whose guns had sufficient range to allow her to anchor beyond the German minefields, well outside the reach of our own artillery, and pound us at her leisure.

My companion and I discussed this problem as we walked back down through the town to the naval harbour, where the *Kaiserin Elisabeth* was taking a day's rest from providing artillery support on the left flank of our lines.

"What we need to do," he said, "is to remove that battleship one way or another. The smaller ships don't have enough range to do the forts a great deal of damage, and they daren't come close in to try sweeping our minefields. If only there were some way of getting at the Britishers . . ."

"Easier said than done. It'd be suicide in daytime, and the Jap destroyers keep a close picket line offshore at night. One of the German torpedoboats tried a few nights back and thought herself lucky to escape with her funnels riddled like colanders. A warship would never get close enough to risk a torpedo."

He laughed. "Perhaps we ought to try a Chinese junk? So far as I can make out the locals take little notice of the long-noses and their precious war. At any rate, I've often seen junks out there among the warships, sailing along as if nothing had happened. It seems that Chinese skippers have sailed these routes for the past four thousand years and aren't going to be put off by the Japs and a lot of mad Europeans fighting one another. Perhaps we could load a torpedo aboard a junk and just creep out one night and try to hit the *Inexorable.* If nothing else it'd be better than sitting here waiting to be taken prisoner."

I was silent as we walked along, thinking deeply. I remembered an item of redundant stores that we had excavated from the holds of the *Elisabeth* a few weeks before, during the first great immobilisation panic. And I also remembered a certain exercise that we had once attempted to perform many years before when I was aboard the steam corvette *Windischgrätz* as a cadet. That evening, back on board the *Elisabeth,* I requested an interview with the Captain.

"Well Prohaska," he said, "on the face of it it seems an eccentric idea. But after giving the matter some consideration over dinner, I can't see why not. Quite frankly, the *Kaiserin Elisabeth* and her crew have taken no very notable part in these operations until now, and as far as I can see the operation which you suggest, even if it were unsuccessful, might help lift morale and do something to restore the prestige of the k.u.k. Kriegsmarine in the eyes of our German allies. Anyway, how many men do you think that you would require?"

"About twenty I should think, Herr Kommandant: the local junks seem to have about that many crew."

"Twenty, you say? It seems an awful lot, particularly since it would be mostly our youngest and fittest men. But there: what else will they do except sit here and wait for the Allies to round them up when the town falls? As for the rest though, do I understand you as saying that you want two 45cm torpedoes and the dropping frames?"

"With respect, yes, Herr Kommandant."

He sucked his teeth for some time and twirled one end of his moustache absent-mindedly. "Two torpedoes would take some accounting for if you lost them—but then again, what earthly use are they to us now, bottled up here in harbour? As for the dropping gear, you're welcome: it's so old that it doesn't even appear on the inventory of stores any longer. I believe that they were all collected for scrap about 1908, but since the ship was already on the China Station no one bothered with ours. Have you ever used them though?"

"Once only, Herr Kommandant, when I was a cadet. We tried launching torpedoes from a fifteen-metre sailing cutter in Castello Bay."

"With what results, if I might ask?"

"To be honest, rather mixed, Herr Kommandant."

He shrugged. "Very well then: you may have your crew and your vessel and the necessary armament. I shall ask for volunteers tomorrow. Personally I think that you're just courting death to no purpose, but if nothing else it'll make something worthwhile to put down in the official history of the siege. Austria's military annals are largely a record of heroic futility, I fear, so you'll at least be part of a long tradition. Anyway, when do you propose taking this junk of yours out for a sail?"

"Perhaps the day after tomorrow, Herr Kommandant, if everything can be got ready in time."

"Excellent. I shall come and watch. There's been precious little else to laugh at lately."

The Habsburg fleet in my day might have been German-speaking, but this had not always been the case, for as late as the 1850s Italian had been its language of command. And why not, when we were legatees and heirs-at-law to the Navy of the Most Serene Republic of Venice? When I was a cadet at the turn of the century a number of the older and crustier naval staff officers still had themselves paddled ashore in gondolas instead of the smart four-oared gigs prescribed by regulations. My first captain, Slawetz von Löwenhausen aboard the *Windischgrätz,* was one such. I was once given the job of returning his gondola to the Molo Bellona before we sailed from Pola, bound for South America. And I still remember the bitter humiliation as the little vessel pirouetted aimlessly in the middle of the harbour, how I sweated with effort and embarrassment as I tried desperately to steer and propel it with the single paddle while the whole k.u.k. Kriegsmarine lined the rails to jeer at my discomfiture. Well, I was to experience exactly the same feeling of impotent rage that next afternoon as my crew and I struggled to master a twenty-metre Pechili trading junk out in the waters of Kiaochow Bay.

Indeed, I think that in all my years at sea I never came across a more awkward vessel or one so totally and mulishly defiant of all the accepted rules of boat-handling as practised in the rest of the world. My crew were mostly Croat seamen from the coast and islands of Dalmatia, men to whom the handling of small sailing vessels was as natural and effortless as breathing. They were well accustomed to the square-headed lugsail, of which our junk carried no less than five, and also to the deep, heavy rudder lifted by a block and tackle, which was standard equipment aboard their native trabaccolos and brazzeras. Yet, superb sailors as they were, the junk entirely defeated them. When we tried to run before the wind the vessel would yaw and roll uncontrollably from side to side, then suddenly broach round head to wind and begin to sail backwards, flapping and clacking her battened sails like some malevolent praying mantis. Yet when we tried deliberately to luff her round into the wind she would keep paying off, or sit sullenly in irons until we had to push her round with the single, huge bamboo stern-sweep. When we tried to sail on a reach she would drift sideways like a crab, wallowing in the wave troughs; while as for going to windward, a cardboard box would have performed better. In the end, after two or three hours of this, we had to admit defeat. Too worn-out and apathetic to mind the hooting crowds on the lighthouse mole—for whom we had provided a rare afternoon's diversion from the monotony of the siege—we submitted to the crowning indignity of being towed back in by a steam pinnace.

A figure detached itself from the crowd as I climbed the steps at the jetty to report to my Captain that the junk was unusable. He stepped up to me, saluted and offered me his hand. I already knew him slightly: Leutnant-zur-See Paul Ehrlich of the Imperial German Naval Reserve. He stood out from the other German naval officers at Tsingtao by reason of being a Eurasian, the son of a Lutheran missionary from Mecklenburg who had come out to North China in the 1880s and married a local woman. His peacetime employment was as a navigation and pilotage inspector with the local German shipping authority, and since he was fluent in Mandarin Chinese, Cantonese and all the local dialects thereof his wartime post would have been aboard a German river gunboat on the Yangtze. However, his ship had been undergoing a refit at Tsingtao when the war broke out and he was now bottled up in a town under siege like everyone else. His position though was rather more isolated than that of the rest of us. For one thing the German professional naval officers had a rather disdainful attitude towards reservists; and for another there was the colour of his skin. For while the Habsburg officer corps was quite marvellously indifferent to the national origin of its members, its German equivalent was extremely touchy on the subject of race, operating an almost explicit ban on Jews becoming regular officers and making it very difficult for Poles or French-speaking Alsatians to obtain commissions. Ehrlich had grown up to think of himself as a German—though he had never managed to visit Germany—but now found himself treated with suspicion by Germans and Chinese alike.

"Herr Linienschiffsleutnant," he said, "I hope that you will forgive me for remarking upon it, but I cannot help observing from your crew's performance out there that you have not the slightest idea how to sail a junk . . ." Thank you, Herr Leutnant, I thought to myself: you may be half Chinese and may never have seen your distant Fatherland, but you have still inherited all that instinctive tact and delicacy for which Prussians are so justly famous. But before I could think of a suitably polite way of saying this, he smiled and continued: ". . . but of course, no European has. To handle a junk properly you have to have been born aboard one and lived your whole life afloat."

"Thank you for that advice, Herr Leutnant. But permit me to observe that it helps me very little in the operation which we are planning."

"May I make a suggestion, then?"

"By all means."

"Let me find you a local crew off the waterfront this afternoon and show you what they can do with the boat. Then if you're as impressed as I think you will be, you can try signing them up to sail the junk for you in the—er, operation, which you are preparing."

"Hmmm. The idea seems attractive, I agree. But there are two problems.

For one thing your local sailors are Chinese subjects and therefore citizens of a neutral state; and for another, even if I could overcome the bureaucratic difficulties and hire them to sail with us, how would I tell them what to do? I speak barely a word of Chinese."

"Simple—I would come with you."

So Leutnant Ehrlich recruited his crew of seventeen Chinese junk sailors. It was not easy. As soon as war broke out most of the local Chinese population had tactfully disappeared from Tsingtao. The German Governor had issued decrees and declared martial law to press-gang those who remained, but he was rapidly discovering that there are times when the laws of supply and demand apply even on the coasts of China. There had been far too few Europeans to run the place even in peacetime, and now that the entire adult male population was in uniform, those Chinese who had stayed on in Tsingtao were demanding and getting quite respectable wages for digging trenches and loading supplies at the harbour. In the end we had to pay heavily in gold coin from the ship's pay-chest to get our crew. But they undeniably gave good value for money next morning, miraculously transforming our floating orange-box of a vessel into, if not exactly an ocean greyhound, then quite a fast and handy small sailing trader. To this day I have no idea how they did it. Certainly to my eye it looked the very opposite of seamanship as taught at the naval training establishments of Europe, consisting as it did of a great deal of confused, ant-like, apparently panic-stricken scrambling about to an accompaniment of that curious Chinese street-noise, a sort of raucous nasal "wang-wang-wang" sound. But, messy and chaotic as it looked, it did the job impressively well. The junk went through her paces under Ehrlich's command as neatly as any European yacht, and even managed at one stage to sail within about five points of the wind, a difficult enough feat for any lug-sailed vessel and especially for a clumsy, flat-bottomed, high-sided scow like ours. I did notice at one point that they were letting her heel so that the almost square chine acted as a sort of keel, but apart from that it might have been by witchcraft for all the sense that I could make of it. I suppose that, as Ehrlich said, it came from living one's entire life aboard a junk and sensing every quiver of its hull as if it were an extension of one's own body.

By evening we had established to the satisfaction of Linienschiffs-kapitän Makovitz that with a locally hired crew, a fair wind, a dark night and a good helping of luck a Chinese junk might be made into an effective torpedo vessel. The problem then arose of squaring this highly uncon-ventional project with the service regulations. Recruiting foreigners to serve the Austrian Emperor was no great obstacle: since the days of Prinz Eugen the Habsburg armies had employed soldiers from every country in Europe and from quite a few outside it, and the *Dienstreglement* said nothing whatever about citizenship. As for the Chinese themselves, so far as we could make out in our negotiations with them via the two brothers who seemed to be the local shop stewards of the seamen's union, they were not at all bothered about serving in a foreign navy, provided they were paid well enough and given red and white K.U.K. KRIEGSMARINE armbands to protect them from any unpleasantness under the Hague Convention. No, the problems only began when money had to be found to pay them. In the end it required two days of agonised and intricate pleading with the *Elisabeth*'s paymaster before he grudgingly agreed to recognise the Captain's delegated authority from the Ministry of Finances and open his safe. Each man got no less than 800 Kronen in gold—about two years' wages for an Austrian naval rating. I was very unhappy about paying this in advance, fearing naturally that once they had the money our Chinese sailors would head for the open sea and vanish without trace, but Ehrlich set my mind at rest.

"The thing to understand about Chinese seamen," he said, "is that they have absolutely no respect for you either as an officer or as a Euro-pean. They're excellent seamen in every possible respect—except perhaps for cleanliness—but they're not doing it because you command obedience from them, in the way that our sailors will work willingly for a tough captain even when they're underpaid and ill-treated. The Chinese find all Europeans quite ridiculous, and the nearest you'll ever get to their affec-tion is when they reach the stage of treating you indulgently, like a parent with a half-witted child. But within those limitations I've certainly found myself that provided you pay them well, they'll always do what they've been paid to do. As for running off with the cash, you need have no fears on that score. No, I can't understand why they don't either. But they just won't; take my word for it."

As for the junk herself, despite her demonstrable sailing qualities she was still an utterly perverse craft to the European eye. In fact, every single thing about her seemed to have been designed back-to-front or upside-down. Take her hull, for example. I think that most people, however ill-versed in naval architecture, would agree that in general, a boat has a rounded bottom and a flat deck. Well, just to be different our junk had a flat bottom and a rounded deck, as if her builders had started out intending to construct an elongated packing crate and had ended up making a barrel. The bottom was flat in section, without a keel and con-structed from massive pine planks stapled together with iron cleats. The chines were almost square and the topsides were planked not European clinker-fashion, where one starts with the planks next to the keel and works upwards so that each strake overlaps the one below it, but Chinese-style, starting at the top and working down. As for the deck, it was whale-backed like the deck of a submarine and topped with a bamboo platform to walk on. And whereas boats in the western world have a pointed bow and a flat stern, the junk had a sawn-off bow like that of a pram dinghy, with a massive windlass mounted across it, and a pointed stern with the rudder hanging from the stern post on sliding hinges, so that it could be raised and lowered with pulleys. Accommodation was a barrel-roofed deckhouse at the stern, rather like a small railway carriage, and beyond the stern there projected a kind of gallery made of bamboo lattice sus-pended between two projecting beams like the handles of some huge wheelbarrow. As for masts, she had no less than five, each carrying a bamboo-battened lugsail made of coarse calico strengthened with matting and controlled by a fantastically intricate system of crow's feet and uphroes and lazy-jacks—so fragile-looking that the lightest breeze seemed fit to bring it all crashing to the deck, and so complicated that a spider would have gone mad trying to make sense of it. Sleeping space consisted of tiers of coffin-like bunks in the deckhouse, and cooking was done on a double earthenware stove. Safety was represented by a stone-and-bamboo anchor, a five-metre sampan which could be hauled up on deck over rollers, and a small shrine to the Goddess of Mercy Kwan-Yin. As for finish, forget about it: there was not the slightest pretence at adornment. The hull was lopsided, the planks were so inaccurately cut that I could thrust my hand into the gaps between them and all the timbers were as rough as if they had just come from the saw-pit. The whole vessel stank most unpleasantly, partly from the stagnant water slopping about in the bilges, partly from the crew (who seemed never to have washed in their lives) and partly from the dark-red sails, which were that colour from having been treated with an infusion of mangrove bark in pig's blood. The vessel's exterior was painted—or rather smeared—black with pine-tar, while for stopping the horrifying gaps between the planking copious use was made of a substance called chu-nam, a kind of putty compounded from lime, hemp and bamboo shavings held together by the oil of some nut or other.

The junk might have been a crude and rather alarming vessel to European ways of thinking, but for our purposes at least she could not have been better designed, for the sloping deck was ideally built for slinging two torpedoes amidships, one on each side, without raising the centre of gravity too much. Junks in those waters, I had noticed, often carried large bundles of bamboo stems slung like a donkey's panniers on either side, partly I suppose for buoyancy and partly as primitive wash-strakes. So it was a simple matter for our carpenters to make up false bundles, hollow inside, to be slung over the torpedoes in their dropping cradles. When the time came we would simply cut a few ropes to discard the bundles. In the end, though I say it myself, it would have taken a sharp eye even when alongside to detect that our junk was anything other than a common north-Chinese trading vessel.

After four days or so of preparation we took the vessel out into Kiaochow Bay for trials under cover of darkness. The bamboo bundles were cut loose, the triggers were pushed to start the engines of the two practice torpedoes, then the levers of the dropping gear were pulled to open the clamps and release the two hissing missiles to splash into the water. We watched them streak away into the darkness, waited—then saw a red lamp in the distance. Both had hit their target, an old wooden barquentine moored eight hundred metres away. The demonstration was so conclusive that we were ordered to make ready for an attempt on the British battleship on the night of 30 September.

The crew for this exploit would consist of myself as Captain, Leutnant-zur-See Ehrlich as First Officer and interpreter and Torpedomeister Kaindel (who volunteered to come along with us) as torpedo and weapons specialist. Our armament, in addition to the torpedoes, would comprise three rifles and a Schwarzlose machine gun, the latter not so much for offence as to defend ourselves (though no one said as much) if our Chinese crew cut up nasty. As for the seventeen Chinese, they seemed perfectly happy to organise themselves according to the hallowed traditions of their ancestors under the direction of the two villainous-looking, dwarf-like brothers who had first negotiated with us on their behalf. Although I was unable to speak with these joint bos'uns, I asked Ehrlich what their names were. He told me. I asked him to write them down, and both Kaindel and I were delighted to find that their family name transliterated into German as something like "bei Wien." The elder and younger of the brothers were henceforth distinguished by us as "Baden bei Wien" and "Mödling bei Wien," after the two last stations on the Südbahn before one arrives in Vienna.

The plan of operation for the attack was that we would be towed out of Tsingtao harbour around midnight and then cast off to run before the breeze until we found our target. I anticipated no difficulty there: the wind had settled to a steady north-easterly for several days past and the Tsingtao meteorological station assured us that it would stay in that quarter for some time yet, although it might get stronger. If we could run before it, then with our shallow draught we could sail straight over our own defensive minefields offshore. We hoped then to be able to run through the Japanese picket lines undetected in darkness and silence. Once we neared our target there should be no trouble: the *Inexorable* had anchored overnight at the same spot for the past ten days and I had arranged that two pairs of lights on shore would give us our attack position. After that it should be easy.

The battleship would be blacked out, but even so a bulk as vast as that would be impossible not to see at five hundred metres' range. We would launch the torpedoes, and then try to run astern of the battleship in the darkness, hoping that in the confusion after the torpedoes hit we would be able to slip past unnoticed.

And after that? We would run down-coast towards Shanghai and then put the junk ashore to get ourselves interned while our Chinese seamen melted into the landscape. To this end, as I made my last preparations that evening, I checked our navigational equipment: a magnetic compass, a sextant, a small watch-chronometer, a set of charts for the north-Chinese coast down to the Yangtze and a nautical almanac. I also checked our navigational aids for use once we were ashore: a cashbox and a canvas money-belt holding 2,000 Austrian Kronen in gold. The Chinese authorities were known to be utterly corrupt, and I was confident that if we were able to talk with the local officials and wave a little money beneath their noses our internment would be lax enough to allow us to get to Shanghai and board a steamer bound for San Francisco.

One last detail remained to be settled, once all the preparations had been made. If we were to enjoy the protection of the Hague Convention on the treatment of prisoners of war, and not simply be shot out of hand as *francs-tireurs* if captured, our junk would need to be officially commissioned as an Austro-Hungarian naval vessel. We combed the naval lists and at last settled on the name *Schwarzenberg,* as being no longer in use by any other vessel. It was appropriate in a way: the steam frigate S.M.S. *Schwarzenberg* had been Commodore von Tegethoff's flagship at Heligoland in 1864 when an Austrian and a Danish squadron had met inconclusively in what turned out to be the last ever sea battle between sailing warships. It was fitting, we thought, that this belated sailing-ship action on which we were now embarking should be distinguished by such a hallowed name.

Midnight neared. A steam pinnace from the *Elisabeth* towed us out past the lighthouse and to the edge of the minefield, then slipped the hawser. Two lamps on shore lined up to give us our initial course, and we sheeted the sails to the wind. With a great creaking of bamboo we were off, running before the light breeze to bear down upon our unsuspecting target, anchored about three miles offshore. The wind had dropped a little since sundown. It was still quite adequate for our purposes, but I was uneasy at a curious, sticky, rather irritating warmth which had crept into the breeze after weeks of Manchurian cold—and at the rapidly falling barometer when we sailed. Still, it scarcely mattered now; half an hour would bring us within range of our target.

The first picket vessel we met beyond the edge of our minefields was a Japanese torpedo-boat. As their searchlight beam caught us, Kaindel and I scrambled out of sight and left the talking to Ehrlich, who was dressed in native clothing and was sufficiently Chinese in appearance to pass muster as a slow-witted local junk skipper. The Japanese had an interpreter aboard.

"What's he saying, Ehrlich?" I hissed from where I was crouching behind the bulwarks.

"Their Captain says that we're a gang of simpletons and if he had his way he'd cut all our heads off, since we seem to make so little use of them. He's ordered us to keep our present course and get to hell out of it as fast as we can before he loses his temper and opens fire."

We sailed on at a steady four knots until the torpedo-boat was lost in the darkness astern. Surely we must be nearly there: the two pairs of lights on shore now lined up perfectly to mark the starting point for our torpedo run. We strained our eyes peering into the murk ahead to catch our first glimpse of the black shape of the *Inexorable,* silhouetted against the faint light of the stars. But where was she? We reduced sail, then hove to. Still nothing. Our target had gone, raised anchor after nightfall and either moved to another position, or perhaps returned to Hong Kong for repairs and more ammunition. We had gone to all this trouble and come all this way for nothing. We loitered for half an hour, but the sea around us was empty. Our quarry had given us the slip.

The typhoon struck us about an hour before dawn, howling down from the wastes of the North Pacific with the suddenness of a tiger's pounce and the violence of a million buffaloes in full stampede. And it blew like that for the next nine days. I was to remember that time many years later when I was a prisoner in Buchenwald: recall how easily a sub-animal existence of fear and privation became normal; how quickly it dissolved one's sense of self; and how soon one forgot that there had ever been anything else. For the first two days I was sure that each wave would be our last, as the *Schwarzenberg* bowled crazily southwards before the screaming wind and the short, brutal seas and we clung to any projection on the deck, so soaked through and cold and terrified that we no longer felt exhaustion and hunger and lack of sleep, just a sick fear combined with a longing for it all to end. Direction and time and distance ceased to exist as we raced along, the whole world reduced to that crazily pitching, wave-swept deck and a grey disc of spray and howling wind and the constant, deafening crash of thunder beneath a low, muddy sky lit with the endless baleful flicker of lightning. Even day and night were abolished, merged into a uniform, sullen twilight as the clouds darkened day and the lightning illuminated night. The end nearly came on the first day, when a towering wave came up astern and broke over us. By some miracle no one was washed overboard, and the junk surfaced and shook herself afterwards like a duck in a farmyard pond. But much of our gear was washed away and the chronometer was put out of action.

It mattered little though: in this primeval chaos any idea of navigation was almost comically irrelevant. The most we could do was to reduce sail to the bare minimum necessary to keep us stern to sea and run before the tempest, hoping not to meet anything in our path. I was going to drop our torpedoes to lighten ship, but the Chinese stopped me, saying that the weight seemed to steady the vessel. Soon we had not the slightest idea where we were, or even which day it was. About the sixth day, the typhoon lessened just enough to give us a glimpse of land—perhaps Formosa, I thought—rushing past a mile or so to starboard. But then the weather closed in again and we ran straight ahead as before, centre of our roaring little world of waves and cloud and spray.

Then it was all over, almost as suddenly as it had begun, and our leaking, battered vessel found herself sailing before a warm breeze across a sunlit sea of indigo, creaking softly to herself as she pitched slowly on the long, gentle waves that follow a far-off storm. We felt our bearded, salt-caked faces in disbelief, astonished that we were still alive. The Chinese got busy with joss-sticks before the shrine of Kwan-Yin, the Goddess of Mercy, while kindling was laid out in the sun to dry and a tin box of matches was found. Soon a fire of charcoal was burning in the earthenware stove to cook the first warm food we had tasted in nine days. Before long a terrible tiredness struck us, as all the cheques which we had drawn against our physical and mental bank accounts were cleared at once. It was as much as we could do as dusk fell to heave to and snatch a few hours' sleep.

The sun came up next morning over an empty sea. It was warm, and the breeze was now a light easterly. But where on earth were we? I had to confess that I had not the faintest idea. I thought that we might be somewhere north-east of the Philippines, but there was no way of telling. We had no charts for anywhere south of Shanghai and our chronometer had stopped days before. As for estimating our position with the sextant, the best that I could do in the end was to fix our latitude by the time-honoured method of taking a series of sights each side of the sun's zenith and working out the average. When I had done this, however, I nearly dropped the sextant in my astonishment. I checked the calculations again. But there could be no mistake: we were less than ten degrees north of the Equator. In which case we had run something like 1,500 nautical miles in nine days.

We were near the Philippines then, but on which side? If we were to the east of Luzon we would make landfall on what was now United States—and therefore neutral—territory. If we were to westward, though, the nearest mainland coast was that of French Indo-China. We had to know where we were: the knowledge might mean the difference between a journey back to Austria via the United States and an indefinite spell in jail as prisoners of war.

Before long, however, the question of which colonial power's territory we were nearest to was to become of secondary importance. For in the mid-afternoon, wallowing our way southward with the wind on the port quarter, we spotted sails on the horizon to north-eastward. I examined her through binoculars as she rose over the horizon. It was a small native sailing craft, a prau of some kind, with two brown lugsails wider at the head than at the foot, and she was moving fast to catch up with us. At first I was glad of this: one of her crew might speak Chinese or a European tongue and we would be able to get some idea of where we were. But as she gained on us, and drew near enough for me to get a good view of her, I became uneasy. She was indeed a prau, low in the water and with two massive outriggers. But her crew seemed to be inordinately large for a trading or fishing vessel. In fact she was fairly crammed with men from stem to stern, and before long, as they drew nearer, we saw the sun glint on steel and heard distant shouts across the water. Perhaps they merely wished to sell us fresh coconuts; but then again, perhaps not.

I ordered the crew to crowd on every available stitch of canvas. The contest in speed between the clumsy trading junk and the pirate prau was by its nature an unequal one, but it was not that unequal. The *Schwarzenberg* was sailing close to her most favourable point, while the shallow, keelless canoe was at something of a disadvantage. They would overtake us within half an hour or so. But that still gave us ample time to make our preparations. I had the crew fill rice-sacks with shingle from the ballast in the hold, then stack them around the outside of the stern gallery to make a crude breastwork with a loophole in the middle. Then I had the Schwarzlose machine gun unpacked from its metal box and brought up from below, wrapped in canvas, along with five hundred rounds of ammunition. We set it up on its tripod with the muzzle pointing out through the loophole, then Torpedomeister Kaindel and I lay down behind it to wait. We had a good view of them now, about a hundred metres astern: not Chinese as I had expected but darker, larger-nosed men with black, wavy hair bound up in gaudy-coloured scarves. They were a fearsome lot to be sure, armed with all manner of swords and daggers and elderly firearms which they were now brandishing in unholy anticipation, little suspecting that Europe's civilising mission was lying in wait for them behind the breastwork of rice-bags. They filled the air with jeers and catcalls as they came within hailing distance. There were a couple of Chinese among them, so Ehrlich was able to parley with them. Not that there was much to negotiate about though, as the two vessels pitched and wallowed across the waves: they were quite patently after our blood as well as the cargo that they imagined us to be carrying.

"Heave to, you miserable scabs!" their interpreter yelled. "Give yourselves up and we may show some mercy to those who join us. Sail on, and when we board you we'll slice up every one of you like gherkins and feed you to the fish morsel by morsel!"

"Go away, you thieving scum, and leave peaceful traders alone!"

"Why should we? Are you going to make us then, oh dunghill cock?"

"I warn you, I have a weapon aboard of such power that not one of you will escape if I decide to use it."

This last threat produced general hilarity among the pirates. "Yes to be sure, oh Emperor of All the Earth! Lower your trousers then that we may all see this weapon of which you speak, and tremble with fear!" The range had narrowed to a mere thirty metres now. At a sign from me Kaindel worked the cocking handle of the machine gun and peered through the sights.

"Can you do it, Kaindel?" I asked. "The ship's pitching like a rocking-horse."

"Don't you worry, Herr Kommandant: I wasn't a Mitrailleur First Class for nothing. Just let the murdering savages get bows-on and I promise you I'll kill the lot of them in three seconds flat. Just say when."

I peered through the loophole at the crowd of yelling, sword-waving sea-robbers packed into the bows of the prau as she foamed along through the waves astern of us. I had a sudden vision of them as they would be a few seconds from now: a floating slaughterhouse of dead and mortally wounded, drifting away in our wake as blood trickled through the holes in the bullet-riddled hull. And something snapped inside me. Perhaps it was the recollection of the slaughter at the Raven Pass a few weeks before, I do not know, but I just could not bring myself to do it. These villains had undoubtedly merited death a hundred times over for their crimes. But who was I to be their judge and executioner? I who had fallen among them from a world so alien that it might as well be on another planet?

"No, Kaindel," I said. "Let's give them a chance, even though they certainly don't deserve it. When I give you the signal put your first burst through the cross-trees of their foremast and try to bring the sail down. After that, only fire in among them if I say so."

"But Herr Kommandant . . . I could kill the whole rotten bunch of them with one burst. We'd be doing a service to the human race . . ."

"Do as I say, Kaindel."

He sighed, clearly disappointed. "Very well, Herr Kommandant."

They were going to try and make us heave to now. Guns were raised. There were flashes and puffs of white smoke and a volley of bullets sang overhead. One hit the taffrail and sent pieces of wood flying. I clapped my hand on Kaindel's shoulder.

"Fire!"

Kaindel had not boasted idly of his skill as a machine-gun marksman. Despite the pitching and rolling of the two vessels, the entire burst of fifty or so rounds went through an area no bigger than a dustbin lid, right at the junction of foremast and lugsail yard. Mast, spar and sail all disintegrated in a most satisfying manner into a shower of bamboo splinters and shreds of fibre, and the sail fell in a billowing heap to engulf the howling pirates on the fo'c'sle. It was plain that they had never met with automatic weapons before. Even at that distance I saw their brown faces turn pale as they stood in aghast silence, staring up at the shattered mast—then at us. It seemed at any rate that they had no desire to trouble us any further. Half an hour later their remaining sail had disappeared beneath the horizon astern of us.

Our brush with piracy, then, had been a highly satisfactory one from our point of view. But it did nothing to resolve the pressing question of where exactly we were. Now, as evening drew near, we were among an archipelago of small islands, rafts of dense greenery floating in the vivid blue sea and fringed with white sand. None seemed to be inhabited. At last the short tropical twilight came and the sun plunged below the horizon to westwards. I had no desire to go ploughing ahead amid coral reefs without charts in the hours of darkness, so once more we hove to for the night. This time though I took the precaution of setting look-outs and arming the watch on deck with rifles and cutlasses, just in case. The night passed uneventfully, and at dawn we set off again. Before long we saw land to southwards—not islands this time but a distant, grey-blue range of mountains. Soon we were within sight of a low-lying coast of forest and mangrove swamp.

Following our encounter the previous day with the local pirates, I was nervous of making a landing on this coast, which might well be their home territory. But at some point, I knew, we would have to take our courage in both hands and go ashore; partly to obtain directions, partly because our food and water was running low, and partly because, after her nine days at sea in a typhoon, the *Schwarzenberg*'s racked seams were leaking badly and needed caulking. I decided that we would look for a settlement, but a small one which could be easily overawed by our firepower if necessary; for not only was there the possibility of running across the pirates in a larger village, there was also the fact that for all I knew we might be approaching the coast of French Indo-China.

About midday our look-outs sighted a native canoe in the distance, along the coast to south-eastwards above two miles away. I doubt whether the man in it saw us, for he was intent on paddling against the current. Soon we saw him turn into the mouth of a wide creek among the mangroves. I scanned the shore through my binoculars—and noticed a faint wisp of smoke above the trees some way inland. There must be a village there, I thought, but not a large one. So we followed the canoe into the creek. The wind had dropped now. It was oppressively hot towards midday as we sculled the *Schwarzenberg* into the sluggish, oily waters of the river, a dozen men sweating and grunting as they worked at the single ten-metre-long bamboo stern-sweep. About a mile into the creek, hidden now among dense forest, I gave the order to drop anchor. The crew would get to work paying the seams with tubs of chu-nam while Kaindel, the Chinese bos'un Baden bei Wien and I set off upriver in the sampan, seeking to make contact with the villagers whose smoke I had seen. Ehrlich would remain aboard the junk with the machine gun and two rifles in case of attack.

The noonday heat hung in a dense, suffocating blanket over the creek and the surrounding forest, stifling even the cries of the jungle animals and the chirping of the insects. We paddled our way upstream for several kilometres, bumping at one point against a floating log which turned out to be a large alligator dozing in the river. I was just beginning to wonder where our canoeist had got to when we saw it ahead of us: a rickety bamboo landing stage with four or five dug-out canoes tied up to it. We landed and moored our sampan, then set off along the path which led away from the creek. We must have cut a strange sight as we sweated along that jungle trackway, two Europeans and a straw-hatted Chinese. Ragged, salt-stained and with nearly two weeks' growth of beard (we had neither time nor fresh water for shaving), Kaindel and I were in shirt-sleeves order with handkerchiefs hanging from the bucks of our caps to protect us from the sun, in the style of Henry Morton Stanley In Darkest Africa. I had my Steyr pistol while Kaindel carried a rifle, and all of us had cutlasses hanging from our belts. Baden carried an Austro-Hungarian naval ensign before us on a bamboo pole as a sign that we were no mere shipwrecked sailors or common criminals but an armed naval unit of a major European power. In truth, however, it must be said that apart from the flag there was precious little other evidence of our status.

The path seemed to lead nowhere. We had been walking for the best part of an hour now in the steam-bath heat. Surely the smoke could not have been a mirage . . . Then they were upon us, quite without warning, emerging like mist from the ground and like ghosts from among the forest trees to cut off both advance and retreat. There were about twenty of them I think: of small stature but strongly built, and a light tawny brown in colour; clean-shaven and naked except for short, dark-blue loincloths fastened about their hips and basket-like helmets of plaited bamboo on their heads. All, I noticed, had an intricate pattern of dark-blue tattooing about the left wrist. They carried short swords and shields decorated about the edges with hair, while several had spears and blow-pipes as well. They stood silent, perfectly composed, regarding us with faces as devoid of expression as so many bladders of lard. At length their leader advanced towards us, arms folded. He was about a head taller than the rest, in his early twenties I should think and really a rather handsome, fine-featured young man. I sensed that we were in a very delicately poised situation; that, while these people were not unconditionally hostile towards us, they might very soon become so if we were unable to explain to their satisfaction what we were doing here. We had firearms of course, but common sense told me that, surrounded and heavily outnumbered, we would all of us be cold pork after the first shot if we tried to use them. Everything depended now on my skill as a negotiator. If I could only explain that we had no hostile intentions towards these people, but were merely lost seafarers seeking directions . . . I tried him first in English, always a safe bet in those days in the China Seas. No luck. So I tried French, then German, then what little Spanish I knew from voyages to South America when I was a cadet. Same response. I tried Portuguese, Italian, even Latin in the faint hope that perhaps Catholic missionaries might have passed this way. Still the same steady, unblinking stare. It was hot and I was extremely tired and exasperated by my failure to communicate with these men. At last I rather lost patience with their leader, standing impassively before me with his arms folded and regarding me with that unblinking stare.

"*Dobře, hnědý ďáble,*" I muttered. "*A možná mluvíte česky?*"

His reply was, I think, one of the greatest surprises of my life.

"*Ano mluvím, ale ďábel nejsem.*"

## 14

# NIGHT ATTACK

THE YOUNG WARRIOR AND I TALKED as we made our way along the jungle trackway towards his tribe's village. Once I had got over my initial astonishment, I found that, while his mastery of Czech grammar was by no means perfect and his vocabulary was limited, his command of the language was still remarkably good in the circumstances. I also noticed that his speech was tinctured with a strong east Bohemian accent and idiom.

"But tell me," I enquired, "how on earth does it come about that you speak Czech?"

"Why ever not? My father does. He taught us when we were children. He says that it's the language of his tribe far away beyond the sea: a very great tribe, greater even than the Dusuns—though he says that they no longer take the heads of their enemies."

"I know; I am of the same tribe myself. But who is your father and how did he get here?"

"My father is the chief of our people. He came here many years ago from across the sea in a great white prau with a fire in its belly and a smoking pipe in its middle. The Toewaks ambushed its men one day when they were paddling in a smaller prau on the river. They killed all of them but my father, who was wounded. Our hunters found him in the forest and the daughter of our old chief nursed him back to health. But his fellow-warriors had long since gone back to their land, so he married the chief's daughter and stayed with us and taught us how to fight like white men, then led us against the Malays of Sulu and the slave traders. We beat them in a great battle and took many heads and they never came to trouble us again. So my father became our chief when the old one died and has ruled over us for many years."

"Do you have brothers and sisters?"

"Yes. My name is Vaclav. My elder brother Jiři is away hunting in the forests. But my sisters Zdenka, Vlasta and Jarmila are with us, in the village." He pronounced these marvellously prosaic Czech names with such gravity, as if they were the most fabulously exotic titles, that it was all I could do to restrain myself from laughing out loud.

We arrived at the village after another ten minutes or so of walking. It consisted of a wooden palisade surrounding a single, long hall built on stilts and thatched with bundles of palm leaves. Raised bamboo catwalks connected it with the lesser buildings of the settlement—a welcome convenience since the ground beneath was a slough of evil-smelling mud in which chickens and black pigs rootled among numbers of noisy, naked infants. The villagers put down their work to witness our arrival, though their faces registered no particular surprise to see our bizarre-looking little colour-party escorted into their midst. A fat, middle-aged man leant against the rail of the gallery at the end of the longhouse. He stared—then yelled something. Before we knew where we were the three of us had been seized by his warriors and a crowd was gathering around us. As I struggled in the grip of five or six warriors—very strong men despite their small stature—the fat man elbowed his way through the crowd towards us. He had drawn his short sword. He advanced on me and held the point under the tip of my nose. I could smell its sharpness. He was dressed like the rest of his people except that his sarong was rather more elaborately patterned while the sword had its blade decorated with a complicated pattern of gold inlay-work. He was—or rather had once been—a European. He spoke to me in bad German, corroded from decades of disuse.

"What does you want an' who is you, speak? If zey comes after me, you not live hour longer! How you knows I here?"

I decided to take the risk, and answered in Czech. "Tell your men to let me go and perhaps we can discuss this more sensibly. I don't know who we are supposed to be that we should be coming after you, but I assure you that we are merely seafarers in distress, asking for directions and supplies—that is, if you wish to sell us any."

He stared at me for some seconds in utter astonishment—then slowly lowered the sword. "Why have you got that Austrian naval ensign then? Tell the truth: you've come to arrest me, haven't you, and take me back to Pola with you." Light began to dawn.

"We haven't come to take you to Pola or anywhere else. We had no idea you were here and I haven't the faintest idea who you are. But if we had come to arrest you—I assume as a deserter—we would hardly have come in a party of three, would we, and one of those a Chinese? Be reasonable. But if you'll forgive my asking, which ship were you from?"

He looked at me resentfully, then motioned his men to let go of me.

"From the old *Sesana,* if you must know: two years round the world. Only I got fed up with Zwieback and the petty officers and decided to make a run for it as soon as we got into a scrap with the natives—only I got grazed by a poison dart instead and nearly died in the jungle before our friends here rescued me. Here, look." He showed me a large, deep, puckered scar on the back of his left arm. Meanwhile I was ransacking my memory. Yes, had it been in 1883 or 1884? The steam gunboat S.M.S. *Sesana* had been reconnoitring the East Indies with a view to claiming a colony for Austria-Hungary, and a survey party had been attacked and wiped out by the natives. But that had been on the coast of . . . Surely not?

"Does that mean then," I asked, "that this is the island of Borneo?"

He looked at me in surprise. "Of course it is. Where did you think you were, then?"

We sat down to a copious evening meal of boiled rice and forest venison—very welcome, I can tell you, after nearly two weeks without proper food. As we ate the two of us talked. I learnt that he had been Matrose II Klasse Jaromir Vychodil, recruit of the 1862 class, from a village near Pardubitz in Bohemia.

"I never was too loyal a subject of the old man in the Hofburg," he said, "being a Czech and a socialist. But tell me, how long has the old fool been dead and who's Emperor now?"

"He's still very much alive."

He choked slightly and went on. "Of course, I sometimes miss the little things about home and long for a good mug of Pilsner now and again. But you can't have everything in this world—and God alone knows I had little enough to go back to in Austria anyway, as a landless labourer's son. No, these are good people and I'm happy with them. And I've got five children to look after me in my old age . . ." He indicated the three sisters Zdenka, Vlasta and Jarmila, bare-breasted lovelies who smoked pipes and chewed betel nut as they sat, cross-legged and stony-faced, endeavouring to follow this conversation in their father tongue. "No, it could have been much worse really; and certainly I did a good turn for this tribe when I turned up at their door. The Sulu pirates and the slavers had cut them down almost to nothing over the years, until they were living in the jungle on roots and tree-bark like the Punans up-country. Still, we taught those bastards a lesson or two, once I'd organised these folk a bit. They never came bothering us again—though I moved the village back from the creek anyway to remove the temptation."

"But where exactly are we?"

He eyed me suspiciously. "Why do you want to know?"

"Because we're lost."

"Lost? An Austrian naval landing party lost? How come?"

"There's a war in Europe now. We were at Tsingtao."

"Where's that?"

"Oh of course, you wouldn't know, would you?"

"Not really; deliveries of the *Präger Presse* have been a bit irregular of late."

"It's a German colony up on the coast of China, under siege now by Japan and Britain and France. Anyway, we escaped in a Chinese junk, but we got blown south in a typhoon until now; we haven't the faintest idea where we are, except that you tell us we're on the coast of north Borneo. Can you help us?"

"How many of you are there?"

"One Austrian and one German officer, one Austrian warrant officer and seventeen Chinese."

"Well, I can't tell you exactly where we are now because I'm not quite sure myself—and anyway, I don't want you coming back later with a larger party looking for me. But we're near the far north-eastern tip of Borneo, that's for sure."

"Is this British territory then?"

He laughed. "Search me. British or Dutch: I couldn't say. We had a party of boundary commissioners along a few years back."

"Where did they fix the border, then?"

"They didn't get the chance: we fixed them first." He pointed up into the smoke-blackened rafters of the longhouse at a dim cluster of objects wrapped in dried banana leaves, objects which, until now, I had assumed to be coconuts. The thought suddenly struck me that what with their long-house style of architecture and their pastimes, these people would have found a great deal to talk about with the Gospodarijca Zaga.

Before the evening was out I had talked Chief Vychodil of the Bohe-mian Dayaks into drawing me a simple sketch-map of the coast, using a stub of pencil from my pocket and a piece of smooth tree-bark. His fingers were clumsy—"About thirty years since I last wrote anything," he said—but the map was a godsend to us, since it sketched out the coast around the north-eastern tip of Borneo and down to the first settlement in what was indisputably Dutch territory, a village called Serikpapan about fifty miles distant, where there was a small police post. I knew from wire-less messages picked up at Tsingtao that in late September at any rate Holland had still been neutral. If we could get on to the territory of the Netherlands East Indies and give ourselves up to the Dutch colonial authorities, then we would surely soon be able to escape from internment and make our way home.

We returned to the junk next morning loaded with rice-balls and a roasted pig by way of provisions. The whole village turned out to wish us farewell, while the three sisters Vychodilovna waved and called out, *"Na shledanou!"* as the sampan pulled away from the landing stage. The whole episode left me feeling rather dazed afterwards, as if I had dreamt it all. But it did happen, and I suppose that it may just be possible that somewhere in the jungles of Borneo the great-grandchildren of the deserter Vychodil still exchange a word or two of Czech without having the faintest idea of why they do so, providing endless puzzlement for visiting anthropologists and perhaps (one hopes) a few owlish doctoral theses in linguistics at American universities.

The supplies provided for us by the headhunters were welcome, but by far the most useful item that we gained from our excursion ashore was Vychodil's tree-bark map of the coast: crude but really quite accurate, as we found over the next two days while making our way through the Sibutu Passage and down the eastern coast of Borneo, hugging the shore and marking off the landmarks one by one: a rocky headland, a prominent clump of trees, the wreck of a ship on a sand-bar and so forth. At last we came to the small inlet which he had reckoned to be the north-eastern limit of Dutch territory. We sculled the junk into the creek and were soon tying up at the landing stage of the tiny settlement of Serikpapan, population about thirty.

The official residence of the District Officer was only to be distinguished from the other huts by the fact that it had a Dutch flag flying above its roof, and that the roof itself was made of corrugated iron instead of atap. The entire population of cripples and pariah dogs turned out to throng around Ehrlich and myself as we straightened our caps, then made our way up the single street to surrender ourselves and our ship to the custody of the Kingdom of the Netherlands.

Queen Wilhelmina's representative in these parts—probably the most God-forsaken posting in the entire Dutch empire—turned out to be a jovial young Irishman called Shanahan, about the same age as myself. There was nothing peculiar in the fact of his national origin, of course: with a country of about four million people attempting to run a colonial empire twice the size of Europe it was inevitable that the white Dutch should be rather thin on the ground, and that the administration of the Netherlands East Indies should have to employ whatever Europeans it could recruit. Like myself, Shanahan owed his presence here in north Borneo to an ill-considered bout of fornication, in his case with the wife of his immediate superior in Batavia. But I found him to be good-humoured, dedicated to the service of his adopted country and far from the popular stereotype of the gin-sodden colonial official condemned to rot away with fever and boredom in some pestilential outpost. In fact he seemed to take a positive relish in being up here, on the furthest frontier of Dutch territory, entirely dependent on himself and a force of six native policemen to impose The Hague's directives on a territory not much smaller than the Netherlands itself.

"Nowadays its mainly head-hunting and tribal warfare we have to be dealing with," he reported as we sat on the verandah, drinking some of his precious stock of bottled beer, "that and the blackbirding schooners pressing labour for the copra plantations. The Navy's put down most of the piracy along this coast, but we still get trouble from the Sultan of Sulu's blackguards—the lot who chased you. The borders haven't been settled yet with the British and the Americans, so no one can decide whose job it is to deal with them. Most of my work at the moment's trying to enforce some bloody silly directive from The Hague about stopping the Dayaks from keeping their dead relatives in the living room until they rot away. I ask you now: how would Wilhelmina like it if they paddled up to Amsterdam in their canoes and tried to stop the Dutch burying people in cemeteries? But tell me, gentlemen, in what may I perhaps be of assistance to you, out here in the back of beyond?"

"We wish to have ourselves interned by the Netherlands government, if it isn't too much trouble. We are 1,500 miles from our nearest base, in a leaking junk with a Chinese hired crew who may soon be getting troublesome, our food and water are low and there's absolutely no military sense whatever in our trying to get back to Tsingtao—which may by now have fallen in any case. So if we could give ourselves up here and disarm our vessel we would be only too happy to be taken into custody."

He smiled. "Well, Captain, I'd be delighted to oblige. But the size of it is that we'd be your prisoners rather than the other way about, considering that there's twenty of you and only seven of us."

"But surely you could contact your headquarters and get them to send a naval vessel to take us in?"

"Not so easy, I'm afraid. We're really out here on our own, I can tell you. We get a visit from a gunboat once every three months, and the last visit was a week ago. For the rest there's no roads and no telegraph. The quickest I could get a message to the residency in Tarakan is by sending a runner, which would take three days there and three days back. As for keeping you here, our supplies wouldn't stand it. Food's none too plentiful in these parts. No, Captain, I hope you won't think me inhospitable, and it's been a fine thing to have you drop in on us like this. But I think you'd best put to sea and make your way down to Tarakan yourselves. It's only about fifty miles, and I'll give you a chart and a letter to the Commissioner explaining why we couldn't keep you here."

I weighed up the situation. Certainly it seemed far preferable to spend another day at sea rather than sit here indefinitely waiting for the Dutch authorities to send a ship and pick us up. After all, it might take longer than I had thought to escape from internment, and to tell you the truth I was anxious to get back to Europe while the war was still on. The last news we had received before our escape from Tsingtao was that early in September the German armies had been within sight of Paris. Surely, then, the war would come to a negotiated end before Christmas—perhaps even earlier. And in the mean time, who knew what great events I might be missing while I sat in Batavia on parole, reading newspapers and fretting to be where the action was? I sensed also that Leutnant Ehrlich was keen to reach his hypothetical Fatherland and continue fighting for his Kaiser. No, I thought, let us press on towards civilisation.

It was late the next afternoon as the Imperial and Royal armed junk S.M.S. *Schwarzenberg* rounded the northern tip of a largish island, about ten miles north-east of Tarakan, marked on Shanahan's chart as "Sekoe Eiland." We were keeping out to seaward of the island because the channel between it and the mainland contained a number of hidden coral reefs. As we crept around the promontory, a shout from Kaindel brought me running to the bows. It was a large passenger liner, riding at anchor in a palm-fringed bay about three miles to southward. She looked strangely familiar. I picked up the binoculars and began to study her. No, there could be no doubt about it. To the inexperienced eye a change of colour scheme can completely alter the appearance of a ship. But I had been at sea for too many years now to be taken in by such trifles. The smart black hull and white upperworks had given way to a coat of patchy and thinly applied battleship grey, but there could be no mistaking those funnel-caps and the curious round-topped arcading along the promenade decks. The ship before us was the Austro-Lloyd liner *Gorzkowski,* aboard which I had come to the Far East three months before and which I had last seen moored alongside the Bund at Shanghai. But what in God's name was she doing here in the East Indies? I looked more closely, and saw a number of eloquent tarpaulin-draped shapes by her fo'c'sle and quarterdeck rails. So that was it: she had been fitted out as an armed liner for commerce-raiding. Well, here was a stroke of luck and no mistake. I knew that in the years before 1914 our German allies had set up an elaborate network of coaling and supply agencies around the world to assist a *guerre de corse* against the enormous British merchant fleet. As one might have expected, Austria-Hungary had made no such provision. But I knew that, in theory at least, Austrian passenger liners could be equipped as armed merchant cruisers while their crews were mostly naval reservists; so evidently Captain Martinelli had displayed a very un-Austrian initiative when war broke out and had armed his ship to go a-privateering. Well, if that was the case there would certainly be a place for us aboard.

But what about our Chinese seamen? It seemed to me as I thought about it that I had no wish to involve them any further in this Europeans' war. They had endured enough these past two weeks, even if we had not managed to get into action that night at Tsingtao, and I felt that, even if they were now technically members of the k.u.k. Kriegsmarine, enough was enough. Certainly I had no wish to see them conscripted for an indefinite spell of further—and much less well-paid—service to the Emperor Franz Joseph. No, we would leave them with the junk and their money to make their way home to China. Ehrlich would stay aboard with them for the time being. Once I had reported for duty with Kaindel we would send a message back to him asking whether he wished to join us. If so, he could jettison the torpedoes, load the machine gun and rifles aboard the sampan, and then bid farewell to Baden, Mödling and the rest after paying them the remainder of their bounty. He told me that north-Chinese junks traded regularly in these waters about this time of year, so they should have no difficulty falling in with a homeward-bound convoy.

I had the *Schwarzenberg* drop anchor out of sight in a small bay and set off with Kaindel in the sampan. By now we were so ragged and sunburnt and generally dishevelled that we might have difficulty persuading the officer of the watch that we were in fact Austro-Hungarian naval personnel, especially if we turned up in a sampan. But that problem would have to take care of itself. It took us well over an hour working at the oar to get within hailing distance of the *Gorzkowski,* approaching under her stern just as I had done that morning off Antivari. I saw that her name had been painted out. And I also noticed with some surprise that the once-immaculate ship was now very much the worse for wear: not only rust-streaked and dirty (which might reasonably be expected after three months at war), but unkempt also in all those little details which distinguish a smartly run vessel from a floating slum—boats slung lopsided at the davits, scuttles flapping open unsecured, untidy lines of washing hanging forlornly at the rails. Something about her made me feel uneasy. There was no sign of life aboard her, apart from a sentry with rifle and bayonet leaning indolently over the taffrail and watching our approach with no very great interest. From an open scuttle near the waterline at the stern came the mournful wailing of an accordion. Suddenly a faint breeze from the land ruffled the still afternoon surface of the bay—just long enough to flap the ensign hanging from the jackstaff at the stern. I caught my breath as I saw it. It was white, with a blue St Andrew's cross: the flag of the Imperial Russian Navy. So that was it: the Russians had captured the *Gorzkowski* as a prize and armed her themselves as a merchant cruiser. I signalled to Kaindel to go about so that we could make our escape. A number of praus had come out to the ship from the cluster of native huts on the distant shore of the bay, so our sampan was not too conspicuous among them, while as for ourselves I hoped that we were sufficiently brown and ragged to pass for Malays. The sentry was taking no interest in us, and the only other crew member in sight was a white-jacketed figure who had just come down to the foot of the gangway to shoot a pail full of empty bottles into the water. The hair stood up on my neck as he paused to stare at us. What were we to say if we were challenged? I looked at him—and recognition struck us both at the same instant: it was Steward First Class Ferdinand Wong, the Trieste-Chinese employee of the Austro-Lloyd line who had befriended me on the passage out. He stared in amazement, then motioned us to come alongside. We scudded the sampan up to the foot of the gangway ladder.

"Wong—what on earth are you doing here . . . ?"

"Don't ask questions now, Herr Leutnant—just let me jump aboard." He looked around and above to make sure that we were unobserved, then sprang across into the sampan. We hid him beneath a piece of tarpaulin and began to scull away, careful not to make our departure look too hasty. Once we were a safe distance away from the liner we could begin to ask questions.

"But Wong, what are you doing here with the Russians? Surely the *Gorzkowski*'s a naval vessel now, and you're a civilian as well as an Austrian subject."

"I know. Herr Leutnant, I told them that, but I wasn't offered the choice."

"What happened?"

"We were still coaling at Shanghai for the return voyage when we got a telegram from Trieste ordering us to stay there and wait for instructions. Then they told us that because of the war we had to sail for Nagasaki instead of Hong Kong. We waited there a week, but then we got another telegram telling us to go back to Shanghai because the Japanese might be coming into the war against us. So we raised steam again and put to sea—right into the arms of a Russian cruiser waiting outside the three-mile limit. We had to follow them up to Vladivostok as a prize."

"What happened then?"

"The crew were interned and the passengers were put on a train for Austria. They were going to intern me as well, but then the Russians said I was going to sail with them as a mess steward, even though they were painting her grey and fitting guns. I told them I was a civilian and an Austrian subject but the Captain just gave me a whack in the mouth and told me I was a dirty yellow kitajchyk and that if I didn't button my lip and do as I was told he'd have me shot. So that, if you please, is how I came to be a steward aboard the Russian auxiliary cruiser *Nikolayev.*"

"What are they doing here?"

He smiled grimly. "Supposed to be looking for the *Emden,* they say—though from what I saw of it they'll be lucky."

"Are they that bad, then?"

"Bad? Bad's not the word. The crew are only about half what they need to run the ship, and most of them are peasants anyway who'd probably never seen the sea before they came aboard her. They shit in the corners and get seasick and drink vodka like mineral water. And the officers—you never saw such a bunch in your life: hardly know one end of a boat from the other, most of them. I reckon we're only here because they got lost. As for our beloved father-commander Blagodaryov, only last week he bit a sailor's ear off for being improperly dressed. I tell you, Herr Leutnant, if you hadn't happened by I'd have jumped overboard and risked the sharks to get ashore. With that lot aboard it's only a matter of time before they tear her arse out on a reef—or perhaps the *Emden* finds us."

As we sculled around the headland to make the bay where the *Schwarzenberg* lay at anchor, we saw a ship approaching from the east. As she drew nearer we saw that she was a warship, a small cruiser in fact. For one wild moment we thought that she might be the *Emden.* Then came disappointment as she turned broadside-on, about a mile to seaward of the liner. I could see that she was a two-funnelled vessel of considerably earlier vintage than the sleek, three-funnelled *Emden.* I did not recognise her at first, but then I realised that this was a Dutch *Holland*-class cruiser. I had seen one at Yokohama about 1905, and although this one had been heavily rebuilt—her funnels lowered and fitted with curious hat-like cowls—the silhouette was still recognisable. She stopped, and a signal lamp began to wink from her bridge: *"Je voudrais vous informer que vous êtes déjà dans les eaux territoriaux hollandaises bien plus que les vingt-quatre heures constatées par le droit international. Vous êtes priés de vous rendre immediatement en haut mer."*

There was no reply. The message was repeated, only to elicit a completely unintelligible reply from the Russian vessel. Stalemate, it seemed.

If I were the Dutch captain I would now be sending a wireless signal for assistance in dealing with this unwelcome and ill-mannered guest. But then an idea struck me: why not save them the trouble? The junk still had her two torpedoes. Kaindel had checked them only the day before at Serikpapan and had found them to be in perfect working order. Meanwhile the *Nikolayev,* ex-*Gorzkowski,* was at anchor and seemed to have no intention of moving—in fact might not even be able to move, since Wong reported that there had been trouble with her starboard engine. It might be worth a try, and it would certainly be a better reward for our fortnight of privations than tamely handing ourselves over to internment without striking a blow for our country. Why not?

It was already getting dark as the three of us boarded the junk once more. I outlined the situation to Ehrlich and we made our plans. The evening breeze was favourable, which was the main consideration for a nocturnal torpedo attack under sail. There was the problem of the crew, however, for I had reason to believe that the attack would be risky. The Russians might hardly be the last word in seaman-like alertness—at least to go by Wong's highly unflattering reports of them—but with the Dutch cruiser in the offing they would surely be keeping watch more vigilantly than usual and sleeping at action stations. We would need to close to five hundred metres for a successful attack, and at that range, on a moonlit night, we would present a good target. Thus I arranged to land all but the bare minimum of crew necessary to handle the *Schwarzenberg* on what might well be her last, brief voyage. Kaindel, Ehrlich and I would stay aboard of course, and also Ferdinand Wong, who was technically a naval reservist—though currently about class E8—and insisted on coming with us to avenge himself for the miserable two months he had just spent with the Russian Imperial Navy. Besides ourselves we took only Baden and Mödling bei Wien and a further six Chinese seamen, all heavily bribed with extra gold coins from the cashbox. The rest we sent ashore in the sampan with instructions to make their way home as passengers on the next junk sailing back to China.

We weighed the *Schwarzenberg*'s anchor about 10:30 and crept out towards the headland. The false bundles of bamboo slung on each beam had been cut loose and the two greasy brown torpedoes gleamed dully in the moonlight, still locked into their dropping cradles, but with the protectors now removed from the nose pistols. The machine gun had been set up on the fo'c'sle in the hope that as we attacked we might at least be able to rake the liner's rails and put her gunners off their aim. But for the present all was silence as we creaked softly on to the open sea, driven along by the gentle night breeze of the tropics. As we rounded the promontory we strained our eyes to catch sight of our quarry. Had she raised steam and left, as instructed by the Dutch? We dreaded a repeat performance of the futile operation off Tsingtao two weeks before. But no; there she lay, exactly where she had been in the afternoon, blacked out so inefficiently that points of light shone all along her hull like cats' eyes in the darkness. And there too lay the Dutch cruiser, still waiting for the help that would be needed to enforce the neutrality rules.

Ehrlich steered and Kaindel manned the machine gun as I crouched in the waist with Wong, ready to start the torpedo motors and open the dropping cradles. Meanwhile the Chinese trimmed the battened sails to catch each last breath of breeze. Slowly we bore down on the unsuspecting liner. Surely they would see us: the moon was bright and seemed twice as large here as in more northerly latitudes. But I suppose that their attention was focused on the Dutch cruiser; or perhaps they saw us but took us to be a local trading prau, of no possible concern to them. At any rate, we got to within six hundred metres or so before the first warning shot rang out and the first beam of light began searching the sea to starboard. Ehrlich had lined us up nicely, about a hundred degrees to port on the liner's bow. Rifle shots were cracking in the darkness now as the sentries opened fire—though what at was far from clear. I jerked a line to break out the Austrian battle ensign at the foretop. It was now or never. I yelled, "Both torpedoes, start!" and swung with a hammer to trip the motor lever on my side. The torpedo's engine faltered, then burst into life with a vicious hiss of steam as the compressed air and oil inside its body ignited to fire the heater coil. It was as if some huge iron bar had been heated white-hot then plunged into water. I heard the same noise from the other side—then heaved at the lever which operated the dropping cradles. For a moment I thought that it had jammed—then felt it give, and was nearly thrown off my feet as the vessel rocked from side to side, suddenly relieved of 1,500 kilograms of torpedo. There was just time to see the twin tracks streaking away towards the anchored liner before we were blinded as the searchlight caught us.

In the end I think it was only the distraction provided by the Dutch that saved us; that and the fact that we were by now too close to the liner for its main guns to be depressed enough to hit us. They certainly tried, and I had a mild concussion and ringing ears for days afterwards to prove it. But their aim was confused. One of our torpedoes hit the *Nikolayev* just forward of the bridge, I know that: I saw the sudden plume of phosphorescent spray and felt the shock through the water. After that it was a free-for-all, with some of the Russian gunners obviously thinking that it was the Dutch cruiser who had attacked them while others tried frantically to hit us as the wind took us across the liner's bows. As we passed I could see that the ship was already listing to port. For a few moments I thought that we would escape unharmed in the confusion, now that the searchlight had lost us and the Dutch cruiser was returning fire, throwing up shell-splashes all about. But just as we emerged from under the liner's bows on the starboard side, one of their gunners was lucky. It might only have been a single shell that hit us, I cannot say; all I know is that when I picked myself up from the deck, dazed and half deaf, I saw to my horror that most of the junk's stern had been blown away, along with the rudder head and the mizzen mast. Worse still, the vessel was starting to burn. A parting burst of machine-gun fire caught us as we drifted away into the darkness, on fire and out of control.

Ehrlich was missing along with the stern of the vessel and Wong was badly wounded, that much I could gather; but there was no time to inspect the damage as I organised the survivors into a fire-fighting party, passing buckets of water to douse the flames which were spreading hungrily forward along the junk's tar-coated topsides, licking at splintered wood and torn canvas. In the end it took us most of the night, passing buckets and working the pump, before we put the fire out. I would have beached the junk, but there was no means of steering. All that we could do was run helplessly into the dark before the breeze as our victim and the Dutch cruiser exchanged shots in the distance.

Dawn found the armed junk S.M.S. *Schwarzenberg* and her surviving crew in a lamentable plight: adrift, on a calm sea to be sure, but without the smallest sign of land in any direction, nor any means of telling where we were since the sextant and compass had gone overboard with Ehrlich. We had managed to put out the fire at last, but not before the flames had eaten the entire stern of the vessel almost down to the waterline. We stood in silence, looking at the blackened, still smouldering rim of timbers, which hissed like a cat every time a wavelet slopped over them. Not that the rest of the ship was in much better condition: shell splinters and machine-gun bullets had riddled the upperworks to a point where only constant and energetic pumping would keep her afloat—and that not for much longer, since the numerous leaks were letting in slightly more water than we could pump out, while as the waterline crept steadily upwards it found still more holes to trickle through. There were only nine of us able-bodied enough to take turns at the pump now, working in pairs. One of the Chinese seamen had been lost with Ehrlich as the shell demolished the stern, while as for Ferdinand Wong, in addition to a number of smaller wounds from shrapnel his right elbow had been smashed by a bullet, so that only a few arteries and ligaments and rags of muscle held the two halves of his arm together. Kaindel had applied a tourniquet and we had laid him out in the shade of a sail on the fo'c'sle and administered our tiny store of morphine from the medicine chest, but he was in a bad way.

Not that it would make much difference, I thought to myself as I took a rest from pumping. The junk would stay afloat for an hour at most now, especially since the pump—a bamboo stem fitted with a crude raw-hide flap by way of a valve—was beginning to come apart. The sampan which might have offered us some faint last hope of survival was gone, and anyway there was no land in sight in any direction. We had scooped out what ballast we could to lighten the ship, but I knew now that it was all futile. I could also see—and knew the others could see, although no one was tactless enough to remark upon it—that in the last few minutes a number of triangular black fins had begun to appear in the water around us. They circled us warily at first, then gradually became bolder, to a point where they would impertinently break surface alongside to show us their white underbellies and ugly mouths. I had ordered Kaindel to shoot one with a Mannlicher in order to drive them off, but the wounded fish's companions had merely fallen upon their stricken comrade and devoured him amid a boiling patch of foam—then resumed their patient circling with their appetites apparently increased rather than sated by this disgusting hors d'oeuvres.

I checked my pistol—not with any intention of shooting another one but rather with a view to our own immediate future. I had already seen a man eaten by sharks, when I was a cadet aboard the *Windischgrätz* lying off Guadalcanal and a young seaman had been foolish enough, during the regulation daily bath, to swim outside the sail that we had suspended in the water as a makeshift swimming pool. I had been in charge of the rescue boat that day and I remembered now how the frenzied creatures had still been biting lumps out of him as we dragged him over the gunwale. In the end we only got about three-quarters of him into the boat, and he had bled to death on the bottom boards as I tried to take down a last message to his family. Well, they would not have us as live meat at any rate. Ten rounds in the magazine. So I would have the captain's dubious privilege of being last to go, shooting each man in turn through the head and then killing myself. It seemed a wretched end; but at least we had done our duty, and performed it successfully. It would never be recorded now—as if that mattered to us.

Suddenly Mödling bei Wien, who was also resting from the pump, began to shout and wave his arms. It was a sail on the horizon to southwards. A small keg of pine-tar was quickly lashed to a spar, set alight with a burning oil-rag and hoisted into the air. We watched the sail until our eyes ached with willing it to creep up over the horizon. But it was no use: within a few minutes it had sunk out of sight. The keg was doused in the sea, three parts consumed, and we returned wearily to our losing battle with the slowly rising waterline.

"Well, Kaindel," I said, "it looks as if they thought we were a steamer."

"Suppose so, Herr Kommandant. But how much longer are we going to pump like this? My arms are near dropping off."

I hesitated. "Go on for as long as you can. Here, let me take a turn on the other handle." It was a pointless exercise and everyone could now see as much: the waterline, which had been creeping upwards by milli-metres, was now rising by a good centimetre a minute. Soon there would be a sudden lurch and plunge as the waves slopped over the burnt-down stern. However, suicide did not appeal to me except in extremis, so we worked at it for another twenty minutes—until a shout from one of the Chinese seamen drew our attention to a plume of smoke to northwards. They were coming our way, but might still pass hull-down below the horizon without seeing us. I decided to take a last chance. The tar-keg was lit again—or what was left of it—and once more the smudge of black smoke boiled up into the clear tropical morning sky. We watched in an agony of apprehension. The tar-keg burnt out and the staves fell hissing into the sea. Then we cheered as we saw the steamer's mast-tops change direction towards us. Twenty minutes later we were hoisting the injured Wong as gently as we could into the rowing cutter, then scrambling across ourselves.

As Captain I was the last to leave, carrying only a hold-all with the ship's log, the cashbox and a few other valuables. As I hauled myself across the gunwale our rescuers backed oars to get clear. I looked back. There was a faint groan, then the noise of someone flushing an old-style water closet as the waves rushed across the remaining deck of the gallant Imperial and Royal war-junk S.M.S. *Schwarzenberg*. She sank, then paused for an instant with the top of her foremast still above water. The red-white-red battle ensign of Imperial Austria fluttered bravely for a few seconds,

until with a last lurch of the wreck it sank beneath the waves—so far as I
am aware the last occasion on which it ever flew outside the confines of
the Mediterranean.

But that was all past now. Our immediate future lay ahead of us,
sitting there on the water like some immaculate white swan as the surplus steam roared from the relief pipe on her black-and-orange funnel.
A blaze of gilt scrollwork adorned her bows and a gold cove-line ran
to her graceful counter-stern, from which hung the red, white and blue
tricolour of the Netherlands. Her awnings were spread against the sun,
and the rails were lined with hundreds of silent brown faces watching
us as the cutter drew alongside. We were about to board the steamer
S.S. *Samboeran,* 1,963 tonnes, of the Holland-Amboina Reformed Steam
Navigation Company, bound for the Arabian port of Jeddah with 350
pilgrims en route for Mecca.

# 15

# SALVATION BY GRACE

I T WAS PLAIN FROM THE VERY OUTSET that Captain Abraham Zwart, master of the S.S. *Samboeran,* was anything but graciously pleased to accept my thanks for having just snatched us from the jaws of death as represented by a half-dozen hungry sharks. In fact, as I reached the top of the ladder to the *Samboeran*'s bridge, he let drive at me with such a furious barrage of maledictions that I almost lost my grip on the handrails to fall on top of the Second Mate coming up below me. His rage was such that he danced a little jig on the planks of the bridge deck as he cursed me in strangulated, guttural English.

"Vat vor de fokking do jou maak mij vor jou to stop, bugger-all goed-for-notting?" he roared. "Whij vor must I also time vor jou to lose, bloddy idjot of a dammfool . . ." I seized the chance to interrupt as he paused to catch his breath, and spoke in German.

"Excuse me Herr Kapitän, but if you would find it easier to curse me in Dutch, then please feel free to do so; I don't speak it but I understand it quite well."

He paused for a moment and regarded me suspiciously, as if he were being offered some poisoned sweetmeat—then proceeded to blackguard me for another five minutes or so in Netherlandish, which to the Austrian ear sounds like someone speaking medieval German while trying to dislodge a fishbone from their throat. At length he ranted himself to a standstill, having run out of objurgations for the time being, so that I had an opportunity to present my compliments and try to explain piecemeal how it was that I, a senior lieutenant of the Imperial and Royal Austro-Hungarian Navy, came to be floating in the Celebes Sea aboard a shot-riddled and half-burnt Chinese junk in the company of eight Chinamen,

one of them seriously wounded, and an Austrian petty officer. He listened
to me incredulously, then gave a derisive snort. He signalled to his Second
Mate, who was accompanied by three or four seamen armed with lengths
of iron pipe:

"Take him aft to join the others. I must decide what to do with
them."

I was led to the poop deck where Kaindel waited with Baden and
Mödling and the other Chinese, who had squatted down on the deck
and were watching events with that patient indifference which is such a
speciality of their people. Kaindel and the *Samboeran*'s Third Mate, who
seemed to have some experience of first aid, were at work applying dressings to Steward Wong's shattered arm. There was little that I could do
to assist them, once we had made him comfortable on a straw mattress
beneath the awnings on the shaded side of the deck, so I leant over the rail.
I was still dazed by gun-blast from the previous night and felt curiously
limp now that the immediate peril had been surmounted and we were out
of danger for the time being. The ship was under way again now, steaming
along at a steady fourteen knots or so as she sliced through the dark-blue
water. The *Samboeran* was one of those smart, medium-sized passenger
steamers which the Dutch used for running services between the myriad
islands of their East Indian possessions, of necessity a fast ship since
the Dutch East Indies extended almost three thousand nautical miles,
from the western tip of Sumatra to the eastern end of Netherlands New
Guinea. I turned around, and for the first time in over two weeks I caught
a glimpse of myself in a locker mirror inside an open cabin—and had to
look twice before I realised that this bearded, filthy, smoke-blackened
apparition with its matted hair and torn clothing was really me. No wonder
then that skipper Zwart had found my story so hard to swallow. But would
the authorities in Batavia be any more ready to take it at face value?

I did not have much time to think about it, however, for the Second
Mate reappeared to summon me once more to the master's presence, this
time in his cabin beneath the bridge. He bade me shut the door and sit
down, like a headmaster about to conduct a severe interview with an erring
pupil. He was still evidently in a very bad mood and stood for some time

with his back to me, staring through a porthole, immersed in thought. He was certainly a most odd-looking man: about the same height as myself, but still strangely squat in appearance, as if a very tall man had been placed in a screw-press and squeezed into himself like a stick of modelling clay. His brows beetled over his narrow eyes; his shapeless nose overhung his frog-like mouth; his neck hung in folds over the collar of his white tunic; while his arms seemed too long for his dumpy torso. And as for his lower limbs, although I could not see them, I got a strong impression that his concertina-folded trousers concealed similarly compressed legs. If anything, he reminded me of a seafaring version of the Michelin Motor-Tyre Man, but without the latter's cheery benevolence. At length he turned to me, regarded me for some time, then spoke in his heavy Dutch-flavoured German.

"Austrian naval lieutenant indeed? Pah!" He leant across his desk and glared into my eyes. "I will tell you who I think you are, mein Herr Leutnant: it is my opinion that you and your companions are nothing but common criminals escaped from a penal colony somewhere along the coast. Otherwise how is it that you were floating in a half-burnt junk full of bullet-holes while one of your Chinamen has his arm hanging off, eh? You were shot at while making your escape, weren't you? Well, my mister lieutenant whoever-you-are, I have to think now what to do with you all."

"Of course, Captain, that is your privilege. You have gone out of your way to comply with the mariner's code in rescuing us, so please land us wherever and whenever is most convenient for you. For my part I promise that once we are ashore and I have made contact with the nearest Austro-Hungarian Consulate I shall see that you are amply compensated for your trouble."

I thought that he was going to burst with rage at this, or perhaps open out like a telescope until he hit the deckhead. "Land you?" he bellowed. "What do you mean, land you! We were already four days late even before we had to stop to rescue you from your damnfool boating adventure! We were due to call at Batavia, but now it'll have to be Jeddah at full speed non-stop even if the boilers blow up!" He paused and got up again to stare through the porthole. I got a strong impression that here was a man wrestling heroically with an acute moral dilemma. At last he turned back to me.

"Herr Leutnant—if that is what you wish to be called—might I ask whether you are a Christian?" I was mildly surprised at this question, so utterly out of context did it seem, but I managed to reply. "Well Captain, I was baptised and confirmed a Catholic—most Austrians are—but I don't really see . . ."

He seemed relieved. "Good. Excellent. So you are not a Christian then, only a reprobate Papist idolater. That means that it doesn't matter."

"But why? I'm afraid I don't . . ."

"Herr Leutnant whatever-your-name-is, I have a proposition to make to you, because I sense that whatever the crimes were that landed you in a penal settlement, you are at least—or rather, once were—a sea-officer of some kind."

"I am, but I haven't . . . I mean, I am a sea-officer, but I was never a convict. Please go ahead though."

"The position is this. The S.S. *Samboeran* is on passage from the eastern Celebes to Arabia with 350 Mohammedan unbelievers on board, travelling to Mecca to practise their abominable rites. We make this trip every year, travelling around the islands to pick them up in tens and twenties, then running from Menado to Jeddah once we have taken our full complement aboard. Normally we arrive at our destination with a good three days to spare before the start of the pilgrimage season. But this year everything has been running late because of you and your idiotic war in Europe. When we were at Amboina the Navy was mobilised and requisitioned all the steam-coal on the island; then we had five men and the First Mate jump ship at Menado; then we were diverted to Tarakan to pick up a bunch of thick-headed Malays who missed an earlier ship. In short, we have to make Jeddah by the 2nd of November, but we can only do it if we keep up a steady fourteen knots day and night for the next three weeks."

"So might I then ask what's the problem? Your ship is fast and she looks very well maintained from the little that I've been able to see of her."

He grunted. "The problem is this: we are a strict Reformed Christian ship and practise rigid observance of the Sabbath. Every year but this we would have hove to from sunset on Saturday to sunset on the Lord's day and done no work. But this year we must steam every day if we are to reach our destination on time. Because if we arrive at Jeddah even a day late these Malay savages are going to be very, very angry indeed with us."

"But surely, Captain, couldn't you just refund their fares and take them next year?"

He stared at me incredulously. "What? These Mohammedans from the jungle kampongs? I tell you they would tear us limb from limb, every single one of us."

"I see. But where do I—I mean, we—fit into this?"

"As I said, we need to run the ship on the Lord's day, but without Sabbath-breaking."

"Might I ask how many crew you normally need to work the ship?"

"Thirty-four, but we have already lost one officer and four crew at Menado."

"Well Captain, there are nine of us altogether, of whom only eight are able-bodied, and of those eight I am the only one able to fulfil the duties of a watch officer, so I think that we would scarcely be enough even if we worked the entire twenty-four hours of the Sabbath without stopping. You must need at least four men in the stokehold alone to keep up even minimum steam pressure, and none of us is qualified to stand watch in the engine room."

"These are not such great problems. You would be able to stand two watches on the bridge and your petty officer the one in between; while as for the engine room, my Second Engineer is a heathen Chinese recruited in Malacca and not one of the Elect People of God, so it doesn't really matter in his case either."

"But the stokehold . . ."

"That can be overcome. This ship carries a hundred tonnes of fuel-oil to spray into the furnaces: we had her converted last year because oil is so much cheaper than coal out here in the Indies. We can reserve the oil for the Sabbath, and then only two stokers will be needed at a time to feed the furnaces."

"I see. So you are proposing that my men and I work the ship for you on Sundays?"

"Not only that: you will also work your passage as deckhands the other six days of the week."

"And might I enquire what we get in return?"

He seemed close to explosion once more, and when he spoke it was with a strained voice. "What will you get? Who are you to ask me what you will get in return? I am a just man and obey the laws of the state as well as those of God. If we were not in our present difficulties I would have no hesitation in landing at Batavia and handing you over to the temporal ministers of justice to suffer retribution for your crimes. But now—well, whatever your offences have been and however justly you were punished, I shall turn a blind eye and not enquire what sort of murders and banditries landed you in jail. I am prepared just this once to break the law by giving you passage to Arabia with free food and accommodation in return for your work. Once we are at Jeddah I promise you that you will all be put ashore and left to go to the Devil as you please."

"And if I refuse your offer?"

He glowered at me from under his pendulous brows. "The hold, in irons, on ship's biscuit and water. Then handed over to the authorities once we return to Batavia."

I asked for ten minutes to think over the generous offer. Certainly he meant what he said about working hard for our passage, I could see that. And I must say that I had to ask myself, What is there to stop this man squeezing every last drop of work out of us, then handing us over anyway to the authorities as escaped criminals at the end of the voyage? But even if Captain Abraham Zwart was not the most generous or the most prepossessing of mortals, I sensed somehow, without quite knowing why, that although this man might drive a hard bargain, he could be relied upon to keep it.

Jeddah though, by early November: it seemed too good to be true. Before we left Tsingtao we had heard that Turkey was favourably disposed towards the Central Powers and likely to enter the war on our side. But even if this were not so, Jeddah was only just across the Red Sea from the Italian colony of Eritrea—and Italy of course, though still neutral, was Germany's and Austria's partner in the Triple Alliance. Surely if we reached Jeddah on this magic carpet so miraculously furnished for us by the hand of Providence, then we would be able to get home either via Turkish Arabia or on an Italian steamer via Suez. No, it was an offer too good to refuse; and all the more so since it involved no money changing hands. I still had gold in my canvas body belt and in the *Schwarzenberg*'s cashbox, but I was anxious to save that up for whatever adventures lay ahead of us from the Red Sea onwards.

I knocked at the door of Zwart's cabin, entered and informed him that, on behalf of my men, I had decided to accept his offer.

"There is just one condition that I would like to add though," I said.

"Hmmph! What is that?"

"That you should take my seven native Chinese seamen back with you to the East Indies and put them aboard the first junk that you meet bound for north China." For a few moments it looked as if an eruption was imminent. But he calmed down sufficiently to answer.

"Bah! Very well then, damn and blast you: the bargain is made."

So I duly signed up myself, Kaindel, Baden and Mödling bei Wien and the remaining five Chinese to work for the duration of the voyage as unpaid deckhands and stokers about the S.S. *Samboeran*. As for Steward Ferdinand Wong, Zwart was adamant that even he should undertake light duties about the ship as soon as he was fit enough to do so.

There seemed to be little enough prospect of Wong's recovery during the first couple of days aboard. In fact the ghastly wound in his arm got worse. He was accommodated for the time being in an empty cabin on the upper deck, which was at least light and airy and on the starboard, shaded side of the ship. We dosed him with morphine from the ship's medicine chest, but it was clear that something drastic would have to be done, for by the second day, when Kaindel and I changed the dressings, a sickly decomposing smell filled the cabin. Gangrene was setting in. There was no doctor aboard, and Zwart was adamant that he would not stop to land the injured man; in fact, seemed to regard the whole thing as our affair and no real concern of his. So it looked like amputation of the arm above the elbow, using only such instruments and expertise as we could muster aboard ship. I consulted the Second Mate, a brown Dutchman called Jan Hendrik Silano, who seemed rather more helpful and sympathetic than Zwart. Would it not be possible, I asked, to canvass the passengers and see whether there was a doctor among them, or at least someone with enough hospital experience to know how to go about the job? He thought not: the pilgrims were mostly simple village folk from the north coasts of the Celebes and the smaller islands to eastwards; not only that, but they were also particularly devout and zealous Muslims, coming as they did from the easternmost extremity of the Islamic world. Not only did a high proportion of women and children travel from these parts each year on the hadj, but the pilgrims took a particularly strict and rigid view of the journey. According to the letter of Islamic law (he said), the pilgrimage only began on arrival at the boundary of the city of Mecca; but these folk regarded the whole six-thousand-mile journey as the pilgrimage, and believed that any contact with an infidel during that time would bring ritual defilement and loss of the coveted title of "Hadji." Of necessity they had to use the *orang belanda*'s steamship to get to their destination; but beyond that they lived completely separate lives aboard, passing through the ship like water through an iron pipe.

There was no help to be expected from that quarter, then. It looked instead as though I was now going to have to add amateur surgery to my list of skills, with only the contents of the medicine chest and a *Seafarer's Medical Handbook* (in Dutch) to assist me, plus whatever instruments we could improvise. Zwart said that we could have a scrubbed table to operate on, and unlimited hot water from the galley for sterilisation, but beyond that he washed his hands of the matter. There was nothing for me to do now but read up all I could on amputations, then roll up my sleeves and get on with it.

Fortunately the *Scheepvaarders Geneeskundige Handboek* was remarkably thorough on amputation, and copiously illustrated with step-by-step diagrams of how to remove practically any limb or bodily organ, from an ingrowing toenail to an appendix. The trick for removing an arm above the elbow, I gathered, was to cut at ninety degrees until the bone was sawn through, then slice outwards at forty-five degrees so that a flap of flesh would be left to fold up over the stump and sew into place. I memorised the veins and arteries of the arm and hoped fervently that everything would be where the drawings indicated. So far the limit of my surgical experience had been to bind up an artificer's crushed finger when I was a torpedo-boat captain, and that only as a temporary measure until we could get back to port.

Where surgical supplies were concerned, the anaesthetic was the least of our problems. The *Samboeran*'s well-stocked medical chest contained two bottles of chloroform, so all that Kaindel and I had to do was to borrow a wire-mesh tea strainer from the galley and stretch gauze across it to make a face-mask. We would put this across Wong's nose and mouth and Kaindel, in the role of anaesthetist, would drip chloroform on to it in sufficient quantity to keep the patient under. Otherwise we were not too well-off. The medical chest had a scalpel and needles and catgut, but where a bone-saw was concerned the best that we could manage was a hack-saw borrowed from the engine room. As for clamps to close off the blood vessels, the electrical store-room yielded a few crocodile-clips and little else. Second Mate Silano provided a cut-throat razor, and also offered his assistance as theatre nurse. He had been a leading seaman in the Netherlands East Indian Fleet during the Atjeh war at the turn of the century, he said, and had watched an emergency arm-amputation aboard a gunboat.

Certainly I felt anything but confident as the hour approached for the operation. In fact your expression "butterflies in the stomach" hardly even begins to describe the churning sensation as I read yet again through the *Medical Handbook*'s instructions on arm amputation and checked yet again that everything was laid out around the trestle table. I was not especially squeamish, but I had a queasy premonition that something would go terribly wrong: that the sutures on the arteries would burst as the flap was being sewn up, or that the blood-clogged hack-saw would fail to bite into the bone, or that the anaesthetic would go wrong—some disaster at any rate that would leave the wretched Wong in an even worse state than before and me reproaching myself for having attempted the operation. The only consolation was that if the dangers of being operated upon by an amateur surgeon were great, the prospects if the smashed and now putrefying limb stayed attached to its owner were even less attractive. They were in the galley now, boiling the instruments in a cauldron. Soon Wong would be brought in and laid out on the table and my self-education as a surgeon would commence.

There was a knock on the cabin door. I opened it to find Silano standing in the corridor with a second figure, draped in scarves and carrying a black bag. "Quick, let us in and close the door."

"Who's this?" I asked.

"A doctor. Don't ask his name. He's one of the passengers: a village doctor from Mendano. I got a message to him and he's agreed to take your man's arm off. But never a word of this, do you understand? He's a poor man and has spent his life-savings on this pilgrimage. If any of the rest find out that he's been in contact with Christians then at the very least he won't be allowed to go on to Mecca, and quite possibly he'll go overboard one night with a kris between his shoulder-blades."

"Please thank him for me," I said, "and tell him that God will surely recompense him for his charity to unbelievers."

The man removed his scarf to reveal a brown, thin, rather sad face with the high cheek-bones and black eyes of a Malay. He smiled. "No need for an interpreter, Herr Leutnant. I studied medicine at Leyden and I know German quite well."

"Well, thank you anyway. But tell me, how can we assist you?"

"Bring the injured man here so that I can examine him. By the sound of it we must act fast."

Wong was brought in, leaning on Kaindel's shoulder. He was thin and hollow-eyed, and obviously frightened of what was to come. As the cabin door closed behind them I began to smell the sickly, oppressive stench of gangrene. I tried to reassure him as we laid him out on the table that we had managed to get a proper doctor now to treat him. The pilgrim-doctor made his examination and assigned us our duties. Then he opened his bag and began to lay out his instruments before sending them to be sterilised.

"It was fortunate that I brought these things," he said; "but then a good doctor should always travel prepared for the worst."

Before long the chloroform was dripping on to the gauze mask and the scalpel was slicing into the mottled purple flesh of the ruined arm, now tied off with tourniquets and masked with towels. It was evening now. The cabin was hot beneath the oil-lamps and before long we were all slightly tipsy from the chloroform fumes. I think that I took it all rather well really, in fact only began to feel sick as the hack-saw started to grate through the bone. My job was to tie off the blood vessels as the doctor severed them, so really the intense concentration on the job in hand prevented me most of the time from realising that this was living flesh that we were cutting through, and not meat on a butcher's slab. It lasted about twenty minutes I think, from the first incision to the last neat stitch around the blood-oozing stump. Then came the awful moment when the tourniquet above the cut was removed. Would it all burst in a torrent of blood, like an ill-constructed dam? But no, it held, though it bulged ominously for a while. At last it was all over.

I placed the severed limb in a bucket and took it up on deck to throw it overboard, holding my face away from the nauseating smell. Then I returned to the cabin. The doctor was already gone, spirited back to join the host of pilgrims bedding down for the night beneath the awnings. He had left a note giving us instructions for looking after the stump during the next week or so, but said that we were only to contact him again if infection set in or if there was uncontrollable bleeding. Wong was taken back to his cabin, still asleep. He suffered greatly over the next few days from the usual post-amputation pains—chiefly (he said) from a maddening itch in the hand that was no longer there—and the stump looked dreadful when I came to change the dressings next day: a blotchy, sausage-like mess of blood-clots and inflammation. But as the days passed the swelling reduced and the stump began to heal. Within the week Wong was up and about engaged in the "light duties" specified by my agreement with skipper Zwart: chiefly pushing a broom about the deck with the handle tucked under his left armpit. I felt badly about this, but he assured me that having something to do took his mind off the loss of his arm.

As for my own duties over the next two weeks, they were anything but light, for in addition to my work as a sick-nurse I had to be a full-time deckhand, a part-time stoker and, on Sundays, bridge-officer for no less than four watches: four hours on, four hours off. For her age—she had been launched about 1905 at Vlissingen—the S.S. *Samboeran* was a remarkably well looked-after ship. But that was always the case with Dutch vessels, both merchant and naval. I served two voyages as Second Mate on a Royal Dutch Shell oil tanker in 1920; and during the 1930s, when I was in the Polish fleet, I spent some time with the Royal Netherlands Navy when Poland was having submarines built in the Fijenoord yard at Rotterdam. These later experiences only served to confirm my opinion that, of all the ships I sailed aboard, those of the Netherlands were invariably the neatest and best-maintained. But aboard the *Samboeran* I experienced on my own calloused knees and with my own aching back exactly how this uncanny smartness was achieved, as I toiled from long before dawn to long after nightfall with bucket and swab and scrubbing brush, scouring corticene decks with wire wool and stripping the skin from my hands as I wiped down the immaculate paintwork with that vicious solution of caustic soda known as "sugi-mugi." In fact I think that I had never before worked so hard in my entire life as during that fortnight.

Worst of all was the stokehold. In coal-fired ships the "black gang" always lived a life apart from the rest of the vessel, toiling away in the suffocating depths like the myrmidons of Vulcan, obeying their own laws and keeping their own watches as they laboured at the bottom of their sulphurous black pit, between the towering walls of bunker-coal on one side and the glowing furnace doors on the other, as the floor heaved and rolled beneath their feet. Even in temperate latitudes it was always a matter of wonder to me that human beings could so much as survive in such conditions, let alone work like navvies shovelling coal and raking out red-hot clinker to fill the ash-hoists. In the tropics, though, surely even a salamander would curl up and die in this inferno? Well, I was now to experience myself the truth of the aphorism, current in those days among the k.u.k. Kriegsmarine's Dalmatian sailors, that the Navy makes a stoker by taking a soft man and baking him hard like a ship's biscuit. For the first few days I thought that I would die of exhaustion and heatstroke. But gradually I got used to it, got to that stage of numbness where I shovelled and barrowed coal without even remembering that I was doing it. As for the Chinese, they endured it with their usual sturdy, uncomplaining patience.

Thus the days passed. And on the Sabbath, as skipper Zwart way above our heads preached his interminable sermons to the rest of the crew, we damned heathens and Romish idolaters toiled down below to keep up enough steam pressure to maintain fourteen knots, shovelling coal hour after hour as the oil-sprays roared like dyspeptic dragons, blowing back every now and then to fill the stokehold with greasy black smoke. Then as soon as I had finished my watch I had to wipe down hurriedly in a bucket on deck, and make my way to the bridge to stand my trick as officer of the watch, weighing (I should think) about two-thirds of what I had weighed that morning through loss of water, but thankful at least to be up in the fresh ocean air under the sun or the stars. All in all, each day of rest I think that I was lucky to get three hours' sleep. But I was glad at any rate that each day we toiled brought us an average of 340 nautical miles nearer to Pola and my duty as an officer of the Noble House of Austria.

In fact as the days passed, and the green-swathed humps of Krakatoa and Half-Athwart Island slid by and Java Head disappeared astern as we steamed out into the Indian Ocean, I realised just how lucky we were to have been picked up by a ship where the Sabbath was strictly observed—at least by the Elect—and which had been too pushed for time to have called at Batavia as intended. It was about the sixth day I think, just as we were leaving the Sunda Strait. We fell in with another ship of the Holland-Amboina Line, the S.S. *Kalipoeran,* on passage from Batavia to Colombo. There was no time to do anything other than ease our speed to steam alongside her for a few minutes, just long enough for an oilskin-wrapped parcel of company documents and Batavia newspapers to be tossed over from one ship to the other. They were brought to me as officer of the watch—and when I opened the packet I was thankful for once that it was Sunday, and that Zwart and his crew were too scrupulous in their Sabbath observance to read a newspaper on the Lord's Day. For the first journal that I saw was a three-day-old copy of the *Batavsche Telegraaf,* and even my imperfect knowledge of Dutch allowed me to read the headlines:

## INCIDENT AT TARAKAN—THE MYSTERY DEEPENS
*FURTHER INFORMATION ON EXCHANGE OF FIRE BETWEEN
RUSSIAN VESSEL AND NETHERLANDS WARSHIP.*

*Bandjarmasin, 13 October*

During the past day further information has come to light concerning the exchange of shots on the night of 11/12 October between the cruiser Hr MS *Overijssel* and the Russian armed liner *Nikolayev* off Sekoe Island.

It was reported today by the office of the Netherlands District Commissioner at Tarakan that a party of Chinese seamen was apprehended next morning on Sekoe Island. When questioned through an interpreter the men claimed to have been landed the previous night by an armed junk, commanded by two European officers, which had made its way south from the besieged German port of Tsingtao. The men said that after putting them ashore the junk, which was armed with two torpedoes, had set sail to attack the Russian liner anchored in Pasar Bay.

Though on the face of it highly improbable, this story, if true, may explain how the Russian ship was so badly damaged by an underwater explosion that she had to be beached in shallow water. The Captain of the *Overijssel,* Kpt Lt W. M. H. Legrange, has since categorically denied that his vessel fired a torpedo, or did anything other than return the Russian ship's fire, suffering three men wounded and some damage to the forward funnel in the process. For his part the Russian captain, Captain IInd Rank N. I. Blagodaryev, is reported to have told the local authorities that a small sailing vessel was fired upon just before the explosion, and was later seen to drift away into the darkness ablaze.

A strongly worded protest at this violation of Netherlands neutrality has been lodged with the Russian minister at The Hague, and the German representative has also been asked to furnish an explanation of the incident. In the mean time the Governor-General of the East Indies has offered a reward of 5,000 Fl. for information leading to the arrest of the mystery junk and her crew.

I destroyed the newspaper as quickly as I could. Captain Zwart might have been stubborn and he might not have been particularly quick-witted, but I had strong grounds for suspecting that with 5,000 guilders in prospect he would have turned the ship around and headed back for Batavia even though he had been carrying 350 demons on a pilgrimage to hell.

Once we had cleared the Sunda Strait, the rest of our voyage across the Indian Ocean was a tranquil one, now that the monsoon season was dying away. My labours about the ship gave me little time for observation, but none the less I did begin to realise as the days passed just how singular a vessel it was that I had boarded. Ever since the first men paddled out in a hollow tree-trunk, each ship has had its own peculiar domestic economy. In my time I have sailed aboard a good many weakly run, irresolute autocracies, and also a fair number of equally ill-run, irresolute floating parliaments. I have known a few ships that were brutal tyrannies, and a few—by far the pleasantest to sail aboard in my experience—that appeared to be despotisms but which were in fact run by a process of discreet consultation with the crew, so discreet in fact that nobody realised it was taking place, and the magic would have been lost if they had. The S.S. *Samboeran,* however, was the first and so far the only example that I have ever encountered of a floating theocracy: Calvin's Geneva reproduced in miniature as it glided across the sparkling tropical seas.

I knew already that skipper Zwart and his crew were strict Reformed Protestants. I had also noticed that only Zwart himself, the Chief Engineer Praetorius and the Third Mate were Europeans. All the rest, apart from the Second Engineer, who was Chinese, were natives of the East Indies. They were not Javanese or island Malays though: their features were somewhat Negroid and their complexion darker and their hair frizzy like that of the Melanesians. I learnt that this was because they all came from the island of Amboina in the Moluccas, referred to sometimes as the "twelfth province of the Netherlands" because, alone among the peoples of the East Indies, its inhabitants had willingly adopted the Dutch language and Calvinist Christianity. They might have been born in atap-roofed huts beneath the waving sago palms on the fringes of the South China Seas, but their devotion to the House of Orange, barrel-organs and black-coated moral rectitude was limitless. However, the peculiarity did not stop there, for Zwart was no ordinary Dutchman and the crew were no ordinary Amboinese.

The story came out one warm evening as I was alone on the bridge with the helmsman and Captain Zwart. He had just prepared a report on the absconding First Mate and his companions, and though a taciturn man he evidently felt aggrieved enough at their desertion to mention it to me. Being a ship's officer myself I felt that some commiseration was called for.

"The usual reasons I suppose," I remarked, "drink and women?"

He looked at me in some surprise. "No, theology: there was a disagreement concerning infralapsarian and sublapsarian predestination, so I excommunicated them." He then proceeded, for the remaining three hours of the watch, to give me a detailed history of the events leading up to this schism, events which (so far as I could make out, given my imperfect understanding of Dutch and his imperfect command of German) had their roots in the early seventeenth century. The gist of it was that Zwart and his crew were members of a small, ultra-Calvinist breakaway sect of the Dutch Reformed Church which, as the result of two centuries of synods and conclaves and colloquia—after which the majority invariably excommunicated the minority—had finally reduced itself to a concentrated, boiled-down, distilled essence of doctrinal purity. The only snag was that in doing so it had also reduced its numbers to a point where, by about 1890, the temporal boundaries of the Exclusive Dutch Re-Reformed Elect Church of God coincided pretty closely with the limits of a fishing village called Gurk on the shores of the Zuider Zee, some way north of Enkhuizen, a community so strict (I was told) that even the dogs were muzzled on Sundays to stop them from barking and people were regularly tarred and feathered for whistling. But then, in 1895 or thereabouts, a missionary from the brethren of Gurk had succeeded in persuading a portion of the Dutch Reformed faithful on Amboina to break away from the rest and throw in their lot with the Elect in faraway Holland. Thus the Holland-Amboina Reformed Steam Navigation Company had been born: a shipping line based on a church. I had assumed when I first came aboard the *Samboeran* that the "Reformed" in the title referred to some purely business arrangement, perhaps after bankruptcy; but I now learnt that this was a mark of the company's religious affiliation. The board of directors was in fact the consistory of the church, while no operational decision was taken without a prayer meeting and due reference to the Holy Scriptures and God in His position as majority shareholder; or, failing that, to a mysterious document called the "Rubric to the Confession of Dordrecht" which seemed to be the touchstone of the church's existence.

I sat enthralled as I listened to Zwart's narrative of the Elect of Gurk. I had never before taken the slightest interest in theology, but there was something irresistibly fascinating about it all, as that seemingly endless procession of grim-faced divines marched relentlessly past before my eyes there under the tropical moon and the indigo vault of the night sky, some in starched ruffs and black steeple-hats, others in periwigs and Geneva bands, all of them with thick leather-bound theological tomes beneath their arms and all with names like Hooftius or Canisius or Hondius.

I soon gathered, however, that this curious fusion of the nautical and the ecclesiastical had its drawbacks. Or, to be more precise, that aboard the *Samboeran* and the other vessels of her line, the little differences of opinion which are an everyday part of shipboard life had a fatal tendency to assume a theological guise. Disputes that would be resolved aboard a normal merchant steamer by the First Mate chasing the Bos'un a few times around the deck with a stoker's slice and no hard feelings afterwards, tended here—as they had recently done at Mendano—to lead to schism and excommunication, with the dissident party trooping down the gangplank reciting the text from St Paul about "Wherefore come out from among them, and be ye separate." It was all very, very strange.

I was a nominal Roman Catholic, and had thus (as far as the Gurk

Brethren were concerned) been specially created by God—like the rest of mankind—to be roasted throughout eternity over a slow fire for His special amusement. But this at least meant that I was neither required nor expected to take any part in these curious goings-on. One point where the crew's religious practices did impinge upon me, however, was the ship's messing arrangements. The passengers cooked their food each morning and evening over braziers on the open deck: they were Muslims on pilgrimage and would of course have nothing to do with the *orang putih* and his unclean foods for fear of defilement. They were very wise, I thought; for as the delicious smells of their own simple meals wafted in through the open scuttles of the saloon amidships where the officers messed, I would be sitting down to face food that would have caused a riot in any jail in Europe. The Gurk Elders held that anything which gratified the senses was displeasing to God and injurious to morals, and of all the senses they believed that of taste to be the easiest route by which Satan might gain access to the heart of a potential castaway. Thus the bill of fare served to the officers and crew of the S.S. *Samboeran* was of such plainness, such a fiendish, unrelieved monotony, that even the sparse rations dished up for us cadets at the k.u.k. Marine Akademie seemed luxurious by comparison. The only thing that could possibly be said in its favour was that it was at least democratically served—or rather administered. The officers (with whom I was graciously permitted to mess) and the fo'c'sle both got exactly the same dreary rations.

It started each morning at eight bells with breakfast: a black, unsweetened fluid described as coffee and a bowl of an awful mush called *zwavelgrutten*—"brimstoned groats"—a breakfast cereal fit for Beelzebub himself. About a spoonful was usually as much as I could get down. Then came the midday meal. On Tuesdays and Fridays it was pea-soup, a greenish-yellow jelly with the flavour and consistency of library paste. On Mondays, Thursdays and Saturdays it was something called *nasi goreng*, consisting of a plate of plain boiled rice with a cold fried egg on top. This may sound rather luxurious, the fried egg I mean, but the Elders had thought of that as well, for the eggs had been preserved in buckets of lime down in the hold, perhaps for years on end, and combined the texture of celluloid with the disagreeable, musty flavour of an old horse-hair sofa-cushion. The *chef d'oeuvre* of Reformed Protestant cuisine, however, was set before us on Wednesdays and Sundays: *stokvis*. This consisted of a flap of greyish-white boiled salt cod reposing like an old face-flannel on the white plate. I had always been rather wary of eating fish in the tropics, after a very unpleasant few hours once in Pernambuco when I was a cadet. But one glance at *stokvis* in its uncooked state convinced me that I had no reason to fear infection. It hung there in the provisions room, row upon row of fish which had not so much been preserved as mummified: transformed from gleaming silvery-white creatures flapping on the deck of a trawler to things which might have come from the lower strata of the Devonian sandstone. Hot food or cold, it scarcely mattered, for Zwart would always intone such a long grace (prayers aboard were supposed to be extempore but were in fact as formalised as those in any breviary) that molten lava would have solidi-fied before we got down to eating. The day was concluded by supper: a ship's biscuit and a cup of the same "coffee" served at breakfast. I later learnt that even the coffee was made by roasting the biscuit left over from the previous evening's supper in the galley oven, then pulverising the charred fragments and infusing them in hot water. My body cried out for calories after my shifts in the stokehold and on deck but my stomach churned at the thought of the stuff that I would have to pack into it to obtain them.

My membership of the reprobate class of mankind did at least have the advantage that I was excused attendance with the rest of the crew at the regular daily sessions of prayer and Bible-study and psalm-chanting (the Elect disapproved of music along with just about every other human activity). Instead I could stand on the bridge and listen simultaneously to the prayers coming from the Brethren in conclave in the saloon, and to the wailing chant of the *muezzin* rising into the heavens from the fore-deck (one of the watch-officer's duties was to give a compass bearing for Mecca each morning). The S.S. *Samboeran* fairly reeked of religion from stem to stern, as a cattle boat reeks of cow-dung. I often wondered what on earth God must have made of it all.

# 16

# PLANE SAILING

Y OU MAY PERHAPS HAVE GATHERED from the foregoing that,
all things considered, the steamship *Samboeran* possessed one
of the strangest ship's companies to have taken the water since
Noah's Ark grounded on top of Mount Ararat. But there was one even
greater and more unsettling surprise to come.

It happened one evening when we were five days out from Java Head.
The great silver platter of the moon had just risen from the smooth,
oily water and the stars were shining with their full brilliance. The ship
steamed on at her steady fourteen knots, as she had done for the past week,
leaving a shining dead-straight trail of phosphorescence behind her like
some giant snail's track across the sea. I had been apprehensive of her
ability to keep up this speed day in, day out without a boiler bursting or a
crankshaft snapping, but my fears had so far proved groundless. The ship
was soundly built and well cared-for, her boilers were in excellent condition and her engines were still thumping and hissing away down below
without the slightest sign of fatigue. It was about an hour into the first
watch. The pilgrims were already settling down for the night beneath the
awnings, spreading their sleeping mats on the deck and organising their
few belongings with the contented hum of a swarm of bees, punctuated
only now and then by the crying of a baby or the high, musical tinkle of
Malay laughter. Skipper Zwart was out on the bridge while I stood over the
chart-room table, comparing our last position with the patent-log reading
and measured shaft revolutions. Zwart strolled in.

"Well Captain," I remarked, "three thousand miles in nine days. That
means we've already travelled an eighth of the way around the world."

He stopped. There was a sudden stony silence. I sensed that I had said something dreadfully wrong. After some moments Zwart spoke: slowly and deliberately, with the air of someone correcting an appalling social faux pas without wishing to publicise it still further. "Herr Leutnant, you mean that we have already sailed an eighth of the way *across* the world."

"With respect, Captain, I said around . . ."

"You mean across: we cannot have travelled around it, because the world is flat and one cannot travel around a flat surface."

It appeared that I had stumbled unwittingly across a subject that aroused nearly as much fervour in Captain Zwart's bulky breast as that of infralapsarian predestination or the technicalities of excommunication. To cut a very long story short, during the course of his monologue—which lasted for the rest of the first watch and well into the middle watch— I realised with growing horror and incredulity that I was afloat in the middle of the Indian Ocean aboard a ship commanded by a man who, on grounds of scriptural inerrancy, totally rejected the twin hypotheses upon which all marine navigation has been based since about 1500: that is to say, that the Earth is more or less spherical and that it revolves in space around the sun. If it had been anyone less serious than skipper Zwart I would have suspected—how do you say?—that my leg was being pulled. But the man had not the tiniest grain of a sense of humour, in fact was manifestly incapable even of grasping the concept of a joke. I tried to raise objections.

"But Captain, if the earth is flat, how does the sun rise and set? If what you say were true, it would be visible all the time from any point on earth."

He smiled patiently. "The earth is not perfectly flat, but slightly domed, like an inverted saucer. While as for the sun, it travels its daily course through the sky at an altitude of about seventy kilometres. When it disappears behind the curvature we see it set."

"How does the sun orbit the earth though?"

"It orbits the point in the centre of the earth which geographers refer to as the North Pole, but which is in fact a giant lodestone. The magnetic attraction of the lodestone acts on the sun—which is only a couple of kilometres in circumference—to keep it more or less on its course, above the imaginary line which we refer to for the sake of convenience as the Equator."

"But what about the seasons?"

"The procession of the equinoxes takes place because the height of the sun's progress above the earth and the radius of that orbit vary during the year, like a boy swinging a ball about his head on an elastic band."

"Tell me though, Captain, how do the moon and stars work?"

"The heavens are in fact a series of concentric domes of a translucent glass-like substance, surrounded by water as the Book of Genesis makes clear. What we call the moon is in fact not a planet, as the carnally minded suppose, but a kind of porthole in the innermost dome provided by God to illuminate the night. The first and second domes revolve inside one another independently, and the stars are in fact lamps hung inside the second dome. The stars, we believe, are about eighty kilometres above us."

It might have been the warmth of the night, but I could feel my shirt sticking clammily to my back with cold perspiration. It is always a disturbing experience to meet a maniac; but the encounter is doubly unsettling when, instead of raving with straw in his hair, the madman presents his crazed opinions with a measured, calm, carefully enunciated certainty, as if only someone very obtuse, very ill-informed or very perverse could possibly disagree with something so blindingly self-evident. I felt compelled to return to the attack, though with a growing sense of desperation.

"Please tell me though, Captain: if the earth is an inverted dish and the Equator is a circle about twenty-five thousand nautical miles in circumference . . ." He nodded magisterially, as if graciously pleased for the moment to consider this as a working hypothesis. ". . . Then how is it that the outer edge of the dish is not about seventy thousand miles around?" His reply was delivered without a moment's hesitation: "How do you know that it isn't?"

"Yes, but if one travels around the world south of the Equator, the distance travelled decreases with each parallel of south latitude."

"How do you know? Have you measured one recently?"

"But people who sail around the world . . ."

". . . In fact sail across it. But have you ever met anyone who has sailed right around one of your precious parallels of south latitude without deviation? I understand that Africa and South America get in the way. No, Herr Leutnant, it simply will not do. They teach children in schools that if a ship sailed right around the world on a parallel of latitude it would arrive back where it started. But none ever has, and even if it could it would maintain its course by compass bearings. And the compass needle would always point to the lodestone at the North Pole, so its crew would think that they had sailed around a sphere when in fact they had described a circle on an almost flat surface."

"Measurements though, by patent log . . . by observation of longitude . . ."

He sighed as if trying to reason patiently with a child of limited intelligence. "Patent-log measurements, as you know, are unreliable over long distances, and are not constant anyway because the density of sea water decreases the nearer one gets to the outer edge of the world. As for your observations of longitude, so-called, permit me only to observe that they are themselves based upon lines drawn on maps on the false and damnable hypothesis that the earth is a sphere—which is really what they have to prove in the first place."

"Surely though, a ship that sails around the Southern Ocean at about latitude sixty degrees South . . ."

"I never knew one that did. But tell me, Herr Leutnant, you are a seafaring man. Have you ever been around Cape Horn, which for practical purposes is the furthest south that ships ever venture?"

"Yes, twice if you must know."

"And how long did it take your ship to travel between, say, what we refer to for the sake of convenience as seventy and eighty degrees West longitude?"

"About four weeks in one case, and six in the other, but . . ." His squashed features assumed a look of quiet self-satisfaction, such as one might see on the face of a prosecuting attorney who has just got the accused to say that he could not have left fingerprints on the vase because he was wearing gloves at the time. "I see: four to six weeks to travel a linear distance which, according to your theories, ought to be about three hundred nautical miles. And why did you take so long, pray?"

I struggled weakly now, like a fish in the net before the gaff is hooked beneath its gills. "Because of head winds and mountainous seas."

"Head winds and mountainous seas be damned: it was because the real distance was far greater than that marked on the chart."

I decided on one last desperate throw. "The edge of the world though: if the earth has an edge, why do ships not fall over the edge?" Before the words had left my lips I knew that I was lost, finally and irrevocably.

"If you take the trouble to consult the 'Lloyd's Register' or some such publication you will see that each year scores of ships disappear in what you erroneously call 'the Southern Ocean.' They sail from Valparaiso or Hobart, then poof! nothing more is ever heard of them: no survivors, no wreckage, no nothing."

"Do you really suppose then that they fall off the edge of the world . . . ?"

"Either that, or they become trapped until the Day of Judgement in the fringe of perpetual ice which surrounds the outer edge of the world, and which the reprobate refer to as 'the Antarctic Continent.' Continent indeed . . ." He snorted with derision. "Another sieve designed by the omniscient God to test a man's faith and separate the wheat from the tares. Your whole 'Antarctica' is nothing but a gigantic hoax, Scott and Amundsen—pah! Godless deceivers and charlatans the pair of them: Scott fell over the edge and Amundsen turned back to avoid a similar fate."

I gave up at this point. There was no way into the fortress of this man's mind, not even the smallest hairline crack in its towering, smooth glacis of black granite, not the faintest hope of getting a scaling ladder against it, not a single objection which could not be explained away as optical illusion or lens distortion or magnetic anomaly. I retired from the field, utterly defeated. But even if I knew that I had lost the argument, curiosity still remained.

"Captain," I asked, "if you will pardon me I must still ask how it is, if you believe the earth to be flat, you still manage to navigate this ship from place to place. After all, every chart and almanac that I have ever seen assumes it to be round."

"Not all, Herr Leutnant, not all . . ." He reached up to the shelf above the chart table and reached down a thick, much-thumbed leather-bound volume. He laid it on the chart table before me and opened it at the title page. It was in Dutch, and read *Reformed Protestant Astronomical and Chart Correction Tables for the Use of Christian Seafarers—Anno Domini 1914*. Underneath this legend was the subtitle, in smaller print: "Compiled by Dominie H. C. F. Van Zanten of the Biblical Seminary of Alkmaar, and attested as conforming to the literally inerrant Word of God and the Rubric to the Confession of Dordrecht by the Consistory of the Exclusive Dutch Re-Reformed Biblical Church of God."

I turned the pages: sheet after sheet of sun-tables and astral tables and lunar tables as in any other nautical almanac—though in this case each page was headed with some suitable proof-text like "Hast thou perceived the breadth of the Earth? (Job 38: 18)" or "And the sun stood still, and the moon stayed, until the people had avenged themselves upon their enemies (Joshua 10: 13)."

"You see?" he said. "The merciful dispensation of God's providence has provided his Elect Nation with a pastor who cares sufficiently for the souls of his people to devote his life to the study of astronomy on their behalf. We could have gone on using the so-called almanacs produced by the minds of carnal men. But instead we can correct their charts with this book, and this . . ." He opened the drawer beneath the chart table and drew out a sort of elaborate slide-rule, about a metre long, beautifully fashioned from boxwood and brass but with four or five minutely inscribed slides instead of one. "We use this to correct the distance between their so-called lines of longitude, since we are still obliged to use charts drawn up by unbelievers. If you ask me one evening when I have more time I shall instruct you in its use. But for now you must excuse me. It is late and I have evening prayers to conduct before I retire for the night."

"Thank you for your time; I have found it most interesting."

"Please think nothing of it. I regard it as time well spent to have set you right on one or two particulars. When I see you tomorrow—God willing—I shall give you some pamphlets which may help to explain matters further. Good-night."

He left me standing on the bridge, alone but for the helmsman at the wheel. I gazed up into the sky at the luminous disc of the moon—or was it a hole? . . . No, no—if I started like that I would lose my sanity completely! Somehow the deck now felt unsteady beneath my feet, even though the sea was glassy-calm. Surely, Fate had not saved me from the sharks off the coast of Borneo only to entrust me to the care of a dangerous lunatic? And what about those other poor souls sleeping so peacefully on the deck? Perhaps I ought to wake them and tell them that for all I knew we might be heading for Tierra del Fuego or the Bering Straits? I even considered lowering a lifeboat and committing myself to the ocean rather than spend another night aboard this floating asylum full of religious maniacs. But after a while I calmed down a little and went back to the chart table—then remembered something. I stole back to the cabin which I shared with Kaindel and rummaged around in the bag of belongings which I had rescued from the sinking junk. Yes, here it was: the *Hallweg and Berndt Nautical Ephemerids, Berlin, Year 1914*. I carried it back to the bridge with me, took the ship's sextant out of its drawer and, when I was sure that no one was watching, proceeded to pull down a star or two.

I did this over the next three days, stealing the odd sun observation as well when I had a free moment. I compared the positions thus obtained with those marked on the chart, and found to my surprise that, however Zwart and his officers had come by them, they corresponded almost exactly with mine as regards longitude. My latitudes though were badly out, and remained frustratingly so however carefully I checked and rechecked my calculations. But after a couple of days I began to notice that they were always out by the same amount. In the end, after taking a few simultaneous sun and moon sights in the early morning, the only con- clusion I could come to was that the *Samboeran*'s chronometer was some twenty minutes fast: surely a most unlikely eventuality aboard so smartly run a vessel. I was quite at a loss to explain this until one day I happened to glance at the tiny print near the bottom margin of the chart and saw that it said "Degrees east of Amsterdam." So that was it: all the other seafaring nations—even the French—had long since gone over to locating zero degrees at Greenwich, but the Dutch chart-makers (or at least, the ones favoured by the Holland-Amboina Steam Navigation Company) still clung obstinately to a prime meridian at Amsterdam. I read somewhere years later that a few of them were still using it in 1940 when the Germans invaded and forced everyone to go over to Greenwich Mean Time.

I suppose in any case, looking back on it now, that skipper Zwart's navigational eccentricities had not a great deal of practical significance. The S.S. *Samboeran* and her sisters of the Holland-Amboina Line spent most of their lives sailing within the tropics, and in those latitudes—up to about twenty degrees each side of the Equator—the difference between treating the lines of longitude on the chart as straight and treating them as slightly curved is so small as to be scarcely worth bothering about. These were the latitudes of what we used to call "plane sailing," so I suppose that Dominie Van Zanten's book of theologically sound tables and the mysterious offset ruler really had little effect on the ship's progress from A to B. I suspect also that, as in the matter of sailing the ship on the Sabbath, doctrinal purity may have been quietly diluted with a measure of practical common sense.

Anyway, across the world or around it, early on the morning of 29 October we sighted land, the first for twelve days. It was the island of Socotra, just off the Horn of Africa and the entrance to the Red Sea. We congratulated ourselves discreetly: at this rate we would make Jeddah late on the first day of November, with plenty of time in hand for our passengers to disembark and start out on the last leg of their pilgrimage to Mecca. For my part I had additional reason to feel quietly pleased. I had no idea what hardships and dangers might lie ahead of Kaindel and Wong and myself on the next stage of our own weary journey, but I knew that we were now five thousand miles nearer home than we had been three weeks ago, and that thought did much to soften the pain of calloused hands and aching back and raw knees. In two days' time we would be landing on the territory of the Ottoman Empire. I knew that a railway now ran from Damascus to the holy city of Medina; and, if I had previously been rather vague on the inland geography of the Arabian Peninsula, the intense Old Testament religiosity of the *Samboeran*'s master and crew had at least allowed me the opportunity to spend my few free moments studying and making sketches from a Dutch *Atlas of the Holy Land and the Near East.* Some of the information had been of limited relevance—for example, the precise route followed by the Israelites during the forty years in the wilderness, or the site of the Garden of Eden—but most of it had been highly informative. The difficult part was clearly going to be the journey to Medina, if Turkish help was not forthcoming. Once we were there, however, then in theory at any rate all we had to do was to buy three railway tickets for Vienna by way of Constantinople.

But it was not to be quite as simple as that, for about midday on the 29th, as we were entering the Gulf of Aden, we fell in with another ship steaming on a parallel course to our own. We took her at first to be another merchantman, but then she altered course to close with us, and we saw that she was in fact a small cruiser: a hideously ugly vessel with a grotesquely elongated ram bow and three squat, unevenly spaced pagoda funnels. She flew the French *tricouleur.* It was the colonial cruiser *Villeneuve.* As the vessel drew alongside us her Captain hailed us through a speaking trumpet.

"What ship are you?"

Zwart bellowed back in French, so loudly that he had no need of a trumpet. "Netherlands steamship *Samboeran,* on passage from the East Indies."

"Where are you bound for?"

"Jeddah!"

"Stop immediately: we are boarding you!"

"Go to the Devil! We are a vessel of a neutral state and we are in a hurry!"

The French ship's reply was simple and unambiguous: with exquisite menace the forward gun traversed round to point at our bridge. Zwart spluttered and swore, but we stopped engines and lay rolling in the swell. The *Villeneuve* lowered a boat and within five minutes a boarding party of armed matelots in sun helmets was clambering over our rail. They were led by a young and rather unpleasantly self-possessed *lieutenant de vaisseau*. Zwart gave him the benefit of his entire repertoire of French invective, but the officer only smiled.

"Aha, neutral? This is perhaps still so in the case of Holland, I cannot say; but Turkey has just broken off diplomatic relations with France and Great Britain. The French Marine will now stop and, if necessary, detain all vessels bound for Turkish ports."

"But what am I to do with my passengers? We have 350 Malay Muslims on board, heading for Mecca, and the hadj starts in three days. We have to go on to Jeddah."

The lieutenant shrugged his shoulders. "I regret, but that will unfortunately not be possible. You must instead follow us into Djibouti. There we shall inspect the ship for contraband and enemy nationals, then you must turn around and go back to the East Indies." I thought for a moment that Zwart was going to burst a blood vessel. "What? Search the ship? Turn us back? This is an outrage! You are nothing but common pirates! The Netherlands is a neutral state . . ."

"Eh, *m'sieur,* what would you? That France and Holland are not at war, it is true; but as for your neutrality, perhaps you would like us to send a wireless message to Batavia to call a *cuirassé* here so that we can discuss the matter? It would only take three weeks or so for them to get here. We could always wait."

So we gave in and dejectedly followed the *Villeneuve* into Djibouti Roads where we dropped anchor. It was evening now, and the sun was sinking below the mountains of Africa. A search party would come aboard in the morning and check the crew and passenger lists, no doubt paying particular attention to the fact that the *Samboeran* had mysteriously gained an extra nine crew members since she left Mendano, and that none of them had any identity papers. I considered how we might get ashore under cover of darkness, but the more I thought about it the less attractive the idea looked. For one thing, the French were keeping a close watch on us and on a German steamer which they had brought in the day before, sweeping the water with their searchlights every half-minute or so. For another, we were over a mile offshore and the bay was reputed to be infested with sharks, so swimming for the land was hardly a promising line of escape, even if Wong had still possessed both his arms. No, we would have to sit it out tonight and see what opportunities presented themselves in the morning. The moon rose: the very thinnest sliver of light now. Tomorrow night and the night after that there would be no moon, then the new moon would rise to announce the start of the Muslim month of Zulhijah and the beginning of the hadj season. If we were not at Jeddah to see it rise then our passengers would miss the pilgrimage for which most of them had saved all their lives and undergone God alone knew what hardships to undertake—and all on account of a white man's war in Christian Europe. The pilgrims were mostly simple, illiterate Malay kampong-dwellers and entirely ignorant of the rest of the world; but even the slowest-witted among them had surely noticed our encounter with the French cruiser and our detour into Djibouti. Even if they were ignorant of geography, they knew the phases of the moon far better than any newspaper reader, and they must have sensed dimly that, wherever this place was where we had dropped anchor for the night, it was not Jeddah. I noticed as I stood on the bridge in the darkness that the normal, gentle hum of the pilgrims preparing to sleep was beginning to fracture into a peevish, irritable buzzing as groups formed beneath the awnings.

It was an uneasy night for us all. The sun came up at last over the eastern, seaward horizon to illuminate the barren mountains, and the voice of the *muezzin* intoned the morning prayers. The *Villeneuve* lay anchored about 1,500 metres to port while a small French gunboat lay some way off our starboard quarter. For the time being it appeared that their boarding parties were fully occupied with the German prize, and with a Norwegian sailing ship which had been brought in during the night. So we lay for most of the day broiling beneath the African sun, still and irritable with frustration. It was murderously hot now that the ship's forward motion was no longer moving a breeze across the decks. The passengers were taking it particularly ill. Children cried fretfully. Women wilted in the throbbing heat. Groups of men were squatting cross-legged about the deck engaged in animated debates. I could not understand a word of it, but I could see that white-moustached village elders in their brimless felt hats were counselling caution while the young men were urging action.

By midday the heat was so intense that nearly everyone, passengers and crew alike, had sought whatever shade could be found. I was under the bridge awnings, but as I looked down on to the foredeck, to a place immediately below where the awnings did not extend, I saw to my surprise that one group of five or six young Malays was sitting on the deck in the full furnace glare of the sun, apparently indifferent to its rays. Curious, I looked down without them seeing me. It seemed to be some kind of game, but for the life of me I could see no dice or board or any impedimenta at all. Yet they seemed as engrossed as poker players gambling for thousands of dollars. At length one of them leant forward and with slow, steady, deliberate intensity described a circle on the scorching deck-planks with the tip of his finger. The others watched, mesmerised, sitting like statues. I mentioned it to skipper Zwart, who was pacing the bridge fretfully, cursing the French Navy under his breath. He had lived in the Indies for many years, so perhaps he knew this game? When I described it to him his eyes bulged and his normally florid complexion suddenly drained of colour.

"He did . . . what?"

"Drew a circle on the deck with his finger, like this. They all seemed very absorbed."

Beads of sweat broke out on his brow, even beyond that which was being squeezed out of him by the appalling heat. "Quick, Silano! For God's sake lower a boat and send to the French ship for help. Tell them to get an armed party here quick. Here," he turned to me, "here's the key to the weapons locker in my cabin. You'll find six revolvers there held by a padlock and chain. Bring them here at once so that I can hand them out, then muster your men. If we hold the bridge you will have to hold the poop and the engine room. Take two revolvers and arm your men with belaying pins, then tell Praetorius to lock the engine-room hatches. If we can confine the savages to the fore and quarter decks we can at least keep them separated."

I ran below to Zwart's cabins and unchained the revolvers in their safe, took two boxes of ammunition, scrambled back up to the bridge to distribute them, then hurried aft below decks to warn the Chief Engineer. Wong was despatched to tell Baden and Mödling and the other Chinese to get down to the engine room and help the crew barricade the companion-ways. Meanwhile Kaindel and the Third Mate and I improvised barriers of boxes and furniture and bales of merchandise to secure the poop deck. A boat had just been lowered and Jan Hendrik Silano and two seamen were rowing at top speed towards the *Villeneuve* to seek help. Assistance came, but in scant measure: a mere section of Fusiliers Marins, consisting of an NCO and ten men. They took up their station on the bridge deck amid-ships, looking very bored indeed and quite evidently wondering what on earth all the fuss was about over a few hundred unarmed Malays, half of them women and children and old people anyway. An uneasy silence had fallen over the ship in the dreary, stultifying heat.

The storm broke quite suddenly, just as the sun was touching the western horizon. I have no idea whether the shot was deliberate, fired by a nervous young French Marine with a delicate trigger-finger, or whether it was what your army calls a "negligent discharge": letting a rifle clatter to the deck with the safety catch off. But whatever happened, there was a bang and a flash from the bridge deck, a moment's silence—then an angry, unearthly scream from a hundred throats as the mass of passengers fore and aft of the bridge began to seethe like a pot coming to the boil. There were hoarse shouts in French and Dutch. Dark figures began to scramble up the ladders to try and mount the bridge. The fading light gleamed on the steel of kris being drawn from their sheaths. There was an order, and a volley of rifle-shots—aimed quite deliberately into the midst of the sway-ing mass below: young men and old, mothers with babies in their arms, the nameless doctor who had treated Wong's arm. Their shrieks were lost in the great roar of anger as they came at us, surging up the ladders and over the poop-deck railings to attack. I saw the Third Mate fire his revolver as a young man in a red head-scarf lunged at him with his knife. The man dropped—and the mate fell on top of him with a kris in his back. A Dutch sailor swinging an awning stanchion laid three or four of them low before he too was cut down.

"Come on!" I yelled to Kaindel and Wong above the uproar. "To the stern!" I remembered that the boat which had gone to the *Villeneuve* for help was tied up there. In the end we slid down her painter and tumbled in just as the brown wave reached the taffrail. A body fell into the water beside us as I cut the painter. There was just enough time to see that it was Second Mate Silano. We pushed away desperately from the *Samboeran,* trying to catch a glimpse of our Chinese among the surging, struggling knots of figures fighting for control of the ship. We had no luck: all were below in the engine room and I never learnt what became of them. Shots were splashing about us now as the Malays seized rifles from the dead. All that we could do was try to get as far away as possible. Boatloads of armed sailors were already pulling over from the *Villeneuve* and the gun-boat. But as they reached the ship's side we saw a sudden flash of light under the starboard wing of the bridge as a kerosene lamp fell to the deck and spilt its fuel. The flames touched one of the sun-dessicated canvas awnings, and began to lick up the varnished wooden sides of the chart-house. Within seconds the whole bridge was on fire as a dense column of smoke and sparks rose into the darkening sky. By the time we lost sight of her the S.S. *Samboeran* was ablaze from stem to stern.

# 17

# ARABIA FELIX

I T WAS THE LAST DAY OF NOVEMBER 1914. We had been here nearly a month now, in the hot, humid, foetid little port of Massawa, gateway to the Italian colony of Eritrea. Four weeks had passed, and four unsuccessful attempts to get ourselves aboard a ship bound for Italy via the Suez Canal. I lay on my bed in our torrid little room in the Pension Grimaldi, overlooking the harbour, listening to the frightful bleating and bellowing issuing from the abattoir next door and thankful that today at least the wind was carrying its stench away from us. Well, I thought ruefully, these Italian colonial officials and their native police force may have a relaxed attitude to Ordnung and Vorschrift compared with us Teutons, but they are certainly a sharp-eyed lot and miss very little. For the truth is that our erstwhile partners in the Triple Alliance had turned out to be nowhere near as well-disposed as we had anticipated towards their nominal allies, not even as embodied in the form of three unarmed Austrian fugitives arriving by dhow from Djibouti. We had not exactly been interned here at Massawa, Kaindel and Wong and I, but we were not exactly at liberty either: forbidden to travel outside the town's limits and constantly met with evasions and procrastination when we tried to obtain travel permits from the representatives of the Italian Governor. Four times we had tried to board Italian or neutral ships—even disguising ourselves at the last attempt as Abyssinian merchants—and four times we had been seized at the foot of the gangplank by the gendarmery and harbour officials and returned, politely but firmly, to our lodgings.

The position was of course—though we could not know it where we were—that Italian emissaries were scurrying furtively from Berlin to Paris and London and back again in order to assess which side would offer the most attractive bribe for Italy's entry into the war. Nor could I know, as I lay there in our frowsty, stifling little room in Massawa, that the needle was now swinging in a very decided manner away from the Central Powers and towards the Allies. We knew nothing of this out in faraway Eritrea, but we did sense that the Italians were not quite sure what to do with us. They did not want to jail us; but if Italy was going to be fighting Austria in a few weeks' time then they did not want to set us free either.

So for the time being, while we were not in prison, we were lodged in the next best thing, a cheap and squalid lodging-house on the water-front, sandwiched between an abattoir on one side and a bordello on the other, with a fine view out over Massawa's dramatically filthy harbour: a heat-shimmering bouillabaisse of dead fish, sewage, oil slicks and floating rubbish, garnished with the odd camel's carcass and with a few ships play-ing the role of stale bread-crusts. The days were made hideous with the noise of the abattoir—which tipped its offal straight into the harbour—while at night the scarcely less noisy brothel on the other side kept sleep at bay. When we arrived I saw Kaindel eyeing this latter establishment and fingering the few lire of pocket money given him by the German Consul. But then he caught sight of some of the "girls" leaning over the balcony: raddled Eritrean harpies with braided hair and collapsed noses and teeth filed to points, worthy of modelling for that waxwork show which used to be so popular an attraction on the Viennese Prater, "The Types and Progressions of the Venereal Diseases." And I saw even his stout seaman's heart falter within him as he took a silent vow to remain celibate a while longer. As for Ferdinand Wong, he remained outwardly cheerful and optimistic about his prospects of being home with his family in Trieste by Christmas. But I knew that he was troubled by the ache of his amputation stump—and also by a very understandable anxiety as to what a Steward First Class on ocean liners would do to earn his living now that half his right arm was missing. Likewise I sensed that although no one had said anything, he reproached himself for our failure to stow away aboard a ship. After all, in a port on the north-east coast of Africa a Chinese with his right arm missing below the elbow is a description such as even the dullest-witted policeman can hardly fail to recognise.

It was the German Consul, Herr Schultz, who kept us alive. The Italian colonial authorities would only provide for our keep at the sub-starvation level specified for shipwrecked seamen, not for armed-forces internees, so the difference was made up by the Consul even though, as Austrian subjects, we were not his responsibility. The most he could do for us out of his limited funds was to provide us with little more than bare subsistence: a roof over our heads and a meal of pasta once a day. Madame Grimaldi, our landlady, was in fact Provençale French—a jovial enough woman, dressed from head to foot in black bombazine, despite the monstrous heat, to signify her status as a widow. It was only by chance that I learnt that she was a widow because about 1890, in Marseilles, she had administered rat-poison to her husband and seven or eight of her relatives. She had been reprieved at the steps of the guillotine, then released under a presidential amnesty some years later to come out to the Italian colonies and begin a new life as a boarding-house proprietress.

After all the excitements and perils of the previous three months, the days now had a depressing sameness about them: the walk to the German Consulate to see whether there was any news, then to the police headquarters to register our presence, then to the government offices to spend yet another morning sipping mint tea and facing the bland, smiling evasions of the Italian bureaucrats with their little pointed beards. This morning it was Signor Rabagliati again: all politeness and compliments on my excellent command of Italian, but with nothing to offer as usual. A passage to Naples aboard the *Civitavecchia,* paid for by the German Consulate? No, that would not be possible: the British authorities at Port Said were demanding passenger lists before issuing permits to use the canal. No, it would not be possible to work as deckhands aboard the *Livorno* either, or to ship aboard a Swedish tramp steamer bound for Portuguese East Africa: the harbour authorities came under the Italian Navy and would not permit it. Regrettably it would not be possible to travel to Mogadishu either and try to find a berth there: the Governors of Eritrea and of Somaliland were at one in their desire to enforce neutrality rules. As for going up to Asmara to argue with His Excellency the Governor in person, no, that would not be of any use: he could not answer for the gendarmery, who were the responsibility of the local military commander (who was on leave in Italy) but he doubted whether I would be granted permission to leave the town. As for my request to His Excellency the Governor, there had not yet been any reply: the post took time in Eritrea. I left the government offices—and ran straight into Herr Schultz. He had news to impart. We went to a nearby café and over an iced coffee (generously paid for by Herr Schultz since it was mid-week and I was already destitute) he filled in the details for me.

"I've managed to arrange it for you, I'm happy to report. A sambuq has been chartered by a ship-owner friend of mine to carry you across to the Arabian side tonight. All you have to do is get to the coast a few kilometres south of here. I've arranged a guide and mules—and also bribed the native they've set to keep watch on you."

"Herr Schultz, we shall be eternally indebted to you if you can get us out of this disease-ridden hole. But what are we to do once we reach the Arabian shore?"

"I'm sorry, but that's as far as I can take responsibility for you or offer you any useful directions. As you have found out, there's not the slightest hope now of your getting through the Suez Canal even if the Italians were prepared to let you. The British are not only demanding passenger lists from neutral shipping but carrying out searches. No, Turkey is at least in the war on our side."

"But where are we to go? I understand that the Arabian Peninsula is quite large."

"The sambuq's skipper will put you ashore at a place called Al Qunfidha. The British and French are blockading the coast quite closely, but he's made several trips across already and managed to dodge them each time. Once you're there and have made contact with the Turkish authorities—I shall give you a letter, by the way—you'll have to make your way north-westwards as best as you can to Medina. Once you're there the rest should be easy."

"And how far is it from Al whatever-it-is to Medina?"

"About 450 kilometres; desert all the way, though there's a caravan route I understand."

"Are we likely to get much help from the Turks, from what you know on this side of the Red Sea? I've always understood that Ottoman rule in Arabia is rather patchy, to say the least."

He sucked his teeth. "Difficult to say. I'd certainly be doing you no service though if I led you to believe that it's going to be easy. As you say, Turkish authority in the Hejaz has always been nominal at the best of times; and from the reports we're getting now they seem to be facing near-revolt in places. I appreciate that I'm dropping you into a viper's nest. But what else are you to do? The Italians are going to come into the war against us before long and when they do they'll just round you all up and stick you in jail for the rest of the war."

Herr Schultz's comments as to the disturbed state of law and order in the Hejaz were borne out almost as soon as we waded ashore two mornings later, boots slung around our necks, on a desolate stretch of beach some way north of Al Qunfidha. The sambuq captain, a one-eyed epileptic, had missed the port in the dark and we had been chased at one point by a steam pinnace, until a providential rain-squall allowed us to shake them off. We each had a Mauser pistol procured for us by Herr Schultz, and I also had a cheap pocket compass, a small-scale map of western Arabia and the canvas belt of Austrian 20-Kronen gold pieces which I had worn all the way from Tsingtao. And that, apart from the clothes we stood up in, was the total extent of our preparation for this latest stage of our journey home. Still, it was good to feel the beach sand beneath my feet and to know that for the first time since we left Tsingtao we were back on friendly territory.

It has to be said, however, that this amity was not immediately apparent, for as we breasted the line of dunes a troop of six or so horsemen appeared further along the shore. They gathered into a knot and conferred for some moments, then set off towards us at a canter. Thinking them to be Turkish scouts sent to meet us, I stumbled towards them waving and calling—until a rifle bullet kicked up a fountain of sand by my foot. We dived for cover in a hollow of the dunes as I fumbled to get the wooden holster which served as a sort of shoulder stock on to my pistol. The horsemen circled us for some time, firing occasionally, and we fired the odd shot or two back. This went on for an hour or so, the riders getting more insolent and coming closer, horses' hoofs thudding on the sand—until they suddenly broke and rode off at full gallop. Puzzled, I stood up and saw a large body of horsemen drawing towards us from the opposite direction. As they came nearer I saw that they were soldiers, about twenty of them. My first instinct was to greet them as our rescuers, but after my earlier encounter I was more cautious. They seemed to be regular cavalry of some kind, rather than mere robbers, but of what nationality was less certain. They wore dark-blue tunics and red breeches, and their headgear, so far as I could make out, was white with a cloth over the neck. The thought suddenly struck me that these might be part of a French landing force, Algerian *spahis* or some such exotic colonial cavalry. It would be a fine joke, I thought, if we had just landed on Ottoman territory only to be picked up by the French Army before we had travelled a hundred metres.

But, whoever they were, we had to face them. Three men with pistols might have been able to hold off six irresolute Arab thieves for an hour or so; they would stand no chance whatever against regular troops armed with carbines and sabres. I strode out towards them as the officer in charge reined in his horse in front of them. We regarded one another for some time. The headdress, I now saw, was not a white *kepi* with a flap but a kind of formalised version of the Arab head-cloth. The officer was also quite clearly an Arab, to judge by his features. He saluted me perfunctorily.

"*Entschuldigen Sie bitte, sprechen Sie Deutsch?*"

He shook his head.

"*Parlez-vous français?*"

Again a shake of the head.

"Do you speak English?"

"A little bit, yes."

"Might I then enquire of what army you are part?"

"The Turkish Army of course: 4th Cavalry Brigade of the Hejaz Division of the 14th Army Corps. I am Lieutenant Nassim-al-Hazri Bey, at your service. But who might you be?"

"My name is Ottokar Prohaska, senior lieutenant in the Austro-Hungarian Navy. We are now allies, I believe."

"How then do you come to be here?"

I told him how we had crossed from Massawa and, as briefly as I could, how we had come to be in Massawa in the first place. At the end of my narrative he looked as impressed as if I had just arrived from next door to borrow a cup of sugar. He considered for a while, then spoke. "Very well. You had better come with us."

Our destination turned out to be the town of Taif, high up in the granite mountains above the broiling shore of the Red Sea: the headquarters of the Turkish Hejaz Division and also summer residence of Sherif Hussein, hereditary Emir of Mecca and guardian of the holy cities. Really I could hardly believe our luck as the three of us rode up into the mountains amid an escort of Arab horsemen. Apart from the little contretemps with the robbers on the shore it was all going splendidly. We were being conveyed to the headquarters of Turkish rule in the Hejaz, and once we were there who could doubt that we would be sent under escort to catch the train at Medina? Vienna by Christmas began to look like a real possibility instead of a vague hope to keep our spirits up.

We were to be disappointed once more. True, Taif was a much pleasanter place to be stuck in than an insufferable, torrid, filthy hole like Massawa. A small walled town built on a granite plateau about two thousand metres above the sweltering littoral of the Red Sea, it was an almost indecently picturesque place, a tastefully arranged cluster of flat-roofed houses and domes and minarets like some illustration from *The Thousand and One Arabian Nights,* or a depiction of Bethlehem in an Austrian advent calendar. Its deep, narrow streets were as smelly as those of most Middle Eastern towns, but the houses were well constructed and pleasingly adorned with balconies and shutters of elaborately carved wood: cedar and teak, whose oils did something to sweeten the odour of the alleyways. And the air at this season of the year was like champagne after the pestilential miasma of the Eritrean coast—cold, but invigorating and so clear that objects many kilometres away had the enamelled-miniature sharpness of the view through the wrong end of a pair of binoculars. As for ourselves, we were decently if plainly lodged, by courtesy of the Turkish Military Governor, and looked after by an Austrian engineer, one Herr Poltenbach, who had come here in 1912 to build and run an oil-pressing mill. He provided us with fresh clothing, pocket money and even reading matter to while away the days, once we had seen all the sights of the town. I got through most of Thomas Mann, sitting in Taif in those last weeks of 1914 as camels rumbled and goats bleated beneath my window and the *muezzin* intoned his prayers from the nearby mosque.

The one home comfort that we could really have done without was the Turkish Governor's military brass band. These rogues were sent to play beneath our balcony from time to time as a mark of honour and special favour since the Governor, who had once been to Berlin, was under the impression that all German speakers were passionately fond of loud martial music. Being a Czech, I was not too averse to brass bands in moderation: the old k.u.k. Armee's military music was of the very highest quality, as well it might have been when its bands had numbers of orchestral players doing their military service, and bandmasters of the quality of Lehár and Millöcker and Fučik. But these Turkish players were quite execrable; so bad, in fact, that it was only seldom that one could so much as make out which piece of music it was that they were butchering. I got in to some trouble early on for failing to stand at the salute for our own imperial hymn, the "Gott Erhalte," simply because I failed to recognise it. The only Austrian march that they could get even approximately right, I remember, was "Prinz Eugen der Edle Ritter," ironically enough, because this piece commemorated the Austrian Army's great victory over the Turks at Belgrade in 1717. Perhaps it gave them less trouble than the rest of their repertoire because it contained a passage in the style of a janizary march—a vogue later imitated by Mozart, among others. I could only listen to the hideous blaring beneath my window and conclude that the standard of Turkish military musicianship had gone badly downhill since those days.

It was some consolation at least that we were tolerably billeted at Taif, because in all other respects it was a repeat of Massawa, except that we were now resident, not in a colonial possession of a western European power, but in a particularly backward and remote province of the Ottoman Empire, a political entity which over the centuries had erected procrastination and delay and evasiveness—not to speak of sheer downright indolence—into principles of state. The Turkish military and civil authorities were polite enough—as well they might be, now that we were fighting on the same side—but trying to conduct any business with them, I soon found, was like trying to wade through the contents of a feather mattress emptied into a vat of treacle. My life in Taif soon resolved itself into a weary, frustrating, treadmill round of visits to Turkish officials to try and make arrangements for our journey to the head of the Ma'an–Medina railway. We sat over endless tiny cups of syrupy coffee as they puffed hookahs and recited to me a litany of mournful, cow-eyed excuses: that really they wished to do everything in their power to facilitate the onward journey of the Austrian effendi and his companions, but I must understand, these things could not be arranged overnight. The country was unsettled and it would be necessary to have us escorted by a company of gendarmes, and there was the matter of permits to be arranged with the Sherif of Mecca before we, infidel Nasranis, could enter even the outskirts of Islam's second-holiest city. I divined before long, however, that there were perhaps other reasons for our being detained in Taif.

The two centres of power in the town were the residence of the Turkish Governor and Military Commander, Ghalib Pasha; and the Sherif of Mecca's summer palace, a modern, Western-style building of outstanding vulgarity on one side of the town's main square. The Sherif was not in residence when we arrived: he had moved to his winter palace in Mecca for the start of the hadj the previous month and would not return to Taif until March or thereabouts, when the weather in that lower-lying city would begin to warm up and the plague season would begin. We were received instead by his son the Emir Abdullah, a genial round-faced man who quizzed us extensively in French about our adventures since we left Tsingtao. He learnt that I had been an airman, and spent several hours questioning me about aeronautics over glasses of mint tea. In general I must say that for someone from such a remote part of the world his grasp of modern technology was remarkably good. I had to explain the principles of wireless telegraphy and the submarine to him as well as those of aerodynamics, and I found him quick and apt to understand. He enquired after the health of our venerable Sultan Fransi Yussuf, and asked me to explain to him the current political state of the Austro-Hungarian Empire, or "El-Nemsa" as it was called in these parts. I tried, but saw his eyes glaze over in bewilderment after about five minutes. The audience ended, and we were commended to the care of the Turkish Governor.

Ghalib Pasha spoke no language other than Turkish, we were told, so our audience was with his ADC, Nabil Bey, a slim, elegant young man, in his late twenties, of Lebanese-Greek descent. He spoke with me in that delicate Levantine French which seemed to be so much in favour among Turkish Army officers of the more epicene variety. Once more I was obliged to sit over coffee and recount our adventures. The Bey was much impressed, nodding and interjecting comments like *"Mais formidable!"* and *"Quelle horreur!"* at suitable points in the narrative. At last, judging the time to be right, I managed to edge in a polite enquiry as to when we might be allowed to proceed to Medina to catch the train for Damascus and Constantinople. He regretted, he said, but it would no longer be possible for us to go to Medina. Why ever not, I asked? Because trains were no longer running that far, he said, but terminating at Al-Ula, over two hundred kilometres to the north-west.

Nabil Bey explained to me that even though the Hejaz railway had been completed in 1909, it was intensely unpopular with the local population along its course down from the junction at Ma'an. The towns and villages along its route had derived most of their scant annual income from the great hadj caravan which would pass that way each year from Damascus to Mecca and back; and now the railway had taken it away to leave them destitute. Likewise the local Bedouin tribes had been accustomed for centuries past to extort protection money from the Pasha of Damascus for allowing the pilgrims to pass with their throats intact, and now that source of hard cash had gone as well. Town Arab and Bedouin had submerged their immemorial hatred of one another in a common detestation of the railway. And in addition, the fanatical Wahabi sect had objected violently to this access of Frankish infidel technology to Islam's second-holiest city. The result of this *derrière-garde* alliance was that scarcely a day passed now without a raid of some kind on the blasphemous iron road, to a point where only the occasional armoured train could now attempt the passage to Medina.

*"Enfin, mon cher Lieutenant,"* the Bey concluded, raising one finely pencilled eyebrow, "surely you cannot wish to take your leave of us so soon? Is not everything to your liking here in Taif? Have you not been treated with all the hospitality at our disposal in this poor and out-of-the-way part of Arabia?"

"Not in the least, I assure you: we have been treated since our arrival with every courtesy, and we are truly grateful to the Governor for having taken such care of us. However, we are anxious to return to our homeland to continue to fight for our country. You are a soldier yourself and must surely understand this."

"Yes, yes, my dear Lieutenant: I understand perfectly your very honourable desire to make your way back to your Fatherland to fight for your Emperor. But Turkey is also at war, and Austria and Germany are our allies. Why not stay here with us in Arabia and continue to fight against the enemies of the Ottoman Sultan? You are a formidable soldier by all accounts. And quite apart from your remarkable bravery I understand that you have a number of special skills which might be of great application here."

"His Excellency the Governor knows that I am an officer of the Emperor Franz Joseph, and that if my sovereign commands me to do so I shall stay here and fight alongside the Turkish Army to my very last breath. However, until I receive such an instruction my clear duty is to return as soon as I can to the war in Europe. But to what skills can you possibly refer, honoured Bey? I am a naval officer and we are far from the sea."

"Yes, certainly. But you are also a qualified pilot, and your servant Kaindel is a man skilled in the mechanical arts. He has already repaired the meat mincer in the Governor's kitchens, I believe, in consequence of which the townsfolk look upon him with awe as a Frankish magician."

"But my dear Bey, there is not a single aeroplane in the whole of Arabia. How then can I be of service as a pilot?"

"Aha, Lieutenant, but we now have an aeroplane: it will be brought here tomorrow. We would like you to put it into working order for us, then fly it for us against our common enemies."

I had to agree, of course; the courtesy incumbent upon a guest demanded as much. But I did so with a sinking heart, realising dimly that my work on this mysterious flying machine might keep us stuck here for months longer. I talked with Herr Poltenbach as we made our way back to my lodgings after the audience. A chill wind was blowing off the desert, scurrying thin snow along with it as we walked through the narrow streets.

"Tell me, Herr Poltenbach, why is the Governor so anxious to retain my services and get this wretched aeroplane of his flying? Surely I can't be that important to the local war-effort? From what little I can see of it, the only fighting the Turks are doing around here at present is against robbers, while as for flying, surely the Turkish Army has its own pilots and mechanics?"

"Yes, but there's more to this than meets the eye I'm afraid. I've lived here two years now and, believe me, there's a lot going on beneath the surface."

"What do you mean?"

"The Sherif for one thing, old Hussein. They say he's been in contact with the British in Egypt for some time past, asking what support he would get from them if he rose against the Turks. The Governor can't prove anything of course, and anyway he daren't throw the Sherif of Mecca and a descendant of Mohammed into jail unless he wants the whole country to rise against him. No, for the time being Hussein and his sons are loyal vassals of the Sultan. But not for much longer, I suspect. They want to keep you here because they think you might be persuaded on to their side if it came to fighting."

"But surely, can't they see that I'm an Austrian officer and will only fight as my government commands me?"

"Not really: their minds don't work that way. The whole Turkish Army in Arabia's riddled with treason. Half the officers and most of the men would go over to Hussein at the drop of a rag. Why not? Most of them are Arabs anyway—like our friend Nabil Bey. They've learnt that you're a Czech by birth, not a German, so they reason that you must be ready to change sides as well."

"But surely, you can't mean that the Governor's ADC is mixed up in all this as well?"

"I do: the man's a Syrian and very intelligent. I suspect he's in contact with the Emir Abdullah already. That's why he's keen to keep you here. The aeroplane is his idea, not the Governor's. Whoever possessed a flying machine here would have a tremendous advantage if it came to an uprising—in prestige as much as anything else. If you ask me, the Bey's watching to see which side to take."

"So what is this aeroplane of theirs that we're supposed to make airworthy? A German Albatros I suppose?"

"No, nothing of the sort I'm afraid. I gather that it's a captured French machine. They're bringing it up from the coast by camel. It should be here tomorrow. They've conscripted me to work on it as well."

The aeroplane arrived next morning as promised—in pieces. So far as I could make out it was a French Nieuport Bébé seaplane. Or rather, had once been, because by the time it reached Taif it was little better than the remains of an aeroplane: more or less complete, but reduced pretty well to its constituent parts by crash damage and inexpert dismantling for carriage. It appeared that the machine had been brought down by engine failure near Quishran Island a couple of weeks before, during a reconnaissance flight from a French cruiser. The pilot had been rescued by one of the warship's boats, but had failed to set fire to the machine before being taken off the beach. The aeroplane had nosed over on landing—hardly surprising in view of the fact that the pilot had tried putting it down in water a few centimetres deep. The propeller had been smashed to matchwood, the wing structure had been pulled apart by the sudden stop and the Clerget rotary engine had been wrenched from its bearers. All in all it was a pretty disheartening experience to inspect the remains, and to realise that our departure from Taif—if indeed we ever managed to leave the place—would depend on putting this ruin back together, giving it a landplane undercarriage and making it airworthy to the satisfaction of our hosts. I sensed that, quite apart from anything else, the prestige of the Austro-German alliance in these parts depended on our technical competence. Word of Kaindel's mechanical skills had already got around the town, while as for myself, once the townsfolk learnt that I was a flying-man they almost reverenced me in the streets as a wizard and a prophet after the manner of Elijah—"the Nasrany magician Bir-Hazaka," as I was called. Rumours were already spreading through the souks of Taif that I was not only able to ascend into the air at will but also to conjure up whirl-winds from the desert and afflict my enemies with haemorrhoids.

So we set to work, using Heir Poltenbach's workshop and technical advice, plus a half-dozen Syrian carpenters and a vehicle mechanic loaned by the Turkish garrison. If nothing else, it gave us something to do for those two weeks. I have always enjoyed working with my hands, and it was good to have some legitimate excuse now for doing so without losing officer's caste, as I would have done in Austria. But it was a hopeless task. We reassembled the airframe as best we could, lashing it together with wire and string where the joints had been racked by the crash and using local resin for glue. The undercarriage was fabricated from bamboo and the wheels of a bicycle once owned by the Sherif's vizier. The propeller was a problem though. In the end I had to laminate it from strips of teak, which I am sure was far too heavy, then have it carved to what I thought would be the right diameter and shape for an 80hp engine—a hit-or-miss process, since even in those days propeller-balancing was a skilled and very exact business.

Likewise the engine was in less than perfect condition when we took charge of it: complete, but clogged with sand and with the crankshaft knocked badly out of true by the crash. We did what we could with it, and managed to get it running in the end. At least lubricant was no problem: the Turkish garrison's medical officer was approached—a dirty one-eyed Albanian rogue to whom I would not have entrusted a sick cow, let alone a human being—and he cheerfully sold us his entire stock of castor oil. This had in fact been the only item left in his dispensary, since he had already sold all the other medicines to the townspeople—except for the surgical spirit, which he had drunk himself. Covering-fabric was an insuperable problem however. The little Nieuport's original covering of doped linen was too badly torn for much of it to be salvagable, so we had to re-cover the wings in bazaar calico, which was certainly too heavy for its strength. This had to be proofed somehow, and the best that we could manage here in the absence of cellulose dope was a sort of French polish made from resin dissolved in methylated spirits. Altogether it was not a very workman-like job of reconstruction, however much Nabil Bey and the Emir Abdullah might express their wonder as the aeroplane took shape.

December 28 was set as the day for the first flight trial of the "steam falcon," as the townsfolk had christened the little aeroplane. A flat stretch of desert outside the town walls had been selected as our flying strip, and the rebuilt Nieuport was duly wheeled out through the gates along a road lined with Turkish soldiers, before an admiring crowd. I would have dearly wished the trials to have been held away from the public eye, but this wish was not to be granted that morning as the townspeople—who had never seen an aeroplane before—lined the walls and crowded every rooftop and even the minarets of the mosques to get a view of the wonders that would be wrought by the infidel wizards. A dais had been set up, and the Emir Abdullah sat there with the dignitaries of the Turkish garrison to watch the show. My heart collapsed into the region of my kidneys as I saw the Governor's band forming up. There followed a brief musical recital: the "Gott Erhalte," by now improved to a point where it was at least possible to recognise what it ought to have been, then "Prinz Eugen" once more, then something (I think) from *The Pirates of Penzance,* finally (just as we were about to start the engine) "Ein Feste Burg Unser Gott ist Noch." Wishing that the latter item didn't sound quite so much like the "Dead March," I signalled to Kaindel to swing the propeller. It took three or four goes to get the engine firing, belching smoke from the poor-quality petrol. A cheer went up from the assembled multitude, who had never seen such a show in their lives. I pushed forward the throttle. The airframe started to shudder violently from a combination of misaligned engine and mis-shapen propeller. Kaindel was lying across on the wing beside me as the barely recognisable strains of the "Radetzky March" filtered through the din and the cheering and the pounding of hoofs and the shots fired into the air by the Sherif's horsemen.

"All right, Herr Leutnant? Shall I tell them to start?"

"For God's sake Kaindel, the thing's going to shake itself to pieces!"

"Best try taxiing a little—I think our Arab friends might get nasty if we don't provide some sort of show."

I looked across at the crowd and saw what he meant: the prestige of the entire Austro-German alliance was at stake.

"All right then, let's go. You'll find my last letter in my lodgings." I pushed the throttle forward for full power. The shuddering increased to a frenzied convulsion as the aeroplane began to bump across the stony plain. If I could just get airborne a couple of metres then touch down again—surely that would suffice . . .

I was told afterwards that the Nieuport did leave the ground briefly—before crashing back again in a cloud of dust to collapse in an ignominious heap on the plain. All that I remember is being dragged from the wreckage by Kaindel and a couple of Turkish soldiers as the wretched thing started to burn. In the end it was only the intervention of troops from the garrison that saved us both from being torn to pieces by the crowd as impostors.

However, as your own proverb says, every cloud has a silver lining, and in the event our public exposure as charlatans meant that the necessary permissions to travel ahead to Al-Ula were suddenly and miraculously forthcoming, now that both the Emir Abdullah and the Governor were keen to avoid the loss of prestige rubbing off on them. We set off at dawn on the morning of the last day of 1914, riding out through a side-gate of Taif as unobtrusively as we could on camelback, in the midst of the escort of thirty or so Turkish gendarmes thought necessary to protect us against the insurgents, bandits, religious zealots and plain honest-to-goodness murderers who infested this part of Arabia.

Our journey to the railhead at Al-Ula was about seven hundred kilometres, I suppose; it merely seemed far longer. The first couple of days were not too bad, apart from the cutting winter wind of the mountains. But once we had descended the caravan trackway to the lowlands east of Mecca, each successive march became a further instalment in purgatory. Indeed, if the damned were offered a day-excursion to the Harrat Kishib I think that most would take one look at it and decide that perhaps things were not so bad where they were. Even in the middle of an Arabian winter the midday heat and glare was intense, made all the worse from being reflected upwards from the sand, which seemed in fact to be a coarse mica of some kind. Before long the caravan track which was supposed to run towards Medina—the old Hadj Road—had all but disappeared, so that throughout the day, when there were no stars to navigate by, I suffered a constant nagging apprehension that either through treachery or incompetence our escort (who were mostly town Arabs) would lose us to die of thirst and heatstroke in the wilderness. Certainly there was no lack of reminders along the way that this might be our fate. Every few kilometres a sad scatter of bones—usually of animals but sometimes also of men—bore silent witness to a caravan that had come to grief.

I had certainly never realised before that the simple word "desert" could encompass so many gradations of aridity, so many types of ground or so many types of weather blowing along above it: sometimes a sort of thin steppe-grassland; sometimes a barren expanse of stones or pavements of bare rock; sometimes convoluted fields of black basalt, like petrified chocolate icing; sometimes the sound-muffling sand dunes of some never-ending seashore. Wherever we were though, wind-blown sand gritted in our teeth and clogged our mouths and nostrils and seeped into our clothing. And always that wind: hot and desiccating on the lowlands, bitter cold and mixed with thin rain or even a little gritty snow when we climbed up on to the mountain plateau once more north of Medina. Nor was camel-riding a sinecure. The three of us were all seafarers of long standing, but even so the queasy swaying lurch of the beasts made us feel permanently half-seasick, a nausea not eased in any degree by the smell of the creatures themselves, each with its constant and attentive entourage of blow-flies which clustered about the animal's revolting bodily orifices, then grew bored and flew to swarm over us and our food. What with them, and the sand, and the constant skin-cracking glare of the sun, and the impossibility of washing, we soon all of us had a fine collection of boils and sores.

Each day was the same: awake an hour before dawn, when the cold and the sharp stones made it impossible to sleep any longer, then up to stretch one's aching limbs, then breakfast of a half-cup of brackish water and some gritty dates, then riding until nightfall with only a short pause at midday, a supper of boiled barley or rice and a little clarified butter, then an attempt to sleep until the brief glory of the desert dawn broke once more over our weary little party, preparing for the hardships of yet another day.

We had to give Medina a wide berth to eastward, having fallen in with a messenger about 10 January who told us that the city was in a state of near-insurrection. If we attempted to enter it, he warned us, neither Christian nor Turk would be likely to get out again alive. Three German merchant seamen had tried it the previous week, he said, attempting the same journey as ourselves after escaping from a HAPAG ship taken as a prize into Aden. Their naked, mutilated corpses had been found dumped outside the walls one morning. Several times as we rode on our journey we met groups of armed riders who would accompany us for a few hours just out of rifle-shot, evidently weighing up whether our party was weak enough to be attacked and plundered. But despite all our hardships and dangers I reckoned that we were making a steady forty to fifty kilometres per day towards Al-Ula and the railway.

That is, until 17 January, by my calculation less than eighty kilometres south of the railhead. It was mid-morning, and we were traversing an area of low dunes in a shallow basin of sandstone hills. We were between the Wadi Jizl to westward and the track of the Hejaz railway a few kilometres away over the hills to the east. We could simply have ridden alongside the railway line, but our guides discouraged this, saying that, with such frequent Bedouin raids on the railway, to follow it would be to invite attack. Suddenly there was a great disturbance and shouting among our escort, then a crackle of rifle-shots in the dry, clear air. We dismounted and lay down in a shallow scrape in the top of a dune, leaving the escorts to take our camels after we had unslung our saddlebags and rifles. The first wave of attackers appeared as if out of the ground, mounted on camel- and horseback and firing from the saddle as they milled around, about four hundred metres away. There must have been about a hundred of them. Shots whined around us and one of our party fell near by. I took his Mauser rifle and bandolier and handed my pistol to Wong, who could fire it with one hand if necessary. Then I began to return the fire as well as I could, given that our attackers were elusive as flies. I had just sufficiently recovered from my initial surprise to wonder what on earth all this could be about when there was a yell from Kaindel. I looked around. Our escorts had not dismounted: instead they were galloping away in disorder, taking our beasts with them! I shouted to them to come back, but within a minute they were a cloud of dust disappearing back down the trackway towards Medina. We were now alone in the Arabian desert, surrounded by enemies: three men with five arms between them; with two rifles and a pistol plus about sixty rounds of ammunition; with their saddlebags and a skin of water; and with a dead Turkish gendarme for company. We used a mess-tin to scoop out a hollow in the dune-crest, and filled our saddle-bags with sand to build a scanty breastwork. Then we settled down beneath the blazing sun to resist our attackers.

Fortunately for us the Bedouin were poor shots, and would anyway persist in firing from the saddle as they circled us. To this day I cannot explain why they did not simply charge and do away with us. Perhaps they thought there were more of us than there really were. At any rate, by nightfall casualties were nil on our side against one man on their side, knocked from his saddle by a shot from Kaindel, and one man wounded by me. We could not hold out much longer though. The afternoon sun had broiled us like fish on a griddle as we lay in our wretched little scraped-out dust-hole, and now the winter night was setting in to chill our bones and freeze the water in our goatskin. Yet we ground our teeth, and endured not only the night but another ghastly day of the sun, until our water was gone and we were near delirious from sunstroke. Yet still they circled us, sometimes drawing nearer, sometimes retreating when we fired at them, wearing us down for the kill and the plundering that was presumably the point of the exercise.

Night fell once more. We finished the last of our water, and chewed some dates while we could still get them down, then settled down to endure what would probably be our last night on earth. By the small hours it was so cold that a sudden insanity fell upon us. Why lie here alternatively freezing and frying until thirst and exhaustion finished us off? Let us at least go out and seek death. We shook hands and said farewell to one another. Then we took up our weapons, loaded only with a clip apiece, and stumbled forward down the dune slope, shouting—or rather croaking—as we went and determined to face the worst death that a tyrant could devise a thousand times over rather than spend another hour huddling like partridges in our shallow scrape in the sand. We must have gone a good half-kilometre and fired several shots in challenge before the truth dawned upon us: that our attackers had gone. We found horse- and camel-dung still warm on the ground. Then Wong stumbled over something. It was a dead man, the one shot by Kaindel the previous day. He was already swollen and turning black from the sun. His teeth grinned up at us in silent greeting beneath the moonlight. Where had the rest gone though, and why? Perhaps they thought that a relief force was nearing; perhaps they had just grown tired of it all and given up, in that half-hearted, inconsequential fashion so typical of warfare as practised in these parts.

Anyway, wherever they had disappeared to and whatever the reasons, we were now left with the question of what to do next in the few hours which separated us from death by thirst. Should we wait for rescue where our escorts had left us or should we press on? The last well, at a fort on the old Hadj Road, was a good half-day behind us even on camelback. We were all disinclined to go back to the dust-hole which we had occupied these past two days. So we determined to press forward for as long as our strength lasted, striking towards the railway. At least we had four or five hours before the sun came up. We trudged on across the plain, then climbed over the low hills in the darkness. But it was heavy going in the loose sand, then on the jagged rock. Just after dawn, we were sitting exhausted and dispirited before a last swell of the hills. We had not found the railway line as I had expected. The burden of leadership was beginning to crush me. I felt that I could keep their spirits up no longer.

"Kaindel, Wong," I asked, "tell me truthfully, is it worth it? Do you want to try further or shall we just give up? I can't go much further myself."

"Nor me," Kaindel wheezed like a pair of old leather bellows. "I'm done for, quite done for." He licked his cracked lips, then lifted his head and parted them in a desiccated, mirthless grin like that of an Egyptian mummy in a museum. "Heh! Funny that—never knew you got mirages in the ears as well."

"What do you mean?"

"Hark, can you hear it as well, Herr Kommandant, or am I really going off my head?"

We listened intently. Then I heard it, faint and plaintive in the distance. For a moment I wondered as well. But surely, thirst hallucinations were not collective . . . It was the far, clear note of a military bugle. In fact I could even make out the call: something like the German version of Reveille.

"Come on, I think it came from that way." With infinite labour we forced our aching limbs to climb over the low ridge. And there it lay before us, about five kilometres off across the plain, but seeming much nearer in the clear, cold morning air. It was a small stone-built fort with a tower at each corner. Tongues hanging out, wild-eyed, willing it not to dissolve into the air, we staggered towards it. It remained fixed to the ground however, and grew more rather than less solid-looking as we approached. I could make out the flag now that was being hoisted on a pole above one of the turrets. It was red, with a crescent moon and star in the centre. We were saved.

# 18

# GUESTS OF THE SULTAN

I SHUFFLED MY FEET IN THE STRAW OF THE DUNGEON. How long had we been here now? Eight days? Nine? It scarcely seemed to matter any longer; and anyway, our only means of measuring the passage of time was the brightening and fading of the dim light at the bottom of the stone air-shaft which led down to our prison. Kaindel scratched as Wong stirred in his sleep and moaned softly, clanking his chains. The Turks had been very rough with him when they brought us down here, evidently regarding it as a severe breach of military discipline for a man to have only one wrist instead of two for fetters to be locked on to. After a great deal of shouting and hitting one another they had solved this problem by attaching two manacles to the same wrist. I had protested and threatened to have them all before the Pasha of Damascus for treating their allies like this, but the garrison Commander, Targan Bey, had been quite adamant: we were British spies and there was an end to it. I was their leader and I spoke English, so that settled the matter, and would we now be so good as to admit as much and allow him to get on with having us executed? I demanded that they should telegraph Al-Ula to verify my story, that we were Austrian sailors lost in the desert. Targan Bey had merely laughed, and said that even if they had the telegraph here he would not waste the Ottoman government's electricity on filth such as us.

I had protested further—then wished that I had not, for the previous day we had all been taken out in front of the assembled garrison and the bastinado had been applied to poor Kaindel until he howled for mercy. I was clearly an officer-spy, and therefore (in Turkish eyes) immune to torture; but that did not apply to my ranker manservants. Wong was to be next, and Targan Bey had hinted darkly that if this failed to extract confession, "other means" would be applied. I had heard just enough during my stay in Taif of the practices current in the Ottoman Army to imagine what these other means might be. I had held a brief consultation with Kaindel and Wong there on the parade ground. Kaindel, lying bound hand and foot in the dust, was for holding out longer if he could, but we concluded in the end that it all seemed pointless. We had been prisoners for over a week now and no help had arrived, so it looked as if no one knew that we were here; that we had been given up as having perished in the desert.

"No, Herr Komandant," Kaindel had said in the end, writhing on the ground, "these Turkish bastards want us dead, so let them get on with it. Say whatever you like and let's get it over with."

I had turned to Targan Bey, standing by smoking a cheroot. "All right then, may the Devil take you, write us down as British spies or Zulu spies for all I care."

He smiled and thanked me. "So good of you to see sense at last, Herr Englisch. You are a clever one, but not clever enough for Targan Bey. You are hereby all sentenced to death for espionage, sentence to be carried out tomorrow morning at first light."

They would soon come for us, I knew. I lay there, aching in every joint, tormented by lice, my skin seemingly hanging on me like an old shirt, and my mind ran back over the previous half-year: the meeting with Pani Bożena on the island and the flight from her husband and his hired ruffians; the Black Hand and the fight at the farmhouse and the mad escape with the Gospodarijca Zaga across Montenegro; then Tsingtao, and the dying Japanese officer I had bayoneted; and the typhoon and the attack on the *Gorzkowski* and the outbreak of amok at Djibouti. And now this: lying in a Turkish dungeon awaiting execution a mere day or so's march from salvation. It all seemed so pointless, such an exquisitely bad joke, so ludicrous to be done to death by our own allies for no better reason than that a young, conceited and rather dim-witted Turkish officer, bored out of his mind in this desert outpost and tired of sodomising his men, had read a newspaper article about British secret agents and decided to fill in his time by executing a few of them.

Certainly I had found during our lengthy sessions of "questioning" over the previous week that it was a futile task trying to get any sense into the head of Targan Bey. He spoke German after a fashion. But he spoke it so ill that I was never at all sure that what I had said had registered with him or been properly understood, however slow-ly and dis-tinct-ly I spoke. He would just smile that infuriating complacent smirk of his, puff at his cheroot and come back again like a compass needle to the same question: "Yes, but if you are not English spy, how come you speak English to my sentry at the gate, eh?" And I would roll up my eyes, count up to ten and try to restrain the urge to plant my fist squarely in his face, then repeat for the hundredth time:

"I spoke to him in English, Targan Bey, because I speak almost no Turkish and because he did not understand German. I thought that he might know English, so I tried that first." He would struggle with this idea for a while, like a dog trying to grasp a football in its jaw, then produce the unvarying reply:

"Ah yes, but if you are not English spy, why do you speak English?"

And I would wearily trundle out the same reply: "I speak English, Bey; but I am an Austrian, not English. You speak German, but that does not make you a German spy, I hope."

"Germany is Turkey's ally, but England is our enemy. I do not speak English because I am not English spy."

And once again, I would see that we were getting nowhere. Not even corruption or slovenliness would save us now; Targan and his men were no disaffected local Arab levies like the garrison at Taif but pure Anatolian Turkish soldiery: head of bone and heart of stone.

I had been suffering from a mild fever which made me more dispirited than ever. They had all trooped through my aching head that night, the Heir-Apparent and the Kaiser and all. I had danced with the Duchess of Hohenberg, until she changed into Major Draganić and Pani Bożena came in to cut his head off. I woke and dozed fitfully, too exhausted to care much now. No, let them kill me. I was a sea-officer of the House of Austria and I had at least the bleak satisfaction of having done my duty to the end. I remembered Draganić's words about his deluded young patriots:

"They have volunteered to give their lives for the Fatherland, so what does it matter whether it's on a battlefield or on the gallows?" I suppose that he was right in a way: I had faced death a dozen times in recent months—by shot, by fire, by man-eating sharks and by stress of weather. Whether I gave my life on the deck of a sinking ship or in the courtyard of a Turkish fort in the Arabian desert, I would be just as dead at the end of it.

It must be getting light now. I wondered what the end would be. Firing squad perhaps? That was the approved way for an officer to die when caught spying; but then again, from what I had seen of Turkish marksmanship in recent weeks I had grounds for suspecting that death by powder and shot at their hands might be a prolonged and untidy business. Soon I heard the tapping of a carpenter's hammer in the courtyard. A gallows? What the devil did it matter anyway? Let them strangle us all with a bowstring if they wanted, so long as they got it over with quickly. A key rattled in the massive lock and the door swung slowly open. The jailers came in and unlocked our manacles, kicking Wong and Kaindel to their feet. Then we were marched up the stone stairs amid a squad of armed soldiers, and led blinking into the early-morning light. Kaindel could barely walk after the previous day's bastinado and had to be supported between Wong and me. Targan Bey was waiting for us, smirking with self-satisfaction. In the middle of the square stood a rickety-looking frame which might have been constructed by children as a makeshift swing. Three halters dangled from the crossbeam and three stools stood beneath them. So it would be slow strangulation. There was not enough drop to break our necks.

But there was something else for us to do before sentence was carried out. We were led past the gallows to the far side of the square and handed a spade each. In the end I had to do most of the work of scooping out the three shallow graves from the sandy earth. Then we were taken back to the foot of the gallows, where Targan Bey read out some lengthy document in Turkish—despite the circumstances, a melodious and pleasant-sounding tongue, I considered, rather like Magyar. He finished, then turned to us.

"Good morning Mister Englisch, how are you this morning?"

"Well enough, thank you," I growled in German.

"Very good. Shall we start then?"

"Please feel free."

"Thank you." He said something to a sergeant and lengths of cord were produced to tie our wrists—or in Wong's case, wrist—behind our backs. "Very good. Have you any last request?"

"Yes," I said. "If it's all the same by you I would like to die last, so that my men don't have to watch."

He laughed. "So, the English spy's courage fails him at last. No, shame upon you: you are their leader, so you must die first. But do you have any other request?"

"In that case, a cigarette if you please." A cigarette was placed in my lips and lit. It was uncommonly good tobacco, I remember, the first I had smoked in weeks. It seemed at any rate to steady me a little. I finished it, its length smouldering away with my life.

"Proceed then!"

I was hoisted up on to the stool and the noose was adjusted about my neck by the hangman on his ladder. Targan Bey had drawn his sabre, and a camera on a tripod had been brought up. No doubt when we were dangling lifeless by our crooked necks he would pose beneath us, that complacent grin on his face, and have the scene recorded for posterity, as evidence for a promotion board of just how zealous he had been in hunting down foreign agents. He raised the sabre—and a smile suddenly crossed my face as I remembered how my father, when I was twelve and had first announced my intention of becoming a naval officer, had sworn at first that he would rather see me hang. Most probably the old boy would never learn that I had achieved both honours.

I had sometimes wondered whether hanging was a painful end. Suffice it to say anyway that the few seconds after the stool was jerked away turned me into a lifelong opponent of capital punishment. First came the agonising wrench as my neck took the weight, then the desperate, bursting red fog and the roaring of a thousand cataracts as the noose squeezed the arteries shut. I willed myself to die, to lose consciousness—anything to end this pain—yet I was still hideously aware of the world revolving before me. Then suddenly I was staring up into the blue sky, gulping and gasping for breath, too dazed to comprehend at first that the noose had come undone. Choking and trembling in every limb, I was hauled roughly to my feet and dragged aside while the Bey pummelled the hangman, who was trying to retie the knot. At last all was ready once more. I was lifted back up on to the stool and the noose was repositioned with a great deal of fumbling and shouting. For God's sake get on with it, I thought to myself. At length the sabre was raised—and flashed in the sunlight as it fell. There was another brutal wrench at my neck. But this time I was not to manage even the three or four swings I had achieved at the first attempt, for I was immediately sprawling on the ground with the ruins of the gallows on top of me. Again I was dragged to my feet as the cross-beam was lifted off me.

By now though a curious thing had happened: fear and resignation had given way to a murderous rage against these helpless dolts and their blundering, feckless incompetence. Targan Bey came up to me; ruffled now and out of breath after kicking and beating the hapless executioner several times around the square with the flat of his sabre. He was clearly much embarrassed.

"A thousand times a thousand apologies for this . . . I am so sorry, but this fool here . . ."

"Spare me your apologies," I croaked, half throttled and neck scraped raw by the rope. "You are a miserable cretin, Targan Bey, and your men are nearly as great jackasses as yourself. In all my years as a sea-officer I have never come across such a wretched, slipshod, un-seaman-like display of ineptitude as I have seen here this past fifteen minutes. For God's sake, if you are going to hang innocent men then at least make a job of it!"

"I am most sorry—we in the Ottoman Army do not . . ."

"Evidently you don't. Here, untie my hands you buffoon and bring me a pencil and paper. I'll show you how to do it properly if you can't work it out for yourself. That gallows of yours wouldn't serve to hang a tom-cat, let alone three grown men."

A notepad and paper were brought, and while Targan Bey looked over my shoulder and made admiring noises I sketched out a sort of sheerleg arrangement which would produce a structurally sound, three-man gibbet from the available timber. Then while they set to work constructing it I demanded to see the halters. It was miserable cordage, barely clothes-line standard. I sent the sergeant off in search of something more substantial. Coffee was served, and in the mean time I set to work on the three field-gun drag ropes that had been procured by the sergeant. Within ten minutes I had produced three hangman's nooses of such neatness that not even the grim old petty officer who taught us bends, hitches and splices at the k.u.k. Marine Akademie could have found fault with them. They were passed from hand to hand for a while so that Targan and his soldiers could wonder at them and congratulate me on my skill. Then they were attached to the crossbeam and the proceedings resumed.

It was to be my turn first once more. I stood on the stool, quite composed now, and watched as the sabre was raised. It would be over in a minute or so, I thought: losing consciousness even if I continued to kick and struggle a while longer. I only wished that the minute would not hurt quite so much . . . The Bey's sabre was raised in the air—and remained poised there. An NCO had marched up and saluted to report something to Targan. There was a brief conference, during which I became aware of a distant buzzing noise. When it appeared at last from over the hills the aeroplane came in quite low over the fort. As it roared overhead I could see that it was a German-built Albatros biplane with Turkish markings— black squares—beneath its wings. Something fell from it as it passed over the parade ground. Men ran forward to pick up the aluminium canister and take it to the Bey. He looked at me suspiciously, then stuck his sabre into the ground as he unscrewed the lid and took out a sheet of paper. He frowned at this for some time, puzzled, then showed it to his NCO. There was a whispered confabulation for five minutes or so. Standing on my stool with the noose around my neck and the cords cutting painfully into my wrists, I soon grew tired of it. The initial wild hope caused by the aeroplane's appearance had soon given way to a more realistic assessment: that since this fort was away from the railway and the telegraph, in hostile country, the Turks were probably in the habit of using aircraft to drop quite routine orders to their outlying garrisons. At length I grew impatient:

"Targan Bey, if you could spare me a moment . . ."

He looked up. "Yes Englisch, what do you want?"

"If it's not too much trouble, I believe that you brought us out here to hang us. Would it now be possible to get on with it and confer with your adjutant later? My legs are going numb up here."

"All right—a moment if you please, just one little moment . . ." He turned back to his mysterious message, scratching his head in bewilderment. I suppose that I might have stood there another ten minutes before a bugle sounded suddenly from the gatehouse. Almost before Targan Bey had realised what was happening the soldiers paraded in hollow square had broken ranks to rush to their posts on the battlements. Was it an attack? No: others were running to unbar the gates. They swung open to admit a cloud of dust and a column of fifty or so cavalry with lances. They were led by a fat man with white moustaches, wearing a sheepskin version of the Turkish fez, and by a thin European in dusty field grey, with a sun helmet and a monocle. They dismounted and walked over to us as Targan Bey stood like a statue at the salute, face white with terror. The fat man spoke to him in Turkish, growing red in the face—then landed him a blow on the side of the head which knocked him sprawling in the dust, before proceeding to administer a kicking of such ferocity that the Bey's previous maltreatment of the unfortunate hangman seemed mild horseplay by comparison. When he had finally exhausted his rage he walked over to address me, leaving the Bey whimpering and grovelling on the ground. He spoke in quite competent German.

"A million pardons, my dear sir. How can you possibly forgive us for this outrage? My humblest, most sincere and most heartfelt apologies. A dreadful mistake, perpetrated by this miserable idiot here. But allow me to introduce myself. I am Yilderim Pasha, Chief of Staff to the 4th Army Corps at Ma'an, and this is my German ADC, General-Oberst the Freiherr Gotz von Stulpitz." The Freiherr bowed stiffly in the Prussian manner. "We received word from Medina that your miserable dogs of gendarmes had abandoned you in the desert. Search parties were sent out—even an aeroplane—but it was not until yesterday that we got word by messenger that two so-called Austrians and a one-armed Chinese were to be hanged here today as English spies. Fortunately for you, this cretin here was so keen to show us his work that he wrote out the report of your execution and sent it to us in advance by courier. We travelled by train to Al-Ula, then rode all night to get here, sending the aeroplane ahead of us. But Allah the Merciful has granted that we should not be too late. If there is anything that you may care to request though, dear Herr Leutnant, to recompense you for your sufferings, you have only to ask for it."

I was taken down and untied, then invited to take breakfast with the general and his ADC. As we left the place of execution Yilderim Pasha gave orders in Turkish. Before I realised what was happening, the wretched, much dishevelled Targan Bey was dragged over, his hands were tied and he was lifted on to the stool which I had just vacated. As the noose was placed over his head I managed to shout to them to stop. Yilderman Pasha turned to me.

"Do you wish to see this cur strung up after breakfast then? Perhaps better so: it might spoil your digestion otherwise, and it will give the dog time to think about it . . ."

"No, no, honoured Pasha, please don't hang him . . ."

"No? Why ever not?"

"The man is a fool, not a criminal. He imagined that he was doing his duty. Please don't hang him."

The Pasha looked doubtful, and stroked his moustache thoughtfully. "Well, military discipline demands it. I really don't know . . ."

"Sir, you promised me anything I wished."

"Oh, very well then. Take him down. But, Herr Leutnant, you must permit us to give him the bastinado and break him to the ranks: that is the very least that the Turkish Army can accept if discipline is to be maintained." I was going to ask that this should be spared him as well. But then I thought, Why not? The bastinado was hideously painful, but from what I could see it did no permanent harm. Blessed are the merciful—but a little vindictiveness now and then adds spice to life. And anyway, I thought, having the soles of one's feet beaten instead of having one's neck stretched is a pretty good commutation of penance at any rate of exchange.

"Yes, Pasha," I replied, "by all means—and hard. I have found it remarkably difficult this past week to get any sense into the Bey's head by way of his ears, so perhaps you will have more success beating some in via his feet."

So we breakfasted as the unfortunate Bey's shrieks echoed around the barrack square, to Kaindel's evident satisfaction. Then we exchanged our tattered rags for new German uniforms brought down from Ma'an for us, and finally bade farewell to the accursed little fort. The ride took us until the evening of the next day. The sun was setting behind the mountains of the Hejaz in a baroque splendour of purple and gold as I heard it faintly in the distance: the most prosaic yet the most blessed sound that I ever heard in my life, I think. It was the whistle of a railway locomotive.

We were still in our new German uniforms as we stepped down on to the railway platform on the eastern shore of the Bosphorus opposite Constantinople, to be welcomed with brass bands and flowers and speeches and photographers and journalists as well as by the entire Austrian and German communities of the Turkish capital. It was the morning of 18 February 1915. I stepped smartly up to the k.u.k. Naval Attaché, saluted and reported us present and correct: one officer, one warrant officer and a naval reservist escaped from S.M.S. *Kaiserin Elisabeth* at Tsingtao, the entire surviving crew of the armed junk S.M.S. *Schwarzenberg*. We learnt that Tsingtao had surrendered to the Allies on 2 November and that the *Elisabeth*'s entire crew had been taken prisoner by the Japanese, apart from a small party who had managed to get to the United States with forged Swiss passports and who had just arrived back in Vienna via Portugal. Our own journey from Al-Ula had lasted ten days and had been relatively uneventful: nothing to report except a derailment near Aleppo and an ambush by brigands in central Anatolia.

The last leg of our adventure, from Constantinople to Vienna, took us three days. But when we arrived at the Staatsbahnhof on the evening of 21 February the whole thing was kept very quiet indeed. It appeared that the Netherlands government had learnt of our arrival at Constantinople and had expressed the wish to interview one Linienschiffsleutnant Prohaska in connection with certain serious violations of Dutch neutrality a few months earlier. The Austrian minister in The Hague had been summoned to the Foreign Ministry to offer an explanation and it was generally felt to be a good idea that the whole affair should be allowed to disappear quietly from public view. Holland was now Germany's only outlet to the world, and the Dutch government's displeasure was not to be risked lightly. For my part I was taken to the k.u.k. War Ministry, interviewed, commended unofficially and given a suitcase containing my belongings from S.M.S. *Tisza,* including the clothes which I had left folded on the shore that day when I began the swim which was to take me half-way around the world and back again. I was then given a month's convalescent leave, along with instructions to spend it quietly in my home town of Hirschendorf and to avoid giving newspaper interviews. Before I left I filed a request with the Marineoberkommando to be assigned to flying duties when I returned to Pola. Instead I became a submarine captain. But that is another story.

Only one incident stands out in my recollection from that train journey home. It was one morning as our train clanked across the dusty, frozen emptiness of the Anatolian Plateau on its way towards Constantinople. I was sitting in a first-class carriage whiling away the interminable journey by reading some old German newspapers provided for us at Adana. The train had stopped now, yet again: moved into a siding to let another troop-train pass carrying Turkish soldiers towards Palestine. I was reading a copy of the *Berliner Morgenpost* from late November. It carried an extensive report of the hunting-down and destruction of the German cruiser *Emden* off the west coast of Australia, and an American journalist's interview with her Captain, von Muller, "the Gentleman Pirate" as he had been dubbed, who had been taken prisoner by the British after the action. His proudest boast, he said, was that in three months in the Indian Ocean he had sunk a quarter of a million tonnes of Allied shipping without harming a single hair on the head of a single civilian. I looked up from the newspaper and glanced through the carriage window at the whistling, frost-bound landscape outside, and saw to my horror that a gang of several hundred skeletal, half-naked wretches—men, women and even small children—were working feebly at the embankment under the supervision of Turkish soldiers with whips. One boy, about fourteen I should think, dropped his pickaxe to wring his frostbitten fingers to me in supplication, pointing to his mouth. Quickly I snatched some bread rolls from my haversack and began to lower the window to throw them to him. But before I could do so a Turkish sentry had walked up, swung the butt of his rifle into the air and dashed the boy's brains out with no more concern than you or I would kill a fly, before returning to encourage the rest of the labourers with his boots. I sat down, sick at heart. I later learnt that these pitiful creatures were Armenians, rounded up by the Turks "for their own protection" during the great massacres at the end of 1914 and now being used up by the Ottoman government in various labour projects across the Turkish Empire. The train started to roll forward once more and we left them behind. Then Kaindel came into the compartment, looking grey and uncharacteristically silent. It was several days before he could bring himself to tell me how he had got off the train at that halt to stretch his legs a little—and had witnessed an Armenian woman giving birth in a miserable shelter of blankets in the lee of the embankment. As soon as the child was born and the cord cut, he said, its father had drowned it in a bucket of water, too kind to allow it to live. They were the new world we were heading into, those starving, typhus-ridden ghosts, advance guard of the faceless legions of victims of the Century of Progress and Rationality; precursors of the tens of millions of nameless innocents over the next half-century who would be enslaved and systematically worked to death: digging canals across the Arctic tundra or building railways through the jungles of Asia; victims of murderous weapons and the even more murderous ideologies that aimed them; of a collective fit of amok on a scale which would make that outbreak aboard the *Samboeran* at Djibouti look the uncivilised and pre-scientific affair that it was. Although we could not know it at the time, von Muller and the *Emden* and our own adventures over the past six months were the last twitchings of the Age of Chivalry.

I arrived in Hirschendorf to start my month's leave—and was greeted by the melancholy news that my brother Anton had been posted missing in Serbia the previous August, after the 26th Jäger Regiment had been all but wiped out in the fighting at Šabac. But there were other matters to be resolved during that month. The first person that I tried to contact was Richard Seifert, in the k.u.k. Danube Flotilla. S.M.S. *Tisza* was no more, I learnt. At the mobilisation she had been sent to join the monitor group at Brod on the Sava, and had claimed the dubious distinction of having fired the first shot of the war: at a Serbian border post near Klenak just after dawn on 29 July. But the subsequent course of the Serbian campaign had not been favourable for Austria. After a fortnight of savage fighting, disfigured by appalling atrocities on both sides, the Serbs had not only chased out General Potiorek's punitive army but had themselves crossed the Sava and invaded Hungary. The *Tisza* and several smaller vessels had been cut off in the loop of the river above Šabac and had eventually been blown up by their own crews to avoid capture. Seifert had transferred to another monitor, so it was not until mid-1915 that my letter reached him. His reply said that yes, there had been a most fearful row in Neugraditz the day I disappeared, and that Pani Bożena was reported to have left for Poland—fortunately with nothing worse than a black eye—while Grbić instituted proceedings for divorce on grounds of persistent adultery. In the event he might have saved himself the trouble. The war was only a few weeks away, and when it came the Hungarian authorities in the Banat set to work with a gruesome relish at squaring accounts with the local Serb population. A Honvéd regiment leaving Szeged for the Serbian front was ceremonially presented with a thousand metres of rope, and with instructions to bring none of it back. Nor did they: in fact they sent a telegram at the end of the first week asking for another thousand metres. Being a factory owner, Grbić was an obvious target, and when the Serbian armies fought their way across the Danube into southern Hungary in the last days of August 1914 they found his body dangling from an oak tree on the outskirts of Neugraditz, along with a few dozen other victims of summary court martial.

As for Seifert himself he did not survive the war either. They sent him with a k.u.k. naval force to the Ukraine in 1918 to try and restore order in that devastated land: not out of any concern for its inhabitants, I might add, but only to secure the railway lines and the rivers so that Ukrainian wheat could be got out of the country to feed the starving cities of Austria.

He was killed in a skirmish with partisans near Kherson in August 1918: a sad waste of a promising young life.

I have little idea of what became of Pani Bozena after that. People I have spoken with in the years since have said that they remember a Bozena Karpińska singing at the provincial opera-house in Lemberg—by then the Polish Lwów—in the early 1920s, but after that the trail goes cold. She was the same age as myself, so that would have made her fifty-three in 1939, the first year of Poland's dreadful ordeal. I hope that she was dead by then, for Lwów fell within the Soviet zone of occupation under the Hitler–Stalin Pact, and late middle age is not the best time of life for a woman to face a three-week journey to Siberia in a freezing cattle-truck, or to endure the horrors of an NKVD labour camp at the other end. But whatever became of her, her indestructible spirit goes marching on. It must have been 1968 or thereabouts, one Saturday morning in a jeweller's shop on Ealing Broadway as I collected my wristwatch from repair. I heard the doorbell, and glanced over my shoulder—only to feel the blood drain suddenly from my face. It was her, Pani Bozena, exactly as I had known her, except that she was wearing one of the miniskirts fashionable in those days (a style which I have to say did not show her muscular legs to best advantage) and a pair of sunglasses the size of ship's portholes tipped up on her glorious golden mane of hair. She had a distinctly sulky expression and was accompanied by a harassed-looking young Englishman a good half-head shorter than herself. It appeared that they were there to select an engagement ring—and that the very cheapest that she was prepared to accept was about four times what her fiancé was prepared to pay. As I left I overheard her: "Vwhat? Do you not zen love your little Irenka after all? I tink I am go to cr-y . . . y . . ." My last glimpse of them was of the young man reaching into his back pocket with an expression of martyrdom. As for myself, I had to go to the Kardomah Café and order a cup of coffee to steady myself. My hands were shaking so badly that the waitress asked whether I felt all right and would I like her to call an ambulance? But at least I could console myself with the thought that, despite wars and the rise and fall of empires, there are some things in this world that never change.

And the Gospodarijca Zaga? I have no idea what became of her after my last sight of her that morning off the coast of Montenegro, swimming for our skiff. The only clue came many years later in a book on French painters which my English wife Edith was reading, in 1963 or thereabouts. It was a brief note which remarked tantalisingly that

> One of Soutine's mistresses in Paris in 1924–25 was a curious figure, a self-styled Yugoslav Princess Saga: a woman of plain features but of strong character. She moved with him to Cap Ferrat, but was later abandoned by him and took to absinthe before dying of consumption at Antibes a few years later.

The trouble with our dreams, I think, is that they have a way of coming true.

As for my two companions on the journey, Stabstorpedomeister Kaindel and Steward First Class Ferdinand Wong, they were both discreetly rewarded for their bravery and fortitude. Kaindel was awarded the silver Bravery Medal for unspecified "gallantry on active service" and then retired from the Navy—only to be called up again in 1916 because of the acute shortage of senior NCOs and put in charge of a marine-supply depot at Pola. This position and the growing wartime misery throughout the Danubian Monarchy allowed him to accumulate a sizeable fortune through selling off government property, but he was not to be able to enjoy it. He died in October 1918, one of the myriad victims of the great Spanish Influenza epidemic which finally brought the war to an end. Meanwhile Steward Wong, as a civilian, faced the authorities with a difficult problem when it came to recognising his bravery and the loss of his arm in action. In the end he was received by the Emperor in a private audience at Schönbrunn and awarded a small pension from the Imperial household purse. This was offered either as an annuity or as a lump sum. Wong wisely chose the latter and used the money to set up a small family café in Trieste, where he remained something of a local celebrity even after that city's transfer to Italy in 1918, regaling all comers with the story of his adventures. I arranged to pay him a visit in 1934 when Polish naval business took me to the Adriatic, but in the event I never managed it since he died from a stroke a few days before I was due to arrive.

Early in 1918, because of the desperate wartime shortage of officers, Linienschiffskapitän Blasius Lovranić, Edler von Lovranica, my disciplinarian captain aboard the *Erzherzog Albrecht* at the start of these adventures, was transferred ashore to command a k.u.k. Kriegsmarine infantry battalion on the Italian front, even though he was far too old for such active service. And in those terrible last days of October 1918 he had found himself in the trenches on that devastated ridge called the Monte Tomba, some way north of Treviso, as the starving and influenza-riddled remnants of the Habsburg armies fought to hold the front line while everything collapsed about them in confusion. In the face of a major Allied attack, with Hungarian regiments on either side of them already pulling out of the line, old Lovranić had gathered together a company of Bosnian Muslims and half a Polish battalion and led them and his surviving sailors in a ferocious counter-attack which had temporarily driven the enemy off the summit of the ridge, himself being killed by a grenade in the process. It was perhaps a mercy that he should not have lived to see the final ruin of the empire and the dynasty that he and his forefathers had served with such mutton-headed loyalty for so many centuries. I can only hope that in their final ragged charge through the barbed wire and shell-craters of that accursed ridge the spirits of Radetzky and Schwarzenberg and Prinz Eugen and all the Emperor's Whitecoats looked down upon him and his gallant handful of men, fighting and dying (although they had no way of knowing it) for a state that had already ceased to exist.

But what, you may ask, of Professor Alois Fibich, the recently deceased American economist with whom this narrative began. How does he fit into all this? Well, it was like this. I was at the Marine Sektion on the Zollamtstrasse late that afternoon in February 1915, having completed my round of interviews and filed my reports and received congratulations on my escape from Tsingtao. I had been closely questioned by everyone from the Chief of Naval Staff downwards about my earlier adventures in the Balkans, and I had told the entire, unembroidered truth in the belief—naïve perhaps in retrospect—that I had only done my duty as best as I could, and that no harm would befall me. Everything had been minutely noted down and was now being typed out in triplicate before being walled up for ever in the War Ministry's intricate filing system. My last interview before departing for Hirschendorf and a month's leave was with the head of the Marine Evidenz Bureau, the Austro-Hungarian naval intelligence service.

"Well Prohaska," he said, "a nice little jar of worms you've opened up here I must say: not only outrageous incompetence at the highest level but also a strong possibility that our own people were mixed up in the plot to murder the Heir-Apparent. I only wish that we could pursue the matter further."

"But Herr Schiffskapitän, why not question Hauptmann Belcredi? I'm certain that he was their 'Prohaska.' I saw him there in Montenegro that afternoon and he recognised me, in fact denounced me to Draganić and his ruffians. If you question him you might find your way back to this mysterious 'Falcon' they kept mentioning."

The Linienschiffskapitän shuffled some papers on his desk before speaking. "Believe me, we would dearly have loved the chance. But there will not be the opportunity now I'm afraid. Hauptmann Belcredi was killed near Limanowa on 14 September: reportedly shot by his own men as he tried to stop them going over to the Russians. Whatever he knew he took to the grave with him. As for your 'Falcon' . . ." He paused for a moment. ". . . We have an idea who he might be; just an idea. But there: we can scarcely ask Conrad von Hötzendorf about it now, can we? Public confidence in the k.u.k. Armee is shaky enough as it is without us running the Chief of Staff in for questioning in connection with a possible charge of high treason. No, Prohaska, in this world we sometimes have to let sleeping dogs lie. The truth is that we're in a world war now, and exactly how we got into it is largely of historical interest. Our duty as officers of the House of Austria is to look to the future and fight to our utmost for our Dynasty and Fatherland. Which, incidentally, brings me rather neatly to this last piece of business which I must ask you to complete before you go on leave."

"What is that, Herr Schiffskapitän?"

"This." He pushed a sheaf of typescript across the desk towards me.

"A solemn undertaking to secrecy which our superiors have ordered me to get you to sign before you leave this building. Don't ask me why: all I know is that the War Ministry and the politicians are scared stiff that stories about the Sarajevo affair will leak out to the newspapers."

I looked at the document:

"I, k.u.k. Linienschiffsleutnant Ottokar Prohaska, do solemnly undertake before almighty God and upon my honour as an officer of the Noble House of Austria" et cetera, et cetera, "never to divulge to any person whatever or to commit to permanent record in any form the above particulars during the lifetimes of the witnesses to this document . . . Signed Vienna the 21st day of February anno 1915."

"Must I sign this, Herr Schiffskapitän? Is my word not considered sufficient?"

"Evidently not. But anyway, how old are you Prohaska?"

"Nearly twenty-nine: 1886 class."

"I see. Well, I'm fifty-eight, so . . . No, we'd better make sure." He got up from his desk and went to the door, opened it and called into the outer office.

"Fibich, damn you: stop picking your nose and come here for a moment if you please." Shuffling with embarrassment, a spotty-faced young Seefähnrich of about eighteen appeared in the doorway.

"Herr Schiffskapitän?"

"Fibich, I have often had cause to remark in recent weeks that you are of use neither to God nor man, and that one of the greatest disasters to befall the Monarchy in this war was the day when you were gazetted Seefähnrich. However, you may perhaps do some small service this afternoon to justify your existence. How old are you, Fibich?"

"I most obediently report, eighteen in March, Herr Schiffskapitän."

"Splendid: that will do nicely. I want you to witness the Herr Schiffsleutnant's signature if you will: the contents of the document are not important and are no concern of yours anyway. He will sign first, I shall countersign, then you will affix the horrible ill-formed scrawl that you dare to call a signature, do you understand?"

"Obediently report that yes, Herr Schiffskapitän."

So we all signed the undertaking, and Fibich returned to his office, and that was the last that I ever saw or thought of him until last week. Well, the head of naval intelligence was fifty-eight in 1915, so he would now be nearly a hundred and thirty if he were still alive—a sufficiently remote contingency (I feel sure you will agree) for me to have been released from my oath of secrecy by the death of Professor Fibich.

But what does it all matter? Not a great deal I think. The story of my tangential involvement in the Sarajevo murders may perhaps have entertained you, but I do not think that it adds much to our understanding of events, except to reveal that there were really eight would-be assassins in Sarajevo that day, instead of the six uncovered later by the Austrian police. I can only assume that Dusić and Kardjejev got away and either kept quiet about their activities or were not taken seriously if they did say anything. Perhaps there was complicity at the very highest level on the Austrian side; perhaps not. We shall never know. For my part, looking back on it now, I think that it was merely a matter of the blundering, blinkered ineptitude of a dying bureaucracy colliding with the theatrical, self-deceiving murderousness of Balkan politics; the two of them as fated to meet as the iceberg and the Titanic a couple of years earlier. In the end it matters very little. I might have got my report to Vienna a little earlier—but then all the evidence is that it would have been disregarded as completely as all the other warnings that the Serbs were planning something; ignored, most probably, because the relevant ministerial registries in Vienna had not opened folders on any organisations called Zvaz o Smrt or Crna Ruka and were therefore unable to file reports of their activities.

I certainly do not flatter myself that I might have averted the World War and the suicide of a whole civilisation. Years after the war, in Prague, I happened to meet an old schoolfriend, a psychiatrist who had attended the Sarajevo assassin Prinzip in Theresianstadt prison-fortress where the youth—who had been too young to go to the gallows with his fellow-conspirators—was rotting away with bone tuberculosis as he served out a life sentence. My acquaintance had asked him once whether he felt any remorse for the carnage going on around him. The boy thought for a while, then said:

"No, I feel no regret at all. They wanted their world war, and if it had not been over what I did, then they would have found some other pretext."

I think that sums it all up pretty well.

So once again I have prevailed upon your patience and your forbearance of an old man's ramblings. I hope that these stories have entertained you. For these tales are as true as recollection can make them at the distance of nearly seventy-five years. I have told you how it was when I was young and in the prime of life, sturdy enough to endure such adventures and still glad to undertake them in the service of my Emperor and my Fatherland, both of them long since turned to dust. Perhaps I have succeeded in picturing to you who never knew it a world that has gone for ever—and of which I must now be one of the last witnesses. For it was dying even then: not just Old Austria but that whole brilliant, proud civilisation of Europe, even as I fought for it there on the plains of China and amid the islands of the East Indies. The defence of Tsingtao was one of the last, fading echoes of the age in which I was born; perhaps the last months in the world's history when war could plausibly be described as a dangerous sport for gentlemen. I would rather that they had never happened, the events that I saw in those final months of the year 1914. But since they did I am glad that I was there to see them, and that I have lived long enough to record them for you.

JOHN BIGGINS CAME ACROSS PHOTOS of the Austro-Hungarian submarine service in 1987. He subsequently wrote the four-book Otto Prohaska series, a cult classic with literary flair and an ironic twist. Biggins divides his time between his native England and Poland.